TRUMBULL PARK

Other titles in The Northeastern Library of Black Literature
edited by Richard Yarborough

TRUMBULL PARK

FRANK LONDON BROWN

With a foreword by Mary Helen Washington

NORTHEASTERN UNIVERSITY PRESS / BOSTON

Published by University Press of New England

Hanover and London

NORTHEASTERN UNIVERSITY PRESS

Published by University Press of New England

One Court Street, Lebanon, NH 03766

www.upne.com

Printed in the United States of America

5 4 3 2

First Northeastern University Press/UPNE
paperback edition published in 2005

Library of Congress Control Number 2005928415

ISBN–13: 978–1–55553–628–2

ISBN–10: 1–55553–628–X

The Library of Congress has cataloged the original edition as follows:

Brown, Frank London

Trumbull Park, a novel.

Chicago, Regnery [1959]

432 p. 21 cm. I. Title.

PZ4.B8774Tr   813.54   59–8460

*Dedicated with pride to the
tenants of Trumbull Park*

FOREWORD

Mary Helen Washington

When it was published in 1959, *Trumbull Park,* one of the first novels to treat the story of racial desegregation struggles in the North, was hailed as an artistic triumph, and Frank London Brown seemed well on his way to literary celebrity. Sales soared to 25,000, and the largest publishing house in Germany, Knecht Verlag, brought out a German translation. The U.S. publisher, Regnery House, initiated a distribution agreement with *Ebony* magazine so that the book could be purchased from the *Ebony* bookshop. The novel was reviewed widely in major newspapers and magazines, to mostly favorable notice. *The New Yorker* called it a "vigorous and exciting first novel."[1] South African Alan Paton, author of *Cry, The Beloved Country* and one of the writers who inspired Brown, wrote a featured review on the front page of the *Chicago Tribune* Sunday book supplement, claiming that *Trumbull Park,* though it would shame white Americans, was a story of courage and not hatred: "An outsider like myself marvels again at the inner resources of the American Negro, which are shown both in Brown's writing and in his novel."[2] Van Allen Bradley, literary editor of the *Chicago Daily News,* praised both the author and the publisher for the courage it took "to bring this book into being."[3]

One of the clearest signs of the novel's popularity in the African American community is the feature-length article on Brown in *Sepia*, a black monthly picture magazine on the order of *Life*.[4] There are pictures of Brown with his wife and daughters, in his study writing, at Chicago's Val-Jac African art shop where artists and writers congregated, at a cocktail party talking to the Hollywood movie actor Lana Turner, and at a radio station where Brown read his stories to jazz accompaniment. Even in parts of the South, the novel was enthusiastically received. Writing for the *Montgomery Advertiser,* Bob Ingram said that although the story was fictionalized, its "feeling of white against black" was "too real not to be true."[5] A rare negative review was penned by black critic Charles Nichols. Brown was clearly a star in the making.

Writing for *Jet* magazine in April 1959, Langston Hughes praised the new author for many of the same qualities often associated with Hughes's own work: for writing about "his own people"—"their warmth, their humor, their language, their blues" with love.[6] But, for Hughes, the real source of the novel's power was the authority of firsthand experience. Brown and his family had actually lived through the trauma he wrote about:

> Brown lived in Trumbull Park. And from his harassed sojourn as a Negro in this troubled Chicago housing project, he emerged with a fictional account of its days and nights of racial tension that is almost documentary. Its account is substantiated by the on-the-spot reports of eyewitnesses—newsmen writing for not only the Negro press but the national press.[7]

As Hughes indicates, Frank London Brown did in fact live the events he fictionalizes in his novel. The idea for *Trumbull Park* was born when Brown and his wife, Evelyn, then six months pregnant, moved with their two daughters,

Debra and Cheryl, to Chicago's all-white Trumbull Park public housing project in April 1954. Though the Brown family was motivated by an entirely personal decision to find affordable housing for their growing family, the Chicago NAACP, buoyed by the 1948 Supreme Court decision against racially restrictive housing covenants, had targeted the Trumbull Park housing project for integration. Built in 1938 by the federal government as part of the Public Works Administration of the New Deal, Trumbull Park had operated from the beginning under the government's stated policy that it did "not intend to accept Negro families in Trumbull Park" and would resist any efforts to allow blacks to live there.[8]

Whites in Trumbull Park did everything in their power to make life unbearable for the Browns and for the several other black families in order to sabotage the desegregation effort. They threw bricks, stones, and sulfur candles through their windows and nightly set off explosive devices, which went off in three- to five-minute intervals with a flash and a deafening thunder. Jazz musician Oscar Brown, Jr., reports that when he visited the Browns during this time, the only person who didn't jump at every explosion was the Browns's newborn infant: "The new baby [Pamela] was so acclimated to the sound that she apparently thought the world exploded every three minutes."[9] With the tacit approval of the police and housing officials who made no arrests and did little to stop the harassment, whites carried on psychological warfare against the black families, congregating on street corners in hostile groups, putting out hate sheets, and making it dangerous for black families to use any community facilities, including stores, parks, and churches. The pastor of nearby Saint Kevin's Catholic Church said he was "powerless" to stop whites who sat behind the blacks at church and called out racial insults during Mass. White mob violence was so threatening that blacks were required to sign police logs to get in and out of their apartments and had to be driven by armed police escort, in filthy wagons, to points of safety beyond the projects where they could then board public transportation. In the late 1950s, Brown began writing *Trumbull Park,* painstakingly documenting the mob violence and intimidation experienced by blacks in the desegregation of the Trumbull Park Homes.

Brown's entire short life seemed poised to write this novel. He grew up on 58th Street, the "Blood Alley" of Chicago's South Side, where his contemporaries included junkies and gang members and where he learned to be both a fighter and an intense chronicler of the lives of the people he knew there.[10] This was also the place where he was exposed to the great jazz and blues artists and to the new music of bebop, which shaped his life and his aesthetic sensibilities. At Morrie's Record Shop, under the "El" tracks on 58th Street, he spent long hours listening to the musical greats he would eventually write about: Miles Davis, Muddy Waters, Billie Holiday, Billy Eckstein, Ella Fitzgerald, Joe Williams, Sonny Stitt, Count Basie, and Sarah Vaughan. As a student at Roosevelt College in the late 1940s, Brown and his college friends staged weekly jazz concerts on campus, bringing in such artists as Charlie Parker, Lester Young, and Miles Davis years before they became well-known stars. There are references throughout *Trumbull Park* to blues, jazz, and gospel music and to the resistant spirit generated, nurtured, and sustained by the example and energies of that music.[11]

Brown's position as the unofficial leader of the Trumbull Park families was inevitable given his commitment to progressive black issues and social protest writing. That commitment may very well have begun at Roosevelt College, where he met and became friends with former congressman

Gus Savage, Harold Washington (the first black mayor of Chicago), and Bennett Johnson, a fellow student activist at Roosevelt—a group that Johnson describes as intensely nationalistic. They formed the Chicago League of Negro Voters, which whites were not allowed to join, and although they worked with the white left periodically, Johnson recalls, "Our priority was our own folks, and that made us 'persona non grata' to the white organized left."[12] As a result of his efforts as program coordinator for the United Packinghouse Workers of America, a union widely known for its commitment to civil rights and antidiscrimination activity, Brown went to Mississippi to cover the Emmett Till trial, an experience he fictionalized in his 1959 short story "In the Shadow of a Dying Soldier."[13] In this early piece we see Brown struggling with the aesthetic challenge that would mark his fiction: how to represent the almost imperceptible shifts in black consciousness brought about by the civil rights struggles of the 1950s. Even when he was gravely ill with leukemia in the summer of 1961, Brown continued his political work, joining in the wade-in at Chicago's Rainbow Beach on Lake Michigan to protest the policy barring blacks from swimming at that beach. At the 1959 First Conference of Negro Writers in New York City, Brown responded to a panelist who decried social protest literature: "Let it be known here and now that you will always be my literary enemy, you or anybody else who tells me not to use my art for protest!"[14]

Published in 1959 when the South was still the major stage for civil rights activism, *Trumbull Park* focuses on what historian Sterling Stuckey calls "the new militancy in the North" and on the internal changes produced by that militancy.[15] At the beginning of the novel, the main character, Louis "Buggy" Martin, is talking to his wife, Helen, and his friend Red about the violence that may occur when they attempt to integrate the all-white Trumbull Park Homes. Buggy tells Red that he is skeptical about the black-run *Chicago Defender*'s accuracy and truthfulness in depicting racial events. When Helen retaliates that she'll believe the *Defender* before she believes the white press, Buggy tries to retract his accusation, insisting that he only meant that "our people are—always exaggerating things." His friend Red, whom Buggy calls "an agitator" because of his leftist politics, counters with, "Boy, you been white folk-ized. . . . That means these folks got you thinking everything *you* do is wrong, and everything *they* do is—well, ain't as wrong as you doing it." Buggy tries to defend his antiblack position as simply one of self-protection: "Man, we stick *out* so much when *we* do something." Again Red corrects him: "You ever see one of them white folk when they come to our part of town, and gets loose in Club DeLisa? Do they stick out, or don't they?" Red's response points to his understanding of the constructedness of difference, that whites become "different" when blacks are the judge and standard for behavior. Over the course of the novel, Buggy moves from a sense of racial inferiority to pride and courage as he and the other black families defy the police and the white mobs. This focus on the change in Buggy's consciousness is Brown's clear reference to racial representation during the period of Cold War conservatism when blackness signified difference and inferiority and when racial integration was widely interpreted as dependent upon blacks becoming as unmarked as possible and therefore more acceptable to whites.

But this shift is not just in Buggy's consciousness. Resisting the single-protagonist story, the novel creates instead a collective narrative voice that includes each of the six black couples who join Buggy and Helen in desegregating Trumbull Park. The novel takes these couples from racial shame and fear to their first acts of militancy, from experiencing blackness as inferiority to manifesting its power to inspire political action. Like Lorraine Hansberry, another Chicagoan of that era whose first play is about black identity and integration, Brown was intent on exploring what the new civil rights movement and a growing militancy meant for representing black subjectivity.[16]

These six couples begin as a distinctly unorganized, contentious group whose political positions range from not wanting to offend whites to planning to arm themselves and shoot whites on sight. For the first several months, the couples live in terror and shame, all of them reluctant to challenge the mobs, which, with the collusion of the police, gather around their homes at night, chanting racial epithets and detonating explosives. In response, the couples initially board up their windows, eat in silence, and sleep in fear. They are forced to ride in and out of the projects in police wagons and sign log books whenever they enter or leave, as if they are the ones guilty of a crime. Finally, with each one of the characters encouraging the others, men and women together, almost in counterpoint, they collectively perform their first acts of defiance. Helen begins, shouting to the police that they will meet whenever they want and without permission; Buggy's voice follows hers; Ernestine backs Helen up; Arthur and Mona join them, then Nadine and Terry. These unlikely "soldiers of Trumbull Park" gradually become emboldened: Ernestine leads the way out of the house through "the ring of uniforms and plainclothes," refusing to sign the log books despite police threats. In the final moments of this scene, signifying her defiance with a rhythm and blues song, Christine belts out, "Let the good times roll, Honey!" transmuting the sexual energy of the song into a force that intimidates the police and reinvigorates the protesters.

In what is the most transformative aspect of this novel,

about halfway through the narrative, the author disrupts the male-privileged narrative voice and begins to focus on women as political activists. If there is anything that marks this novel as progressive, it is Brown's rejection of its male-centered narration and his characters' subsequent reliance on women's strength and leadership. I consider this a remarkable feature of a text produced in the 1950s, a decade in which male narrators and authors generally sexualize and silence women without awareness or censure. About halfway through the novel, Buggy begins to question openly the way the narrative has represented women:

> What was getting wrong with me? Women were beginning to be on my mind more and more. . . . the women had done something that we men didn't have to do. They had put in twenty-four hours a day in good ol' T. P.—no husbands, no nothing—and had faced up to the mob and the policemen, all day, every day.

In the chapters following this awakening, women are given the two major political speeches. The first, delivered by Mona Davis at a downtown church to dramatize what is happening in Trumbull Park and to enlist community support, frames anger in a collective, public space. In the second speech, Helen reminds Buggy that their struggle is a part of the national push for desegregation and part of a larger international network of political activism represented by the 1955 Bandung Conference.[17] In acknowledging the moral and political importance of the women, *Trumbull Park* confirms what civil rights activist Ella Baker said in 1970: "The movement of the 50s and 60s was carried largely by women."

It is important to note how Brown uses music to signify another form of collective action in the novel. As Buggy leaves his house at the end of the novel, determined to stage a one-man walk-in and refuse police protection, Helen begins a call-and-response by singing the first line of a Joe Williams song, "Ain't nobody worried!" Buggy answers her with the second line, "And it ain't nobody cryin'!" Throughout the rest of the chapter, the song serves as a counterpoint to the taunts of the white crowd. When Buggy imagines them calling out, "We dare you to walk, nigger!" he sings out a line from the song, "Noooooo-body wants me. Nobody seems to care!" Finally, when Buggy and his buddy Harry have made their way through the mob without backing down, the words come pouring out, this time with Harry joining in. The song assists—perhaps even compels—action, creating an antiphonal relationship between music and action, much as it did in many civil rights demonstrations. The chapter ends with the words of the song inscribed in italics on the page but unmediated by any character, with the result that the blues voice, the characters' voices, and the authorial voice all seem to be speaking as one: "Every day, every day . . . Well, it ain't nobody worried, and it ain't nobody cryin'!" Many of the images of *Trumbull Park* explicitly anticipate the aesthetics of protest of the 1960s and 1970s. The characters in the novel, who are sustained in their efforts by the powerful blues rhetoric of the singer Joe Williams, will be replaced in just a few short years by singing demonstrators whose victory will be to march *into* police vans rather than out of them.

Trumbull Park is a novel that defies categorization. Despite the echoes we hear of Richard Wright in the story of class exploitation and urban racial violence, *Trumbull Park* represents a break with the tradition of social protest as defined by Wright in the 1930s and 1940s. Brown neither focuses on black victimization nor is he interested in appealing to or threatening a white audience. In fact, he said explicitly that he wrote the novel with black people in mind, constructing Buggy Martin as a kind of Everyman who could encourage black political change: "If I could get the Negro reader to identify himself with this man, then, at the end of the novel, the reader would be sworn to courage—if the trick I tried to pull on Negro readers worked—." But *Trumbull Park* also seems out of place as a 1950s novel. The focus of nearly every black novel of the 1950s is on an individual main character and on his or her growth toward consciousness. I am thinking here of Ralph Ellison's *Invisible Man* (1952), James Baldwin's *Go Tell It on the Mountain* (1953), Richard Wright's *The Outsider* (1953), Alice Childress's *Like One of the Family* (1956), and Paule Marshall's *Brown Girl, Brownstones* (1959). In contrast to this individualistic imperative, Brown's novel portrays the growth of a community. Like Sterling Stuckey, I believe that Brown was exploring and creating a new narrative, motivated, at least partly, by Brown's own activist engagements— his work in progressive unions, in civil rights protests, in desegregating the Trumbull Park Homes. If there is a category for *Trumbull Park,* I would call it a "civil rights novel" because the northern civil rights movement provided both a subject and a method. It gave the novel a collective protagonist, a community of couples acting (like most civil rights activists) in spite of being fearful and unprepared. It inspired the novel's representations of black musical traditions as assisting and nurturing political action, and made absolutely necessary the portrayal of women as major actors.

But in some ways *Trumbull Park* exceeds even the category of American civil rights novel. In the penultimate chapter, Helen tells Buggy that she has heard a radio story about the Bandung Conference, where "a whole bunch of people from all over the world are getting together," and she tells Buggy that they too should be doing some pushing. That reference to the 1955 Bandung Conference in Jakarta, Indonesia, and the subsequent "walk-in" at the end of the

novel internationalize the fight in this Chicago neighborhood, linking "the soldiers of Trumbull Park" to an international community of nonwhite people.

In March 1962, on the cusp of national recognition,
Frank London Brown died of leukemia at the age of 34.
Gwendolyn Brooks, who knew Brown well, eulogized him at
his funeral and in a poem published in *Negro Digest* in
1962, "OF FRANK LONDON BROWN: a tenant of the world."
The title signifies that Brown's "tenancy" in the larger world
could not be constrained or controlled by the viciousness of
a parochial white mob in South Deering, Illinois.[18] In words
that suggest Brown's revolutionary vocation as well as his
moral integrity, Brooks paints a portrait of a person not
unlike Malcolm X, a prophet who combines the severity of
revolution waged with love and political action carried out
with religious conviction:

> Always
> Love and the pledge of the curtain to fall
> Erected such reverence of vagabond View after all.
> . . . .
> Our Liberator and our insevere
> Armed arbiter, our scrupulous pioneer—
> . . . .
> His stars, that stare so certain-silverly;
> His trees, that stretch in hard and lofty pride;
> His clouds that sail a vari-tempered sea.

The legacy this warrior leaves is lush with "stars," "trees,"
and "clouds," but the lushness of the landscape is combined
with hardness and "lofty pride." In the poem's final stanzas,
Brooks unites images of religious mysticism and righteous fury
as she urges those left behind to carry on Brown's mission:

> We've given our Goodbyes.
> There are no further choices.
> There's nothing left to know.

> But carry back the fact
> Of the stone in his Voices.
> But carry back the storm
> Of the organ in his eyes.

As the Brooks poem indicates, Frank London Brown was at the center of intellectual and political circles in 1950s Chicago—to his friends and comrades he was "Liberator," "Armed arbiter," and "scrupulous pioneer." As a writer and activist, he cultivated and maintained these deep connections to his local communities, but his activism also produced a larger and more radical perspective—what Brooks calls his "vagabond View"—that inspired his writing. As Brown's close friend Sterling Stuckey said in a 1968 tribute to Brown, *Trumbull Park* and his superb short stories "marked him as a writer of major talent."[19] Critic James C. Hall provided what is perhaps the most fitting commentary about the loss of this young writer-activist at the very beginning of his artistic and political life: His death "just prior to the dawning of the Black Arts movement in Chicago is one of the major tragedies of contemporary African American literature."[20]

NOTES

I would like to thank Oscar Brown, Jr., Bennett Johnson, Sterling Stuckey, and Evelyn Brown Colbert for extended interviews with me about Frank London Brown.

1. *New Yorker* (April 25, 1959), p. 174.

2. *Chicago Tribune* (April 12, 1959) Part 4, pp. 1–2.

3. Van Allen Bradley, "Trumbull Park, Elm Street Politics and AP," *Chicago Daily News* (April 15, 1959), p. 18.

4. *Sepia* (June 1960), pp. 26–30.

5. Bob Ingram, "A Novelist Studies Trumbull Park," *Montgomery Advertiser* (April 19, 1959), p. F2.

6. Langston Hughes, *Jet* (April 2, 1959), p. 52.

7. Langston Hughes, *New York Herald Tribune* (July 5, 1959), p. 5.

8. My documentation of the history of the desegregation struggle at the Trumbull Park Homes is based extensively on the information in Arnold R. Hirsch's article "Massive Resistance in the Urban North: Trumbull Park, Chicago, 1935–1966," *Journal of American History* (September 1995), pp. 522–550, and on interviews with Sterling Stuckey, Bennett Johnson, Oscar Brown, Jr., and Evelyn Brown Colbert. On July 4, 1954, the Eric Sevareid show, *American Week,* produced a half-hour film, "On the Integration of the Trumbull Park Housing Project of South Deering, Chicago," featuring an interview with Frank London Brown, but I have not been able to locate this film. Television broadcasting apparently did not keep film as far back as 1954.

9. Phone interview with Oscar Brown, Jr., May 14, 2004. According to Evelyn Brown Colbert, the Browns' fourth child and only son, Frank London Brown, III, was born three months after they left Trumbull Park and died forty-five minutes after he was born, his death, she believes, probably caused by the tremendous stress of their lives during their years in Trumbull Park. Evelyn Brown Colbert, "The Works of Frank London Brown," unpublished manuscript presented in fulfillment of course work at Chicago State University, March 31, 1980.

10. Evelyn Brown Colbert, "The Works of Frank London Brown," p. 1.

11. Maryemma Graham, "Bearing Witness in Black Chicago: A View of Selected Fiction by Richard Wright, Frank London Brown, and Ronald Fair," *CLA Journal* (March 1990), pp. 280–297. Graham says that growing up in Chicago, "one of the major centers of bebop music in the 1950s," deeply influenced Brown's life and his writing. According to Graham, the new music of bebop was "based on the same revolutionary impulses as the written literature of the thirties and forties" and reflected "a more assertive dynamic in cultural expression." For the writers and artists who came after Richard Wright, this music functioned as an "abstract expression of a militant political mode that would become a central theme in the black experience in the 1960s."

12. Phone interview with Bennett Johnson, May 21, 1997.

13. Frank London Brown, "In the Shadow of a Dying Soldier," *Southwest Review* (Autumn 1959), pp. 292–306.

14. Evelyn Brown Colbert, "The Works of Frank London Brown," p. 4.

15. Sterling Stuckey, "Frank London Brown," in *Black Voices: An*

Anthology of Afro-American Literature, ed. by Abraham Chapman (New York: New American Library, 1968), pp. 669–676. Phone interview with Sterling Stuckey, April 9, 1997.

16. It is worth noting the striking similarities between the two Chicagoans, Lorraine Hansberry and Frank London Brown. Both Hansberry and Brown lived for thirty-five years: Hansberry from 1930 to 1965; Brown, from 1927 to 1962. Both died from cancer. Their first major published works—*A Raisin in the Sun* and *Trumbull Park*—were published in the same year, and both are about families struggling to escape the ghetto and to integrate all-white Chicago neighborhoods. Both writers managed a delicate balance between being politically on the Left and being included in elite establishments—Hansberry in Broadway circles and Brown as a graduate instructor and doctoral student at the University of Chicago.

17. Malcolm X gave literary and political prominence to the Bandung Conference when he referred to it in his speech, "Not just an American problem, but a world problem," given at Corn Hill Methodist Church in Rochester, New York, on February 16, 1965. He hailed Bandung as the first time in history that the dark-skinned nations of the world had united to reject colonialism and racism and to promote unity among the colonized. No European nation was invited, nor was the United States, their very absence, he claimed, signifying them as the world's colonizers. In *The Color Curtain: A Report on the Bandung Conference* (New York: World Publishing Co., 1956), Richard Wright, as one of the attendees, gives a first-hand view of the conference. Adam Clayton Powell, then a U.S. congressman, attended the conference and asserted that far from being oppressed, Negroes in the United States were a privileged group. According to Lloyd L. Brown, the press praised Powell for his patriotism, and Congress passed a resolution commending Powell (letter to MHW, October 23, 1998).

18. Gwendolyn Brooks, "OF FRANK LONDON BROWN: a tenant of the world," *Negro Digest* (September 1962), p. 44.

19. Sterling Stuckey, "Frank London Brown—A Remembrance," Introduction to Frank London Brown's *The Myth Maker* (Chicago: The Path Press, Inc.), 1969.

20. James C. Hall, *The Oxford Companion to African American Literature,* ed. by William L. Andrews, Frances Smith Foster, and Trudier Harris (New York: Oxford University Press) 1997, pp. 101–102.

TRUMBULL PARK

"Gypsy woman told my mother just before I was born I got a boy child comin', gonna' be a son-of-a-gun . . ."

MUDDY WATERS singing WILLIE DIXON's
Hoochie-Coochie Man

1

WE CALLED the building we lived in the Gardener Building, after Mr. Gardener, the owner. He didn't live there, but it seemed like he did, because the Gardener Building was old—real old, like Mr. Gardener, and rotten. Rotten from the inside out. Rotten toilets. Rotten window sills. Rotten lamp cords. Rotten porches.

The Gardener Building had its own special smell: baby milk and whiskey, fried chicken and cigarette smoke, perfume—and the sick smell of rotten porches.

Mr. Gardener looked and smelled just like his building, and that's why we called it the Gardener Building.

Babydoll, my girl Diane's little playmate, called the Gardener Building the "Darder." Babydoll was two years old, same as my girl Diane, and very pretty.

I was in the kitchen, with the back door open, when I heard a soft cracking sound, and before I could turn I saw Babydoll, through the corner of my eye, fall off the porch through a hole in the bannister.

I broke over to the porch and grabbed my baby, Diane.

Babydoll hit the ground four stories down. What an awful sound Babydoll's body made! Babydoll screamed once, something like a groan. Then she was quiet. I stared at her body for what seemed to me to be a long time, but I know it wasn't. Then I screamed Babydoll's mother's name:

"Bertha! Bertha! Oh, my God! Bertha, Bertha!"

Mr. Jackson down on the second floor hung over his bannister and took one look at Babydoll and jumped all the way from his porch to the ground.

Helen, my wife, was downtown with Louella, my oldest girl. I ran down the four flights of stairs holding Diane tight in my arms.

People started running down those steps like the place was on fire—as it had been, lots of times: sometimes people were burned; sometimes they died. I knew Babydoll was dead.

Bertha was upstairs over me on the sixth floor. She caught up with me and pushed me out of the way. She kept screaming:

"Oh Lordy, no! Oh Lordy, have mercy! Kind Jesus, have mercy! Oh Lordy, no!"

I ran down the twisting, rickety, wooden steps behind Bertha. Diane started crying. I heard a baby somewhere else crying, too. When we got to the bottom landing, Bertha just jumped and fell down beside Babydoll.

Mr. Jackson was already there, and Bertha pushed his hands away from Babydoll and put her face on Babydoll's back. Mr. Jackson was crying, and he stood up and looked around him.

Everybody in the whole building was down there standing around. Some of the women were out there in their underslips, and some of the men had on stocking caps. They were all talking under their breath.

Mr. Jackson's whole face was wrinkled and wet with tears. His eyes were red: I don't know whether from crying or drinking—I think from crying. He stretched his arms up toward my porch. One board hung loose, and even from

2

way down where I stood I could see the orange, rotten, wooden-jagged edge of the board. I got dizzy and I closed my eyes.

Mr. Jackson said:

"Oh Lord, she's dead!"

I heard Ol' Mrs. Palmer cry:

"Lord have mercy!"

I heard a lot of people answer:

"Lord have mercy!"

Mr. Jackson just stood there with his arms stretched out to the board hanging from my porch. He said:

"She's dead!" He said that in a very loud voice. He said it again.

"She's dead, Mr. Gardener. She fell off your porch, Mr. Gardener, and she's dead!"

"Lord save her!" said Mrs. Palmer.

"Lord save her!" the people said.

Bertha tried to pick Babydoll up, but Babydoll's blood got all over her hands, and Babydoll's head flopped back, and Bertha put her back down. Bertha started screaming:

"My baby's gone! Call a doctor somebody; call a doctor; my baby's gone!"

Somebody said:

"You mean didn't nobody call a doctor? That's the first thing shoulda been done!"

Somebody else said:

"Did you call one?"

"Why no, but I will. I just said . . ."

"Well, stop all that goddam gabbin', Negro, and go call one!"

Bertha stood up, her arms hanging limp at her sides, her shoulders drooped. She started to cry. Mrs. Palmer put her arms around Bertha's shoulders:

"Honey, the Lord do as he see fit. Have faith, Honey. Please have faith!"

Bertha's big, fat, dark-brown body started shaking all over. She closed her eyes and started shaking her head from side to side. She started moaning as though she was getting ready to start singing. Then she screamed and broke away from Mrs. Palmer and ran over to the porch and started up the stairs, screaming:

"Babydoll, Babydoll, Babydoll, Babydoll!"

We all just stood there looking at her for a minute, then I thought, She's going to jump! I put Diane down and started after her. She was already past the second floor and heading for the third.

"Bertha!" I hollered.

"Bertha, come here; come here, Bertha!"

"Babydoll, Babydoll, Babydoll, Babydoll!"

"Bertha!"

I took three and four steps at a time; once I slipped and fell, but Bertha kept going. I climbed to my feet and ran, and ran, and ran.

"Catch her!" a lady screamed down below.

Bertha stopped at the top floor, out of breath, crying, and still calling Babydoll's name.

I ran even harder. She heard me coming and made a break for the bannister.

"Bertha, come here!"

She lifted one leg high, trying to lift it over the bannister, but her fat stomach got into the way. She was breathing heavy, gasping for air, and trying to climb over that bannister. I reached the top step. Everybody downstairs was hollering:

"Grab her, Buggy, grab her!"

"Get up them steps after her, Buggy. Lord Jesus!"

I climbed up to the top landing and almost fell again. When I got there she was leaning over the bannister—her big fat rear end looking me right in the face. She was crying:

4

"Babydoll! I'm going with you, Babydoll! Just wait for me, Honey!"

I leaped for her ankles, just as she swung herself over. I missed one but I caught the other.

The folks downstairs:

"Grab her! Grab her, Buggy! Save her, Jesus!"

"Let me go!" she screamed.

I held on to one thick, soft leg with both hands. Bertha's body hung over the bannister, her head aimed straight down toward where Babydoll was. She squirmed and screamed and kicked my hands with her other foot, but I held on. Then I heard the sound of wood breaking. I looked around, and there in front of me, underneath Bertha, was the bannister breaking in two places.

"Bertha!"

The bannister under Bertha tore loose from the rest of the porch. I heard Mrs. Palmer screaming:

"Go help him, somebody! Go help him! Save her, Lord Jesus!"

I heard feet running up the steps. I heard the bannister hit the ground six stories down. I thought I was going crazy. Bertha fell over the edge of the porch, her dress flying every-which-way, but I held on to her leg; I felt myself sliding over toward the edge, but I hung on to Bertha's leg. Bertha kicked and screamed, and the people downstairs were screaming. I heard feet stomping up the stairs. I felt a rough, hard hand fold around mine; I felt it tighten up; it gave me strength.

"Pull, Buggy!"

Mr. Jackson's voice yelled, close to my ear.

I pulled, but all my strength was gone. I felt another hand on mine, and another, and then someone pulled my hand away. I crawled backwards between the feet that stood astraddle me, and all around me. I crawled until I was far away from the feet. Then I stood up.

5

Mr. Jackson and three other men pulled Bertha back on the porch. She was calm now—and quiet. They rolled her on her back. She stared straight up at the porch ceiling. She didn't blink her eyes. She didn't make any expression. Mr. Jackson unloosened her blouse, and one of the other men pulled her skirt down. She closed her eyes and shook her head from side to side.

"Babydoll . . . Babydoll . . ."

The police wagon rolled up a half hour later, and two policemen walked over to where Babydoll was lying. Someone had spread a sheet over her, and they pulled the top back.

"Second one today, Pete. What is this, kiddie day?"

Everything had gotten quiet. Folks were talking in whispers.

I found Diane around the corner on State Street, playing with two little girls. When she saw me, she ran to me squealing:

"Daddy, Ba'doll fall; Ba'doll fall—go boom!"

I looked around me to see if Helen and Louella were coming. I wondered why it was taking them so long to get back home.

"Daddy! Mommy! D'look! Mommy and Du'ella!"

I don't know how Diane saw them on a moving street-car, but there they were, standing in the door, stepping off as the car stopped: Helen, smiling, carrying downtown packages; Louella loooking just as grown-as-you-please, for a five-year-old.

Helen was just the right size for me—tall—just the right color dark-brown, with a face that reminded me of something sweet and warm to drink, maybe like hot chocolate. She had two dimples, and eyes that kind of jumped when she smiled. She wore her hair straight and combed back. She looked fresh, like early-in-the-morning. Her blue-and-white striped dress blew in the wind and wrapped against her legs. Her figure was full in that dress—full and, well, it just didn't seem she was three months along. She was so pretty.

The police wagon rolled out of the yard behind the building and turned the corner in front of Helen and Louella. Helen stepped off the curb and tiptoed to peep through the grating as the wagon hesitated briefly at the corner:

"Bertha?"

The wagon moved on, and she hurried across the street. I grabbed her around the waist and took the packages.

"What's the matter with Bertha? What did she do? What happened?"

I pulled her closer to me as the people filed out from behind the Gardener Building. Seeing Helen, some of them ran to her. A little girl, new in the building, got there first:

"Helen, Babydoll fell off of your porch! And she's dead! Dead, Helen, I saw her!"

Louella frowned up and looked at Helen.

"Shut up, child!" I yelled at the little girl. "Come on, Helen and Louella; come on upstairs. Helen, I'll tell you about it."

I pulled at Helen's waist, but she wouldn't move. Louella held on to Helen's hand for all she was worth.

"Come on, Helen."

Mrs. Palmer, out of shape and old, with gray eyebrows, gray hair, and a faint, kind of gray moustache, had reached Helen by then. She put her arm around Helen's shoulders:

"Honey, it was awful—broke every bone in that child's body. Pore thing's head flopped back like a kilt chicken when Bertha tried to pick her up. Bertha, pore thing, tried to commit suicide. 'Hadn't been for Buggy here, Bertha'd a jumped off the top floor herself. Lord

7

Jesus, girl, didn't you call Mr. Gardener 'bout your porch? I knew that plank was gon' fall out by and by. Helen, Honey, it was off your porch she fell. It's a wonder it wasn't your Louella or little Diane!"

Helen grabbed my hand. Louella went over to Diane, standing beside me. Helen looked at Mrs. Palmer; then she said in a low voice:

"I did call Mr. Gardener about that bannister. I told him time and time again that somebody was going to fall off of that porch. He just said, 'Okay, I'll fix it, don't worry, I'll take care of it.' Take care of it, he said—take care of it. Oh poor, poor Babydoll! Lord, help her, and poor Bertha! Lord in heaven *knows* I told Mr. Gardener about that porch. I swear I did!"

I looked at Helen and got a pain in the pit of my stomach. My wife's pretty face was all wrinkled and tight, and there was such misery in her eyes I thought she would just fall out right then and there. Her voice got hoarse, and wrinkles ran across her forehead like runs in a silk stocking.

I looked around at my neighbors as they milled around us. Most of them I knew—most of them were from the Gardener Building. There was Lukey—she was Helen's good friend, almost as good as Bertha was. Lukey lived on the second floor. Lukey was short, fat, and light-brown skinned. Her long hair just sort of sprayed out from her head like—well, like light-brown water.

Then just behind her was Lukey's cousin, Mae Jean, from Oxford, Mississippi; she lived down the hall from Lukey. Her mother—Lukey's mother's sister—lived with her. She kept kids for people in the building for a dollar a kid. She was sixty-five years old. Now, she was standing in back of the crowd, leaning on a cane, moving her mouth as though she were munching on a piece of tough meat or something—not saying anything—just munching. Indian-

8

faced and shriveled, with straggly, thin, short, white hair, balding in the front of her head—munching on nothing and shaking her head.

Helen squeezed my hand around her waist. She looked at the crowd—all people she had known all her life. She looked at me like she was asking what it all was about. I looked away from her; I didn't know what to do, I swear.

Mr. Jackson said in that loud bodacious voice of his:

"Somebody should burn that goddamned building to the ground. Look at it."

No one moved to look, and he shouted again:

"Look, look, at that big, ramshackle, firetrap. Look at it, look at what killed Babydoll. Look at it, Buggy!"

How come he had to pick me out? I turned and gazed at the building. It truly was a fearsome thing to look at—six stories tall; high ceilings in the inside; big bay windows on the outside, shooting straight up, one bay window right on top of the other.

Mr. Jackson said:

"That damned building been the cause of many a man dying."

The red brick was covered with smudgy streaks, and the gray mortar had oozed from between the red bricks and dried, looking like ashy icicles in the summertime. Down below there were six entrances. The building covered half a block going north and south, and a quarter of a block going west from State Street toward Lafayette.

Windows, windows, most of them with only one pane. A lot of the windows were broken out completely, and in their places were weather-stained, yellowing pasteboards. In some windows there were jagged green strips of shades that the wind had torn and eaten. In other windows there was nothing—no curtain, no shade, no nothing—just an open window without a glass.

9

Mr. Jackson was saying things we had all said many times before:

"He's just out to get our rents, that's all. When the faucet won't turn on, when the hall lights are out, we can't find his tail nowhere; but just let rent day come, and, hell—it don't get too early in the morning or too late at night for that gray-headed old money-grabber to come pecking at your door with his big, bony hand sticking out! Burn it, I say. Burn the bastard down!"

Some of the young boys in the crowd hollered:

"Burn it!"

Mrs. Palmer hollered back in her screechy old voice:

"Then where will we go? Huh? To another Gardener Building down on 56th Street? You know, they's one down on 33rd Street that burnt, but it was peoples in that one, children! It was peoples in it, and they got burnt up with it! Lordy, where we go if we burn this scoundrel? Besides, the law would put everybody in the building in jail and throw the key away!"

Louella said:

"Daddy?"

I said:

"Hush child!"

I looked at Helen. She had closed her eyes and had put her thumb and her forefinger in the corners of her eyes on either side of her nose. Tears were smeared over her nose and under her eyes. Her hair had gotten messed up somehow or other, and she looked real tired now—not fresh and spring-timey, the way she did getting off the streetcar.

"Helen, Honey, let's go home."

I pulled her away from Mrs. Palmer and toward our entrance. Lukey followed us, and so did her cousin and her old Indian-faced aunt. The others started going back into their entrances. We lived on the fourth floor. There was a row of store-front apartments on the ground level; then above them was the regular first floor—actually it was the second floor.

Children, and probably some grown-ups, had written on every inch of the wall on that first floor stairway. I read them as I went up. They only now seemed to mean anything. *Lukey loves Larry.* Now Lukey and Larry were married, had three children—Lukey expecting number four—Larry bussing dishes down at Walgreen's in the Loop. *Sam is a nigger.* Sam driving a Yellow Cab now. Sam was a fighter. I saw him in many a picket line, protesting this, protesting that. None of that ever seemed to do much good—not so far as I could see. Sam even picketed Yellow Cab, before they started hiring Negroes. Now he was working for them, that Sam, grown up, driving a Yellow Cab, still not married, still living in the building with his mother.

Further up, I saw *Buggy hates Helen.* Fifteen years had passed since the time I saw Helen on 58th Street in Dixie's drug store, sitting at the soda fountain beside Big Junior, and wrote *Buggy hates Helen* on the wall.

We reached the fourth floor. Helen still held my hand tightly. We went down the hallway, leading to our apartment. Diane had slipped away from us and come upstairs and fallen asleep on the couch. Louella went out on the back porch. I hollered quicker than I could think:

"Louella! Come off that porch!"

The house seemed strange to me. The maroon flat water-paint on the walls had seemed real beautiful when Helen and I first painted the living room (we never did get to the kitchen), but now it seemed like a mourning color—the shadows in the high ceiling were gloomy and dark.

Helen pulled her dress off, and hung it in the alcove we used for a closet. Then she sat on the couch beside Diane, and pulled her shoes off:

11

"Poor Babydoll. I told Mr. Gardener about that porch. It's two or three places there that need fixing. I don't know why the health department don't do something to him, to make him fix this place up."

"'Cause they're getting a pay-off," I said, "that's why. You remember when I called them last winter? I think it was January, after Mr. Gardener wouldn't put no heat in. They told me they would be around here to see about it. Hell, if we hadn't burnt the gas kitchen stove all winter, we'd have froze to death. You know that?"

I watched her face while I talked. She didn't seem as tall as she used to. She looked pure-D beat—I mean beat. Her slip was torn at the seam that ran along the side, and her stomach poked out more than yesterday. Her arms were beginning to get wide, up near her shoulders. I turned to look into the mirror over the dresser to see what being married six years had done to me. There wasn't enough light for me to see *that* good, but there were red lines running across my eyeballs—that hadn't been there before—and lines around my mouth, and I seemed to be getting thin in the face, and my skin, dark brown as it was, seemed to be even darker under my eyes. Lord, it looked like there was a gray hair right on the top of my head! I opened my mouth to look at my teeth. Helen said:

"I went by the Chicago Housing place today. Remember that application I put in last year?"

"Oh yeah, what did they say?"

She got up from the couch. She was holding something back from me. I knew she was.

"What did they say?"

"They said we are in a relocation district, or area or something. Anyway, the lady said we can get a place soon, if we want it."

"If we want it?"

A feeling swelled in my stomach and shot to my heart. My ears started to ring. Move? Move! Lord, bless the woman, the weaker half, or whatever it is. Here I'd been walking the streets trying to find a place big enough, where I could pay the rent, make the down payment these real estate people wanted, but I couldn't make any headway, no kind of way. Oh, how the room brightened! Move!

"If we want it? Good Gordon's gin! You know yeah. I know you told her yes."

"Un-uh . . . " She shook her head.

"What?"

"No, I didn't."

I sat down on the couch. Diane moved uneasily. All these things happening so fast just kind of left me confused. Now Helen was acting like she wasn't particular about the place the Housing people said we could move into.

"How come?"

"How come what?"

"How come you didn't tell them we'd take it?"

" 'Cause the lady said she wanted me to talk it over with you first, and *then* decide and let her know."

I got up and started walking—walking nowhere especially, just walking from one wall to the other.

"Well, Baby, you just go back there early tomorrow, and tell that lady, 'Yes ma'am, thank you, ma'am.' "

"You ever hear of a place called Trumbull Park, Buggy?"

"Trumbull Park?"

"Yes, Trumbull Park."

"*Trumbull Park!* Girl are you crazy? Do you know what's going on out there?"

Helen started rubbing her hands in and out of each other like she was at the washbasin. She kept staring down the hall toward the kitchen, toward the back door where the porch was, where Babydoll and our Louella had been. I watched her hands, and I watched her eyes, and then I watched the back door she watched, and I waited for her to tell me that she didn't know what was going on in Trumbull Park so that I could tell her. But she said:

"Yes, I know what's going on in Trumbull Park. But that stuff can't last long. It just can't. Those people are just trying to put up a bluff to scare the colored people out of that project; and, Buggy, I'm so scared of this building I'd go anywhere. Suppose that had been Diane instead of——"

I didn't want to hear any more about Babydoll so I cut her off:

"Helen, the *Defender* said that just thousands of white people gather around the colored families' houses and break their windows. I even read somewhere that they've tried to set somebody's house on fire a couple of times. Suppose we jump out of this frying pan into that fire? What have we accomplished anyway? Besides, isn't there some other project we can get besides Trumbull Park? That place is so far out that it would take us a whole day just to go downtown and back."

Helen got up from the couch and walked to the hallway leading to the kitchen. Then she turned around and walked back. When she sat down this time she turned her side to the hallway, but still, as she talked, she kept glancing down that long black room toward where Babydoll . . .

She sounded weary when she spoke, and I thought I heard a half-mad sound in her voice:

"Buggy, I know how far Trumbull Park is. I read about it in the papers. I know about the fires, the mobs, the broken windows. But I want to get out of here! We're getting just like everybody else in this building. We're making the best of it. We're getting used to all this stink, and dirt and . . ."

14

"Well, why not? You've lived here almost all your whole life. You ought to be used to it by now! I was raised in this building just like you. Everybody we know lives here. My mother died in this building. My sister was born in this building. So was my baby brother Ricky. You and me got married in this building. Even this apartment we live in has been in the family for a long time."

I was hollering at that girl. And she was huffing and puffing and getting madder by the minute. I went on:

"I know a lot of people who wish they had a place this good to live in."

That girl slipped her come-back on me so fast it made my head swim:

"Well, you got it wrong when you said this apartment has been in your family for a long time. What you mean is your family has been in this apartment for a long time. And I'll tell you this one thing—it's nothing to be proud of! Just look at this place!"

The first thing my eye caught when I looked around was a new hole in the wall along the baseboard that one of those big country rats had made overnight.

Helen caught my eye, and I caught hers. She knew I was cut down. What white mob could be more frightening than that black rathole? I swallowed hard and tried to think of something to say. Helen put her hand over her mouth and started to snicker. And that made me laugh, and I said:

"Well, I know one thing we ain't goin to no Trumbull Park, and that's that."

2

I DIDN'T KNOW we had so much junk. That moving-truck was *full*. We had a hard time convincing Diane and Louella we'd come back to see their little friends. We'd had a hard time convincing our friends that we'd come back to see them.

We left the building in fear. I didn't believe that anyone *could* leave that place—big and dreary red, the Gardener Building, a live thing that was almost human itself, eating and sleeping—always a restless sleep, but still sleeping. Then, like real people do, a lot of times killing—killing more than any one man or woman I know of.

We had gotten up early in the morning, almost tiptoeing around our three-room apartment, sometimes knocking over brooms and buckets trying so hard to keep quiet. Didn't want to disturb the kids. Didn't want to disturb nothing. Oh, we were getting away, and we couldn't believe it: getting out of jail through the front door. The great, big, raggedy door with chalk-and-crayon writing all over it swung open for us to run through; but we walked through, telling everybody goodbye as we went—walked, not because we didn't want to run, but because we didn't want something to happen at the last minute to draw us back behind those big, stinking walls. So we walked, and said goodbye, and climbed into Red's big, open-end truck, and ran! rode! ran! to Trumbull Park.

The first stop was the parking lot in the garbage dump at 103rd Street and Stony Island. Mr. Green, the project manager, had told us to wait there for him, saying that he would escort us in. We hadn't even seen the apartment we were to move into.

Helen sat between me and Red as the truck bounced over the curb in front of the garbage dump and stopped. She held Diane close to her, and Louella stood up between my legs and looked out of the window, taking in everything as we went along, looking around at that garbage dump with her nose turned up. I didn't blame her.

"Helen, do you suppose it's as bad as they say?"

"What?"

"You know what—this Trumbull Park."

Red said:

"Well, this is a hell of a time to be talking like that. You out here now."

I said:

"Yeah, I know, but I don't think the *Chicago Defender* had the story straight, talking about mobs of hundreds surrounding that colored family's house, and throwing bricks and everything at it, and trying to set it on fire, and all that. You know how that *Chicago Defender* is."

Helen said:

"The *Defender* ain't got no reason to lie. I'll believe the *Defender* before I believe a lot of these papers in this town."

"Aw, I didn't mean the *Defender* lies, but you know how our people are—always exaggerating things."

Red said:

"Boy, you been white folk-ized. You know what that is?" I didn't answer. Red went on:

17

"That means these folks got you thinking everything *you* do is wrong, and everything *they* do is—well, ain't as wrong as you doing it."

"Man, we stick *out* so much when *we* do something."

"You ever see one of them white folk when they come to our part of town, and gets loose in Club DeLisa? Do they stick out, or don't they?"

"Aw, you're getting off the subject! I was talking about I wonder if these folks act toward colored the way people say they do."

"Look," Red said, "this housing project been white since it was built. Now all of a sudden a bunch of 'you' is going in there. You know they gon' raise sand. If they'd wanted you in there, they'd have let you in when it was first built."

A bronze and brown Ford had pulled into the garbage dump, without our noticing it. A short, slim youngish man got out. He wore glasses, a part in his brown hair, a single-breasted brown suit, almost the same color as his hair. It was Mr. Green. He walked over to the truck. He wasn't smiling:

"You folks are late. The kids are out of school for lunch now, and the men are coming from the steel mills to eat. So I'm afraid you'll have to wait for another hour, until they finish. I'll be back in an hour."

Then he turned around, went back to his car, and drove off. We didn't know what to say: he'd caught us by surprise. I watched his car start up the high bridge at 103rd Street. It crawled up the hill like it was so tired it just could make it. When it reached the top, it kind of hesitated, then dropped out of sight on the other side of the bridge. Underneath the bridge, I could see a lot of train tracks, and a boxcar or two, here and there, sitting on the tracks. Beyond the tracks were a row of tall, bushy-topped trees. Beyond the trees, I could see big, black smokestacks, and I remembered that once Mr. Jackson took a bunch of us kids on a trip to Gary, and we had come this way and had passed smokestacks like those. He had said then that those smokestacks lined up beside each other like tall, black soldiers were part of the steel mills. Fire gushed out of one of the stacks and shot way up in the sky.

I looked for Trumbull Park, but I couldn't see it.

"You know," Helen said, "it's a shame we can't live like other people—have to sit out here with this baby in a garbage dump! Just because white folks don't want us in a *government* housing project. It's a wonder the police don't arrest everyone of them, and bury them *under* the jail."

Red laughed. I looked at him, then at Helen.

"Well," she said, "I know one thing, if they start messing around with us, they're going to catch more hell than they ever dreamed of. Now what *you* bet?"

"You ain't lying a bit, Honey," I said.

"Talk is cheap," Red said. "You two better wait till you get there before you do all that big talk."

I got mad at Red, just that quick:

"Red, you talk like you're scared of white folks."

"Hell, I ain't scared, but I know what trouble is. You're still a boy compared to me. You ain't never seen no trouble—but I have. I seen fifty white men and fifty Negroes battle for a solid hour—shooting, fist-fighting, knife-fighting, and everything else, right down on 31st and Wentworth. That was back in 1923; and, boy, wasn't *nobody* the best in *that* scuffle! It was man to man, chest to chest; and blood was flying every-which-way. I was just a young snot then, but I'll never forget *that*. Man, a race fight ain't nothing to sneeze at, and I want to think long and hard before I get anywhere *near* one."

I said:

"Well, do you think we're trying to start a race fight by moving out here in Trumbull Park? Listen, Red, you know how that Gardener Building is. Can anything be worse than that? Do you know how many people died in that building last year from pneumonia? From T.B.? My mother died in that building back in '42. Can white folks kill you any deader than T.B.? Listen, I'll *kill* anybody that tried to stop *me* from getting out of that—that rathole!"

"If you hated that place so much," Red said, "how come you stayed there this long?"

I was afraid he was going to ask me that. I knew I could tell him my job at the airplane engine factory was paying me just enough to get by on; that having two kids ate up every nickel I made. But, with overtime and all, I wasn't starving. Me and Helen had our Saturday night, like everybody else. We bought a suit or a dress every now and then. If we'd really wanted to, maybe . . .

In the first place, why did I stay in the Gardener Building after Momma died and Daddy went off with that 61st Street girl? Why didn't I get out when my brother Ricky left?—Who would have thought that bad thing would up and join the police force?—Why didn't I leave when my sisters moved? Johnetta, now a beautician doing good, living out on the west coast. Doris, in the WACS, traveling all over the country doing real well.

Why? Was it Helen that kept me there? Because she was so, so—I don't know—helpless? No, not because she was really helpless, but because she liked me, came up to see me all the time, even when folks started talking about her running after me. Helen—was that it? Maybe it was be-

20

cause I never really knew anybody else but the people in the building. Bubba—Lukey—Little John—Little Joe—Dickie—Bernard—Maurice—all good buddies: we fought, stole from each other, lied on each other; but there was something that made us need each other, in kind of reverse English. The building was a boogie bear that ate anybody it caught alone.

I remember Momma was alone in that building for a while—just a little while. That was when Daddy met the 61st Street girl, and Momma's friends wouldn't tell her, and Momma found out, and sat and cried all day, and fussed and argued with Daddy all night, and cried long after we were supposed to be asleep. I would lay in the bed and stare at the lights that ran across the ceiling when the big trucks came rolling and rumbling down State Street. And in between the noise the trucks made, and the clank, clank of those streetcars, and the honk of the big diesels going by on the tracks back of Lafayette, I would listen to Momma crying. In between Daddy's snoring, and Ricky's, Johnetta's, and Doris' coughing and heavy breathing, I would listen to Momma crying. Alone.

She wouldn't eat breakfast, she wouldn't eat lunch, and she would only nibble at dinner, when we had dinner. That 61st Street girl liked a lot of things, I guess. Momma was alone, and the big, dreary, damp Gardener Building got her, gave her T.B., and ate her up.

I guess maybe it was Helen, then; and maybe I felt that Mrs. Palmer, Helen, Johnnie-down-the-hall, Lukey and Lukey's aunt with her bald-headed Indian face—were my family. Maybe their being around me was the only thing that made me anything. Seeing them around me, hearing them call my name, sort of made up what I knew as me—like it wasn't any me without them. . . .

Red hunched me:

"Boy, you off in a trance? I asked you a question ten minutes ago. You ain't answered me yet!"

I looked at Red. What was there to tell him? How could I say everything I was just then thinking?

"Man, I didn't hear you," I said. "What did you say?"

Helen said:

"Hey, here comes Mr. Green's car!"

I turned:

"Hey, you're right."

I felt like I was on an elevator that was rushing up—up—up! My stomach shimmied, and I had to hold it still with my hand.

The car whipped a turn after it hit the bottom of the bridge and pulled up beside our truck. Mr. Green, all dressed in brown, hopped out—well, stepped out.

The sun hit his glasses, and a stinky wind pushed his brown coat back from his stomach and pressed the front of his pants against his legs. One hunk of hair kind of raised up from his head and sat back down again. He squinted his eyes, as dust gathered in front of him and formed a cloud that almost hid him.

"Well, folks," he said, his hand holding down the unruly plug of hair, "this is it."

He tried very hard to make his voice sound heavy, snappy, angry-like.

Red waved his hand. I said:

"All right, you want us to follow you?"

"Yes, that's right. Follow me."

"All right," I said.

Diane sat up on Helen's knee. She and Helen had been pretty quiet, up to now. I looked at Diane. She was straining her neck, trying to look over the hood of the truck beyond the hump of the bridge. Helen just looked, with no special expression on her face—just looked. The sunlight hit her eyes as the truck turned out of the garbage dump and started up the bridge beyond Mr. Green's car. I stared at Helen's eyes, and the brown seemed thick; and deep, dark specks way down at the bottom of her eyes seemed like dark clouds just ahead of a storm.

"Helen," I said, "what's the matter? Are you getting nervous?"

"I just don't want none of those white folks messing around. I'd hate to have to kill a bunch of them."

"I don't think it's that bad, Honey. Do you, Red?"

"I wouldn't be knowing, Daddy-o."

"Well, anyway, Helen, things like this never last long. You remember when we used to go out to see Mrs. Mary out in the Altgeld Gardens housing project, we used to pass this house on the bus going back and forth on South Parkway out to 130th Street, where Altgeld is—and back? There used to be a lot of white folks standing around a man's house who lived out on 74th Street—remember?"

Helen nodded.

"You remember, don't you, Red?"

"Naw."

"Well, I remember. Used to be policemen guarding that house night and day. But there ain't no policeman out there now. And now there's Negroes all in that block. Listen, Honey, our folks are like the old-time pioneers: we're moving on down the line. Shux! We're the last heroes this country's got! Just look at us—only thing we ain't got is a covered wagon. Don't you worry, Honey; these folks know they can't keep us back."

Red said:

"What you talking about, Buggy Martin?"

Helen put her hand to her mouth and started snickering.

23

Diane looked at her, and then at me, and then at Red, and *she* started laughing. Red looked at them, and then at me, and damned if he didn't break out. I don't know why *I* started laughing, but I laughed and laughed, too.

The truck pulled up to the top of the bridge, and Mr. Green's car rolled down in front of us. I could see the smokestacks from the steel mills good now. They looked like long black stogies, just puffing away.

The light from the wavy, silvery train-tracks underneath the bridge had the look of a whole row of tiny streams flowing side by side, out of sight underneath boxcar after boxcar, and beyond the farthest boxcar, way up the tracks, right up to a great big misty lake—Lake Calumet, "Gateway to the Great Midwest."

Straight in front of me, the street went down and down, fenced in part of the way by a low, flat-front metal fence; and beyond the fence a swamp-looking patch of land lay on both sides—nothing there but black rocks and water puddles, and yellowish-green grass.

The fences dropped off the street as we hit the bottom of the big bridge. Now the steel mills were hard to see through the high young trees. Vacant lots were on both sides of the street, and houses right past the vacant lots. Most were new houses; frames for others were going up.

Further down the street, there was a park, and at the far end of it Mr. Green's car turned south. We turned, too. The sign at the corner of the street said *Bensley*.

The park was about two blocks across; there were two baseball back-stops at each corner. Smooth brown-dirt paths cut through the short grass. Lines ran from home to first base, around second, third, and back home again. A bald spot sat some ten or twelve paces from home plate, and similar patches were at the corners of first, second, third, and home. I don't know why I noticed a thing like

24

that, but it caught my eye and stayed with me, even as we passed along the edge of the ball park and looked at the smoky brick houses opposite, then gray, slat-board frame houses, unfixed fences, and further on, yards with junk piled almost up to the first floor windows—rusting parts of cars, fenders, crankshafts leaning against old, old trees.

Several more vacant lots, a store on the corner to our left —and to our right was the Trumbull Park public housing project. What a serious, sad, worried-looking bunch of buildings!

Some were high apartments like the Gardener Building. These had green balcony-like porches, and mops hung over them, water streaks staining the green.

Others were long, two-storey row-houses, running down Bensley as far as I could see. Every one exactly the same as the other, a tree stationed in front of each entrance—and policemen!

Lord, there were hundreds and hundreds of tall, fat, short, skinny, wide, narrow, white, and colored policemen! They seemed to have popped up out of the air around us. Nothing, but nothing but blue uniforms with dingy brass buttons, moving this way and that way, walking away, walking toward, cutting in front, crossing behind.

"I'll be damned!" said Red.

"Me, too!" said Diane.

Louella snickered.

"Shut up, Diane," said Helen.

"Helen, do you see what I see?"

"The *Chicago Defender* was right, huh?"

"And then some."

"*Get out, Nigger!*"

Red slowed the truck down.

"Who said that?"

Helen said:

"Come on, Red, I got these kids in here. Don't you start no foolishness!"

I looked out of my side window. Two policemen were riding beside the truck on motorcycles.

"Helen," I said, "we've got two bodyguards on my side."

Red looked out of the window on his side:

"There are a couple of them over here, too——But look!"

I said:

"Where?"

"Coming from between those houses—look!"

There were about eight houses in a row, heading away from our truck. A crowd of women and some teen-agers and old men pushed out of the eight gangways.

"Get out of here!"

I looked at the policemen standing across the street from where the crowd was coming. A sergeant looked around at his men, then at Mr. Green's car, then at our truck. He yelled at the crowd across the street:

"All right, you people, let's not have a disturbance!"

Bang! A rock hit the hood of the truck. *Bang! Bang!* Two more hit the fender. Red said:

"Aw, hell, naw! This ain't happening to me!"

He slammed his foot down on the brake pedal and kicked the door open, climbing down almost in the same motion. Helen said:

"Red!"

I fumbled with my door handle, watching Red all the time, trying to see what was going to happen. One of the motorcycle policemen screeched his machine to a stop and grabbed Red by the front of his jacket, yelling right into his face:

"Get back into that truck! What are you trying to do—start a riot?"

Red bellowed back:

"Start what goddamned riot? Shee-it, look at them son-of-a-bitches throwing rocks at my truck, *my* truck. I don't stand for that from nobody!"

"Who threw rocks at your truck?"

"Who? Who! Hell, wasn't you riding right beside the truck? It's a wonder they didn't hit you!"

Two women moved up to where Red and the policemen were arguing. Several teen-age boys followed them, then two old men hobbled up. One of the women yelled:

"Just drive that junk right out of here, blackie!"

"Kiss my black——"

"Stop it!" yelled the officer.

He grabbed Red's arm again. Red snatched his arm away. I climbed out of the other side of the truck. Mr. Green was out of sight. The two officers who had been riding their motorcycles beside me pulled up right under the door. One shouted:

"Stay in that truck!"

Helen yelled:

"Well, do something about those people throwing at our truck!"

Red climbed back into the truck. People in the crowd started yelling in cadence, like a bunch of evil cheerleaders:

"*Get out, Africans—get out! Get out, Africans—get out! Get out, Africans—get out!*"

Diane started crying and buried her head between Helen's shoulder and neck. Louella began to whimper.

"Follow me!" shouted the police sergeant on my side of the truck.

27

Red was sweating. His eyes were shiny, and his bottom lip poked out above his hard-set chin. I saw the muscles in his jaws moving about as though he were chewing his tongue or something.

"Ain't this a bitch!" I said.

Red said nothing. He started the truck. The yelling grew louder. The crowd kept up its sing-song:

"*Get out, Africans—*GET OUT! *Get out, Africans—*GET OUT!"

Red drove slowly, and the crowd followed on the other side of the street.

Bang! Another rock hit the cab, right behind where Red sat.

"All right, you people!" a heavy voice yelled. "Let's not have any trouble here! No more throwing rocks, now!"

Bang! went a rock against the back of the truck.

The sergeant, walking along the street, leading the truck, turned into a side street, right off Bensley. He beckoned for Red to follow. Red turned into the side street, off Bensley, between 106th Street and 107th.

The side street was a short one, and at the end of it was a kind of a round parking lot, closed in by wire fences. Behind the fence were back yards, and then more of those long, low, two-storey houses—all connected, all the same color, all the same height, like barracks, or maybe a jail.

"All right, stop here!" The sergeant was hollering at Red again. You know, it looked like he had a pick on Red.

Mr. Green was standing beside his brown car over on the other side of the lot. I almost didn't see him, the way his car was tucked all up and in between those other cars. His voice sounded right cheap when he crooked his finger at me and hollered:

"All right, Mr. Martin, come on over here and I'll show you where your apartment is!"

"Shee-it!" said Red.

"Red! Diane and Louella are in the truck. Remember?" Helen said.

Red grabbed his mouth and slapped his other hand down on the top of his head. Then he reached over and laid his hand on Louella's shoulder:

"Honey, Big Red sorry. He forgot all about you and Diane sitting there so quiet, but them bastards——"

"Red!"

"Lord, I'm *sorry!*"

I opened the door and climbed down from the truck, and Diane slid off of Helen's knee. I reached up and took both Louella and Diane in my arms and stood them on the ground.

Helen climbed out next, and Red sat there looking at Mr. Green. I said:

"Red, ain't you coming?"

I don't believe he even heard me. He just sat there staring at Mr. Green.

"Look at that scary scown, will you? Just look at him, a good woman could beat his brains out."

Mr. Green shifted from one foot to the other. He was the impatient type. Me and Helen and the kids started walking over to where he was. He then started walking toward the red brick houses.

"*Hey, nigger!*"—a woman's voice from one of the apartments.

"*Go back to Africa, nigger!*"—a man's voice from somewhere behind us.

Louella looked at Helen; then she looked at me:

"Whatsa' matter, Mommy—huh?"

Helen pressed her hands against Louella's ears. Diane poked two fingers in her mouth and started sucking. Red yelled from the truck:

29

"Don't hold her ears. Let her see how these pecker-woods really are!"

Mr. Green stopped and looked back at Red. His eyes were all squinched up and his face just one reddish frown. I looked at Helen and she avoided my eyes. I don't know; it just didn't seem right for Red to be saying all these things. I said to Helen:

"Helen, Red agitates too much, don't he?"

That girl didn't even look back. I said:

"You hear me, Helen? I said that Red just agitates too much, don't he?"

"I wouldn't be knowin'."

3

WE CAME TO a vacant apartment where eight or ten policemen were standing. The sergeant had gone ahead and was standing there surrounded by the rest, talking to one fat policeman who had shiny bars on his shoulders and a white shirt on, instead of a blue one.

Mr. Green hollered at the policeman in the white shirt:

"Howdy, Captain!"

"Afternoon, Mr. Green."

When we came closer, he smiled at us:

"Well, folks, here's your place. I'm the captain out here, and here's Sergeant O'Grey."

The sergeant, a tall, beefy, thick-necked man with ice-cold eyes, wrinkled his face up in a smile and said:

"Hello, folks. Now don't worry. We'll have this situation under control soon."

He pointed to a group of policemen standing near a patrol wagon in front of a vacant apartment:

"Mrs. Martin, whenever you want to go out or come in, just let one of those officers know. They will escort you to the wagon and take you to 95th Street, Cottage Grove, or State Street."

I said:

"95th Street! Why that's almost three miles from here!"

31

Helen said:

"I'm not riding any patrol wagon. I'm no criminal!"

The policeman said: .

"Well, it's only for your own protection. We can't allow you to walk these streets. It's not safe yet."

"How do our friends come out here to see us?"

The captain stepped up:

"Just call Essex 5-5910 and we'll pick them up."

Mr. Green coughed, and started toward the door.

"Hey, nigger! Get out of here!"

It was the same woman, hollering from one of the apartments right close nearby. I looked around, but I couldn't tell where that voice was coming from.

Mr. Green took out a ring of keys and slid two off. He handed one to Helen, and opened the door with the other one.

"Well, Mr. and Mrs. Martin, here's your new home. I—uh—hope you enjoy it."

I said:

"Yeah?"

Helen said:

"Thank you."

There were about eight policemen in front of the door. One came toward me, holding a thick tablet in his hand:

"Sign here, Mr. and Mrs. Martin."

Helen let Diane's hand go and reached for the pen that the policeman held out to her. Louella started to reach out for the pen too.

"Helen," I said. "Hold it! What's this?" I asked the officer. "We got to sign in to get into our own house?"

The policeman looked at the captain. The captain said in an extra-loud laughing voice:

"It's orders from headquarters, Mr. Martin!"

Helen started writing. When she finished, I took the pen and signed my name.

"It's worse than being in jail," Helen said. "I guess we have to sign to go out, too, huh?"

"Yes, ma'am," the captain said.

"*Nigger, nigger, nigger!*" That woman again.

"Mr. Green," I said, "can't you do anything about those people calling names like that?"

"Well—uh—yes. That is, if you can properly identify the person molesting you. There is a ruling in your hand-book—uh—I'll get you one, which expressly prohibits actions by tenants to intimidate other tenants. Uh—I'll get that handbook for you, if you'd like."

"Yeah," I said, "because somebody's gonna get hurt, acting like that. Hey, Red, let's go!"

Red climbed out of the truck and headed for the back. The crowd that had met us out on Bensley started coming into the lot. I started back for the truck. Helen started behind me. I said:

"No, you stay here!"

"You must be crazy," she said, "I'm not going to let you go over there by yourself."

One of the policemen looked at the police chief. The chief looked at me, then at the crowd. I started walking toward the crowd. The chief said:

"Mr. Martin, you'd better wait here, till we do something with that crowd."

"So what are you going to do with them?"

"Don't get smart! You just stay here!"

He started walking toward the truck. One of the old women in the crowd started screaming at Red:

"Go back to Africa, Blackie! Get out of here. Get out, get out, nigger! You're not wanted!"

Red turned to face her. A couple of other women moved in behind her. Then, a couple of teen-agers came up. Red reached for his back pocket, turning at the same time to face the whole damned crowd.

I walked past the police chief real fast. He was so busy looking at Red and the other people that he didn't hardly notice me. Red stood his ground. He was about six feet, with that funny looking kind of red hair—actually, it wasn't what you would call red—it was more orange, I'd say. But Red was a big one. His arms looked like a whole lot of rope was underneath his skin, and every time he moved, one of those ropes would start to poke out like it was going to break through. Red didn't like a whole lot of clothes; he had taken his jacket off in the truck, and he had on just a pair of khaki army pants and a green open-neck shirt with the sleeves cut off high on his arms.

He had that one hand stuck down in his back pocket, and the other he was pointing right in that little screaming woman's face. She was short and skinny, and had sunk-in jaws and some of that *bad* brown hair. I mean it was all *over* her head.

But she sure could holler a while. And she just hollered, right in Red's face:

"Get out of here, nigger!"

Splap! Right against Red's face—a rock! Red fell back and grabbed his face, and then made a mad break for the woman. That gal screamed and broke out. I mean she disappeared!

Red started after her, right in that crowd, and they started running this way and that, and the captain hollered at his men standing up there, watching it all like they were at a baseball game, or something:

"Hey, you! Hey! Come on men. Break this up!"

By this time, I was up with Red. He glared at me:

34

"Shee-it!"

The captain ran a few steps past Red; then he turned around and started back. He hollered at his men:

"You men keep them out of here. That's an order!"

Red rubbed his cheek, and blood smeared on his hand, from a long cut. The captain grabbed Red's arm. He started to pat Red down. Red knocked his hand away:

"Git your hands off me!"

The captain said:

"What you got in your back pocket?"

"What you mean, what I got?"

"What I said. What've you got there? I saw you reaching for something. What've you got—a knife?"

Red straightened up. I ain't never seen Red stand so tall. He just bellowed at that captain:

"What do you think—all Negroes carry a knife? That what you think! Just because I'm colored, and you white, officer, I carry a knife? Is that what you think? *I* got a knife? How come you stand there—let that bunch of bastards gang up on me, and then you come running, after *I* get hit in the face with a brick and start after that bitch! How come you——"

The captain was about to blow up. I mean *up!*

"That's all, fella! That's all outa you. One more word and I'll run you in for 'disorderly!' "

"Run *who* in!" Red was screaming for all he was worth. "Run who in!"

"You, fella!"

The captain reached for his club. I grabbed Red's arm.

"Come on, Red," I said. "You're making it bad for me and Helen. You ain't got to live out here, man; come on, let's get that stuff off the truck!"

Red's big, mean face, full of freckles, looked at me, and those eyes of his were glassy, and that wide-kind, pointed nose of his going in and out like to scared me to death. I stepped back from that man. I couldn't look at him, and I was scared not to—no telling what he might do. Red just stared at me—looked like it was for a year! Then he turned around and started walking toward the back of the truck. I just stood there a minute, trying to get myself together, thinking I didn't know what was wrong with Red. He knew he couldn't whip none of them white folks, especially with the police acting like they were. Red was really a fool— didn't take time to think things out. I mean, a few names called—hell, I've been called worse than that many a time. But, then, I could see Red's point: it all depends on what the person means when they call you a name, and who's calling you what.

Anyway, I started to helping Red unload the truck. Mr. Green handed Helen the extra door key, and left.

"*Hey, nigger!*" That same voice from one of those buildings.

Red acted like he didn't want me to help him. We went back and forth, into the house and back again, till finally we were almost through. The captain stood right alongside the truck, near the back, just watching Red, trying to stare Red down. Red didn't pay him any attention.

I started feeling like I had let Red down. That he had been in a tight spot, and I let him tough it out by himself.

But then, I thought, didn't nobody get hurt, not really, except for that little cut—well it wasn't so little—in Red's face.

Helen was bringing stuff in and out, too. Even she had a funny look when I caught her eye. I said:

"Do you think you ought to be carrying that stuff. I mean in your condition and——"

"Don't mind me. I'm all right!"

I didn't know what to think. Did I do something? Hell, I thought, *I* didn't hit Red with no brick!

One of the policemen who the captain had sent out behind that crowd was running toward us from the street where the crowd was. The captain had his back to the policeman and didn't see the man till he was right up on him.

"Captain—uh—Captain!" The policeman, a young rookie-looking guy, with a brand new uniform and a black bushy moustache under his nose, was out of breath. "Captain!"

The captain turned quickly:

"Yeah?"

"A couple of the people out there said that they're going to bomb out the niggers, uh——"

He looked over at Red. Red didn't blink an eye; he just kept sliding a big chair off the edge of the truck. The rookie-looking-cop-with-the-bushy-moustache stammered:

"Uh—I mean, colored families. They said they were going to dynamite them tonight! Captain, the sergeant told me to report it to you!"

"Well, do you have the people who told you that in custody?"

"I don't know, Captain. The sergeant just sent me to tell you, sir."

The captain looked at me, then at Red, then at Helen, staring at each one of us, slow and steady-like. There was something cold and hard in his face. Something that made me get a chill right down my backbone.

He just looked at us and walked away.

4

I T WAS WARM for October, but I was cold. Night time was all over everywhere. Even inside it seemed like night time. Red was long gone, and the junk we had for furniture was laying every-which-way. Helen was in the kitchen, sweet thing, tired as she was.

Everything had a gloomy look, like somebody had died or was going to. You ever been in the country looking out of the window at night, and there ain't nothing out there *but* night, and moon and tree shadows? And then, like a sick old woman, one of them long, lanky meat hounds climbs up on one of them lonesome, I mean *lonesome* hills and stretches its long, lanky neck and points its head dead at the moon, and lets out one of them backwoods howls—one of them sad, loud, moaning howls? Momma used to say a dog howling like that meant somebody was going to die, maybe not that night or the next, but soon.

Lord! That's how I felt there in that house in Trumbull Park that night. We hadn't put the curtains up yet, and all we had was the shade pulled down, but the moon was bright, and I could see the policemen in the moonlight, through the crack between the shade and the window.

Lots of policemen, walking back and forth in no kind of order—not in single file, not two by two—just walking, walking. Helen got quiet in the kitchen. Louella and Diane were asleep on the mattress on the floor. I could hear the cops walking outside my window, feet hitting heavy on the sidewalk.

I looked in the kitchen because Helen was so still in there. She was leaning on the sink, not looking so tall now, kind of poochy in the middle. Her brown skin was shiny at the nose and on her forehead. Her dimples were sort of spread out now—not deep and all like they are when she's happy. Even her hair had got straggly. She caught me looking at her and started to smile. Narrow little face tried to brighten up. Long Indian-nose, I called it—had a little hump at the top—wrinkled when she smiled. Dimples came back into her cheeks. She looked at me, then looked away at the floor.

"What are you looking at?" I asked.

"What are you *thinking* about?"

She got one of those real fake smiles, when I asked her that!

"Oh, nothing, Honey."

She came easing up to me, smiling, and put both arms around my neck and sort of leaned in—you know?

"Don't 'Honey' me," I said. "What's the matter?"

"You remember what the policeman said about them trying to blow this place up tonight?"

"Did *he* say that?"

"You know he did."

"Aw, those guys probably put him up to say that— just to scare us."

"I don't think so."

"Why?"

"I just don't think so. Anyway, I'm waiting to see what's going to happen."

"You're waiting for the bomb?"

"I'm waiting to see what happens."

"Well, what else are you waiting for, if you're not waiting for the bomb? That's what the man said was going to happen."

"Okay, okay, then! So I'm waiting for the bomb," Helen said. "Now, come on, let's eat."

"How about the kids, Helen?"

"They ate a little something while you and Red were bringing the stuff in. You come on. I'm getting ready to put it on the table."

We dug around in those boxes and bags until we found the dishes; then we dug some more, until we found a couple of knives and forks.

I looked around the living room. It was painted cream, with green paint at the baseboards and around the doors and windows. No cracks in the ceiling, no cabbage stink seeping under the front door. Black-tile floor, big windows and trees outside right in the yard. I needed a deep breath to help me take in all this cleanliness, fresh paint, and all. I took that breath and let it out, saying:

"Well, one thing, Baby. This sure beats the Gardener Building."

Helen rummaged around in the boxes of groceries we brought with us, and in between stowing things in the icebox fixed up some hamburgers and a salad; and we sat down at the kitchen table, alongside of a mop and a broom, in a room full of boxes and bags.

Boom!!

Helen screamed. Her hand flew up to her face, and her fork flew out of her hand and hit the kitchen window. I closed my eyes and covered them with my hands. I waited for the roof to start falling. Helen jumped up and ran over to me.

"Buggy! Buggy! What is it?"

40

"I don't know, Honey!"

I hugged her tight—more for my sake than for hers.

Boom! Boom!

There was another explosion, so loud and close that it rocked our house and made the table bounce. Diane and Louella came into the kitchen, crying and pushing their knuckles into the corners of their eyes. Diane seemed tiny for two years old. Her little dress was wrinkled, and her crying had started to spot the front of it with tears. She went to Helen:

"Momma, what that? Huh, Momma?"

"Firecrackers, Honey. It's a holiday; it's Fourth of July. Those are firecrackers, Honey. Now, come here; let Momma take your clothes off, so you can go to bed."

Louella stood there, looking around the room like she was lost in all that junk and noise and all. I went to the front window. The policemen were in a huddle now, like sheep trying to hide in each other from a gray country wolf. I opened the door. One of them turned toward me. I said:

"What was that noise?"

"Don't worry. We'll take care of everything."

"Yeah, but that noise! Was that dynamite—or what?"

One of the cops walked a bit away from the crowd, toward me. He stopped and hollered:

"Don't worry about our business. We're out here to protect you. Don't worry about noises."

"Well, after all, I——"

"Don't worry 'bout it!"

I shut the door. Helen said:

"What did he say the noise was?"

"Oh, I don't know, Helen. Don't worry yourself about it."

41

I didn't eat my hamburger. Helen didn't eat hers, either. We went upstairs to bed. Outside, we heard voices of people. A lot of people were yelling. I made out some of the words.

"*Nigger!*"

"*Jungle bunny!*"

"*Eight balls!*"

"*Let's go in and get them!*"

"*Yeah! Yeah!*"

"*All right, you people. No trouble here!*"

There was a sharp thud outside, against the brick wall of our bedroom.

"*Goddammit!*"—it sounded like the cop outside— "*now them niggers got 'em throwing bricks at us!*"

Thud! Thud!

I jumped out of bed and ran to the window. I saw a whole bunch of people standing down there. Man, I was scared!

"Helen! Helen!" I called before I could stop myself. "Look here, will you?"

"What is it?"

She jumped up and came to the window. She stared down on those people moving around down there. There were two lines of police—one line in front of our house, and the other line right in front of all those people, about five or six hundred it looked like, pouring into the parking lot where Red's truck had been, dribbling all the way back into the street. It was dark, but the moon lit their faces, and every single one of them looked as hot as a pistol. That reminded me, and I turned toward the dresser and opened the top drawer. Helen laid her hand on my arm, kind of light like.

"So, what are *you* going to do?"

"Do you think I'm going to let them bastards get

upstairs here in our bedroom, before I think about protection?"

"So what happens if you shoot one of them? All the cops would do would be to throw you in jail."

"Throw *me* in jail—for protecting myself?"

She turned to face me, put both hands on my arms:

"Honey, don't you know that white policemen ain't going to let colored Negroes like you shoot white folks—no matter what? Huh?"

"White policemen won't what!"

She kissed me.

"Stay away from that dresser. You hear?"

I went back to the window, and looked out just in time to see an arm raise up above the crowd and swing fast toward our house. I didn't know, at first, that it was a brick flying toward the window—not, at least, until it was right up on me. Then, I pushed Helen off to the side, hollering at the same time:

"Duck, Helen, a brick!"

Crash!

That thing threw glass every-which-way. Then it rumbled across the bare tile floor, like one of them big-foot, well-fed rats in the Gardener Building.

"*Get out, niggers!*" It was a woman's voice.

"Momma!" Diane from the other bedroom.

"Mommy!" Louella screamed.

"*All right now, folks, no violence! Move back. C'mon, move back!*" Must have been a policeman talking, then.

Helen started to get up from where I had pushed her. I crawled over to where she was, and grabbed her around the waist. She knocked my hands away:

"Hey, don't you know I'm pregnant? You hurt me when you grabbed me like that!"

43

Louella called out again:

"Mommy!"

"*Get out—nigger, nigger, nigger, nigger!*" Same woman.

Diane began again, too:

"Momma! Momma!"

Helen made another start for the kids' room. I said:

"Helen, those fools might throw something else. You get over there by the wall. I'll go in and see about the kids."

She didn't open her mouth. Just stood up from the dark where she was and walked out through the moonlight, leaving the moonlight behind her sliding off on the edge of the bed and onto the floor where the brick and all that glass was.

I got up and looked out the window. The crowd had pushed the policemen back closer to our house. One policeman was tussling with a tall, sloppy fat man, with kind of silverish-looking hair, the way the moonlight was hitting him.

Helen called from the other room where Diane and Louella were:

"Louis, what's happening out there?"

"Some guy is out there fighting with a cop."

Louella said:

"Daddy, why are they fighting? What was that noise, Daddy?"

The big, fat gray-haired man grabbed for the cop's neck. Louella said:

"Daddy, why are they fighting?"

The cop side-stepped the man and hit him smack dab in the belly with the side of his club. The fat man twisted to the side, grabbed his stomach with one hand, and caught ahold of the cop's neck with the other. Two other cops ran

44

over to where they were fighting, but a couple of women jumped in front of them, and the cops had to stop to get the women out of the way. The fat gray-haired man pulled the long lanky cop forward with one arm and the cop dropped his club.

"Daddy!" Louella called, "why are they fighting? What was that noise, Daddy?"

One of the cops pushed the women who had jumped in front of him down on the ground. Then he snatched out his club and raised it way, way over his head. People started screaming and shoving. Some of them ran toward the policemen. Some of them ran the other way.

Louella had come up behind me while I was watching the commotion outside. She touched my leg. I turned around:

"What are you doing in here? Go back to bed. I'll bet you haven't got any shoes on."

I felt dizzy and scared. I wanted to go back to the Gardener Building—any place—just get out of all this mess before it was too late. Here we hadn't been in this joint twenty-four hours, and we'd been cursed out, Red was mad at me, we'd got our window broke, and folks were threatening to bomb us. Now this crowd was outside my window fighting the cops to beat the band just to get at us.

"Louella!" I said. "Get back in that bed! Helen, what'd you let Louella get out of the bed for? Don't you know there's glass on the floor in here?"

"Come on to bed, Louella," Helen said.

Louella didn't move. She was watching the fight. The light of the moon, even brighter now, was hitting her in the face. There were old woman's wrinkles in her face that I had never seen before. I got scared. My baby looked like a little old lady! I sounded whiney to myself when I said:

"Go to bed, Louella! *Please!*"

She let my leg go. I looked out of the window, just as the policeman's club went down on top of that fat gray head. People hollered, and I saw an arm chunking something toward the window again. I snatched Louella away from the window just as a dull, thump booped against the side of the wall, and a scattering noise followed from the dirt yard underneath the window.

"Helen!" I screamed at that woman, I had to. She wouldn't pay the *devil* no attention! "Helen, Helen!"

She came stomping in the room, her bare feet smacking against that bare tile floor:

"What you want?"

"Get this girl out of here! She's going to get killed! These bastards are throwing bricks like they're crazy! That's the second or third one tonight!"

"Come on, Louella."

Louella grabbed Helen by the leg. She and Helen left. I called Helen:

"What's Diane doing?"

"She's asleep."

I looked out of the window again. The crowd had thinned out. The cops had surrounded the gray-haired fat man and were talking to him. A dark smear spotted his silvery hair. He was rubbing his head with one hand. He rubbed his stomach with the other one.

A red light started flashing down toward the end of the driveway. Headlights lit up the bodies of the few people still standing around, and they moved aside as the headlights came closer. The red flashing light turned on the buildings it touched like a revolving Christmas tree. It hit my room and turned it red, then left it black again when it moved on. Round and round it went like there was a car wreck or something. Two policemen climbed out of the car. One had on a white shirt under his dark uniform. They went over to where the gray-haired man and the other policemen were, and the captain started waving his hands and talking loud. I could only make out part of what he was saying. For the first time I noticed the rushing sound of trains going by in back of my house, the loud sound of big freight cars banging up against each other, and the *shhhhh!* of steam near the tracks. I thought it must be a freight yard. In between all this I heard the captain blowing his top:

"Well, whaddid you have to hit 'im for, officer?"

Shh! went that doggoned steam from those trains, and I couldn't hear a word the long, lanky policeman who had gotten into the fight with the gray-haired man said. The steam died down and the captain's voice rose up again:

"That's no reason for vi'lence! I to' you men a hunnert times. Dooon't rough up these people! They got rights!"

"Yes, sir, captain, but this man here was——"

Shhhhh! bang! went one of them big-mouthed freight cars. *Shhh! bang!*

Then a faraway horn started honking without stopping— just one steady *honnnnnk.* The sound came closer. I had heard those big diesels down at the Gardener Building, back on Lafayette Street where that viaduct was. Same sound that I'd been listening to ever since I was a little snot, laying in bed listening to Momma crying over Daddy and that 61st Street girl. Same sound like something real big was coming. Something real big and fast, and bad, and mean, running at you so fast that you couldn't even think about running away. And you just lay there and waited for it to hurry up and come. Except it wouldn't hurry up. It just went *hooonnnnnnnk!* taking its own good time getting there and drowning out everything but itself as it came, until it caught you in its bigness, and fastness, and

47

hooonnnnnk!, and you just wasn't you or nothing else but that big-ass train until it got ready to let you go and move on down the line.

By the time the train passed the captain had gotten back into that car with the emergency red light going round and round, and the long, lanky policeman had started walking toward my house, and the fat, sloppy, gray-haired man had gone.

5

STARED OUT of the window at the other two-storey apartments around me. The lights were out in most of them. It was quiet except for the *shhh* of the trains in the train yard, and that didn't really seem like noise. It seemed more like part of the quiet. The moon was still bright like it hadn't seen all the commotion that had gone on downstairs right underneath my window. I began to feel things again, to see things around me.

The long smokestacks of the steel mills poked like black fingers with fire for fingertips at the black bottom of the sky, and I got lonesome and sad. Fire just leaped out of those smokestacks, leaped out and broke away and hung in the air with nothing holding it up and disappeared, but not before some more fire took its place. It began to get hot, or maybe it had been hot all the time, and I was just beginning to feel it. It's funny: at first I'd been cold, and now I was hot. A smell like steel burning was in the air, and everytime the wind would shove some of that hot air through the window, that hot, steel-tasting smell would come in with it. I wondered what the people in the Gardener Building were doing right now. Probably having a ball. But somebody in that evil scoundrel was probably dying too, or getting ready to.

I turned and climbed in the bed. Helen was already there, and asleep too. I wondered how she had gotten there without my hearing her. I pulled the sheet over me and snuggled up against her. She grunted and turned toward me and raised up for me to put my arm under her head. She always laid on my arm, and I always snuggled close to her. I closed my eyes, still seeing that fat gray-haired man and that long lanky cop scuffling down there, still hearing the window pane breaking and the sound of that brick rolling across the floor, sounding so much like one of those Gardener Building rats on a rampage. I felt my heart beating heavy and kind of fast, and I felt the blood in my ears washing back and forth like one of those laundromats. I felt things slipping away from me—sounds, smells, thoughts even. Slipping, slipping . . .

Then a loud knocking at the door downstairs. Sounded like the back door. Helen jumped straight up. I hollered:
"Who is it?"

There was no answer. Only that loud knocking. I got up, went downstairs, cracked the back door, and peeked out:
"Sorry to disturb you."

He was real tall. The kitchen light in his face showed me a tired face with a thick moustache, and straight black hair hanging down halfway across his forehead. Beside him stood a woman who looked a lot like him—keen features, full lips, straight black hair and glasses.

The man stuck his hand out, shook mine, and walked in all at the same time. The woman pushed in behind him. She was pregnant. It's funny, but I had to look back at Helen standing there in the kitchen doorway—to see who was the largest. Helen was.

The man stepped inside, and two little kids came up from behind him. Both of them had been crying, and

50

crooked little dirt stains ran from their eyes to their little chins. One, a little girl about six and just a little taller than Louella, said, looking up at the tall man:

"Daddy, can we stay here? Please, Daddy?"

The woman said:

"Hush, Sharon."

Then the woman looked at me, kind of embarrassed like:

"Don't mind her."

The tall man said:

"I'm Arthur Davis."

I said:

"How you doing?"

He said:

"This is my wife Mona."

Mona was real pretty, but she had that same sad look that her husband had. Honest, it didn't help her looks at all. Still she was that kind of nice girl, pretty, with the honey-brown face of hers, oval as an olive.

"And this," he put his hand on the little girl's head, "is Sharon."

He put his hand on the head of the little boy—short little squirt with a part in his hair and a face just like his mother's.

"This is Bobby."

The little boy smiled and sort of looked off in space.

Arthur Davis—sounded like I had heard that name before—*Arthur Davis* and that woman, his wife—seemed like I had seen her before—where?

Then I knew:

"Hey, you ain't the first family that moved out here, are you? The one whose picture is always in the *Chicago Defender?* Is that you? Aw, sure it is! And your picture is in the *Defender* a lot too, ain't it, Mrs. Davis? Well, Helen, we got celebrities in the house tonight!—Oh, this is Helen, my wife. And I'm Louis Martin—everybody calls me 'Buggy.' Come on in, come on in!"

Arthur Davis said:

"I know it's late, and I'm sorry to disturb you, but we just don't have any place to go—at least, not right now. What I mean is can we sit here awhile with you until—until——"

I looked up at him. There was water in his eyes. His wife stepped up:

"Well, what we mean is—these people are awful. They are over at our house right now throwing bricks and iron pipes at every window in the house. Little Bobby here just missed being killed by a piece of pipe that they threw through the kids' bedroom window." Her voice started to get wobbly. "You're new here, and perhaps they won't . . . You don't know what we've been through. We have had to sleep with our clothes on because we never know when they are going to rush in on us. Poor Sharon has been crying all night, she's so scared. None of us have had any sleep at all since yesterday. We don't want to bother anybody, but we haven't anyone else to turn to. The Turners aren't at home and Burtons didn't answer. One of the colored cops told us that you lived here. We just took a chance that you'd be here."

Helen went over to Mona Davis. They looked funny, in a way—both of them sticking out. Yet there was something that caught on between them that seemed to leave me and this tall cat Arthur outside. Helen put her arms around Mona's shoulders:

"We haven't straightened this junk out yet, but we've got a couch that lets out, and you are welcome to use it. Buggy, will you fix the couch for Mona?"

She pulled Mona into the living room.

The little boy said:

"Daddy, can I have a drink of water?"

The little girl said:

"Me too, Daddy, can I have a drink too, please?"

Arthur looked at me, frowning helplessly. I pointed to the dishrack on the drainboard beside the sink:

"Right there, Arthur."

I followed the women into the living room and fixed the couch. Helen said:

"See, Mona? It's plenty large enough for you and your husband. Your children can sleep upstairs with our kids."

"I don't know how to thank you, Helen. You just don't know these people."

"I'll go and get some covers."

Mona said:

"I even heard that they were supposed to try to dynamite our house tonight, Helen——"

"Buggy, where's the cover we used on this couch?"

"——and the police are right in with them, in all this——"

"Look under those boxes near the window," I said.

Helen said:

"You come here and look."

"——and the cops just stood there and watched them throw bricks at our windows. For two months this has been going on. Bombs going off every night. Almost drives you crazy. Once a man tried to break in while Arthur was gone. Broke the window at the door with his fist and tried to reach in. I had a lighted cigarette and I mashed it against his forehead. Honestly, that's the only thing that stopped him. I was so afraid I——"

Arthur Davis came into the living room with the children. Mona stopped talking. There was something funny between them. Boy, I could tell that right away. Now don't ask me what—it was something. Was she scared of him? Still, she had to do the talking when he got all choked up in the living room. Was that swollen place on her cheek a black eye, or was it just from crying? She was such a pretty thing. Smooth skin, and big, round, sad, sad eyes that looked as though they had just finished crying. Poor, poor pretty thing. Yet and still—I swear I'm going crazy— yet and still, she was strong. I mean *real* strong. It was in her voice, it was in those eyes, even through those tears. You didn't want to cuddle her. You just wanted to help her.

I sort of sized her up as I went into the living room—you know how men do—and this Mona had a tallish lean-type figure, but she wasn't skinny-looking by no means. Just big—oh, big-little. Yeah, I guess that's it. She was a little-looking big woman, a weak-looking strong woman. Anyhow, she shuts up when Arthur steps into the room; and Helen, seeing that something was getting out of step, said with one of those snappy voices of hers:

"Arthur, you and Mona are going to sleep down here. Do you think you will be all right down here?"

Arthur put both hands on his forehead, and locked his fingers together, and slid his hands back across his hair. I watched it ripple as his hand slid back. Then he closed his eyes tight. Little bitty folds caved in all around his eyes. His skinny face drew in at the cheeks, and he poked his reddish-wet lips out like he was pouting, or maybe hurting. Then he said, almost whispering:

"Yeah, Helen, yeah. Thanks, folks. I mean it. Thanks."

I heard bare feet trying to tiptoe down the stairs. I listened hard, trying to figure out whether it was Diane or Louella. Helen didn't waste no time—she knew:

54

"Get back in that bed, Louella!"

The feet skittered back up the stairs and I heard the springs squeak. Mona said:

"Have you heard that they are supposed to try to dynamite the house tonight?"

She had that dynamite on her brain. Well, I had it on mine too. After all, I was standing right there when this policeman comes up to this captain and tells him that "they're supposed to bomb the niggers' house tonight." Get that—"*niggers!*"

But this chick—oouee! That's *all* she's talking about. I guess maybe I must have been thinking too loud or looking at Mona funny or something, because she answered what was in my mind just like I had said it out loud, and I hadn't opened my mouth. There was a dryish-tired sound in her voice, and she looked straight at me:

"I guess you think I've just about blown my top, talking about——"

Well, naturally I didn't want her thinking nothing like that, so I cut her off right there:

"Oh, naw! Don't nobody here think nothing like that. In fact, I heard the same thing today. A policeman right outside said——"

If I'm lying, I'm flying. Mona didn't even as much as slow down talking. She just kept right on talking right over what I was saying:

"——talking about dynamite, and men trying to break in and people throwing iron pipes through the window, and all——"

I knew it was going to happen. Her voice started getting wobbly again. Only this time she was just getting wound up and I knew there was no sense trying to stop her. I hate to hear a woman start to get wobbly. But all I could do was stand there with a man's kind of helpless feeling, watching Mona start to tune up, and her voice got wobblier and wobblier:

"——Arthur and I didn't know what was happening out here. We just needed a place to live. Sharon was always catching a cold at the other place we lived. Bedbugs and roaches all over the kitchen table, and in the pillows and cabinets and everywhere. They thrived on insecticides. I never knew when I might wake up and find one of the kids dead in the bed, eaten up by a rat."

She turned to Arthur Davis:

"You know that, Arthur! We used to have to sit up all night to watch the kids while they slept, just so the rats wouldn't get them, didn't we, Arthur?"

She sounded like she was trying to apologize for being out in Trumbull Park, like she had to explain why she was out there. Hell, I didn't need no explanation. I could still see Babydoll falling. I could still hear her body hit the ground four stories down. I could still feel Bertha's soft ankle slipping out of my hands when she tried to jump off the top floor, after Babydoll died.

Arthur Davis didn't answer Mona. He sat down on the couch and started to take his shoes off. His little boy Bobby sat down beside him. Sharon went over to Mona and laid her head against the tall woman's leg.

Boom!

"Aiiieeee!" Mona screamed.

Boom! A yellow flash slugged the house like the fist of a heavyweight. Glasses slid off the kitchen sink and broke against the floor. I got so excited I didn't know what I was doing. The first thing I thought about were the kids. I started up the stairs, and then I remembered Helen downstairs. I heard her crying out loud. I started back down the steps when Louella started crying and calling Helen:

"Momma, Momma!"

"Shut up," I screamed.

Then Diane started crying. And then I heard Arthur downstairs; he had opened the door, and the outside sounds were coming in with his voice:

"Goddamn you! Goddamn you bastards!"

"Get back in that house!" It sounded like one of the policemen.

"Momma!" Louella again.

Helen was still crying. I ran upstairs to the kids' room. They were both sitting straight up; right beside each other. Louella had her arm around Diane. Diane was squeezed against Louella. I turned the light on in the room, and Louella closed her eyes. Then she opened them, blinking. Tears were all over her face. I ran to Diane and Louella, and hugged them.

"Goddamned bastards," I said.

"I told you once. This is the last time! Get back into that house!" It was the cop again.

Arthur wasn't backing down though:

"What the hell are you cops doing out here? You're not enforcing the law!"

I got scared for Arthur. I'd never heard anybody talk to a cop like that and not get hit. The cop hollered back. I could just picture his red face by the way his voice sounded:

"Anyway, it's not your house that got blown up. It's that tavern you been going to!"

Arthur screamed back:

"Who been going to?"

The cop's voice sounded like it was going to break loose from his throat and take off like an airplane:

"You heard me—you! If you hadn't been so smart, going into that joint it never would've happened!"

57

Arthur was screaming, but he was thinking. I could feel
the next thing he was going to say:

"You talk like you knew it was going to happen!"
The cop didn't say nothing. Arthur hollered:

"Did you? Did you know they was going to blow
up the tavern tonight because they served me?"

"Davis, I'm warning you!"

"Did you know? Did you know?"

"Davis!"

Oh my god! I just knew he was going to hit Arthur Davis.
Maybe shoot him even. I let loose of Diane and Louella and
ran downstairs.

"Answer, cop! You knew, didn't you?"

"Davis!"

Arthur slammed the door in the cop's face and walked
back over to the couch. Again he locked his fingers together
at his forehead and slid his hands back across his hair. His
own two kids were holding on to Mona for all they were
worth. She had her arms around Helen. Helen was crying.
Outside police cars and fire engines screeched around corners, and sirens went and bells danged like everybody was
having a hell of a good time.

I felt loose and weak inside like all of my bones had got
unhooked some kind of way, and I sat down on the couch
beside Arthur.

"Momma! Momma!"

It was Louella again. I swear I thought that child was
going to drive me crazy. I breathed hard and called as easy
as I could:

"Go to sleep, Louella. It's all over now. Go to sleep!"
Helen pulled herself loose from Mona and started up
the stairs. She had the same tired slump in her shoulders
that Mona had. But, I thought, Mona's been here two
whole months; we just got here—how come Helen's like

58

that already? Then I remembered that Helen was pregnant. Then I remembered that Mona was pregnant. I said:

"I'll get that cover for you. It's just upstairs in the dresser. I don't guess there's going to be any more dynamiting tonight, huh?"

Mona didn't answer. She sat down beside Arthur and started rubbing his hair back. He laid his head on her shoulder. His shoulders started shaking like he was cold or crying or something. The kids, Bobby and Sharon, looked at me real funny-like. They weren't mad, and they sure weren't glad, just had that funny kind of look. I didn't know I was staring until Mona looked up at me and said:

"It'll happen to you too. It doesn't take long. It'll happen. You'll understand then. Then you'll understand."

I felt like that woman had put a curse on me. I don't believe in all that old-fogey stuff, but I sure felt like she had put a curse on me.

6

I DON'T KNOW whether I slept that night or not. I guess I did. In fact, I'm sure I must have. But still, off and on all night, I found myself staring from the bed out of the window at the flames puffing out of the tips of those smokestacks. The gray in the sky got lighter, and the dark gray of the clouds around the smokestacks got mixed in with the orange-red of the steel-mill fire. The room felt strange to me, and I had to turn around and look at Helen to make sure I wasn't caught in one of those nightmares where everybody knows you and you know nobody, and everything looks strange to you even though you've lived there all your life.

Helen was there. There was a deep frown on her face, and her lips were drawn tight. She was breathing heavy, and there was a trembling in her breath. I listened for sounds in the kids' room. Pretty soon the sound of Louella's half-snoring kind of breathing separated itself from the other noises—of Helen's breathing, the trains in the train yard outside, and the whispery squeak of birds just waking up. I listened to the even in-and-out of Louella's breathing and knew that she was all right. Then I listened for Diane's breathing. It was harder to make out, but I heard it, and I knew that both of the kids were sleeping like two logs. I listened hard. There was nothing except the noises that Diane and Louella made. I made a motion to ease out of bed. Helen stirred, and I stopped and lay real still. She started breathing heavy again, and I sat up and slipped out of bed.

I tiptoed into the kids' room. There on one twin bed were my two girls just as asleep as you please. The other bed was empty. The cover that I had gotten out for the Davis kids was spread neatly over the bed and tucked in at the edges, but the bed was empty. I went half-way down the stairs, just far enough to see in the living room. There was no one on the couch, and it had been made up into a couch again—something to sit on, not to sleep on. Only the sheets and quilts folded neatly at one end of the couch showed that the Davises had been there at all. It worried me—how they had come after dark and gone before light, hauling those two little kids around after bedtime and getting them up again before get-up time. Poor little kids—how had Arthur and Mona gotten them up and away so quietly?

I thought of my own two and went upstairs again and sat on the empty bed looking at them. Diane seemed to have grown up overnight. One day she was a wrinkled little red thing frowning up in the first daylight that ever fell upon her, wriggling and huffing and blowing in the nurse's white-uniformed arms; then all of a sudden up she jumps and gets to be two years old. She lay close to Louella, her arm out from under the cover plopped across Louella's arm, and Louella's arm hugged her tight, and they were just about breathing each other's breath. It was hard to think of Louella as only four. She had been the big sister from the day Diane was born, taking to the job like a little old lady. That bossy thing would just as soon try to spank Diane for acting bad as I would.

The house seemed so quiet around us, the air seemed so

clean—no garbage or sewer stink, no thumping juke-box music bouncing down the streets, no heavy footsteps on loose noisy stairs, no flushing of ten toilets all at once, no porches with rotten bannisters—that I got scared just sitting there looking at Louella. Just looking at her, and thinking of how she'd soon be big enough to know that a boy was a boy, and that she was a girl. I got scared remembering myself when I first figured out that boys were boys, and girls were girls, and—worst of all—that people were people, and Daddy was Daddy, with a girl friend from 61st Street.

I was nine years old and soaking wet behind the ears, watching everything that went on, in the house and out. Momma was alive then. Helen was the "new girl" in the building—on the tall side already; dark, with those keen features even then; eyes shaped like almonds and colored like almonds. Helen—I sure thought she was fine, with her hinkty self walking so straight and smiling so grown-up and quiet when she talked to you.

Daddy was a big man then—inside, I mean. He kept on being a big man outside. At least he was the last time I'd seen him underneath the El on 58th Street in front of the packaged-goods store. Big man—Daddy-boy! That cat could carry a bushel basket of coal under each arm and run up the stairs at the same time. Big man Daddy, about the color of a paper bag, smooth-skin devil, a real cool moustache—still had *that* anyway. Thick wavy hair parted on the side and swinging long and low down on his face into a pair of the sexiest sideburns you ever saw.

Nine years old—what a long time ago! I had a family then—I mean a brother-and-sister-and-momma-and-daddy kind of family, you know? Now Momma was dead. Daddy, a stranger—a lushhead 58th Street stranger. Johnetta, in business for herself somewhere out west. And Ricky—my baby brother Ricky, Ricky the loafer, Ricky the con-man, Ricky the one we expected to be visiting once a month behind high walls and bars—a policeman. And Doris? In-between. Doris never was a child. Nobody ever saw Doris, never paid her no attention. Oh, she ate and laughed and played with everybody else, but no one ever really saw her. She wasn't the oldest, she wasn't the youngest. She wasn't even in-between in any kind of set way. She was next-to-Ricky-the-youngest, just as I was next-to-Johnetta-the-oldest. Doris was a ghost when she was born, and she was a ghost when she left home and joined the WACS.

So I wound up being the only thing left of the Martins down on the fourth floor. Helen was Helen, and I was Buggy—nobody called me Louis. We were the Martins after we were married—and yet we weren't the Martins. We weren't a new family—grown-ups equal to grown-ups. We were just carry-ons of "Zelma-Martin's-family-if-she-hadda-lived." Helen's folks had not left the Gardener Building. They couldn't—just like we couldn't—not until Babydoll. They were "the second floor front." They were the letters that lay on the bottom step, saying *Mr. and Mrs. Johnny Reed and Family.* They were the light-brown skinny cripple man and the dark plump lady with the gold in her teeth. They were Helen's mother and father to Helen's friends, and Helen was Johnny and Marion's girl to their friends.

"What's your name, girl?"

Seven-year-old girls looked big then. Momma wasn't even dead.

"Helen."

"Helen? Helen what?"

"Helen Reed. What's yours?"

"Buggy—Buggy Martin."

How can you like somebody and hate them too? And how can they look at you and make your ears burn even when they're only seven and you're only nine?

Daddy met this 61st Street girl when I was nine. That was when Momma started crying at night in the room by herself. And that was when Daddy started staying out late. Daddy drove a truck. *Jack's Movers,* the sign painted on the side of it said. It was Jack's truck, but Daddy drove it most of the time. Jack would come by early in the morning when it was still dark. Jack's loud, rusty-sounding truck-horn would go:

Honk!

Daddy was a tall big man.

"Hurry up with that coffee, Baby."

Momma was a small, slim woman.

"It's right beside you, Charlie."

Daddy loved Momma, but he just had to go and meet this 61st Street girl.

"Why didn't you say so, Zelma?"

"I thought you saw it, Charlie."

Momma loved Daddy, and she knew about the 61st Street girl. Now Daddy knew she knew. Mrs. Palmer had found out from Sam the cab driver, and told Lukey's mother because she knew Lukey's mother would tell Momma, and Lukey's mother did.

"If I had seen it with my own eyes, would I be asking you about it, Zelma?"

Momma's eyes were light brown, and her hair was light brown and parted in the middle, and her voice was soft and easy.

"I guess not."

Daddy's voice had scrape in it, and it scraped and hurt and bruised, and sometimes it got real low and mumbly:

"I'm—uh—not coming home this evening, Baby. The twentieth ward is having a smoker for——"

And sometimes Momma's voice broke and she had to fix it:

"Okay, Charlie."

And sometimes Daddy's voice broke, and he had to shout to fix it:

"You act like you don't believe me! I get that funny way you're acting. Why don't you believe me? Huh?"

Honk!

"It's all right, Charlie."

And sometimes Momma's light-brown eyes would stare at the fire behind the door of the pot-bellied stove in the living room and get glassy and blink and dry up.

"Jack's blowing for you."

And sometimes Daddy would stare at the fire behind the door of the pot-bellied stove in the living room too, and try to see if there really was fire behind that door, just by looking real hard at it. And he wouldn't be able to know for sure if there was fire behind that door, and would clench his fists and open them, and catch me peeping at him from the let-out couch in the living room, and would wink at me and look away real quick when I wouldn't wink back. Gulp his coffee and push the table away from him, and make the same scraping noise every day as the table scooted over the linoleum. And kiss Momma's forehead— sometimes she would fold her lips between her teeth so that he couldn't kiss her when he tried to kiss her on the mouth—and out the door he'd go. Big man with a plaid lumber-jacket, black-wool cap over his ears, red-plaid scarf, and the smell of cigarettes stirring around the room as he shook the pockets in his pants hanging across the chair to see if he was leaving any money behind.

"Take something for that cold, Baby."

"I did."

"Take something else. You coughed all night. I couldn't sleep."

"Okay, Charlie."

That's when Momma would cry, and cough, cry and cough, cry and cough! cough! cough!

And that's when I would dress fast and quiet and slip out of the back door and run down to Helen's back porch and cough and stomp like I was playing a game until Helen would come out to see what the noise was and would come out to play, wearing that green summer dress that first made me think about boys being boys and girls being girls. And summer would come and go and come and go again, and I would turn ten and Helen would turn eight, and I would turn eleven and Helen would turn nine; and I would run from Momma's cough to Helen. Didn't she ever wear anything but green dresses in those days, or did I just remember her that way? What is it about green dresses anyway that makes little girls who are nine act the way they do? What is it about little girls who are nine that makes you want to run up and down the stairway in the Gardener Building and jump five or even ten steps down to the sidewalk on State Street?

"Helen, don't you think you're cute!"

She wouldn't let my hand go.

"No."

She wouldn't let my hand go.

"You do."

"I don't."

"What are you holding my hand for?"

"Huh?"

"I'll break your back! I'll grab you around the waist

like this, and pick you up like this, and squeeze you so hard that I'll break your back!"

"Put me down, Buggy! You're wrinkling my dress."

She was so warm. She was so soft, soft like hot rubber, soft like hot dough, soft like hot feathers.

"Buggy, stop!"

The soft green-dress thing pulled out of my arms, and ran out of the hallway, smoothing her hair, smoothing her dress.

I broke up those stairs, didn't even feel like I was moving a muscle. Strength took me up—not me. First floor—second floor—past Helen's house—third floor—fourth floor. Down the hallway, cabbage cooking somewhere—past the toilet in the hallway, time for somebody to scrub that thing! Through the door, and—where's Momma?

Into the kitchen—no. Into the living room—no. Into the bedroom.

Momma was in the bed.

Something surprised me. I didn't know what. I said:

"Hi, Momma."

I flopped in the chair in the hallway in front of her door. I could see her real good from where I sat. I blew and puffed trying to keep air in my lungs after all that running after Helen. That syrup in me was hot now, running fast through my veins and making them jerk and jump every time my heart beat. Talk about feeling like summertime! I was a young tree on the lagoon in Washington Park, a hunk of that foamy water behind one of those motorboats out in Jackson Park, a bouncing ball, a flying baseball bat about to knock a home run from State Street all the way to South Parkway.

But Momma was in the bed.

"What's the matter, Momma?"

"I want you to go to the store for me."

The head of the bed was against the wall near the door. I could see her head and shoulders but not her feet. There was a dresser against the wall across from the bed, and while I couldn't see it, I saw that the lamp on the dresser was on. There was a window on the other side of the room right opposite the door leading from the hallway where I was sitting.

Momma's bed was between the window and the door. The shade was halfway down, and the light from outside, dimmed by the shadow from the tall Gardener-fied building across the street, was weak and gray and cold-looking.

The shade on the lamp on the dresser was red, and the light that came from the lamp was red, and the spread on Momma's bed was red, and the red light disappeared when it hit the red spread, and only looked red when it hit the sheet that Momma had pulled over her, and when it hit Momma's face.

There weren't any real shadows on Momma's face as she lay there. She only looked that way, with the gray sun lighting up the back of her brown hair and her thin brown neck, and the red light from the lamp pushing deep red curves underneath her eyes and around her straightish nose and below her narrow moist lips. But it looked like shadows along the high bones that swooped down from her temples and vanished in the shallow cheeks and pointed chin—not black shadows, but red ones, with deep red taking the place of black, and pale red taking the place of light, and gray light curving around her head and neck: silver-spray paint, running into pink and red-water color.

Shadows—real shadows—hung like hot fog on top of the ceiling, and under the bed, and behind the bed, and in front of the bed, and on the chair where Daddy's sport shirt hung, rising out of the shadows like plaid fog and fall-

ing back into them before the shape of the shirt was clear.
I must have not answered Momma that first time. Must have not even seen the shadows the way I do now. Must have seen those shadows long after Momma died, but not then. Maybe right after she died, but not then. Must have been too full of that summer syrup and Helen's green dress. Momma asked me again—I was only eleven then, but I remember well, so well, that she had to ask me again:

"Buggy, will you go to the store for me? I need some things for dinner tonight."

Too full of Helen's green——

"Aw, Momma. Can't I go later?"

Red shadows tiptoe behind me now sometimes and cough and laugh, like some crazy wino on 58th Street.

"It'll only take a minute." *Cough! Cough!* "I—I— Momma doesn't feel too well." *Cough! Cough! Cough!*

"How come Johnetta can't go? She right in the back. You never tell her to go any place. Just because she's the biggest."

"It'll only take a minute, Buggy." *Cough! Cough! Cough! Cough! Cough!* "I'd go myself if I—please Buggy, I can't——" *Cough! Cough!*

"Aw, Momma."

"Okay, Baby. You don't have to go."

Sometimes those red shadows get in between that great big diesel that runs downtown along Lafayette and that diesel starts buzzing, and those shadows start laughing, and I can see Momma's face sunk way down in the pillow of those shadows, and I can see her eyes brighten from the tears in them, and hear her voice say:

"Okay, Baby. You don't have to go. . . ."

I got up from the chair in the hallway and ran to the bed and sat on the edge of it and hugged her head in the crook

of my arm and laid my head on top of that soft brown hair
with the part in the middle.

"What's the matter, Momma? What are you crying
for? I'll go. I was just *saying* that. I'll go, Momma."

That wasn't what she was crying about. It wasn't what
she had cried about for a long time. It wasn't what she had
cried about late at night when the house was quiet except
for the streetcars clanging down State Street and cars hush-
ing over the smooth part of State Street away from the
cobblestone tracks, and I would lay there listening to her
crying and ask her what was the matter and she would say,
"Nothing, Baby, nothing."

She wasn't crying about what I had said, not even really
about what Daddy had done, not really about anything in
particular. She was crying because she was going to die,
and yet not even because of that either, but because she
had told me and Johnetta and Doris and Rickey, not in
words but just by being what she was that we wouldn't
have to suffer the way she had. That we wouldn't have to
suffer to go to the store, suffer to scrub the floors, suffer to
bow to old Mrs. Palmer when she needed someone to boss
around, suffer to kneel to any man, woman or child for help,
or protection, or love. We, she had said, not in words but in
blood that she never let us see, would never suffer as long
as she lived.

"I'll go, Momma. I was just *saying* that. I'll go to
the store. What's the matter, Momma?"

She pulled out of my arms and raised her head and
straightened the pillow underneath her head. I reached to
help her, but she was finished by then and was turning toward me; and that red light clung to her face every way she
moved, clung like water does when you're in it—under it.
Her face didn't jerk, nor did her eyes flutter the way you do

when you're crying about something that hurts just your flesh, just your pride. The tears fell out of her eyes like something inside was broken and crying and wouldn't be stopped by pulling a muscle in the face this way or that. No sobs, no gasps, no deep in the throat moans, no whines— just tears flowing, even and steady and quiet. Flowing.

"Momma, what's the matter? Don't you feel good?"

"No, Honey, Mother doesn't feel good. Mother's sick . . . very sick."

"Do you want me to call the doctor?"

"No, I went to see the doctor today, while you were outside playing. Buggy, Momma's . . ."

"Huh, Momma?"

"I'm sick, Buggy—like I told you. And the doctor said that I'm going to have to . . ."

She pulled her hand out from under the cover, and touched my knee and squeezed it: it hurt. She turned her face to the pillow and started coughing, a dry hacking cough and a deep ripping one. Her whole body jerked about in the bed as though something was knocking it first this way, then that way. Her hands gripped the edges of the pillow, and then the outside edges of the bed as she coughed and jerked and pushed her face deeper and deeper into the pillow. She sounded like she was choking. I hit her on the back, but she shook her head violently from side to side telling me *no*; and after a while the coughing let go a little bit, and she lay there breathing hard, her chest raising the cover up and down, her arms stretched out, hands barely reaching the edge of the bed, hanging limp over the edge. There was a torn place on the sheet at the edge of the bed nearest me, where her fingers had gripped the sheet, and pulled, and scratched, and finally tore it.

I patted her back and rubbed the back of her neck and

started to lay my head in the curve between her neck and shoulders, but she shook her head real hard and raised up from the pillow just enough to say:

"No! Move!"

When she raised her head, I saw that there was blood on the pillow. I remember I had seen it before, without seeing it—had heard Momma cough before, without hearing her—at night when the fire was out in the pot-bellied stove and the house was cold and dark and damp.

Sometimes late at night after Momma died, when John-etta and Ricky and Doris and I would be crowded in some strange bed in some strange room with some strange "new momma," I would hear that coughing and that crying and that buzzing diesel train filling up the room and grinding all other sounds into itself and letting them back down to earth, and buzzing more and more softly until it was gone and only Momma's crying and coughing was there in my mind the way it had once been in Momma's room.

Had I ever really seen Momma at all? Did she ever live for me? Was she ever more than a hot cup of Ovaltine ("because Little John downstairs had some, Momma, honest")? Ever more than a soft hand rubbing Vick's salve on my chest on a snowy night? Ever more than some place to go to get things?

Did I ever hear her voice other than when she was saying:

"It's time to get up . . . It's time to eat . . . It's time for school . . . It's time to go to bed"?

Did I ever hear my mother's voice—really hear it?

"No, no, no! Move, I said!"

And she raised her head out of the blood, and it was smeared on her sweet cheek—my Momma's cheek—and I jumped up and ran to the dresser to find a clean cloth for her to wipe her face; but when I got back she had pulled one from underneath her pillow and had wiped her face and was smiling in the red light from the lamp on the table, the gray light from the window. Her voice was stronger now. She patted the bed, and I sat down.

"Mother's going to have to go away to a—a hospital."

Was she waiting for me to say something then? I didn't open my mouth. She said:

"Mother has a bad cold——and the—" *cough! cough! cough!* "—and the doctor said that Mother has to go away for a little while—to a hospital."

"Why do you have to go away? Can't you stay here? I'll take care of you. I'll go to the store, and Johnetta can cook, and Doris and Ricky can keep the house clean."

"I wish I could stay, Honey, but the doctor said that I have a bad cold and that I have to go so that you and Ricky and your sisters won't catch it. You don't want to have a cold like I have do you?"

"I don't want you to go, Momma."

"I have to, Buggy."

"Momma, who going to take care of us if you go? You can't leave us, Momma. Who'll cook dinner and all of that?"

"I want you kids to go over to Aunt Bobbie's house when I go. I've already talked to her, and she said that you can stay with her until I get back and . . ."

The tears started flowing again. I felt myself getting ready to cry. I felt myself crying. Momma's voice got weaker and weaker, and she breathed harder and harder—pumping air into that little chest underneath the white sheets and the red spread.

"I don't want you kids to be bad, hear? And I want you to mind Aunt Bobbie. I know she sort of loses her temper every now and then, but don't pay that any attention. Just do what she says until I get back. I—I won't be gone

73

long, Buggy. I want you to take care of your sisters while I'm gone and don't let them get into anything, Buggy I–I . . ."

Then the cough got her and the shadows leaped and danced on top of the spread—on top of her, as she coughed and twisted and fell into the black hole in the pillow and gripped the edges of the pillow and the edges of the bed and then lay still, and finally raised up from the pillow with blood around her mouth and the cloth in her hand. She wiped the blood away, and she rubbed at the tears that were still flowing from her eyes and went on to say:

"Now I don't want any cry baby here. You know you're too big to cry. You should be busy trying to keep me from crying. But I'm not going to cry either. I'm too big to be crying myself. Now I want you to go downstairs and bring up your sisters and Ricky. I want to tell them while I'm not coughing. I want you to help me, hear? Just tell them that Mother is sick and that she has to go to the hospital and that they shouldn't cry, because you're not crying, and that Mother will be back real soon, hear? Now you tell them that just the way I told you, hear?"

But I couldn't hear her now. My insides had pulled aloose—my stomach, my throat, my heart, my lungs—all pulled aloose and floating around in there and burning from the salt that ran into my mouth from the tears that ran down my cheeks. My ears were stopped up and ringing, and the red fog and the old diesel were buzzing and laughing to beat the band. And when I ran out of Momma's room out of the apartment and down the stairs and out into the street and around the corner to the back of the building where Ricky and Johnetta and Doris were, I was running to get away from that buzzing and that coughing and crying and the red lamp-light and the gray sunlight and the blood on Momma's pillow.

74

7

By the time I shook myself up from where I was sitting on the empty bed in Louella and Diane's room and went downstairs, the gray outside was lighter—light enough for me to see the note laid on the arm of the couch where Arthur and Mona had slept, but not enough for me to read without turning on the wall light near the door:

Dear Louis and Helen: Thanks for putting up with us. We hope we didn't disturb you too much. Sincerely, Mona.

"Disturb you"? That word "disturb" disturbed me greatly, believe me. I mean, did she mean disturb me by telling me all the stuff that had happened to her and Arthur since they moved in?

I went to the window and looked out. Five policemen stood in a huddle. Two or three of them were rubbing their hands together, and standing on one foot and then the other. A couple of them were standing side by side looking at a big notebook—the one Helen and I had had to sign to get in our house the night before.

The gray was moving away a little from the sun, and a misty pink was beginning to show up in spots through the clouds. The *shhh* of those trains in that train yard started up again, or maybe I was just beginning to hear that steam swooshing out of those trains again. Maybe it never had stopped going *shhhh*.

Then I heard the banging freight cars, and pretty soon the humming kind of growling sound of one of those dog-goned diesels flying down the line toward the train yard behind the house. *ZZZZZZzzzzzzzz* it came, getting louder and making things shake and shimmy and filling every corner with noise, a loud sort of background noise that was everything and yet just part of everything else. I felt myself getting in tune or maybe in rhythm with the trembling under my feet, and the *ZZZZZZZZZZzzzzzzzz* in my ear. I stood still and the train took me over, and held me up in the air almost. Then it let me down easy, and got quieter, and quieter, and growled on away until it was gone. But I stood there for a minute because I wanted to make sure it was gone.

That damned Gardener Building—that's what had me goofed. That's where that train got its bluff in on me. I got mad and shook my head and wiped my mouth with the back of my hand, and my lips were so dry I could feel them scratching my arm. I licked them and put my hands on my forehead and locked my fingers together and rubbed my hands backward on my head across my hair, the way Arthur Davis had done last night. Damnit! Why did I do that?

"*It'll happen to you too.*"

Now why did I have to start thinking about Mona saying that? What'll happen to me? I hollered:

"Helen!"

She didn't answer.

"Helen! Helen!"

"What?"

"I got to go to work. Come on and fix me something to eat!"

"Well, what are you hollering about?"

What was I hollering about? I rubbed my hands to-

76

gether. They were damp. I held one of them out in front of me. It was shaking. I hollered back at Helen:

"I'm hungry. That's what I'm hollering about!"

"Okay, I'll be down. Have you washed up already?"

Do you know I had forgotten that I hadn't even washed yet? That Helen knows every trick in the book: *she* knew I hadn't washed up yet. I just didn't answer her.

She said:

"Come on up and wash up. I'll have breakfast ready by the time you finish."

Did you *ever* see a woman like that in your life before?

Well, I went on upstairs and turned on the water in the tub. Boy, what a *big* thing that tub was! And white? The tub in the Gardener Building was so dingy that, even after you scrubbed it, that dime-store enamel was about as bright as the bottom of my shoe. Hell, I was scared to wash in it half the time, what with everybody and his brother, up the hall, down the hall, and—when somebody was in one of the other bathrooms—even folks from other floors, plopping their fat behinds in that tub. I just stood up over that clean tub for a minute watching that ripply clear water fill up that big pretty white tub. My tub—well, mine and Helen's and the kids'; but not Little John's and Bertha's— poor Bertha—and Johnnie's-down-the-hall, and half the other people in town.

I got in the water and stretched out. Nice warm water. No muddy grit shaking aloose from these pipes and filthying up my bath water now. What a difference such a little thing makes! Nice clean bathroom. Nice clean tub.

"Breakfast is ready!"

That woman!

"I just got in the tub. I'll be down in a minute."

I slid down in that tub as far as I could go. Then I remembered what the captain had said yesterday:

"It's not safe, right now, to walk to the car lines, so

we'll take you in the patrol wagon to 95th and State, or 95th and Cottage Grove, whichever you choose."

The patrol wagon. Boy, that hit me square in the stomach. I didn't even feel like staying in the water any more. I hurried up and washed and threw on some clothes and ran down the stairs. Helen was standing by the stove stirring some cereal she was fixing for the kids. When she saw me she said:

"I hope it's not too cold, Honey. I guess I should have waited till you were almost through."

I stopped.

"Aw, I shouldn't have hollered at you the way I did in the first place."

I sat down at the table and picked up a knife to cut the ham with. Helen had sort of got me off guard being so nice and all. Not that she wasn't always nice. She was. Hell, I guess it was me. I guess I just wasn't fit company for Helen or nobody else that morning.

I cut the ham into little squares and triangles and then I started mashing the eggs up. Maybe, I thought, I ought to explain to Helen about how scared I got this morning for no reason. I looked at her. She had on that blue housecoat I bought her for her birthday last July. It was different shades of blue, and it had flowers on it—light-blue flowers, dark-blue flowers, medium-blue flowers. The sleeves were short and kind of flared out at the ends. Boy, I sure did like that housecoat, the day I first saw it downtown. And I picked it out all by myself too. It didn't have any buttons in the front and Helen kept it closed with the wide, silky-looking, solid-color blue belt that went with it. Right now it kind of poked out in the front, but that didn't make any difference, that woman carried herself so tall and dainty. She even looked good when she was sleeping.

Helen had her hair combed back and rolled up into a

78

little ball in the back. Her hair wasn't very long, and it was easy for her to just comb it this way or that, or squeeze it up into some kind of little ball, and she was ready to go—looking as pretty as any woman in the world. Her skin was that *rich* brown that you don't get just from putting powder on, and when she smiled, boy, those eyes would just about close up; they just turned on like little lit-up marbles. Longish nose sort of wrinkled up, and those roundish poochy lips cherry-red. *Ooouuueee!* Something in me tingled just then! I said:

"Woman! You are a temptation!"

She laughed and came over and pushed my head.

"A fine time to be thinking about me being a temptation! Where were you last night when the lights went out?"

"Ahem! Well, Honey, I was so tired, I didn't know what to do."

EEEEEEeeeee! went a factory whistle, probably from the steel mills. Helen looked at her watch. She said:

"You'd better hurry. It's seven o'clock."

"Already?"

"It sure is."

I tore into those ham and eggs, and downed the coffee, and started looking around for my jacket. Helen went into the living room. She came right back, holding the jacket high and away from her.

"Here it is, you baby you."

I grabbed it and then grabbed her with my free hand, kissing her hard and giving her a little squeeze.

"Bye, Baby," I said.

Then a fear hit me in the stomach again. *I'm-leaving-Helen-and-the-kids-alone-here-in-Trumbull-Park.* That thought just came up from absolutely nowhere. I got weak in the knees. I sat down on the couch. Helen came over.

"What's the matter?"

"I can't leave you and the kids out here by yourselves."

"We're not by ourselves. There's cops outside. And besides, don't think I don't know how to use that gun upstairs!"

"Aw, you get so excited whenever anything happens, you wouldn't even think about that gun!"

"Don't fool yourself about women! We just put on that helpless stuff when we have to—shoot, you big baby, men wouldn't know what to do if we didn't—and when it comes to business, we know just what time it is. Do you remember when Little John got drunk and came in the house, back at the Gardener Building, and tried to get funny with me, while you were at work?"

I had forgotten all about that. I laughed. Boy, that woman took a poker and gave that Negro a poker fit! Then she got a gun and would have shot him if Bertha hadn't heard the noise from upstairs and broke downstairs and grabbed Helen just before she pulled the trigger. And I mean Bertha had to wrestle a while with Helen before she got that gun away from her too. And Bertha is *not* a little woman. Little John was down on his knees with his hands stretched straight up at the sky, begging Helen not to hit him any more, not to shoot him. I mean, Helen was mad that day! I looked at that cute little brown cookie sitting beside me, and she laughed and looked at the floor. I guess she was remembering it too. I said:

"Still, this is not like at the Gardener Building. These folks are cowards, and they wouldn't think about jumping you one at a time. They are the kind that gang up on one person when they catch him alone, and run like hell when the odds start to getting even halfway even."

Helen knew I was right. I could tell it. Her face kind of wrinkled just for a minute, and then she smiled. I felt a

80

pulling in my neck and I coughed to clear my throat. She slid a little closer to me and touched my hand, then held it. She turned to me, real close to my face, and I saw that worried look there again. I swear it hurt me to see that look in her face. Her voice was soft, and still just a bit husky from sleep.

"Honey, I know we aren't out of the woods yet. You know what might have happened to us if we had stayed in that Gardener Building. Anything might have happened. We might have gotten sick and died there like——"

I drew up. I knew that she was going to say "your mother," and I knew that she was right, but I drew up and prayed that she wouldn't say it. It still hurt me too much to think about Momma being dead. Dead from living in the Gardener Building. Helen saw me flinch, and she ducked the subject and started out on another track:

"It's no telling what would have happened to the kids if we had stayed there," she said. "I know you're not talking about moving out of here, but I just wanted to bring all this in so we both know what we're doing this for. Sure, we could have waited and maybe gotten another project somewhere else later on. But how much later? Could we have stood it much longer? Remember old Mr. Horton on the second floor? Remember how the cops beat him when he started shooting his pistol at the rats in his bedroom after they bit his daughter's little boy? It was the only boy they ever had, Buggy. Remember how that baby looked when they brought him out? All blue where the rats had got at him, and puffed up like a poisoned pig? Honey, we got to live out here like business-as-usual. You know what I mean? We got to take this foolishness of these white folks in stride. Live in spite of them——well, not in spite of them either, but because of the Gardener Building."

I felt all tore up. It seemed like I should have been the

one telling her that instead of her telling me. After all, I was the man of the house. But she was so right. So right it made me mad. I said:

"You didn't talk like this when we were on our way out here in Red's truck."

She looked at me real hard.

"It wasn't time for talking then, especially after we got here. I felt like Red: it was time for action then, not talk."

I *knew* she had been mad at me about not helping Red! I shot right back at her:

"Red didn't say anything like that!"

"No, but he sure thought it."

How could I argue back at that? I said, sort of sulky:

"I'm going on to work then, since you say you don't need me here."

She squeezed my hand and leaned up to me.

"I didn't say that."

I moved away from her.

"That's what you meant."

She moved closer to me and kissed my cheek.

"You know I need you—in every way, Baby."

"You'd better stop that. I got to go to work."

"I don't think I'll let you go."

"Aww, come on; stop that!"

I got up from there right quick. I swear to goodness, that woman is as full of devilment—pregnant and all that—as any five women I've ever heard of. I gave her a quick kiss on the mouth and started for the door. She laughed and got up, following me. I hugged her, and she kissed my cheeks again, and said:

"Hurry home."

"Oh, you're silly."

"Oh, yeah?"

"Yeah."

"Silly like a fox!"

"You're not lying about that, Helen Martin."

I thought about the policemen with the book stirring about, and the warm bubbling inside me got cold and sticky. I stood in front of that door for a minute, thinking about that patrol wagon, then I snatched the door open and stepped out into the cold and the policemen and the metal smell of the steel mills. I expected to see a crowd of white people pop up from behind the buildings there in front of me, but nobody did. One policeman walked toward me. He was the one with the big notebook in his hand. He was about my height, but very fat, and red, with about three chins hanging from underneath his open, wet-pink lips. His voice sounded like a diesel—close up—when he said:

"Sign here, Mr. Martin. Captain's orders."

He poked a ballpoint pen at me. I took the pen.

"What's all this for?"

"Captain's orders."

I wrote my name.

"What time do you expect to be back, Mr. Martin?"

Now I don't know why I answered that man the way I did, but I was so mad at having to sign in and out of my own house like *I* was the one being kept under control and not those screaming meemies that had been out there last night, I said:

"I'm not coming back. I'm leaving my wife."

I walked away. I had taken about five steps when I heard one of the policemen say:

"That nigger needs a good education."

Another one said:

"In the lockup."

Another said:

"With one light on."

Another said:

"And with a hard rubber blackjack."

I walked to the end of the driveway and turned to my right. About a block down was another driveway, and in it were about four squad cars and one big black box-looking thing I knew was the patrol wagon. I wondered if it was the same one that they took Babydoll away in. I wondered if the same two policemen were driving it.

Between me and the police wagon were about fifteen policemen, all along the narrow sidewalk that led to the other parking lot. I looked around at the place and felt sort of let down. To tell you the truth, I had thought from hearing about all the trouble the Davis family had had out here that they had moved into a new swanky exclusive neighborhood, like the kind me and my sisters Johnetta and Doris, and my little brother Ricky used to see when Daddy used to take us out to Gary to see his brother, and we used to drive down Jeffery Boulevard, and see the houses with the big windows, and the pretty pictures on the walls inside, and would *ooh* and *ahh* over and green smooth yards that looked like no one even ever dreamed of walking on them.

But Trumbull Park was nothing like that. From the outside, where we came in, it looked like a great big prison. Red bricks everywhere. Windows all the same height. Doors all the same distance from each other. Steps all in the same place. Yards the same size. Everything the same—all the same, and half-worn out. White streaks from the cement between the bricks running down the walls, and brown rust splotching up the bannisters of the tall buildings that stood looking so serious way over on the other end of the project.

On the inside of the project there was a long courtyard

84

that ran between two rows of two-storey buildings like the one I lived in. A couple of streets cut across the courtyard at 107th, and at the street that led to the driveway behind my house. Just behind the set of row-houses on my right arose a real high smokestack, looking something like the smokestacks of the steel mills over on my left. That smokestack just leaned over at me from behind the row-houses that ran alongside the sidewalk I was walking on to the parking lot where the patrol wagon was.

It was a cold, damp October morning, and the sun was nowhere to be seen. The brightest thing in the sky was a smudgy patch squeezed in between a whole bunch of smoky-looking, rolling clouds that looked like rain.

"*Hey, nigger! Whatcha lookin' at, huh?*"

It was that same airy, high woman's voice that had raised so much sand yesterday. I looked all around me, but I couldn't see where that voice was coming from to save my life.

"*Hey, nigger! Niggerrrrr! Can't you see, nigger?*"

I looked and I looked, and I couldn't see a thing. I said real loud:

"You go to hell you white bi——"

"Hey, hey, hey there, boy! Let's not have that kind of talk out of you!"

I turned around to see who belonged to that big booming voice bellowing in my ear. It was the same fat, three-chin policeman that had made me sign the book to get out of my house.

"You got to conduct yourself better than that if you want to get along out here!"

"What are you talking about? That chick been picking at me since yesterday. How come you guys don't shut her up?"

"Where are you going?" the fat policeman said.

"I'm going to work."

"Have you signed in at the office?"

"You mean I have to sign something else now?"

"That's right. Captain's orders."

He grabbed my shoulder and turned me all the way around to face the row houses on the side of the courtyard.

"That's the office over there—right about midway between here and the parking lot at the end of this walk. Just walk into the door where all the policemen are." He gave me another shove. "Go on, Martin. If you want to talk to the captain, he's in there."

I started to say, "Don't shove me," but the cop stood with his legs spread out and one hand on his club, like he was just waiting for me to say something so he could start in on me the way they do on the boys down on the corner of 58th and Calumet.

I got mad way down in my insides, and it started right on up to my face, and I clinched my fists, and let them go, and clenched them again. What could I do? I'd asked for this. I was even glad to be out here. I knew what was going to happen—at least, the *Defender* had told the story about what was happening out here enough times for anyone to get the message if they wanted to. Still there was the Gardener Building standing behind it all like a big skeleton head—a red-brick backdrop that was in the background of all of this—of everything, at least as far as I was concerned.

I walked into the apartment which the cops had turned into a police headquarters. It was just like mine—stairs right in front of the door leading up to the bedrooms and bathroom. The living room off to the right was the front office, and in the back, where the kitchen was, was a row of radios sitting on the side of the sink. A table sat against the wall near the stairs, and a white-haired man in uniform, with a white shirt underneath, sat at the table with a cup of coffee in front of him on one side and a *Chicago Tribune* on the other. I started toward him. He didn't look up. Another policeman sat at a desk in the corner of the room, opposite the table. He said:

"You want an escort?"

I said:

"Escort?"

The policeman, a dark-haired guy with a long, hungry face and small frowning eyes, said:

"Yeah. You want the wagon to take you outa the project?"

I started to say no, but I remembered the crowd outside my window the night before, and I could just see myself walking down that street by myself trying to get to that car line and looking up at about five hundred of those screaming women, old men, and kids.

"Yeah," I said, "I want the wagon to take me out of the project."

"Okay."

I do believe this guy smiled when I said "Yeah."

"We'll get one of the men down here right away." He raised his head toward the ceiling, and I heard feet walking this way and that upstairs in what would have been our bedroom. "Hey, Johnson! Lapski!" he hollered. "We got a trip. Come on down!"

It sounded like a couple of horses tromping around up there. Then footsteps sounded on the stairs, and finally two real big white policemen came into the room. Their uniforms were rumpled, and their ties were loosened as if they had been sleeping in them all night. One, a youngish-looking guy with high round cheeks and real whitish skin, ran his fingers through his straight brown hair and jerked his head back at the same time. The other rubbed his eyes with the palm of his hands like the gray dingy morning light was

87

too strong for his eyes. They both looked me up and down and turned the corners of their mouths down, and then looked at each other and gave that dry kind of laugh you give when you want to say a bad word but there's company around. The policeman at the desk said:

"You're Martin, aren't you?"

"That's right," I said.

"Okay," he said, "just follow these men. . . . Oh, where do you want to go—95th and State, or 95th and Cottage Grove?"

I worked at an airplane engine factory over on 79th and Cicero, and I figured that the best thing would be to go over to Cottage Grove, because that way I'd get a seat before the crowd from the "black belt" which started from South Parkway and ran to State Street began piling in and squeezing each other and everybody else on those streetcars until you could die if you fell down on one of those things. And the people weren't all colored either. A lot of them were white folks who lived all bunched up right on the edge of the colored part of town, like the foam of one of those big rivers that's spreading and spreading and running over and pushing the banks farther and farther back, but never quite breaking through the river wall—never quite breaking over the banks, just pushing it farther and farther back. I guessed right then that that was probably what was wrong out here in Trumbull Park. We weren't pushing the banks anywhere, we had leaped all the way over the banks and were on the other side; and the banks were ripping and dodging, trying to keep from becoming islands.

"I'll take 95th and Cottage," I said. I was smiling this time: we on the other side of the bank—never thought of it like that before. Not really.

The policemen walked in front of me. When they reached

the patrol wagon, one of them climbed in under the wheel and the other one went around to the back of the wagon and unlocked the door—didn't open it or nothing—just unlocked it and went around to the front and got in.

The driver started the motor and I pulled the big stiff door open and peeped inside. It was dark in there, and it smelled awful, like some alley where drunk men go and sick dogs crawl to die. I stopped in front of that dark, terrible-smelling hole. I just couldn't go in. Not yet. The driver hollered:

"Okay, get in! Let's go!"

His partner got out of the front and came around to where I was standing:

"Well, what are you waiting for? Get in."

I said:

"Can't I ride in the squad car? I mean, this wagon, it's—it's . . ."

"Look, buster, if you don't want a police escort say so. If you do, get in. That's all!"

I got in, and he slammed the door. It made a heavy clang when it shut. I felt like I was going down to jail. All these years I had prided myself in never having been in one of those "Black Marias."

Inside was like being in one of the revolving rooms out at Riverview. There was a skinny little board that folded up against the wall of the wagon, and I figured that you were supposed to pull this thing down if you wanted to sit down, and I did—and just in time, for the wagon made one of those mad turns and I almost fell on my face. I'm telling you, it was one of the roughest, bumpiest, stinkiest rides I've ever had in my life. We finally stopped, and the driver's partner climbed out of the wagon and unbolted the door, and I half-climbed, half-staggered out of that thing.

"Whew!" I said.

The policeman slammed the door and started back toward the front.

"Hey," I said, "how do I get back in?"

The driver stuck his head out of his window.

"How do you what?"

"How do I get in touch with the police when I want to get back into the project?"

"Oh," he shouted back, "just call Headquarters Nine —Essex 5-5910." A streetcar was turning around the corner from 95th and heading north on Cottage Grove, and I started running to be at the safety island in time enough to catch it. I repeated the number over to myself and hopped on the streetcar, and turned around to watch that big stinky scoundrel whip around the corner of 95th and Cottage like a square black bat going back to hell.

8

I was forty-five minutes late when I got to work. The foreman sent me to the pass-room to get a late pass, and then I went upstairs to the production floor to work. It took awhile for me to get settled in the everyday grind. My machine was a high-speed drill press. With it I reamed holes in a big light-weight metal casting that covers part of the engine on those big bombers you see flying all over the town. I felt kind of proud to think that something that I had something to do with could actually fly—later on, of course.

The machine itself was a tall, harmless-looking deal, with about five or six drills and two buttons—one for starting and the other for stopping. I would grab those big castings and swing them into position on a platform underneath the drill, and put a brace inside the casting—we called it a "chuck"—and then I'd clamp that chuck down tight against the casting so the thing wouldn't slip, and then push that "go" button, and ZZzzzzz those drills would go! Down they would come slow and hell-bent for that casting—couldn't stop them then if I wanted to. ZZzzzzz they would go, eating into that casting like it was cream cheese, boring little holes right through it, all the same size, all perfect. It wasn't the kind of job you had to strictly concentrate on because once you pushed those buttons it was all over as far as you were concerned. I had been working for about a half an hour when it hit me:

Suppose something happens to Helen and the kids while you're here at work?

At first I pushed that thought out of my head. I started singing, real loud and in rhythm with the bearings underneath the link-belt over on the side where the castings were being taken to other jobs—drilling jobs, reaming jobs, beveling jobs. But as I sang to the rhythm of that link-belt, that damned thought got in step too, and it drowned out the tune that I was singing, and it pounded in my head as loud as those machines had. Loud and regular, loud and regular—just like that all-day-long noise on that link-belt:

Suppose something happens to Helen and the kids— while you're here at work?

It was in perfect time now. Every beat of the machine fit a word—like the machine was a song without music, without words, and had just been waiting for these words to make it complete:

Suppose something happens to Helen and the kids— (da boom, da boom) while you're here at work!

Suppose something happens to Helen and the kids— while you're here at work!

Suppose something happens to Helen and the kids— while you're here at work!

SUPPOSE SOMETHING HAPPENS TO HELEN AND THE KIDS —WHILE YOU'RE HERE AT WORK!

I stopped my machine and put my fingers in my ears. That noise, that idea was filling me up like that doggoned diesel train did. I began to hum out loud; but the rhythm was still there, behind my fingers, behind my ears, down inside my brain, down inside my chest, and in my throat.

It was swelling me up like someone was pumping me full of air. I felt that I was getting short of breath, so I breathed real hard, but it didn't do any good. That damned noise was filling up everything around me, and I felt tears coming into my eyes, and my mouth felt dry, and that noise kept getting louder and louder and louder, banging out the same damned thing over and over again:

SUPPOSE SOMETHING HAPPENS TO HELEN AND THE KIDS (DA CRASH! DA CRASH!) WHILE YOU'RE HERE AT WORK!

I caught the foreman looking at me and I started my machine up again. He came over to where I was:

"What's the matter, Martin?"

He was a tall guy, with a big sagging stomach, and a crew-cut the same color as his narrow brown eyes. His face was like a box—flatish and square, and he pressed his lips together in a one-sided scowl when I explained:

"I don't know. I guess it's a headache."

He looked at me like he wanted to say, "Your story's so touching it sounds just like a lie." But he didn't say anything—just looked. Then he did say:

"If you're sick, you'd better go see the doctor. We can't have any rejects on these castings. Uncle Sam's on our necks as it is."

"It was just a headache. It's all right now."

I'm telling you, it was all I could do to get through that day. Even at lunchtime, downstairs where the fellows all sat together to lollygag and fool with the girls, all I could do was think about that big fat gray-haired fool trying to get into my house. Helen had said that she could take care of herself, and I tried to believe she could. After all, didn't she teach Little John a lesson? But these folks weren't no Little Johns, and they weren't drunk—at least not off of whiskey.

93

They were drunk off of something that only white folks could get a hold of, I thought—something that made them hate all colored folks.

The cafeteria was lit up with a faded yellowish light bulb stuck here and there. It had a gloomy look about it. It was jam-packed, though, with people hollering and laughing all over the place. Everything was in fast motion.

I had a buddy named Robert Miller. He was white, but he was nice. Everybody called him Pete. He and I sat across from each other at the table, and before long we were talking about Trumbull Park.

"Buggy, believe me, those pricks couldn't even get along with each other! I used to live out there, believe me, in the project just like you—and the trouble I had with those guys! I was the trash and they were the Mister Bigs. A low crowd, I'll tell you."

He leaned across the table and whispered, not smiling a little bit:

"Listen, Buggy, if anyone of them bastards ever do anything to you, you just let me know. We'll go out there, you and me, and"—he put one hand to the side of his mouth and pushed his eyebrows way down into his eyes—almost closing them—"and catch one of them bastards late at night and whip his ass in good fashion! Huh?"

I looked at him hard, trying to see did he mean what he was saying. Trying to see did he *know* what he was saying. He kept his eyes fixed right on mine, and *he* wasn't smiling either. I stared at his eyes and he stared right back at mine. Then that fool broke out into one of the most rambunctious laughs that I've ever heard. He reached over and slapped me on the shoulder with that oversized baseball-mitt-looking hand of his and almost broke my collarbone. He just roared:

"We'll kick their asses, Buggy—me and you!"

I heard him, but I didn't believe him. Yet something in the sad look behind that barnyard laugh said that the white people in Trumbull Park had hurt him, and bad; that turning up their noses at him because he lived in the housing project had touched him where he couldn't stand being touched. He was the first white man I ever saw who had the kind of hurt-pride hate in his face that I knew so well among my own folks.

I didn't know what to say. The bell rang and I was glad when Pete punched his palm with his fist and slid back from the table complaining:

"I think these bastards are stealing some of our lunchtime!"

As it got close to time-to-go-home the old machine song that had hit me in the morning came back like a pulled tooth with the medicine worn off:

Suppose something happens to Helen and the kids *—while you're here at work!*

I started calling myself every name I could think of, leaving Helen and the kids home by themselves that way, and the day after we moved into that jungle. You simple bastard, I cursed under my breath, leaving her alone like that. You were too scared to stay out there—that's what you were—so you left her. Now suppose something has happened to Helen and the kids while you're here at work!

The go-home buzzer went off. I ran to the time-card rack, punched out, cut out the side door, and ran over to Cicero and waited there for the CTA bus to show up. It seemed like it took that thing one solid hour to get there, and when it did, it ambled up Cicero about as fast as a Model T on a muddy road. I squirmed and coughed, but it didn't do any good. That bus driver was ahead of his schedule, and he was going to kill time if he had to stop the bus and take a nap to do it. I read every sign on every window on 79th Street. I read every sign in that bus. I counted the number of drygoods stores from Cicero to Western. I even closed my eyes and tried to sleep the time away, but I kept hearing those wheels underneath that link-belt back at work, chanting the same thing over and over again:

Suppose something happens to Helen and the kids— while you're here at work!

Finally the bus reached Western, where the Westside buses finish their trips and the Eastside buses begin theirs. I jumped off of the bus and ran and hopped on the east-bound bus just as the doors were closing. More drygoods stores. More chanting. More time dragging by.

"Cottage Grove!!"

I broke for the side door. One more streetcar ride and then home! Then I remembered that I'd have to call the police department to take me home in a patrol wagon. It didn't take the southbound bus long to get to 95th and Cottage. Now it seemed to me I was getting home too fast. I went to the phone in the filling station at the northwest corner and I dialed Essex 5-5910. It rang a few times; then a voice belched from the other end:

"Headquarters Nine. Officer Street speaking."

"This is Buggy Martin."

"Who?"

"Uh—*Louis* Martin."

"Where are yuh, Martin?"

"95th and Cottage Grove."

"We'll send the wagon after yuh within fifteen min-utes or so."

Thirty minutes later that dusty black patrol wagon rum-bled around the corner of 95th. The same two guys were driving it. They didn't open their mouths. One of them un-locked the back door and went back to his seat beside the driver. I pulled the door open and climbed in, and the long ride began. We bumped around corners, bumped up hills, bumped over cobblestones and railroad tracks. Then I smelled the garbage dump and knew that I was almost home.

It reminded me of the day before when we moved in. I tried to imagine that the patrol wagon was Red's truck and the policeman driving was my buddy Red, and that Helen and I were sitting in the back of the truck moving to some place nice where folks would be glad to see you, where there weren't any policemen at all. But I couldn't imagine that. Not any of it. All I could imagine was Helen crying and the kids bleeding and the house all tore up and the cops standing around trying to explain where they had been when it all happened. I began to dread getting home.

I knew I was on Bensley when somebody yelled:

"*Hey, jailbird! Jailbird nigger! Scared to walk the streets like a man? You'd better not come out of there, nigger! nigger!*"

My ears started burning so bad I thought they were on fire. I peeped out of the grating at the back of the patrol wagon, and there was a crowd of about fifty people lined up along the street—some of the same people I had seen in back of my house the night before. I pushed my face hard against the grating to get a better look at them. Standing in front of the crowd was that gray-haired old man—tall, fat, and needing a shave so bad it looked like some of his old gray hair had slipped down onto his chin. I didn't know whether he saw me or not, but he was just laughing away. His big droopy round stomach jiggled like a bag of foam rubber—oh, he just fell out laughing! I gripped the grating with both of my fists and squeezed them tight. I had to choke something. I squeezed my eyes tight. I felt water on my face and ran my forearm across it and swallowed real hard.

97

The driver's partner climbed out of the front and stomped around the back of the wagon and unbolted the door and pulled it open.

"Okay, kid, you're home."

Even he was grinning at the monkey in the cage. I jumped down from the wagon and spat hard on the sidewalk and started for my house.

The first thing I looked for when I hit the back yard was broken glass and holes in the windows—some sign that the mob had been there.

But there weren't any windows broken.

I ran to the back door and kicked at it with the toe of my shoe.

Nobody came to the door.

I tried to peek through the kitchen window, but the kitchen was dark, and so was the living room beyond.

Then I saw Louella skitter across the living room doorway real quick, like she was hiding or running or something.

I ran around to the front door and kicked it hard.

A couple of policemen ran up to me.

"Hey, what the hell are you doing? Trying to kick the door in?"

I yelled back at this character:

"Where's my wife? I can't get in. I can't get in! I see the kids inside, but they won't open the door! Where's Helen, huh? Where's my wife?"

The door opened. Helen stood there. She wasn't smiling. She wasn't frowning. She wasn't doing nothing but standing there.

For a minute I didn't know her. Her face wasn't that changed; but something had changed, and I'm telling you I didn't know her.

I couldn't help myself from calling her name:

"Helen?"

Louella's round-eyed face stuck out from behind Helen. Then pushing her way through the space between Helen and the door came Diane—narrow-faced as the edge of the door and no taller than the door knob. She ran to me and grabbed my leg. I picked her up and started inside. Helen, looking *so* tired, her cheekbones quivering, turned around, closed the door behind her, walked over to the couch, and sat down. She hung her hands between her legs, and her blue housecoat spread open, and her shoulders fell forward and down. But she kept her head kind of upwards looking at me—round, brown eyes sort of blank and a weird, I mean weird-looking grin spread out across her face.

"Baby, I got here as fast as I could! That damned bus took so long, I had to wait so long! Honey, what's wrong? What happened?"

She pushed her hands further down between her legs and squeezed her legs tight against them and raised her head even higher, fixing her eyes on that blank wall in front of her. She pressed her lips together and rolled them between her teeth. But not a mumbling word did she say.

"Honey! I kicked at the back door—and the front! Didn't you hear me?"

Her chin tightened and started to tremble. I closed my eyes. Lord, I said to myself, don't let her start crying. Not now. Not after all this. I opened my eyes. The Lord must not have heard me, or maybe I didn't ask him in time. Tears were just pouring down her cheeks. Still she kept her chin drawn up, pointed up and out in a tight hard knot. I hugged her. I got worried—her being pregnant and all. I rubbed her stomach in circles, real light and slow. She sort of fell against me and put her head against my chest.

Louella sat on the edge of the couch, sucking her fingers real loud. I didn't like it, but I couldn't get enough words together in my mind right then to tell her to stop. So I just stared at her and listened to that *suck, suck, suck, suck,* and rubbed Helen's round, hard stomach and wondered what was wrong. Why wouldn't she answer me?

I got mad just like that:

"Look, Helen!" I said. "I can't help you if you don't tell me what's wrong!"

She mumbled back at me from the little hole she had burrowed in my jacket with her head:

"I was upstairs, cleaning up. Diane saw it first."

"Diane saw *what* first?"

"The snake . . . Somebody put a snake through the mail slot in the front door."

She started crying hard now. Her stomach just jiggled. I rubbed it a little harder. Louella started sucking her fingers a little louder. I got burned up. Helen mumbled something else:

"They said that they didn't see anybody do it. Said they were out there all morning, and that they hadn't seen anybody all morning. I heard the mail slot slam. Diane screamed. When I got down here, I saw the snake crawling across the floor."

"Where is it? Where's the snake now!"

"One of the cops got it out. The kids had a fit. They were scared to death. I probably scared them by screaming so loud myself."

I jumped up from the couch.

"Where in the hell were the cops when it happened?"

Helen closed her eyes and shrieked at the top of her voice:

"Don't holler at me! Go out there and ask them for yourself! Only don't holler at me!"

Then she fell over on the couch. She laid right on her

stomach and pushed her face into the pillows and just moaned and cried.

I went to the front door and opened it. Four or five cops stood near the door talking. They stopped when I stepped out. The short fat one with the three chins looked at me curiously. I stared right back at him. I was beginning to hate this roly-poly slob. He finally opened his juicy lips:

"Goin' out, Martin? You'd better sign the book if you are."

He seemed to get the biggest kick out of saying that. His whole porky-pig face absolutely lit up. I wanted to beat that man so bad my hand started itching. I took a deep breath. I wasn't surprised to feel my chest trembling when I let the air out. I answered as snappy as I could:

"Who put that goddamned snake in my mail box?"

The fat cop didn't answer—just blinked his big marble-looking eyes once or twice and shifted his feet and hitched up his gun belt—in self-defense, I guess.

"Some kids were playing around here. Maybe they did it," said one long, pimply-faced cop with horn-rimmed glasses.

"Hey, Louis! It won't do no good. They did me the same way. Nobody ever sees them. They're invisible!"

I looked around. Arthur Davis was standing behind me. Helen had let him in the back door. His hair was all down in his face, and he was holding himself up in the kitchen door. He looked a little twisted, almost like he was trying to keep from falling.

The tall skinny cop took one look at Arthur and squealed in a little boy's voice:

"Hey, don't you know you're supposed to sign in? C'mon out here and sign the book!"

"Aw, sign it your damn self! Who you protecting? Us from the white folks or them from us? It looks to me like you're protecting them from us—and me in particular."

He turned around and took a couple of shaky steps back into the kitchen. I followed him. I was sick at the stomach, and my head was beginning to hurt like hell.

Helen was upstairs now. That cry had done her some good, I guess. I guessed she didn't want to say anything more about that snake, and I *sure* wasn't going to bring it up.

Arthur sat on the couch with his legs crossed and his hands folded on his knees. He started patting his foot to a rhythm in his mind. I asked him:

"Would you like to hear some records?"

"Don't mind if I do."

I remembered his wife and kids and I blurted:

"Hey, where are your kids and Mona?"

He didn't stop patting his foot to that music—that music that nobody but him could hear. Finally he said:

"They're over at my mother's."

I plugged the record player in and got my good blues records out of a box. I pulled out a soft number by Billie Holiday and put it on. Her voice made even that cold messed-up living room seem warm and like I'd lived there all my natural life. Arthur stopped patting his foot as Billie got groovy:

". . . . *you're down to my size. It's over and done. So, highness, step down from your throne . . .*"

Arthur stood and walked to the front door and peeped out of the little window there. Then he stepped over to the front window and looked out of it. Then he sat back down at the couch. I thought that maybe it was something that Billie had said that made him so restless, so I said:

"Man, it sure gets you, don't it?"

He had a funny half-mad sound in his voice:

"Naw, it don't get me. Why should it? That's what they're trying to do, but I'll be damned if they will."

Billie's record had run out, and I put it on again. I went for the way she wailed so soft and mellow.

".... *from my window skies ain't gray no more ... no how.*"

I was surprised at what Arthur had said and I asked him, "Get you? Who's trying to get you?"

Then it dawned on me that he was talking about all this stuff out here in Trumbull Park, and I was thinking about how Billie Holiday gets you. This cat was either twisted or nuts or something!

He got up and started for the door. I thought he was going home, but he stopped and looked out of the window and walked over to the very same place he had just a minute before. He peeped out of the front room window, sort of standing off to the side like he thought somebody was going to shoot something through the window at him. His tall, lanky frame drooped into a slouch and he hooked his thumbs in his back pockets. He took his coat off and laid it across the couch. Then he stared out of that window— stared and swayed and stared and swayed.

I stared at him, and he stared at the cops standing near the door outside. The back of his head was oval shaped and his hair came down in a dark taper below his shirt. I thought to myself, This cat needs a haircut. That man was waving like a tall tree on top of a mountain away off somewhere else. I followed his eyes around the room. It was like a one-man show he was putting on—a show without words.

"Hey, man!" I said kind of loud. "What's on your mind?"

He jumped. You would have thought that I had woke him up from a sound sleep.

"Huh?"

"I mean, you been just standing there swinging and swaying like Sammy Kaye and—uh—looking out of that window like the boogie man's gonna come in after you. What's happening, Dad?"

He looked at me real hard like he didn't believe I was sitting there. He frowned his face all up for a minute and then, believe it or not, he picked up his coat and hat and started for the front door saying over his shoulder:

"I'm going to bring Kevin back here. I'll see you later, Buggy."

And with that Arthur Davis stepped on out and shut the door softly behind him.

9

HELEN, what color snake was it they put in the mail slot?"

"Buggy, if you'd seen me running around this house fat as I am, you wouldn't be asking me what color that thing was. Why do you want to know?"

Something hot and shaking rose up in my chest:

"If I ever find out who did that I'm going to kick his pure-D ass. That's just what I'm going to do."

Helen looked at me with those round dark eyes and shook her head.

"Buggy, I told you you'd be sorry you ever asked me to marry you. Look at us—nothing but babies and trouble."

She sat down on the couch. There she went again: poking those arms down between her legs, holding that head so unnaturally high, getting that tired look about the face once more. I wondered what was on her mind.

"Am I making you feel that way, Helen? Like I'm sorry I married you?"

I looked around the house. Not much to show for all my scuffling and scraping. Kitchen table and chairs bought on credit last year, no money down and two years to pay. Seat in the chairs worn out already and one of the table legs wobbling like a loose tooth.

I sat beside Helen and put my hands on both sides of her face. She was such a pretty girl.

"Helen," I said quiet-like. "I love you, Baby. I'm the one to blame for us not having anything by now."

I could feel her eyes searching for mine and I couldn't move mine away. I tried to stare her off, but there was too much love in her eyes. I smiled, not because I felt like smiling at her but because I was begging her not to ask me what I had done with those eight years. She smiled, and I felt that smile right down to the bottom of my natural soul. She put her hand on mine and rubbed the top of my hand once or twice. I looked out of the window. It was dark outside. I said:

"I'll straighten up the living room this time. I'm not too tired."

Helen got up quickly, and I noticed that her eyes were glassy. I blinked mine.

Boom! Boom! Boom! Boom!

Blue-white lights set my living room on fire. I closed my eyes. My ears rang.

Helen turned and ran back to me. I hugged her and looked around the room. I knew that the wall was going to cave in for sure. Then Helen pulled aloose from me and ran upstairs.

"Louella!"

"Momma!" Louella whined.

Then Diane started crying. I ran upstairs. Both Diane and Louella were sitting up in the bed hugging Helen around her waist.

Boom! Boom! Boom!

From the window the sky was welted with smoke streaks and upshooting red-and-blue fire—oversized rockets that shook the house and sounded exactly like they were in the room with you. I sat down beside Helen and Diane and

Louella. Then I got up and ran to the window. I just had to see what it was that they were shooting off that was so hellish and bright and made so much noise that it pulled at the muscles in your back and made you feel like crawling under something to hide from it.

The police had gathered around the house. I looked down at them. They weren't trying to find out who was setting those things off. They didn't even seem half-way concerned about the bombs going off near my house. They wandered around, appearing and disappearing, just like they were a bunch of blue-skinned snakes somebody had stirred up, just enough to make them crawl out from under one rock, straight under another one.

Boom! Boom! Boom! Boom! Boom!

Blue lights. Yellowish-gray lights all over the whole dingy sky. First came a whiny whistle, then a soft explosion, and then that hard blue-white light, and a roaring, spreading, jarring *boom* like one of the stars had swung too close to the earth and blown up. Then before you get time to think about that, another one did the same thing, and another one, and another one. I didn't know whether somebody was aiming them at the house and had just missed so far, or what.

Helen got up from the bed and turned the light out. I pulled the shade down and peeped out of the side. More policemen were gathering. Louella said in a sleepy voice:

"I'm scared, Momma. I want to go back home."

Helen stepped back from the window and hugged Louella to her stomach. Diane moved close to her, and Helen hugged her too. Her voice was low and she seemed not at all excited:

"We are at home, Baby. We don't live at the Gardener Building any more."

There was a fire in her voice, a trembly angry-sounding

fire. I can tell you that I knew right then and there that there wasn't going to be any packing up and leaving.

There was a knock on the door downstairs. I ran down the steps and peeped out of the front window. There was no one there. I ran through the kitchen and looked out of the back door. Two policemen were standing just outside the iron fence around the yard, and four or five people were standing jam up against the back door. I recognized Arthur Davis by his being so tall. I opened the door for him to step in, and another man stepped in behind him. He was about Arthur's height, only much thinner. His features were keen, and his bushy hair was piled up right at the front of his head. There was practically no hair along the sides or at the back. He made me think of a citified Indian brave.

Mona and her two kids, Sharon and Bobby, followed this guy in. Mona and Arthur were still just as nervous and jumpy as they had been the night before. I wondered if they planned to stay all night again. Mona pointed her open hand at the tall bushy-haired guy and said:

"Buggy, this is Kevin Robinson. His and Carl Burton's and Terry Watson's families moved just a little before you did."

Kevin smiled and nodded, and Arthur took up where Mona had left off:

"His wife and kids are in town tonight, and he wanted to meet you and Helen so we brought him over."

That tired look hung around Mona's eyes like smoke in a small room. The bushy-haired guy smiled again but turned it off as soon as I looked at him. I said:

"Glad to meet you. Come on in the living room. Helen is upstairs with the kids. You know we're not used to all this commotion, and the kids are scared to death. Helen will be down in a minute."

The tall guy led the way into the living room and stood up alongside the wall. I sort of swung my hand at the couch:

"Have a seat, everybody."

I figured that this Kevin would sit down and relax himself. Even though he was holding himself in, I could see he was pretty keyed up. Mona and Arthur sat down, and Sharon and Bobby sat down beside him. Bobby looked up at Kevin and slid over to make room for him, but this cat wouldn't sit down.

All in all, this Kevin was just about sharp. That is, he had on a light-blue top coat that looked like it was made of some pretty good material and it was unbuttoned and hung open just wide enough for me to see that he had on a single-breasted tan suit. He wore a white shirt and a tie with a very small knot. I said:

"Will somebody please tell me what all that noise is about? It's going to drive us to Kankakee."

Arthur answered in a carefree know-it-all tone of voice:

"I don't let it bother me. It's just those fools out there trying to get on our nerves."

I waited for Mona and Kevin to say something. Mona finally said:

"Well, they *do* bother me. But I don't think that *those* will hurt you. Just wait until they start throwing cans of sulfur through your window. That's when you'll feel like blowing your top."

I caught my breath.

"Sulfur? Through your window? Awww, come on!"

Mona turned to Arthur.

"Am I lying, Arthur?"

Kevin shifted his feet from one foot to the other and said in a heavy rolling voice:

"She's not lyin'. These people will do anything. Broke my windows two or three times right in broad daylight. Wish I'd catch one of them."

"Where are the police while this is going on?" I asked.

Kevin shifted his weight again and looked at Arthur and gave out with a little laugh like "Is he kidding?" Arthur laughed back, and then asked me:

"Look, do you know that they made us sign a record book before we could come in here to your house tonight? Yet and still, peculiar-looking white folks can go in and out of white folks' houses all day and all night without having to sign anything. Buggy, this police department is strictly for laughs."

Helen came downstairs with Diane and Louella behind her. I stared at Diane and Louella hard, but they didn't flinch. Helen explained:

"They just don't want to stay up there by themselves, and I don't blame them. It's no telling when somebody might throw something through the window the way they did last night?"

Then she caught sight of Kevin:

"Oh, excuse me! I haven't any manners at all."

She looked at Mona.

"This is Kevin Robinson, Helen."

"Hello, Kevin. Do excuse me. I have really had a time today. These bombs, and snakes, and God knows what else."

Mona got excited:

"A snake!"

Sharon slid farther back on the couch and mumbled:

"I'm scared of a snake."

Bobby said louder:

"Me, too."

Kevin shifted his weight to his other foot. Helen eyed him, and then the empty space on the couch.

"Don't you want to sit down?"

He shifted his weight from one foot to the other again and said,

"No, thanks. I'm all right here."

I got irritated, but I didn't say anything to him.

Helen gave me one of those sideway looks and that quick smile, and I looked quickly at Kevin to see if he was looking. He was. He was an out-of-sight-looking guy if I ever saw one.

Helen went into the kitchen and came out with a chair. Arthur jumped up when he saw her and took the chair away from her. I don't know when she had found the time, but she had combed her hair and put on a white maternity blouse and a black skirt. She sat down and took a long breath and then turned to Mona:

"How long have you and Arthur been out here?"

"Two months and twenty-three days today," Mona said. "And that's two months and twenty-three days too long."

"How long has all this three-six-nine been going on?" I asked.

Boom!

That blue-white light flashed, and the walls just trembled. Mona flinched. Arthur started talking and his voice cracked two or three times while he answered the questions which had slipped out of my mind when that bomb went off:

"I think we had about a half a day's peace before these people found out we were colored. Then they started getting together in gangs as big as from fifty to two thousand people."

Kevin backed up Arthur:

111

"That's no lie. I've seen two thousand people out here myself. Right in front of Arthur's house, throwing bricks, pipes, everything they could lay their hands on. Hours at a time around Arthur's house, hollering and throwing things at both Arthur *and* the cops. Two or three cops have been hurt since this stuff started, but still they let the mobs gather."

He pulled his famous foot shift again. I asked Arthur:

"Don't any of the mob ever get hurt?"

"Not that I ever heard about." Arthur turned to Kevin: "You ever hear of any of these people getting hurt by a policeman?"

Kevin said:

"By a policeman?"

I said:

"I saw an old gray-haired man get hit last night, but the captain seemed awful mad about it."

Mona seemed to remember then:

"A colored police officer caught one of them once when he threw a pipe through our window. He knocked the devil out of that man."

Kevin almost smiled:

"That's right."

Arthur put the finishing touches to the tale:

"Yeah, and they sent that cop out of here so fast it made his head swim."

This thing was getting goofier and goofier by the minute. Send a cop away from here for arresting a guy that throws an iron pipe through somebody's window? I said:

"In other words they don't want the cops to arrest the troublemakers out here, do they?"

Kevin answered:

"I wouldn't say that."

Arthur came back at him:

"Well, I would. And I ought to know. I've been out here longer than anybody else."

Kevin stiffened.

"Well, so what? It doesn't mean a thing that you've been out here a few weeks before us. We're *all* catching hell."

Arthur snapped back—madder, it seemed to me, than he should have been:

"Look, Kevin. Your house is way back here in the middle of this project. Do you know where *my* house is?"

"What do you mean, do I know where your house is? Sure, I know where it is. I just said that you're always——"

"You don't know how it was those first six weeks. We were out here *alone*. You were down somewhere on 63rd Street not *thinking* about Trumbull Park, while these bastards were chasing Mona home from church, spitting at her and everything else. And you have nerve enough to tell me that I——"

"Like I was saying, Arthur, you bragging like this is your own private fight, like nobody is suffering but you——"

"Bragging? What in the hell have I got to brag about? Did you ever have to carry a gun to church so that your wife could pray? That's right, a gun. I've had to take my forty-five to that St. Kevin's over on Torrence and sit behind my wife while she got on her knees and prayed to God. Did you ever have to do that? No, you *never* had to do that. If that's anything to brag about, I've got a *right* to brag!"

You could feel that something had blown up between these two. They were getting madder and madder and talking louder and louder. Kevin wasn't leaning on the wall now. He stood straight up. There was a sort of a getting-

113

ready-to-fight look about him. His right eye started jumping and twitching to beat the band, and his face seemed extra bright. His eyes moved around the room like he was trying to see how everybody was taking all this.

Arthur was sitting on the edge of the couch, his fist doubled up. He kept pointing his fist at Kevin, and all the while his voice got louder and squeakier, and it kept breaking everytime he hit a high note.

It seemed like a crazy talking contest. Helen looked from one to the other, like she was watching a ping-pong game out at Washington Park. Diane scooted down on the floor and laid her head against the side of Helen's leg. Louella stood with one arm behind the back of Helen's chair, and sucking the fingers of her other hand like they were lollypops.

Sharon slid closer to Mona, and Mona slid farther back on the couch and just sort of hung her head, shaking it from side to side and rubbing her hand across her face. Little Bobby stood up beside Arthur and stared up at Kevin with that screwed-up mad-look on his baby face. His little golf-ball fists were doubled up so tight that his knuckles were cherry red.

Kevin took a step toward Arthur, swinging one arm behind his back and resting his weight on one foot and pointing his finger in Arthur's face:

"Look, man, if you'd lay off that bottle, you wouldn't have such a hard time out here. One of the colored cops told me that you got all the cops out here down on you, even the colored ones, because you're always blowing your top at somebody."

Arthur knocked Kevin's hand away and jumped up from the couch, trembling all over. Every breath he took sounded like a gasp. He had both fists doubled up now, and standing that close to Kevin showed him to be at least three inches shorter.

Kevin stepped back and slid one hand into the side pocket of his suit. His eyes were moving from the left of Arthur to the right of him, but not another muscle of his face moved. His voice was growly and yet on the soft and quiet side when he said:

"Man, if you ever make a break at me, mean it. You hear me, goddammit! Mean it!"

Arthur tuned up like he was going to cry. Mona stood up and put her arm around his shoulders. She looked at Kevin and then at me:

"You have to excuse Arthur, Buggy and Helen. He's been drinking and——"

She turned to Kevin, and her face got another expression now—hurt, and some anger—disgust. She looked pitiful. I hated to see that look on her face.

"And, Kevin, you know how Arthur is. I don't know why *you* had to carry this thing on."

I could tell that Kevin was listening to Mona. His mouth stuck out just a little, and he took his hand out of his pocket.

Arthur pushed Mona's hand away from his shoulder:

"I don't need you to stand up for me! I don't care what the son-of-a-bitch is carrying in his pocket! I know one thing—if he hasn't got anything in there, he'd better get something, because"—Arthur turned to Kevin; he didn't realize that he was tiptoeing—"I'm going to call your bluff next time."

I was so surprised at all of this that I hadn't done anything but watch, but now that things were settling down, I got mad that they had caused all that commotion, and I said:

"You guys better go home if you're going to act like

115

that. I mean I got kids here, and they're not used to hearing all that kind of talk."

Helen said:

"Aww, Buggy."

I cut my eyes at her and then turned away to say something to Arthur. Mona had sat back down, and her head was pushed down between her hands. She was shaking and crying so hard that before I realized what I was doing I sat down beside her and put my arm around her shoulder. Then as soon as I did it, I felt Arthur tighten. I moved my arm and stood up again. I felt my ears burning and my skin felt like somebody was rubbing it with sandpaper. I had to say something, so I jumped on Arthur:

"Man, you're going to make your wife sick, acting like that."

Talk about blowing up! He about blew my head off!

"What are you talking about? You don't know anything about my wife, and," he added for good measure, "you *don't* know *me!*"

Kevin started for the front door, and little Bobby started out behind him. Mona got up and walked over to Helen, her stomach sticking out more than ever now. Her face was wet in streaks, and there was a smudge where she had wiped the tears away with the palm of her hand. She simply touched Helen lightly on the shoulder and turned her head away from me and started out of the door behind Bobby and Kevin. Sharon smiled at Louella as she passed by her. Louella smiled back and whispered:

"Bye, li'l girl."

Arthur Davis was the last to go. He didn't look me in the face as he passed, but he did mumble:

"I'm sorry, man. Guess it's my nerves." He turned to Helen. "I'm sorry, uh, Lorraine, isn't it?"

Helen took a quick breath and huffed it out:

"Helen."

"Oh, yeah. Helen. I'm sorry, Helen."

"That's all right."

He walked out. I heard the policemen outside telling Arthur to sign the book. I heard him say:

"Hell, no."

I heard a scuffle, and I ran to the front door just as Arthur pulled aloose from a tall white policeman about as wide as my kitchen door.

"And you can't make me!" Arthur shouted.

The policeman turned his back to Arthur and started back toward the door. I heard him mutter:

"Smart goddamned nigger."

I liked that Arthur Davis. He seemed to have something I didn't have. He was on the reckless side—just enough to make him a man. And it takes something to be reckless enough to be a man, especially if you're colored.

I turned to say something to Helen. She was in the kitchen. Diane was stretched out across the couch asleep, and Louella was sitting on the edge of the couch sucking her fingers and looking like she was going to tune up and cry. I sat beside Louella:

"What's the matter, Puddin'?"

"I'm hungry."

Do you know I had forgotten all about eating? Helen said:

"I'm fixing some hamburgers now. It won't be long."

I got up and peeked into the kitchen. She was smiling.

Boom! Boom! Boom!

I could see the blue-white light slap against the wall. It shook from the hollow, booming explosion. Helen dropped a dish and the pieces sounded like scrap iron hitting the floor.

"Damn it to hell!" she blurted.

117

I said, mainly to relieve my nerves:

"Going to have to buy some new dishes soon."

"With what?"

I didn't answer. Louella was sucking her fingers again.

"Take those fingers out of your mouth!"

She did.

I slid back on the couch and closed my eyes. I wondered if I would wind up like Arthur and Kevin. There was something about Arthur, though, that was different. There seemed to be something on his mind. I decided to talk to him the next day after work. I wanted to hear the whole story from beginning to end. What had he done that made the colored cops turn against him? Why did he run to the window and the door every five minutes? Why did he buck up to the cops so strong? Why did he stay in Trumbull Park? I wanted to go over to his house and ask him these things right then, but I decided that I would wait until tomorrow.

Helen scared me when she called:

"Come on, Buggy, you and Louella. Come on and eat. It's almost ten o'clock. I should have *had* your dinner ready. Come on and eat."

Louella sat there looking at me. I looked at her. She started smiling, and I smiled back. I felt a little hitch in my throat. Louella seemed to take everything so cool, right now. She looked so grown up. Not even half as tall as I was. One little braid balled up right at the top of her head, two in the back pinned together. Her round little brown eyes looked just like Helen's when she smiled—and she *was* smiling. I laughed when she blinked her eyes at me and opened them real big. I felt guilty at the same time, though. It seemed that I hadn't paid Louella much attention lately. Now that I was looking at her and smiling and all, she seemed so glad about it. It made me feel guilty.

"Are you two coming?"

"Right away, Honey."

Helen had fixed up a real good meal—hamburgers and tomato-and-lettuce salad and mashed potatoes, and a big cup of hot coffee for me. Louella sat down first. I sat at the head of the table, and Helen stayed at the stove putting the mashed potatoes in a bowl.

"Helen, I thought that maybe tomorrow I'd go over to Arthur Davis' house."

"What for? Haven't we got troubles enough already?"

"How will that cause trouble?"

"You know how."

She sat at the table. I waited for her to scoot her chair closer to the table, but she didn't, and I remembered the baby. Can't upset her, I thought. So I said:

"Okay, just thought I'd ask."

To tell you the truth, I was just going to go on over there anyway, without telling her. I mean after all, they had been to my house twice in a row. Why couldn't I go over there? But that Helen is no fool. She could see by the way I gave in so quick that I had something on my mind. She sounded just like some old lady when she said:

"If you want to slip over there and take a chance on running into that mob that they said hangs around Arthur's house, it's all right with me. You know what they say: 'A hard head makes a soft you-know-what.'"

I got the message, and on second thought it didn't seem quite bright to be asking for trouble—I mean by going over to this guy's house and maybe getting into a whole lot of trouble when I could talk to him just as well right here at my house. Still, I wanted to ask him some questions that I wouldn't want Helen to hear—I mean like if he ever got scared the way I had when they got Red out there on the parking lot the day we moved in and things like that. I was going over to that guy's house tomorrow and that was all there was to it.

Once again Helen read my mind:

"You don't even know where he lives."

Louella cut in:

"I'm through, Momma."

She got up from the table, still chewing on a piece of hamburger. She started yawning. Helen stared down into that mouth full of food and smiled.

"You don't look like you're through. Sit back down here until you really get through."

Louella started a frown and then stopped it and sat back down. She yawned again. Helen said:

"Anyway, you can't go to bed right away; you've got to let that food settle first."

I started yawning. Helen said:

"That goes for you too, Buggy Martin."

"Yes ma'm, Miss Ann!"

She tried to reach over and hit me, but her stomach stopped her short. I laughed:

"Wow! Honey, you ought to do something about that appetite of yours. You're gaining all kind of weight. Why, you can't even reach across the table."

Louella giggled. Helen really tried to hit me then, but she couldn't reach me to save her life. I broke out laughing:

"Yes, sir, Honey," I said, "you're just gonna have to reduce. I mean *re*-duce!"

"Don't worry about a thing." The girl started signifying with me. "I'm going to get my figure back, and when I do, boy, I'm not losing it for you or nobody else."

"Did you say 'nobody else'?"

"That's right."

"Uhhh—like who?"

120

"Like who? What are you talking about, Buggy Martin?"

"You said you weren't going to lose your figure for me or nobody else. Now what I want to know is who is this 'nobody-else'?"

That fast thing laughed. And do you know what she said then?

"Oh, there are several others. Let's see—uh—there's Joe Louis, Ralph Bunche, Paul Robeson, Frank Sinatra——"

"Frank Sinatra!" I reached for her but she leaned back. "Woman, I'll kill you!"

Louella just fell out, and Helen was laughing to burst, and I started laughing. Louella said in her tweaky little voice,

"Daddy, you're silly!"

That tickled me even more, and I took a deep breath that almost burst my sides. Then Helen said:

"Don't you get out of your place, Louella! You're just a little girl. I don't ever want to hear you say your daddy is silly again. Do you hear?"

Louella stopped laughing and nodded her head. I stopped laughing and stared hard at Louella. I wasn't mad, but Helen saying what Louella had said wasn't funny, and sounding so serious about me being Louella's father made me figure I'd better straighten up. Do you know I never thought of it like that before? All at once I felt like being a father was something, and being Louella's father was *really* something. Isn't it funny how all of a sudden you can find out there's something new about what you are or what you're doing?

Helen got up from the table and started cleaning the dishes. I looked at her, thinking about what she had said, Then I thought, You should get up from here and help her.

But then I thought, Hell, I'm tired, I'll help her tomorrow. Louella yawned as Helen turned back to the table.

"Okay, both of you go to bed."

I said:

"Are you sure you don't want me to help you?"

She laughed under her breath.

"I'll clean up, but"—she gave me one of those naughty looks—"I would like for you to stay down here and keep me company."

Deep dimples in her cheeks looking like great comma marks. Eyebrows like black rainbows curving around those deep-set night-time eyes, looking brown then black, and nothing but soul in them. Before she knew it, I kissed her. She moved away.

"You can't hug me tight the way you used to. Little Louis Martin Junior won't stand for it."

I heard a sucking sound behind me. I had forgotten all about Louella. I turned around and there she was, standing in the door looking as sad as a wet little kitten. I said:

"Why don't you go to bed, Bright Eyes?"

"Can I sleep down here on the couch until you and Momma go upstairs?"

I wondered whether Louella's fear had gotten to Diane yet. I wondered if it was the same kind of fear that made Arthur and Kevin and even Mona act the way they did. Louella started sucking her fingers again. That finger sucking was just like a language. That girl could talk to you, just by sucking her fingers. She waited for me to tell her whether or not she could sleep on the couch.

"Sure, you can sleep on the couch, Honey. But don't worry. Daddy won't let anything happen to you. Don't you worry."

"I can sleep on the couch?"

She hadn't heard a word I said.

"Yeah, go on. We'll be in there in a minute."

I went over to the sink. Helen had scraped all the dishes and was getting ready to wash them. I reached into the dishwater and found her hands. She was holding a dishrag, and I grabbed it and pulled it away. She didn't try to hold it.

"You sit down," I bragged. "*I'm* washing dishes tonight."

She smiled and pulled her hands from the water. She was smiling when she said:

"Well, I'm not going to fight with you."

I felt pretty good after that. But then all hell broke loose. Bombs started going off like a string of economy-size firecrackers.

Boom! Boom! Boom! Boom! Boom! Boom! Boom! Boom! Boom!

I'm not kidding; bombs went off there for thirty minutes straight. The whole sky was white with their lights. The house shook like it was on the back of a truck with fifty or sixty wheels going *boom-flat, boom-flat,* one right after the other. I ran into the living room to Louella because I knew that she must be just about scared out of her skin. She was sitting on the edge of the couch when I got there, covering her face with her little hands. Helen came into the living room behind me. There was that wild scared look in her eyes again. I grabbed her hand and pulled her down beside me on the couch. Her hands were cold and damp.

What to do? What to do?

I hugged Louella, and I squeezed Helen's hand, and the bombs kept on going: not one, not two, but bomb after bomb after bomb. Aw, you can't imagine it! You'd have had to have been there and seen the sky light up and see the light flash on your wall and feel the explosions splitting deep down in the hollow of your ears—not once or twice, but three, four, and a hundred times more than that—one after the other for minutes and minutes.

Boom! Boom! Boom! Boom!

What to do? What to do?

Boom! Boom!

What to do? What to do? What to do?

I had to go over to Arthur's house tomorrow. That's all there was to it. I had to ask him what he had done. What I should do. What we could do.

Boom! Boom! Boom! Boom!

I got up and went to the window. There was a red fire burning just beyond the parking lot. I turned out the lights and went to the door. I opened the front door just enough to see. I could see the policemen standing in front of my house, shuffling and restless, but not going anywhere. The red flare burned steady.

"Shut that door!" Helen snapped.

"Keep quiet. I'm trying to see what that light is."

I opened the door a little wider. I heard an even drone like people talking, like an audience in a hall before the show starts. I stepped out of the door. Now I could see to the end of the parking lot. Hundreds and hundreds of people—all white, standing in the street in front of the project, with the light flickering and brightening up their faces. The sides of the two buildings looked like they were on fire. The steel-mill smell blew in with the cool air jostling the hard cracking leaves in the row of trees that ran along the edge of the courtyard. The air was cool, but the steel-mill iron-smell seemed hot. The fire made all outdoors look hot, but I felt a chill at the back of my neck, and I shuddered and folded my arms around me.

Then that little tattle-tale pop in the sky and then—*Boom!* Then another pop and—*Boom!* And then those gray smoke-ring clouds hanging up there in the dark, letting you

know where the bombs were coming from, letting the police know, letting the whole world know, and the whole
world not giving a damn.

Boom! Boom! Boom! Boom!

"Buggy, come in here!"

She sounded like she was crying. One of the cops turned
around and said something to the other cops. They started
walking toward me, and I turned and walked into the
house and slammed the door—hard.

I had to do something. I went over to Helen. She moved
over, and I sat on the couch. I sat down on Diane's foot,
and she whined and moved it. She sat up and started whining, and with her eyes closed tightly felt for my face and
found my neck and hugged me so hard I could barely
breathe. I said:

"They've got some kind of red flare out there, and
they're just standing around in that red light like a bunch
of devils. I swear it looks like it's one great big fire out
there."

Helen mumbled just loud enough for me to hear her:

"I wonder if we're going to have to move."

"What do you mean?"

"Oh, nothing." She paused. "Come on, Buggy, let's
go to bed. I'll finish the dishes tomorrow."

Louella started sucking those fingers again. My mind
was working like a bowl of yeast. I was scared all right, but
I was madder than I was scared: making my wife cry,
making my baby start sucking her fingers. Oh, I was mad
all right. And when I thought about that snake, I got a
choking feeling right at the bottom of my throat. I said:

"What kind of country is this?"

Helen started unbuttoning Louella's dress:

"Don't blame the country. Blame these people."

I started untying Louella's shoe. I said:

125

"I blame everybody. What do you think would happen if those were a bunch of Negroes out there setting off bombs in front of white people's houses, and hanging around to watch them explode? How long do you think they'd let us get away with that?"

Helen stopped messing with Louella's clothes. She took a deep breath and sighed.

"Let's go to bed."

"Helen, you know I'm right! Why, they'd have the whole doggoned Army, Navy, and Marines down on us if we did anything like that."

"In the first place, Buggy, we wouldn't do anything like that. When did you ever hear of Negroes doing a thing like that? Come on, let's go to bed before they start those things again."

Louella was still sucking her fingers. I boosted her back up on my knees and started to get up with her from the couch when my ear caught that little pop, and then the blue flash streaked around the edges of the curtain, and the *Boom! Boom! Boom!* flashed and shook the floor.

"Goddamn it," Helen said—so tired and sadly. "I'm going to bed, Buggy. My stomach is starting to hurt."

I picked Louella up and started up the stairs. I kept thinking as I went up the stairs, I'm going by Arthur's house soon as I get off work. Even after I was in bed with Helen and hugging her and kissing her soft-wet lips, yearning to be closer to her, feeling things wake up inside me that I had been trying to put to sleep, I thought about visiting Arthur's house and what he would have to say and how we would get a scheme together to fight back. Yet feeling the way I did beside Helen made me want her to be just me, and me just her, and us to be not Buggy and Helen, but Buggyandhelen. But I knew as sure as I was in bed, snuggled close to Helen and breathing her warmth and her faint kind of sweetness, that come tomorrow I'd get to Arthur's house and we'd somehow or other figure out what to do.

Helen went to sleep, and she jumped and hugged me when another bomb went off. I guess I had dozed myself. I hugged her tightly and felt a pounding all over my body. I didn't know whether it was her or me. Probably both of us.

10

THE WEATHER had changed during the night—the way it does in Chicago—just like that. Fast change. Quick change. But, oh, so much happening underneath! Wind and cloud . . . Wind and cloud . . . And all of a sudden—*wham!*—it's cold.

I half-woke up and felt the cold trying to get right down into the pores of my skin. But it couldn't: something else was in the pores of my skin coming out the other way—from inside me. Worry. Cold wet worry. Things are happening, the worry said. Things, things. Get your boots on, the worry said, your hip boots, your hep boots. The wind and the worry said: Something is not cool. Something is running—*cold*. I opened my eyes and sang in my head:

"Early in the morning, and I can't get right!"

I reached over and pulled the covers up; but the bed didn't feel good any more. Nothing felt good. I looked over at Helen. She stirred, turned over on her back, and pulled the covers up on her. She bent her arms under her head and took a long breath and opened her eyes. She slid her arm under my head and then she snatched it back and sat straight up:

"Hey, you're going to be late for work!"

I teased her:

"Awwwwww, crack that whip, pretty momma!"

"You like it."

She slid her leg next to mine and pressed hard against me. I said:

"You devil you!"

She climbed out of bed.

"What do you want for breakfast?"

Now that question caused more argument in my house than any other question I know, just about. I knew that if I said bacon and eggs, she would ask, "With toast or biscuits?" Then if I wanted biscuits she'd accuse me of being thoughtless, asking her to fix biscuits that early in the morning. On the other hand, if I asked for toast, she'd ask me if I wanted butter or margarine; and if I said butter, she'd say that she was going to make a cake with the butter, but that if I'd rather use the butter on the toast and not have cake that was all right with her. And then I'd get mad and ask her why the hell she had to get so economical with the butter when she spends money like it was going out of style. And she probably wouldn't be able to think of anything snappy to say after that, and that would make her mad—and boy! the battle would be on. So in order to keep from ruining the day before it got going good, when Helen asked me what I wanted for breakfast this time, I said: "Honey, whatever you desire to fix me, I will be truly satisfied."

"Fine. Then I'll fix you bacon and eggs. Do you want toast or biscuits?"

I turned the water up in the bathtub and eased the lock to on the bathroom door. Then I took my pajamas off and climbed into the tub and started kicking the water around.

"Buggy?"

I didn't open my mouth—just splashed that water in the

129

tub and started humming loud enough for her to hear me. When I finished my bath, I climbed out of the tub and stepped over to the mirror above the face bowl. It looked to me like my face was getting the same hollow-jawed look about it that Arthur's had.

"Buggy, breakfast is ready!"

I jumped. I guess I was lost in thinking about my face. It seemed like the only time I was ever really alone with myself was when I was in the bathroom.

Only a few days in Trumbull Park, and it seemed like a million years already.

"Okay, hold your horses!"

Helen wasn't looking so sporty herself when I got down stairs. I mean she had a peakish down-in-the-dumps look about her. I sat at the table. Sure enough she had fixed bacon and eggs and toast—with butter—I think. I started eating. She poured my coffee and then sat down across the table from me.

"What's the matter, Helen?"

"Oh—you know how pregnant women are."

"Are you worried about something happening again today?"

"No, not really. I'll know now what to do if I do catch anybody fooling around this house—man or boy."

She meant that thing.

I tore into that breakfast, and every now and then I would catch Helen looking at me with a pleased kind of smile on her face. I said:

"Pete, the white guy at work, said that if anybody bothered us he'd come out here with me and we'd kick some butts."

"Who said that?"

"Pete."

"Do you believe that?"

"No, I don't believe it. Hell, blood is thicker than water anyday."

She agreed:

"And like Al Benson says, 'Thot's f'sure!'"

I laughed and got up.

"That was a good breakfast, Helen. I see you're learning how to cook."

I guess we'd been doing all that talking to drown out our thoughts. Now it was time to go to work, and everything was just like it was before. I wanted to stay, but I had to go. The rent man doesn't want no explanations—just cash— even the CHA rent man. I tried to keep laughing and kidding with Helen and kiss her goodbye before she got a chance to ask me not to go over to Arthur Davis' house. Helen caught the look on my face and asked:

"What time are you coming home today?"

"I don't know."

Her face changed when I said that. For a while we had both been dreaming or pretending that we were out of the Gardener Building in a nice clean quiet place where we could start saving to get on our feet. Part of the dream was true, and that's what made it so bad. We were out of the Gardener Building, but now the world around us was icy and mean with the evil stares of the people we had to live with. And the noise of those bombs made the diesel train behind the Gardener Building and the broken bannisters seem like maybe I had exaggerated how bad it had been in the first place. I had thought that diesel meant to me the death, dirt, and gloom of the Gardener Building, but it seemed to have caught up with me in a different way in Trumbull Park. It looked like there was no place for a broke colored man to go. No hiding place. No place to run. I felt choked, trapped, and boxed in. Helen seemed to know what I was thinking:

"I was just thinking, Buggy. If we had all stuck together in that Gardener Building and made that old moneygrabber Mr. Gardener fix up that place, maybe Babydoll would be alive today. Maybe we'd still be there. Maybe poor Bertha's heart wouldn't be broken right now."

"Our folks stick together? When did they ever?"

She got quiet when I threw that one at her. I didn't believe that stuff about Negroes not sticking together, but it was so easy to say. I had heard it so much in my lifetime that it had become the most natural thing in the world to say. Helen didn't say much else; and I couldn't think of a thing funny to say as I walked out of the door and signed the book the police thrust at me, and climbed into the patrol wagon, and started off to earn a living.

I got to the aircraft plant on time. It was a monster of a joint. Machines everywhere—big ones, little ones, medium-sized ones—all kinds of machines. And for a good two blocks alongside the wall ran a long, long row of time clocks.

"Hey, Buggy!"

It was Pete. Man, that cat had muscles he hadn't even used yet! When I grabbed his hand it felt like I had grabbed a two-by-four.

"Listen, Buggy. I've been worried about you. How'd things go last night?"

"They didn't!"

Now, why did I snap Pete up?

"Okay." He sounded hurt.

I cut between a double row of cement pillars with numbers marked on them until I got to 20B. I got to my machine just as the buzzer went off. It sounded like a sick calf. I pushed the "on" button on the machine and looked at the conveyor belt on my right. That thing was loaded with castings. Somebody sure planned to use a lot of airplanes. I hadn't started to think about what those engines were going to be used for, with the war over and all. As far as I was concerned airplanes were airplanes, and I was making them to make me some money. Pete's machine was next to mine. He came up, and we sort of smiled at each other and then went to work drilling those castings for the engines that would send those airplanes about their business.

We drilled castings *awhile* that morning! Noontime caught me in the middle of a daydream about Mona—now why was I doing *that?*—with a half-finished casting still in my machine. I hurried through with that thing and broke down the long yellow-brick corridor to the lunchroom.

The lunchroom smelled of stew, mixed in with the smell of sweat and lubricating oil, of milk, and of coffee boiling on a grill behind the counter. Five or six white women ran back and forth behind that counter like the floor was on fire. Dishes clinked, and knives and forks and spoons twanged on plates and metal trays. The bus boy zoomed in and out of the swinging door that led to the kitchen. He was colored—and very dark, with a process that had seen its best days. Sweat slipped off his face like his skin was crying, and he had one of those Down Home frowns on his face that showed that he wasn't a bit happy about having to scuffle that way.

A short fat white woman got in front of me, and dragged her tail just like she was out taking a stroll somewhere. I started to tell her to get a move on, but decided, Why start anything? Then the idea came to me that she was taking her time just because I was behind her. Then I thought, This chick would waste time if the Lord Himself was standing in line behind her. Then I thought, Maybe I'm just making excuses for this woman because I'm afraid to tell her to get a move on. Hell, I thought, that's what they tell me when I can't decide what to buy. "Get a move on," they say; and I get a move on. Now it was my turn to say, "Get a move on!" and I wasn't saying it. Why? Wasn't it my turn? I got all balled up inside. I saw Pete across the room. He didn't see me. I was glad he didn't.

"Okay," somebody behind me yelled, "let's get a move on!" I looked in front of me. There was a wide space between me and the short little fat white woman in front of me. I looked behind me. A tall, grinning white guy, with short brown hair sticking straight up, nodded toward the woman behind the counter. I turned toward her. She wiped her forehead with the bottom of her apron and leaned forward over the steam table where the stew boiled and half-empty trays of mashed potatoes and green peas and dried-up hamburger patties stared me in the face.

"What'll you have?"

"Stew."

"Hey, Buggy!"

It was Pete. I picked up the plate of stew and made it to Pete's table. He had a mouthful of food and chawed it something awful while he talked:

"Did I ever tell you about when I lived in Trumbull Park?"

"Well, no, you never told me much, ol' buddy! But then people don't brag about being from Trumbull Park."

Pete plopped another blop of stew into his mouth, agreeing between chaws:

"At least white people don't. Or at least they shouldn't. I suppose there are some dopes who think it's something to brag about pushing colored people around. Naw—I'll tell you this. I'm not happy about having lived in that goddamned——"

I helped him.

"Jungle."

"You said it. The Association's got a big racket going out there, and not one out of ten of those goofs know what Mascari is pulling."

"Masca-who? Association? What are you talking about, Pete?"

Pete frowned and swallowed and looked away from me.

"You mean you haven't heard about the South Deering Association?"

Pete laid his fork down and crossed his elbows and leaned toward me.

"Mannnnnn! You *are* late! I thought you knew what you were into. There's been a big fight over whether Trumbull Park should even remain public property, for years! Man, there's millions of dollars hanging in the balance depending on whether that project stays private or public property. Didn't you know that?"

He didn't make any more sense to me than if he was making a speech in algebra.

"Why, when we moved off Maxwell Street into that place, those kids called us 'slum bunnies' and everything else. Compared to the dump we came out of we were in heaven, but we had to fight to stay in that project. That was back in 1939. I was in my last year in grade school, and when I transferred to Bright School, I had a hell of a lot of fights with those kids. It was a bitch, I'll tell you!"

"Well, what has millions of dollars and all that got to do with the kids bothering you?"

"Well, Buggy, a guy finds out a lot of things when he lives in the same neighborhood for fifteen years. If the Association guys can keep the property-owners scared of having their property values lowered—and they don't care what they have to do to keep the property owners scared—

135

I mean, they'll blame white project-people just the same as they blame Negroes. Then who's going to cash-in on the panic, once the Association boys set it off?"

I was getting the message:

"What is it? Tell me what's happening, man!"

Buzzzzz!

That doggoned buzzer shot through me. I jumped. Pete got up real fast.

"Let's go to work, Buggy."

I said:

"You act like you're glad to go back to work."

"You just don't know the half of what you're into—that's all."

This puzzled the hell out of me. The whole thing looked as funny as two left shoes. There was something goofy going on. Why would Pete clam up in the middle of something that it looked like he was dying to tell me? Maybe Arthur Davis knew something. I knew one thing, I was sure going to find out.

The quitting bell caught me in the same mood I had been in at lunch time. I felt my chest thumping hard from the blow in my heart. I felt my throat tighten up, and the water in my mouth gathered alongside my jaws so fast that my jaws ached. I opened my mouth wide to shake things up in my jaws and to ease that hurting, but it only got worse. Not since I had hit Clarence Murphy back in Colman Grade School after he hit me on the head and I heard the kids gasp that he was the leader of the roughest gang between 45th and 47th Street and I had sat in the last class before time to go home, waiting for the last bell to ring, had I felt the kind of stomach-upsetting, headaching, jaw-hurting, slow dread that I was beginning to feel when that quitting bell at the aircraft factory rang.

136

I was still feeling that way when the patrol wagon pulled into the project. The driver's partner got out and unbolted the door. I climbed out and brushed the dust from my jacket and turned my collar up to guard against the sharp October wind that tingled my face and ears. The driver's partner pushed his finger against one nostril and blew hard, then dragged his blue-sleeved elbow across his nose. The red splotches around the curve of his nostril wrinkled as he frowned at me and complained:

"You didn't check in the station yesterday. Go check in before you go home."

"And then sign the book at my door too?"

"That's right."

He walked away, and I walked behind him, not knowing whether to report to the headquarters, or to go home, or to try to find Arthur Davis' house. Even as I tried to decide, I turned into the apartment where the door stood open and the sweat stink—the kind that seeps through heavy clothing—floated into the nippy outdoors. The two policemen in front of me went to the policeman at the desk in the corner of the room. He wrote something in a big book. Then looked over at me.

"You Martin?"

"That's right."

"Whyn't you sign in yesterday?"

And right that minute a bomb went off.

Boom! Then another. *Boom! Boom!*

The policeman at the desk dropped his pencil. His face got that ashy-pale color and his eyes bucked and his mouth dropped loose like a spring somewhere inside it had broken. Only for a real quick moment though. Right away he picked up the pencil and bellowed like some drunk just waking up.

"Wheeeee! Merry Christmas! Them things'll wake you up—huh, Martin?"

But he knew I had seen him afraid. I had jumped and felt a shudder ripple across my skin like a cold fingernail, but the policeman had been scared too. I stared at him. I wanted him to know that I had seen the little boy's dread on his long wrinkled face. I didn't laugh at his joke, and he dropped his eyes and scribbled something else in his book.

"Okay!" he snapped. "That's all. Be sure you check in here from now on—okay?"

I didn't answer. I felt like there had been a test to see who the man was between us, and that I was the man. I mean, the most man—the real man. I turned to go out and bumped into a Negro policeman who was coming downstairs. He was a squatty dark-skinned man, with stubble on his chin and a ragged heavy moustache. His uniform coat was unbuttoned, and his tie hung loose from his shirt. He grabbed me by the shoulders and smiled.

"I'm sorry, man."

"That's okay. I should have been watching where I was going."

"You're that new family aren't you?"

"Yeah."

He hitched up his gun belt as though the weight of the guns was pulling his pants down.

"Jim, this is hell! And that ain't no lie." He looked behind him, and seeing nobody near, walked a few steps away from the station and said, "They don't give us no kind of break."

I knew that this cat was talking about us colored folks, but he was a cop, so I said:

"You mean, you cops?"

He laughed:

138

"Daddy, I mean us colored folks."

"Man, you sure said it! What they need to do is to whip a few heads out here the way they do us down on 58th Street. This stuff would break up in no time."

"Listen, you'd better not let one of the colored cops out here start anything like that! They'd have him making out every report in the book, and then they'd most likely suspend him. The least they'd do would be to send him back to the station."

I was surprised at the bitter way this policeman talked about the police force. To me all policemen had seemed to be just one big family of bullies, no matter what their color was. More than once I'd seen some colored policeman teaming up with his white partner to beat the devil out of a Negro. But now there seemed to be a difference—a big difference. This Negro policeman showed that he didn't go for what was happening no kind of way. I asked:

"Do you know where Arthur Davis' house is?"

"*That* somitch? Who don't? That's where all the trouble's coming from."

He pointed with his thumb:

"It's right behind that house over there."

Then he changed the subject quick:

"Do you know where they keep most of the colored cops out here?"

"Where?"

"In the power house behind the project. That way they make sure we don't accidently enforce the law." He laughed, but I could tell he wasn't tickled. "But I don't care. It's not us that gets thrown at, and cursed out every night, while the sergeant hollers, 'Take cover men! They're stonin' us! Take it easy men! These are citizens!'"

He laughed again, but there was too much worry in his

eyes, too much embarrassment, too much shame for being a "colored policeman." He wasn't tickled worth a damn.

Boom! Boom! Boom!

The cop hitched his belt up and squeezed the inside corners of his eyes with his forefinger and his thumb. When he took his hand away he still had that worry in his eyes, and his face—dark where he needed a shave and crude behind that rough moustache—was tired and pained and wrinkled with some way-down-deep misery. I knew that misery. I knew that it was my misery, that his misery was mine. There was something in that tired face that was kin to me.

Boom! Then another: *Boom!* And another: *Boom!*

The cop hitched his belt with that arm-swinging shoulder-twisting movement and mumbled disgustedly:

"I gotta go, man. Cool it."

"Yeah," I agreed, feeling as drug as the cop looked. "I gotta go myself. These bastards might have put another snake in the door."

The cop looked surprised:

"A what?"

"A snake, Daddy."

"Goddamn!"

I tried to sound don't-care-ish:

"Well, take it easy."

He headed back toward headquarters, answering over his shoulder:

"Yeah."

I called him:

"Hey!"

He stopped—turned.

"Why did you call Arthur Davis a son-of-a-bitch?"

He looked at me for a minute and raised his hand like he was trying to say something that his mouth couldn't handle. Then he dropped his hand, and walked away.

140

I yelled at him:

"C'mon, man. Give me a hint. What's wrong with the cat?"

He didn't stop walking. I started for my house. *Boom!* went that blue light and that ear-hurting ground-shaking noise.

Boom! Boom! Boom!

I walked a little faster.

"Nigger, nigger, nigger!"

It was that chick hidden in one of the dingy buildings around me. I turned to shout something back at her. But the word never came out. From my right came a crowd of men and teen-agers and old women and young women and little kids. They caught sight of me at about the same time I caught sight of them. Somebody screamed:

"There's a nigger! Get that nigger!"

Four or five of them broke away from the rest and ran toward me. I walked fast. I couldn't run—my pride wouldn't let me. I walked faster, trying to run while walking, but these wild-looking white folk came at me in a full run with that scared-mad kind of look that meant they could kill me, just because they were scared. I broke out into a run. Three men had almost caught up with me, as I stretched my hand out for my door knob. I knew that it would be locked and that Helen would be in the bathtub or upstairs in the bedroom—not at the door to let me in.

"Catch that nigger! Catch him!"

Something hit the ground in front of me. I pulled at the door, and it opened. One more step carried me inside, and the door slammed. I fell on the floor gasping for breath, feeling dizzy and light in the head. Helen was already bending over me as something banged against the door. It was a brick. I had gotten to know how bricks sounded against doors and walls and the sides of police wagons.

141

Somebody outside hollered:

"Hey, what are you people doing out here? Please don't congregate here. All right now, move on!"

Helen hovered over me, feeling all over me, rubbing my head, hugging me against her stomach, questioning me:

"Buggy, Buggy, are you hurt?"

I shook my head. She pulled my arm.

"Come on, don't sit by the door."

I got up. Louella, upstairs, cried down:

"What's the matter, Daddy? Huh?"

I opened my mouth to answer, but my throat swelled up just that quick, and my neck felt tight and my eyes started burning and my nose seemed to stop up, and I felt hot water growing on the rims of my eyes and slide down across my skin to the ridges of my upper lip and into my mouth, salty and warm. I felt like the lowest worm in the ground, the filthiest bum on skid row—undressed, stripped buck-naked, and covered with stinking horse manure. Me, a man! Chased—chased home into my pregnant wife's arms, into my little girl's hands. Chased and cursed and thrown at like a roach caught sneaking across the kitchen floor. They chased me, and I ran.

I looked at Helen. There were no tears on her face, just a stern hardness. She wiped my tears with the palms of her hands.

"Don't cry, Honey. Don't cry."

"Helen, what's wrong with me?"

"Nothing's wrong with you. Nothing at all."

"There must be. I should have stayed out there and fought. I mean it. I should have stayed out there and died. Not be chased home and halfway through the house. Why didn't I stand there and fight? What kind of man am I? Huh, Helen? What kind of roach did you marry? Huh, Helen?"

142

Helen sat on the couch beside me, rubbing my face, hugging me hard against her face and patting my wet cheeks with the palms of her hands. Low voice almost trembling, lips against my ear:

"I love you Buggy. I always have. I always will love you. Buggy, I . . ."

"Helen, please tell me what's the matter with me! I let white people get in front of me in the lunchroom, and I won't open my mouth."

"Don't bother yourself about all that stuff, Honey. I love you and that's all that counts."

"I didn't even jump in and help Red—my best friend—the day we moved in."

"You did the right thing, Baby. You couldn't start trouble. We have to live out here."

"Live out here? How? Live like possoms, foxes, mice, bedbugs—shot, chased, squashed on sight? Maybe next time they'll shoot *me* on sight. Honey——" I got too filled up to talk. I slapped my face. "Honey, I get mad—I swear to God I get mad—but I can't *do* anything! I can't fight back. I'm a coward. A goddamned——"

"Hush! Don't talk silly. You're not a coward. You remember how you caught that man who tried to snatch my purse down on 43rd that time? You didn't know what he had. He could have——"

"But he was colored, Honey, colored."

"And the time that bus driver was going to drive off with me after you got off the bus in front of me? You—you were great that time, Buggy. You weren't scared. Remember how you pulled the door open with one hand and jumped in while the bus was still rolling and got that driver told? Don't you remember how scared he was and how we laughed about it afterward?"

"Colored, colored, colored! Everybody that I ever

143

stood up to was colored! I can't even stand up to Pete at work. He called me 'boy' and——"

"But Pete's your friend."

"Sure, he's my friend; sure, he is; and he calls me 'boy,' and I could tell Pete—tell him, and he wouldn't mind. But I'm scared even to tell Pete not to call me 'boy.' My own friend! I'm scared of him. And why? You know why, Helen; and I know why. Because his skin is white and his hair is straight, and—and because he's white—that's why! Helen, what's wrong with me?"

"You're talking crazy."

"Am I? Didn't you start acting funny when I let Red down?"

She bent her head and picked at a piece of ravel on her dress.

"Awwww, Helen, Helen, Helen, I want to die! Die right now. I'm sick. I can't make it. I can't make anything. I'm nothing. They say a nigger ain't worth shit. And they're right as far as I'm concerned. I ain't worth shit. Awwww, Helen, what should I do? Help me, Baby. I don't know what to do."

Louella climbed on the couch beside me and squeezed her arms hard around my neck. She whined while she sucked her fingers.

"Don't cry, Daddy! I love you. Diane loves you too. Don't you, Diane?"

Diane climbed up, too. I tried to push her away, but she wouldn't loosen her arms.

Boom!

That bomb sounded like it was meant just for me. Like it was saying, "And you'd better not come back!"

"Those bast——"

Helen put her fingers on my lips.

"You don't want the kids saying that, do you? We've got to live for them too, you know."

144

"Haven't we *been* living for them, Helen?"

"I know *I've* been."

That one hit me at the bottom of my stomach. I must have made a face it hurt so bad.

"Oh, Buggy, I didn't mean it like that! I just mean that I've had to be with them every day, and I know how they feel about a lot of things—not everything Buggy, but a lot of things—and I know what's important to them. No, I'm saying it wrong. Sure, sure, you've been living for them, Buggy."

Boom! Boom! That house trembled like it had a chill. The blue-white light licked the walls like a snake's blue tongue and disappeared. Helen squinched her eyes like the wind was blowing in them, but she kept on talking:

"It's just that—Oh, I don't know, Buggy!"

It was the first time she'd kept talking while one of those things went off. I stuck that away in my mind: she kept talking.

"I just meant that we can't do things the way we did when there weren't any Diane and Louella. We can't say what we would say if they weren't here. We can't *not* say what we wouldn't say if they weren't here. We can't, can't, I don't know—do anything the way we used to. We can't even . . ."

She looked real hard at my eyes, and then looked at Louella and patted her head.

". . . die if we want to, like maybe we could before, before things happened. I mean before—— Louella! You and Diane go back upstairs! Daddy and I are talking."

Louella got up and started for the stairway. Diane went right behind her.

Helen was telling me something—something deep that I understood, and yet didn't understand. But it was not only what this woman was saying; it was the very idea that *she*

145

was saying it. I searched for her eyes and found them:

"Are you telling me to fight?"

"You do fight. You've always fought. No Negro lives who doesn't fight, early and late, with himself and everybody else. It's the only way we live."

"But do we fight white folks? That's the thing!"

"We fight whoever fights us. Everybody don't fight us, you know."

"I know that. It's just that I feel like that damned song—'tired of livin' and scared of dyin'.'"

"Wait a minute! That song says '*I'm* tired of livin'.' I'm talking about *us* now—Diane, Louella, and me and you—livin' for *us*; and if *we* can live for us, then *we'll* live; and if we have to . . ."

I finished it for her:

". . . die for us?"

And she finished it for me:

"Dying ain't that bad. People do it every day."

Oh, I had to hold that woman close to me—*had* to! I pulled her close.

"Helen——"

Boom! Boom!

Those two scared me. But it was a fenced-in scare this time. It bounced around in my chest, but it didn't spread to my fingertips and snatch my heart the way it had been doing, and I kept on with what I was saying:

"——I'm going over to——"

"I know." She pinched my nose. "You're going over to Arthur Davis' house."

"Some gypsy woman must have showed you how to read my mind."

She laughed.

"Don't need no gypsy woman for that. Your face tells me everything I want to know about you."

146

I got up and picked my hat off the floor and zipped up my jacket, and walked toward the door. Helen called me:

"Buggy?"

"What?"

"I love you, Buggy!"

There was soul in those words. I mean it. There was a new-yet-old something she hadn't ever used before in the way she said it. Something had changed between us. I don't know what. Maybe I had changed—maybe she had. She got up and walked toward me. I put my arm around her waist. That worried look eased back into her eyes.

"Buggy, there's a lot more to this stuff than you think."

I leaned forward toward her and laid my forehead against her forehead.

"You mean, than *you* think. I'm going to find out just what's happening on this scene."

"You don't even know where Arthur lives."

"Try again, Bright Eyes. A cop told me."

She smiled and poked her mouth out.

"Well, then, you be careful."

I opened the front door.

"Don't worry."

"That's not in the deal. I can't help worrying about you. Don't you know that?"

I stepped outside, and a shudder ran across my cheeks as I saw myself a few minutes before, leaping for that door like it was the only thing I'd ever do in my life again.

"See you later, Baby. I won't be long."

"You'd better not be."

It was dark outside and the street light by my house made me easy pickings for anybody with a good eye, a brick, a bottle, or a gun.

11

Arthur Davis peeked around the side of the window shade when he heard my knock.

"Hey, Buggy, come on in."

I stepped in the back door. He waved his hand around the kitchen.

"Come on in. Take a seat here. We don't use that living room much any more."

I sat down at the kitchen table, and Arthur sat down across from me.

"I'm glad you came over. I was thinking about you today. What do you know good?"

"Not much, man . . . Hey, where are all the cops? I thought I'd have to sign in, punch in, swear in, and every other kind of in when I got to your house. I didn't see cop the first out there."

"Oh, they're around. You want to see them?"

"Yeah, I'm game."

I looked around the room. On the floor was a faded linoleum smeared with pasty blue designs; but standing in the middle of that walked-out linoleum was the prettiest kitchen table you ever saw. You could tell it was new. The chairs had thick pink-flowered backs and seats, and the same design was on the table: pretty pink flowers, and dark- and light-green leaves, and an ivory-white border running around the big heavy-looking oval top. The chrome legs were shiny, and rubber tips kept the chairs from scraping as we slid out from under the table. Arthur walked ahead of me. He was really a long lanky brother. He smiled when he walked into the darkened living room.

"Well, Buggy, here we have the same old story. Here"—he moved his arm like a wooden pointer—"is a window that has been broken four times in five days."

I looked for the window he was talking about. I saw only a great big piece of board that reached to the ceiling and stretched halfway across the front of the room. Arthur looked at me and laughed.

"Looking for the window? Well, Buggy, behind that board there are some windows—at least, window frames. The windows have been broken so many times that the Housing Authority put this board up instead of glass. They can't keep replacing the windows, and they *won't* make the cops keep the people from breaking them, so they do the next best thing. It's the same old story."

I looked around the room, it was just about empty. Arthur answered the look on my face.

"Man, you don't think we'd put furniture in *here* do you?"

I saw an orange crate in the corner near the big board leaning against the front window. There was another big board leaning against a side window, and near that board stood another crate.

"We use those for chairs. They threw a burning sulfur candle through the window, and it landed on our big chair."

I looked around for the chair. Arthur nodded toward the upstairs.

"It's in the kids' room."

"Where are the kids?"

"At Carl Burton's. Mona took them over there. He lives right behind us. You passed his house on your way over here." He tugged at my jacket. "Go take a look out that front window, and you'll see why Mona and the kids went over to Carl Burton's house."

I went to the window and peeped out of the space between the board and the wall. The first thing I saw was a whole lot of policemen standing around a little shack that sat on the ground between the sidewalk and the street. There was a fire burning in a can in front of the shack, and some of the policemen were standing in front of the fire holding their hands over it, rubbing them together and stamping their feet hard against the ground. The fire threw light in their faces in wobbly oranges and blacks and yellows. There was one dark face around the fire; the others were white. The wind pushed the fire this way and that, and it jumped at the policemen and fell back into the can and jumped again whenever the wind shook the leaves and jerked the branches hanging over the fire. The smell of the fire swooshed through the holes in Arthur's window, and the cold wind and the burning steel of the mills went up my nose and tickled my throat. I stepped back from the window.

"Hey, Arthur, there's nothing but policemen out there. There's five or six standing over that fire and a whole bunch of them walking up and down the street."

Arthur said casually:

"Take another look across the street."

I went back to the window. The crowd across the street seemed to be marching in two-by-twos—which is why I had thought they were policemen. I stared hard at them, but I couldn't make them out. Pretty soon they marched under a street light. Then I saw that they were not policemen, no kind of way. They seemed to be walking in some kind of picket line—two by two. The longer I watched the more they came: men and women, and even some kids. I never saw the same person twice. More and more of them passed under that light. I saw something in a man's hand flash when the light hit it. It looked like one of those chrome legs under Arthur's table. I began to notice the hands of the others. One tall fat guy with black bushy hair had something in his hand that looked like a brick. I watched them walking by, not speaking to each other, just walking and carrying things in their hands—things that looked like bricks, iron pipes, chrome table legs. I looked back at the cops. They looked like they were washing their hands in the fire.

Arthur, getting mad and edgy, snapped:

"Now ain't that a bitch!"

I replied with kind of a stupid joke:

"Maybe the cops and the crowd are trying to get a Mambo line together."

Arthur corrected me:

"That's not a crowd. It's a mob."

I bypassed what ever *that* was.

"How long have you been out here?"

"How high is the moon?"

"Does it seem that long?"

"Longer. It seems like three hundred years instead of just three months."

He turned away from the window and sat on the orange crate in the corner between the front and side windows. He pointed to the other crate against the wall.

"Grab a seat, rest your feet. Don't ask for nothing to eat."

I laughed and sat down on the crate.

"Say, man, you sound like you've been where I've been!"

Arthur chuckled, resting his elbows on his knees.

151

"Where have you been?"

"Oh, down on 43rd and Prairie, 50th and Forestville, 57th and State—all over."

"You ever go to the Owl on——"

I cut him off:

"47th and State?"

He laughed:

"Yeah, and do you know who sells the best chili in
town? I mean, the entire town?" Arthur was really getting
warmed up. "Come on, now. I thought you were one of
the boys!"

I got tickled and couldn't think of the doggoned name
of the place.

"Just a minute; give me time. I know—uh—oh, hell
yes—Chili Mack's—47th Street between Michigan and In-
diana. Right?"

I decided to throw him one:

"Now, I'm going to see how down with it *you* are.
You ever skate at the——"

He caught it on the run:

"Savoy? You *know* yeah. And how about when old
Todd used to play 'Boogie Woogie'? Wasn't that a kick?"

I couldn't see his face too well in the dark room, but his
voice had lost that angry edge, and he was squealing like
any young no-shaving DuSable sophomore. Here was Arthur Davis—the "somitch," the "nigger," the "black bastard"—just another cat excited over meeting somebody
from "The Stroll" who knew about the Savoy and the Peps
Dance Hall on 47th Street and the stage shows at the Regal
and the side door by the stage where you could slip in with
the musicians, if you wanted to risk having Mr. Bluett set
"Two-gun Pete" on you. Yes, Arthur was excited, and I
was too—a couple of "cats from the shorts" out here in
Trumbull Park. I felt now that I could ask him some of the

things that were on my mind. He was a friend, a straight guy—not a jive stud the way Kevin looked to me. I was glad I'd come to Arthur's. Glad I'd come to Trumbull Park. Now there'd be someone to fight with; someone to help me understand all the new things I was finding out about myself; someone who may have had the same tongue-tied mouth when it came to getting serious with white folks; someone who had had to watch a white man call him "nigger" and not "bust him dead in the mouth," the way we used to say we'd do when we were safe on the steps of the Gardener Building. I wondered where or what Arthur's Gardener Building was and asked:

"Arthur, man, what caused you to come out to this lame joint?"

"Same thing caused you, I guess—bedbugs, roaches, and high rent."

I laughed and added:

"You forgot a couple of things—rats and"—this *had* to go on the list—"broken bannisters."

Arthur didn't know how much those two words meant and he answered carelessly:

"Uh-huh."

The cold air blowing through the crack between the board and the broken windows scooted around the room in a gush that lifted a piece of paper from the floor and sent it sailing into the kitchen. The wind made its way down my back, and I hunched my shoulders and rubbed my hands together.

For a minute or two we sat silently, not saying anything, just sitting there on those orange crates, feeling the wind. Then Arthur started talking softly—slowly, as though he had a lot to say and wanted me to get every word of it.

"It's the same old story, Buggy—you know?"

I didn't know. What was the same old story? He had

153

said that once or twice before. I decided to ask him what the same old story was. I took a breath and opened my mouth, but he had started into something else now and raised his voice over mine when I asked:

"What is this same old sto——"

"Yes. I quit college after just one year . . . going to make some money . . . get ahead in life, get a car, some nice clothes. You know how it is, Buggy."

"Yeah, but this same old——"

"Sure—you know." He stood up, raising up on his toes and stretching his arms up high and out. Then he let his arms fall to his sides and walked over to the window and peeped through the crack. "Me and Mona were making it for a while. A nickel in the bank . . . getting along with each other. Then Sharon and Bobby and that rent too— well, something had to go and it wasn't going to be Sharon and Bobby, so Mona comes out here and applies for a place, and—— well—here the hell we are."

He tried to laugh, but a bomb caught him right in the middle of a "ha," and he gritted his teeth instead, and patted his chest and his side pockets and pressed his hands against his cheeks on each side of his face like he was trying to keep his head from coming off.

Boom! Boom!

Two more even louder than that first one. Jagged blue snapped around the window boards and struck the brass-looking doorknob like lightning. I couldn't shake loose from the stab it made at my chest and the sweat it squirted out of the palms of my hands. I couldn't help closing my eyes like flying splinters and brick dust were sailing at my face, and when I opened my eyes, I saw that Arthur had closed his too and was just opening them. I shook my head.

"Arthur, I gotta go home."

Arthur got up and walked into the kitchen, his hands still hard against his cheeks.

"Don't go yet."

He sounded almost like he was giving me an order, yet at the same time he seemed to be pleading.

"Mona'll be here in a minute . . ."

He paused and frowned.

"I don't know what happened to Carl Burton and Kevin. They usually come over every night 'round this time." He frowned and sounded a little hurt. "Especially Carl."

Then he brightened up and looked over at me as I stood in the kitchen door, both hands in my pockets, leaning on the door watching, feeling sorry for him.

"Did you meet Carl? No, you never met Carl . . . Don't go."

He walked to the kitchen window and peeped out along the side of the shade, wrinkling it in his fist like crepe paper. The place where his hand squeezed the shade grew wet from his hands, and he squeezed it and let it go, and squeezed it and let it go. He just kept doing that. It made me nervous. I said real calm-like:

"I gotta go, man. My wife's gonna be worried."

He let the shade go and turned around. His face was soaking wet with tears, running along the wrinkles laid in his skin in half-a-dozen lines under his eyes and mouth and nose. He tried to smile, and it only made it worse.

"Buggy, they're after me. And they're gonna get me. They're gonna get me and Mona and Bobby and Sharon—all of us, Buggy."

He had said it so flatly, so like it was someone else he was talking about—and yet with his face so full of pain—it scared me.

"Who's after you?" I blurted. "What are you talking about? That crowd outside?"

He jerked his arm back from the shade when I said that. The shade fluttered and clattered up and around the roller at the top of the window, and he screamed out at me, his voice cracking like a ten-year-old's:

"Don't call those bastards a crowd! I've *told* you over and over again! They're not a crowd; They're a *mob!* A crowd is somebody put next to somebody else. A goddamn crowd goes shopping, goes to Soldier's Field to a DuSable–Phillips football game—a bunch of people that's all at the same place at the same time. But this bunch of crazy son-of-a-bitches are together for just one thing—to get me! They hate me. I don't mind that, but they add up their hate, pool it, squeeze it into a ball like a kid does a snowball, and then they throw it at me. Don't you understand that? Only hate keeps them together. And I can feel it, Buggy! It burns me like fire in hell! Don't go, Buggy. Wait till Carl or Kevin gets here. Wait till Mona comes back!"

I sat down at the kitchen table. This was a strange guy. Yet and still, he wasn't any stranger than I was. He was scared, and I was scared. The weight of everything white—suddenly knowing that it was a weight—was what scared me: white bosses, white working buddies, white policemen, white housing authority, white people, white mobs. But what was it that scared Arthur? Mona? Marriage? His kids? Himself? Dying? Living? I went back to the thing that had started it:

"I guess you're right. This is a mob. I've never thought of the kids coming across the bridge from Soldier's Field as a mob. They're rough and ready, and they'll fight in a minute, but they didn't meet to fight. I never thought of them being together because they hated somebody."

Boom! Boom! Boom!

Loud rocking noise shaking everything, like a drunken hand as wide as the sky had drawn back and knocked against the house.

Arthur spat.

"Goddamned bastard cops! Could stop this if they wanted to. If that fat son-of-a-bitch downtown told them to. It's the same old story."

The anger in his voice seemed to give him courage and he sat at the kitchen table across from me, stretching his hands in front of him and locking them together.

"It was a bitch after the first few days, Buggy. Things started off real small. The first day we moved in, some white kids came out and asked us if we wanted them to help us move in. I said to Mona then that it was nice of them. We didn't think too much of it though. We were sure that there were *some* Negroes around—you know?"

As Arthur talked, voices outside started up that whining high-school-cheer kind of chant:

"*Get out, niggers; get out, niggers; get out, niggers!*"

It sounded like a train getting started, getting louder and faster. Arthur got up from his seat and stretched and tried to yawn but didn't make it. He whispered in a sharp phlegmy voice:

" 'Get out, niggers!' Ain't that a bitch?"

He walked into the living room and looked through the crack. Then he came back into the kitchen and climbed up on the ledge beside the sink and pulled the up-rolled shade down, and peeked out along the side of it. He sat down at the table. The chant got dim, and then loud and fast again:

"*Get out, niggers; get out, niggers!*"

I asked myself, more than I was asking him:

"I wonder what's happening to people, man?"

He didn't hear me—just started talking again like he had been talking all the while:

". . . but the *next* day holy hell broke loose—I mean, loose! People started bunching up in front of the house, throwing bricks, paving stones, bottles—everything they could grab ahold of. Me and Mona were floored! We didn't know *what* was happening. The first thing I think of is to call the project office—but then I remember a queer little scene we had had with them after we moved in, and I changed my mind. Mona had just signed the lease, and we had already moved into the project when this chick in the office asks me to come in. Well, things hadn't started happening yet, so I go on up there, and the broad asks to see my discharge papers. I said okay, because, after all, having to work, I hadn't had anything to do with the application and all: Mona took care of that while I was at work. But then this chick starts looking at me real funny like she's trying to figure out what I am—you know, white or colored. Well, I could see what she wanted to ask, but I knew she didn't have enough nerve to. And besides"—Arthur laughed—"I thought that anybody could just about look at me and tell that, so she just stares at the discharge and takes another hard look at me and hands it back. I sign the lease and that's all—so I thought. But when this mess broke loose I knew that she was nobody to run to."

Arthur went to the cabinet and took out a bottle. It was empty. He sighed and hunched his shoulders, then he sat down again.

"The next thing I know two men who said they were from the Mayor's office came to the house and started asking a lot of questions. They hem and haw for a while and end up asking me, like I had done something wrong, 'Do you know you're the first colored family that ever lived in this neighborhood?' Mona said, 'So?' Then these two guys— one was white and one was colored—started explaining, 'Well, if you have any trouble just call us—anytime, day or night.' Talk about crap! When the bombs started going off for the first time, I jump on the phone and call the Mayor's office and tell them about the bombs." He gave a nasty laugh. "Are they still going off?"

I opened my eyes wide and stretched my arms out, palms turned toward the ceiling.

"Like gangbusters!"

"I called the Mayor's office about the mobs outside. Seen anybody out there tonight?"

"Only a streetfull."

Arthur and I seemed to have started a chant, all our own.

"I called your Mayor——"

I cut him off:

"Don't put that on me. That man ain't *my* Mayor."

He talked right on over me:

"——about these goddamned cops getting outside the window, and calling me and Mona and the kids 'nigger,' and 'black bastards.' And if they stopped, then Skippy's a sissy."

"And I hear that Skippy——"

"Yeah, I know. Skippy *is* a sissy. And these cops still call me anything they get ready to. I almost got into a fight with one of them—sitting right under the bedroom window, calling me out of my name like a son-of-a-gun. And the lies they tell the colored cops about me! Man, you'd think I started the Chicago Fire! 'Arthur Davis reports the cops to the Commissioner's Office for just breathing too loud.' Arthur Davis, this—Arthur Davis, that. And, man, a lot of these simple Negroes believe that crap, and even *they* get down on me."

I remembered the cop who had called Arthur a son-of-a-bitch. I began to see Arthur was like a roach riding an ice cube in a pan of hot water—and I mean *hot* water. Only now he had company—me, and all the rest of the folks from "The Stroll" who had had the nerve to move onto the white folks' ground.

Arthur went to the cabinet and looked behind a stack of dishes. Reaching back, he took out another bottle. It too was empty. He sat it on the utility table next to the other

159

empty bottle, and came back and sat down. Outside, the chant rumbled like the all-night grinding of an old refrigerator.

"*Nigger, niggers! Get out, niggers!*"

Arthur looked in the direction of the noise and rolled his eyes and turned his lips down in a sneer, and just as fast he turned it off and said:

"The only decent white man out here is old Mr. O'Leary." He poked his middle finger toward the apartment next door.

"He's crazy as hell. Sneaked over here the first day all this crap was happening to bring me a can of beer. Didn't even mention those folks outside, and they were cutting up too. You should have seen him—no bottom teeth at all and two long yellow curls growing right out of the top of his spotty old bald head! Those folks broke out every window in his house the next night; but the old bastard just sat there as quiet as a mouse while it was going on, and as soon as it stopped, trotted right over here. He was the only thing I had that even looked like a friend before they finally decided to move more colored families out here . . . Actually, they were waiting for us to break down and move out, and then that would be that! But, man, I'm Arthur Davis."

Boy! How he said that!

"Buggy, do you know how long we had to stick it out before the Housing Authority finally moved some more Negroes out here? Two and a half months! That's right; and, man, we suffered too! I mean, *suffered*. Things started happening so fast after a while that the whole world seemed to be going crazy. The NAACP—you know, the National Association for the Advancement of Colored People—came out. 'Stick it out!' they said. The Washington Park Forum—the Catholic Interracial Council—everybody: 'Stick it out! Stick it out!' And still no more colored families. The *Defender*—I've spent more time talking to them than anybody I know—they've really been on the ball; blasted the Housing Authority for not moving more Negro families out here, blasted this alderman for going along with these people out here. Shee-it! The more the *Defender* blasted, the more things happened. The NAACP sued the Housing Authority for discriminating against Negroes in the other all-white projects. The clerk out here who handled Mona's application was transferred downtown. And to top it off, one of the Housing Authority commissioners lights in on me saying it was a mistake to bring my family into this project, that putting colored people in what he calls 'white projects' should be done by bringing in 'good citizens.' It's the same old story—when you start asking for something that white folks don't want you to have, you're not a *good* citizen any more. Man, this bugged me more than anything else. Me and Mona were all the more determined to stick it out then. I may not live this thing through, Buggy, but they're not sending me back to 50th and Forestville just because my color don't suit them! That's crap. I spent too much time and worry in the army fighting to save democracy and all that jazz. Shee-it!"

Arthur's eyes were glassy, and his skin seemed to have tightened around his bony olive cheeks.

"Man, this mess is a gas! The first time I heard one of those bombs, I liked to ruint my pants. The kids ran around the room yelping like a puppy with a can on his tail, and Mona just sat at the table—we'd been eating—like she was stuck to the seat. Her eyes were big, and her mouth was open, and she was straining like she was trying to scream, but couldn't get nothing out. Then it *did* come out! Man, it made me sick at my stomach to see that woman scream like that! It was pitiful . . . in this day and age . . . in this country."

Arthur closed his eyes.

"Awwww, the crap I had to take waiting for you guys to move out here! Bombs every night. Bombs, bombs, and more bombs. No place for Mona and the kids to run, and only poor Mr. O'Leary to talk to. I felt sorry for him. His wife has had some kind of stroke, and the one or two times we hid in his house she would sit there slobbering and nodding, trying to keep her head from falling off—nod, jerk, nod, jerk all the time. He had enough trouble without taking on mine. The mob broke his windows two or three times; and every night for a while they'd march by his house shouting, 'Nigger-lover O'Leary! Nigger-lover O'Leary!' They made a sort of song of it. I heard that thing so much that I'd catch myself humming that goddamned tune! 'Nigger-lover O'Leary!' "

Arthur laughed bitterly.

"And the folks on the Southside—shee-it! Every week they'd have a picket line around City Hall. And meetings, meetings, meetings—everybody who could rent a hall had a meeting. But no action, Daddy. Just lollygag and meetings and 'Stick it out, boy, we're behind you!' "

He stood up and put his fists on his hips and stretched to his tiptoes and laughed again, breathing deep and closing his eyes and shaking his head. He sat down and stared way off somewhere.

"I don't know whether it was the meeting or picketlines or what, but one morning about a quarter to ten I looked out there and saw a mob of white women looking like they were being pushed backwards down the street. I said 'What the hell is this?'; then I see others running forward and some sideways—not at my house—just down the middle of the street. Then comes about twenty squad cars in a row, cruising down Bensley Avenue, red lights just agoing. Then a couple of priests, another crowd of policemen on foot, and some newspapermen with cameras raised

162

over their heads flashing pictures and fighting off those women at the same time. I thought these folks had all gone cuckoo. I called Mona and she came running downstairs with soapsuds all over her head and hands. Bobby and Sharon came racing down past her. We all ran to the door."

Arthur's breath came fast and noisy, and his lips were raised high over his teeth. He sounded like he was preaching.

"A couple of policemen raised so much hell about our being outside that we went back in; but not before we saw—I never will forget that sight—a great big green moving van, one of those closed-in kind, with two Negroes driving it and right behind it a car full of nothing but beautiful dark faces. I swear I like to cried! I felt a funny feeling all over my body. Talk about glad! Mona said—I'll never forget it—'Arthur, the Lord has answered my earnest prayer!' I mean, Mona's a Christian, all right, but she had never said anything like that before. I can see it just as clear! I hugged her and hugged the kids and jumped up and down and cheered those folks like they had been sent out there just for the purpose of saving me and my family. I'll tell you I've never been so glad to see anybody in all my life!"

This tall, skinny, angry cat seemed to be going through stages right before my eyes. First he'd been all slump-shouldered and down in the dumps; and then, when he couldn't find anything in his bottles, he'd gotten nervous and upset; but now he seemed to be another man altogether. He was happier than he should have been, his eyes were brighter, his voice was louder and harder, his words came faster, than they should have been. He was not the same Arthur Davis. I got itchy and jumpy as he stood there walking and talking like an old-time sanctified preacher.

163

"These hunkies never were so mad! Man, they had regular suicide troops out there! Mostly women, too. People were running and hollering at the truck, throwing bricks, tomatoes, bottles, rocks, at everything and everybody: cops, truck, and that car with those beautiful colored people in it. You got to give it to Kevin—he's a goof, but he sure had to be a man to come on in when he saw what met him. There was one old hag—looked like she was seventy or eighty years old—too old for any foolishness like that—this broad actually falls down in front of the car—I mean, underneath the bumper, man! But Kevin just kept on driving, slow and easy, pushing that crowd back with the front of his car, windows rolled tight, going steady like a snowplow pushing through a wall of snow—push-push-push with this old woman clinging to the bumper, letting the car drag her down the street. I don't know how she kept from being run over, because Kevin wasn't thinking about stopping. Then other women started falling in front of the car. I tell you you've never seen anything like it in all your life! As fast as the cops would pry one chick off of that car another one would fall down—right in the street in that dirt and dust—and slide, hands clamped around that bumper while Kevin pushed that car on through. Man, it was a fearful sight—I mean, fearful. And the noise! A herd of wild cattle couldn't be any noisier! Sirens screaming, women screaming, men screaming—even the babies some of them were carrying, screaming. Awwww, man, you've never seen anything like that in your entire life!

"When Kevin's car passed my house, it had dents from bumper to bumper. Smashed tomatoes, apples, grapefruit were plastered all over the windows. The top was loaded with bottles, rocks—I even saw a carrot up there. Kevin's car passed, and then another car of Negroes, and then a third—all full of folks from home. Shee-it! Talk about religion—Daddy, I had it that morning! Bombs went off all day, and my phone rang all night. The hunkies had gotten hold of my number, and they called every minute on the minute, cursing and spitting over the phone. They hollered and they screamed outside and broke out three of my windows. But do you know what me and Mona and the kids did? We cheered! We stood in the corner—and in the closet when the rocks came too fast—and cheered every time a window broke. We had made it and we knew it! We had held on until other Negroes came out, and now they'd never be able to keep us out! We knew that we had beaten them, Buggy! We knew it, and they knew it! The Chicago Housing Authority knew it! The whole world knew it! Or else why all the newspapermen and television men and photographers and all, Buggy? Why? Awwww, man, nobody slept that night. All the crap we had taken seemed worthwhile. We had held our breaths under water for two and a half months until other families came. Stood on our heads on top of the Empire State Building for two and a half months and walked backward across a tightwire two and a half thousand feet high! Awwwww, man, man, man! I was high without taking a drink!"

Suddenly he stopped talking and walking, and sat down like he had gotten tired and heavy all at once. He stared at the pink flowers and the green stems buried underneath the clear smooth top of his new kitchen table, and traced the design of a stem with his little finger. Then he rubbed the back of his neck and twisted his head from side to side, like a man just out of bed in the morning trying to wake up.

I suddenly remembered I had a wife and kids that probably wanted me home right now. I got up and shuffled my feet.

"I gotta go, man."

He kept staring at those pink flowers and green stems.

I could hardly hear him, he whispered so low when he answered:

"It's you guys' turn now, Daddy. I did mine. I held this raggedy-ass fort till you got here. It's you guys' turn now. I'm tired. I'm sick. I can't hold on much longer." He laughed hysterically. "Hey, that's just like a church song—ain't it? I'm tired. I'm sick. I can't hold on much longer. It's you guys' turn now, Daddy!"

I got cold all over. Turn for what? Turn to do what? It got cold in that kitchen. I walked toward the door. He didn't move. He looked tired. He looked sick. He couldn't stop staring at those pink flowers and green stems on the table. He didn't even raise his head when he said:

"Where you going, man? I thought you said you were going to wait here until Mona came back?"

"It's late, man—real late. Helen might not even let me in." I tried to laugh. "I gotta go."

"But you *said*—yeah, yeah, I know—it's the same old story. You and Carl and Kevin and Terry—all you guys—just alike. I know there's no such thing as real friendship any more. I know that. Why should you stay? Who am I? Arthur Davis. So what? Who are you? Buggy. So what? People—just people—just names—just bodies floating around in the middle of a whole lot of other bodies, bumping into each other. It ought to mean something to them—just because they bump into each other! But I've tried, and I'm tired. I'm sick of that boom, boom, boom every night. It's meant for me—and you, too, my friend."

I opened the back door.

"I gotta go, man."

I knew he was going to cry again. I knew it; I knew it, and I didn't want to hear it. I had my own worries. I wanted to cry myself, so why stay there and listen to *him* cry? I wanted out of there before he started. But I didn't make it.

166

A deep coughing grunt, and a gasp for breath, and another grunt came out of his back and arms and legs and head—from the table he stared at, from the room, from outside. From me, too, damn it! I knew he was going to cry. I pulled in all the air I could through my mouth and nose. I held my breath and pushed the air inside me hard against my chest, and tightened my stomach and pulled the muscles in my neck tight, and bit my teeth against each other. And the crying inside me loosened its fingers from around my throat, and I swallowed it and let the air out; and all that was left of the cry was a little water under my eyelids. I tried not to blink my eyes—didn't want to push that water out from under the lids, out of my eyes onto my face.

I pulled the door open and stepped outside. Arthur still hadn't moved. That grunt-gasp, grunt-gasp kept coming up from him like a fume, and the fume followed me like smoke as I closed the door behind me and stood for a minute in the darkness trying to get myself together.

"It's you guys' turn now!"

Son-of-a-bitching Arthur Davis! Why did he have to say that?

12

During the next day autumn really backed out, and by evening old man winter had started easing in like nobody's business. A gray kind of sadness had been hanging over everything all morning, and at work Pete hadn't half-talked all day. Even the mob in the street along Bensley hadn't sounded up to it with their "nigger, nigger, nigger," when the black and dirty paddy wagon hustled me through their ranks back home.

Helen and the kids and I ate dinner silently for the most part, and dark couldn't wait to fall. Soon Louella and Diane were upstairs in bed, and I was lying across the length of the couch, my head in what was left of Helen's lap, listening to the extra heartbeat of the baby inside the warm hard bulge against my cheek. I told Helen what Arthur had told me the night before, and I could feel a tightness grow inside her, and her deep and easy breathing change to trembling in-and-out little spasms.

We heard talking outside our door, and I sat up—waiting. Then a knock. I got up and opened the door, and there stood Arthur, Kevin, and one very short, skinny, dark cat with the meanest frown you ever saw. I saw a policeman close his sign-in book and walk away.

"Hey, Arthur, come on in." I turned to the other guys. "How you doing, fellas?"

They came in one by one, Arthur leading, then Kevin—stooping like he was afraid he'd bump his head against the ceiling, which was a healthy seven feet high. Then came this mad-looking little guy with glasses on, and both hands pushed in his overcoat like they were sewn to the bottoms of his pockets.

"Uh—Buggy, this is Kevin—oh, you know him, don't you? And this"—Arthur looked down like a proud father at the little guy standing behind him, the steam silvering his glasses and a hook of that straight hair curling down across his forehead and stopping just short of his eyebrows—"this is Terry Watson. I told you about Terry, didn't I? He moved in the same day as Carl—you haven't met him, yet—and Kevin here did."

Helen, on her feet now, smiled and said hello. Terry nodded, saying nothing. I took their coats and hung them in the closet. Arthur threw his weight on one foot and pinched his sharp, shiny, olive nose.

"We just thought we'd drop by to see how you were getting along. It's been pretty quiet out tonight. Mr. O'Leary tells me that the South Deering Improvement Association is having a meeting over at the fieldhouse tonight."

Kevin cut in:

"That's probably why everything is so quiet—they're all at the meeting trying to decide what to do to us next."

We men all laughed to show that we had heard him, but Helen said, getting mad just that quick:

"We ought to start having a few meetings of our own—figure out something to do to *them*. No need to always be fighting defense."

Terry frowned like he didn't go for that idea:

"What kind of meeting, Mrs. Martin," he asked in a signifying tone of voice, "could we have with five families against four hundred families here in the project and literally thousands outside the project? How could we implement our decisions? I mean, suppose it was moved, seconded, and unanimously agreed that we stone one of the houses across the street every time they stone one of ours? How could we carry out the mandate of our august body—without getting killed, that is?"

Arthur looked at me and jabbed his thumb at Terry.

"A *smart* nigger, huh?"

Helen frowned up like she was going to cry, then bit her lip and burst out:

"Arthur, haven't you got enough of being called 'nigger' by these white people without calling other people 'nigger' yourself?"

Arthur touched his mouth with his fingertips:

"I'm sorry, Mary—uh, Helen—I wasn't thinking."

Terry went on talking. I had to go along with one thing Arthur had said: this guy was pretty smart, frown and all. You could tell by the way he put words together. His voice dropped two or three keys lower as he explained:

"Now, I'm not adverse to organization. In fact, organization is the only salvation of the Negro here in this country. But let's remember that as a race in the United States we are a minority, and a minority can't act like a majority. And here in Trumbull Park the ratio of us to them is so disproportionate that we are hardly even a minority."

This guy was sailing. But I caught on to what he meant, and I didn't go for it no kind of way, so I leaped in on him with both feet. Besides I just didn't like the way he looked.

"Do you mean we should just sit around and do nothing except get our——I mean, ourselves kicked, just because we're outnumbered! I don't care if it's only two families out here, we still ought to get together to fight these silly somitches, even if we got to get them one at a time."

Terry sat real straight on the edge of a kitchen chair near the couch. Kevin had settled down at the far end of the couch with his eyes closed. He looked sound asleep. Still, something about the stiff way he held his neck and the way the veins on the back of his hands leaped and fell against his coarse brown skin told me that this stud wasn't near about sleep. Terry Watson's voice rumbled on like a big Mack truck idling:

"I probably didn't make myself clear. I'm not saying that we *shouldn't* organize ourselves. I simply pose the question of how much good it would do? Wouldn't it appear that a group had organized before moving out here and then come out to spearhead what some people like to call 'a Negro invasion' of this community?"

Arthur strolled to the couch and sat heavily beside Kevin, answering Terry at the same time in a nasty tone of voice:

"Well, maybe it's a good thing for Negroes to look like they *have* plotted something for a change! Maybe white folks will start to thinking twice before they jump on one of us. Maybe they'll think that whatever organization we're part of will step in and raise hell if they start anything—which as you damn well know, is *not* the case."

Helen eased in her two cents:

"I think it's a good idea for us to stay in touch with each other on a regular basis. There's no telling when the mob might attack one house and head for the others, thinking that the cops are off guard."

Arthur amened that.

"Which they usually are."

"And thinking too," Helen went on, "that we wouldn't have sense enough to defend ourselves as a group."

Terry tried to knock that argument down:

"And exactly what kind of defense could we, twenty-five people at most counting the children, put up against that howling mob of armed hoodlums?"

Helen answered him with a woman's kind of squeaky-voiced disgust:

"What kind of defense could we put up one by one?"

Terry cocked his head toward Helen and laughed. Helen had made her point—my point. He was backing down. His laugh showed that he was. I was glad that he was, and still I was mad inside because it had been Helen who had made this guy say uncle instead of me. I was surprised and ashamed, but there it was: I was actually jealous of Helen. Maybe I had been all along. Maybe I was just then coming to know it. Trumbull Park, I thought, sure brings funny things out of you.

"Mrs. Martin," Terry sounded like he was about to award her a diploma or something, "your point is well taken." Then he turned to Arthur, that frown flickering across his forehead, making deep shadows between his eyebrows and around the edges of his small marble-looking eyes. "Arthur, what do you think about the idea of forming a"—he laughed—"a poor man's vigilante unit, or something?"

"It's cool with me, man."

Arthur turned inquiringly toward Kevin. That cat still had his eyes closed, his legs crossed, his body bent over, with his arms folded on his knees. His bony nose hanging down like a sharp brown icicle, his brush haircut coming to that everlasting point right over the middle of his forehead, that long, hard jaw-line running to his chin—all added up to make him a cold, hard, feelingless-looking something. His profile was nothing but a lot of sharp-edged angles. There was hardly a curve anywhere in that lean, stern face. Even his closed eyes formed a dark gash under the jut of his forehead.

I didn't go for him sleeping in my house like that, and I called him in a tone that I tried to make let him know it:

"Hey, Kevin! Wake up and live, Daddy! Hey, Kevin, do you want to organize a club—huh?" Why was I sounding so damned meek and silly? "A vigilante or something? Hey, Kevin! Hey, man, wake up! This ain't no hotel, Daddy!"

He didn't move a thing but his eyelids. Up they went, slow and ever so solemn. His voice was soft and on the heavy side, not rough and growly like Terry's.

"I heard you, Buggy. I heard you the first time. I'm not asleep."

I waited for him to explain, but he didn't. He just stared with those eyes at the wingtips of his shiny brown shoes, stayed bent over with his legs crossed and his arms folded on his knee-tops. He seemed to be able to keep quiet forever and ever if he wanted to. I got mad at him, just that quick, and blew a question at him in a tone so harsh that it turned his head toward me:

"What's the matter, man? Cat got your tongue? Or don't you care about what's happening out here?"

He lifted his head just a bit and stared sideways at me. He must have stared for half a minute, before he laid out what was to be his opinion of the whole mess. He never changed that opinion.

"If it's going to be action, I'm for it. If you're just going to lollygag, to hell with it!"

Arthur stood up, rubbing his hands together, looking satisfied.

"Well, well, well! That's that." He looked around as

though he suddenly missed somebody. "Maybe we ought
to tell Carl about our new club. Have him here at our first
meeting." He turned to Terry. "Say, when are we going to
have our first meeting, Terry?"

Terry shrugged his shoulders:

"I don't know. It was Helen's idea. When do you
think, Helen?" Then he smiled and clinched his fist lightly
and unclinched it. "I'm sorry—Mrs. Martin."

Helen smiled at the ugly-looking little guy:

"You can call me, Helen. There's nothing society
about *me*."

"Well, I wouldn't say *that*, but I *will* call you Helen."

I don't know whether I was kidding or not:

"All right, all right, you two! Cut that crap out!"

Helen cut her eyes at me and smiled.

"Why, Buggy, I didn't think you still got jealous
over your wife!"

"Jealous! Jealous over what? Bugs Bunny here?"

Well, the man *did* look like Bugs Bunny—I guess it was
the way his two front teeth sort of hung over his bottom
lip. But I was sorry the minute I said that. Terry frowned
real quick; he was hurt. He smiled a bitter smile from under that everlasting frown of his and confessed:

"Well, Buggy, I guess you're right. I'm no raving
beauty. I admit that."

Arthur waved his clinched fist toward Terry as though
there was a bottle in it:

"Hell, man, you don't have to admit it! I think about
Bugs Bunny every time I look at you!"

Terry cut us both down:

"Well, well! Out here you get it from both ends,
don't you? Even from your own color."

Silence rushed into that room like somebody had left a

174

door open. Nobody said a thing for a while. I felt an icy sadness creep along my insides. Everything was back in place now. We were in Trumbull Park, and white people were throwing bricks, bombs and everything else at us, and we were in my house trying to figure out what to do; and here we had turned our fear—that's what it was—on each other: neighbor against neighbor, race against race—even me against Helen.

Yes, I was back on earth again—and right then I suddenly felt I was beneath the earth instead of on top of it:

Boom! Boom! Boom! Boom! Boom! Boom!

I gulped a deep breath, and the cold air that rushed into my chest made me sick at the stomach and I huffed it out with a hissing noise.

Arthur snarled:

"Goddammit!"

Helen complained to no one in particular:

"Those bombs will be the death of me yet."

Terry tried to explain his fear away:

"The meeting must be over. Now they have their instructions for the month."

Kevin mumbled:

"I say we go out there and kick some asses! They'll let us alone then—what you bet?"

I asked Arthur:

"Hey, man, where's Mona and your kids?"

"They're over to Carl's house."

Boom! Boom! Boom! Boom! Boom! Boom! Boom!

The house shimmied and flinched each time one of those things went off. I felt afraid—yes; but not as afraid as I had been when there was only me and Helen in the house. I glanced around at each of the other guys. They seemed sort of unconcerned—cool and collected.

I looked at Helen. There was a slight wrinkle in her brow as she looked around at each of us. I caught a faint, relieved smile easing her lips, and I took another deep breath.

Boom! Boom! Boom!

Arthur started getting nervous. I knew the signs by now. He got up and walked to the front window and peeped along the side of the shade. Then he came back and sat on the couch. Then he got up again and went to the front door and peeked along the shade at the small window in the door. Then he came back to the couch and sat down.

Helen started picking at her hands, pulling at a hangnail on her thumb, cutting the cuticle on her left thumb with the side of the fingernail of her right thumb.

Arthur got up again. *Boom!* He staggered and bent forward as though that blast had hit him in the stomach. He grabbed at his stomach and quickly snatched his hand away—mad at himself for grabbing in the first place. He tried to speak, but choked up, and had to grab with his hands at his throat before he could get the words out.

"Goddamned bastards!"

Terry cursed in his own way:

"And these are the United States of America—'Land where my Fathers died . . .' "

Kevin said:

"Shee-it!"

Terry said:

"You can't beat the syndicate."

Seemed like Terry had to keep coming up with those off-the-wall remarks. I was getting sick of this cat:

"What goddamned syndicate?"

"Any syndicate—race syndicate, crime syndicate, big business syndicate, police syndicate—they're all the same. You can't beat them. The Negro has been trying for a century and a half to beat them and look at us—still under attack."

Arthur agreed in a choked-out-of-breath voice:

"It's the same old story."

"So that's what you meant by that 'same old story' jive, huh?" I said, finally figuring out his favorite little saying.

"I thought you knew. What did you think I was talking about—a backward waltz at the White City Rink?"

"I didn't know *what* you were talking about."

For the first time since he came in, Kevin stood up. Now that he was on his feet again, he looked so lanky and frail I felt I could beat his butt any time I got ready to.

"I gotta go."

Terry walked to the door in front of Kevin; then he stopped and turned around:

"I must be getting absent-minded. I forgot my coat."

I got all their coats. Terry took his and looked it up and down, then shook it and started brushing the back and sleeves, and seeing me looking at him like he was crazy, laughed and put it on.

"What's the matter?" I asked, not digging the business with the coat.

Kevin put his coat on.

"Nutty—that's what," he mumbled.

Terry stepped back into the room, and from the way he drew himself up inside that long trailing coat and put on his deep voice, I knew he was about to say something serious:

"You know, my wife and I went through college together. She was going to be an economist, and I a political scientist—not knowing what one was at the time. We married while we were still in school, and we knew that children were out of the question—then. We were contraceptionalists deluxe. Slept in dingy one- and two-room kitchenettes for almost three years. Once Nadine's economics professor invited us to visit his home. We did, and when we were preparing to leave, the old guy, trying to be polite, held Nadine's coat so that she could slip her arms into it. And, while I watched, I swear, not one but two big family-sized roaches crawled right out from under the collar of Nadine's coat and galloped right across the back. She saw them, too. I don't know whether the professor saw them or not. He didn't act as though he had—kept us talking there a good fifteen minutes before we could get away, while we thought we'd die. We both knew that those roaches had come from our dump of a room. When we finally got away, Nadine rushed to a street light, and we searched that coat inside and out for a solid fifteen minutes, but we couldn't find a trace of them. We knew we'd left them behind.

"Nadine cried all night that night. We laugh about it now. Yet and still, both of us shake and brush our coats whenever we put them on. At first we did it because we wanted to make sure that the 'professor incident,' as we called it, would never happen again. But as the years have gone by, it has become a fetish, a ritual, a compulsion. Now we're trying to break the habit, and we can't . . . Yes, I think we should organize, Buggy. I think we should do it right away. What do you say, Kevin? We're going to form ourselves a protective association, okay?"

Kevin mumbled something, slipping his arms into his coat at the same time.

Terry scowled at him in disgust. Then he shouted at Kevin, and the loud bossy tone of his voice made me jump:

"Okay, Kevin?"

"I *said* 'okay.' What more do you want me to say?"

How did Terry do that—little Bugs Bunny Terry with the voice that was two sizes too big for him, bossing long, tall Kevin around? This Trumbull Park thing was a mess.

Arthur took his coat off of my arm and slid his arms into it. Then he walked to the door and waited. Terry said:

"Well, Buggy, take it easy. I'll get hold of Carl, and line up a time when all of us can meet together. Soon the vigilantes will ride again!"

Helen, putting her arm on my shoulder, leaned forward from behind me. Her toasty face was shiny around the nose and forehead, and her hair was falling down again around her ear. She smiled a strong, confident kind of smile. She seemed to feel good about something. Maybe it was because we had found out that we were not in the mess alone—I don't know.

"I'm glad to have met you, Terry." She sounded so good that at first it made even *me* feel good.

Terry smiled and said nothing. Even Arthur looked better when he turned to her:

"Good night, uh—Helen. Helen! Hey, I got it right!"

Kevin just kept walking. He didn't open his mouth. I sure was beginning not to go for that guy.

"Well, fellas, don't forget to sign out when you go."

Arthur laughed:

"Sure, Buggy, sure."

A short cop wearing eyeglasses without rims came up:

"Sign out fellas? Sign out?"

His high little airy whining voice made him sound like he was out at Comiskey Park in a white jacket with a tray in his hands: "Peanuts, fellas? Peanuts?"

Arthur snatched the book.

"All this goddamned crap with a riot going on!"

I shut the door as Kevin took the book.

Helen called to me from the kitchen.

"Heigh-o, Silver! The vigilantes ride again!"

She sounded like she was ten years old again, playing cowboys in front of the Gardener Building. I went in to her:

"Hell of vigilantes we are! One Bugs Bunny midget, one dumb mute, and one lush. I wonder what's wrong with this guy Carl? Probably has two heads or something."

She looked at me seriously:

"It's too bad we can't pick the people to help us fight, Buggy. But it always seems that the most likely ones never come through, and the least likely ones always do. What'll we do—refuse help because it's not from the right people?"

"Oh, I'm glad about it all, you know that. I just said—aww, you think you're half smart, don't you?"

Helen was staring at me. She wasn't cracking a smile when she said:

"I don't think I'm smart, Buggy—I wish I were."

I lay in bed that night thinking. Thinking long after Helen had gone to sleep, and the more I thought about being in Trumbull Park and getting together with Arthur and Kevin and Terry, the more I felt something nibbling away at the walls of my chest. This was the beginning of trouble. Somebody could go to jail from all of this. Somebody could get killed.

The clang of the boxcars rose over the sound of the far-away machines in the steel mills; but the sound of the boxcars sank beneath the sounds of Arthur's and Kevin's and Terry's voices. The pictures of the steel-mill fires were blotted out by Arthur's drunken olive face peeping out of the window, by Kevin's sharp and bony face cleaving down towards his knees, and by Terry's college-looking Bugs Bunny face, standing higher somehow or other than Arthur's or Kevin's.

180

Then these pictures faded, and I felt the bed tremble, and I heard a hard toneless buzz, and I knew that that goddamned diesel was coming. It had sung or rung or buzzed or something as my mother lay there in the bed, night after night, coughing, and crying and dying. Now it was after me. Death—that's what it signified to me. Death with a buzzer the way a rattlesnake has rattles, telling me it was coming after me, daring me to try and hide and finding me when I tried to hide, chasing me because it knew that I was afraid of it. As it came at me it wailed at me, without one drop of life's blood in it, without the slightest melody, without the slightest beauty. Wailed and buzzed and got louder—wailed and buzzed right through the pores of my skin into my blood and up the holes of my nose and the hole of my mouth and throat and ears and out through my hair, until it was me, and I was death and we were not different one from the other.

13

WHEN I GOT HOME from work the next day
Helen met me at the door looking as worried as she
could be.

"Arthur was arrested today."

"What?"

"They say he shot at some people this morning."

I felt like laughing. I don't know why.

"Did he kill any of them?" I asked.

Helen gave me a sharp look. She didn't answer that. Instead:

"He's out on $1,000 bond. The man from the
NAACP got him out."

"Yeah? This I got to find out about!"

I felt a nagging gladness tugging at my cheeks, and I
had to hold my lips tight to keep from grinning all over
my face. I knew what Helen was going to say before she
said it, and I wasn't going to be stopped from hearing about
this from Arthur in person. If I acted too happy about Arthur
shooting at somebody she'd try to stop me.

I turned to go over to Arthur's house.

"Wait, Buggy, there's been a lot of bombs going off
today. I wouldn't run around here tonight. You know these
people walk through this project like there aren't any cops
around at all."

182

"And I'm going to do the same thing! Don't worry. I can look after myself."

Before she could answer, I had closed the door behind me. When a man makes up his mind there's no use arguing with a woman.

All the same, I was glad to see that there were a lot more cops out there than usual. A bunch of them were hanging around the sunken courtyard in front of my house, stamping their feet and hunching their shoulders in the cold of the gray November evening. All up and down the courtyard between the row houses I could see the in-and-out and back-and-forth movement of dark police uniforms, blending with the dark loom of the buildings and the gloom of the sky. As I walked down the courtyard past the policemen, the wind began to blow hard and biting against my face.

It seemed extra dark when I got to the narrow gangway that led through the inner line of houses to Arthur Davis' back yard. I went straight past Arthur's into the street where the mobs gathered.

Boom!

The thick grayness of the sky split open in a thin lightning-looking jagged streak. I felt like I was going to ruin my pants, right then and there. I'm not lying. It seemed to me that bomb had been set off right behind me, and up ahead of me the flash showed me the figure of a man at the top of the short flight of steps at the end of the gangway leading into Bensley. I felt my stomach shrink and my fists clamp shut.

It was a cop. As I stopped, caught between going forward and going backward, and peered ahead into the double blackness that followed the flash, I saw the fat, tall silhouette of a cop, the brass buttons on his uniform reflecting the glow from the street. He turned around and walked down the steps and out of sight before I had even moved from my tracks. I don't know if he ever saw me. I began to sweat; and my shirt was wet against my back, cold as the night was, when I knocked on Arthur's back door.

It wasn't Arthur, but Carl Burton who answered. I'd never met him, but I knew it had to be Carl. He looked like his name—Carl—big, tall, round-faced, with a certain squareness about his head. The guy grinned real wide when he saw me.

"You must be Buggy. I said to myself soon as I saw you, 'That guy must be Buggy. He looks like his name wouldn't be nothing else *but* Buggy.'"

He stuck his hand out without letting me in, and I shook his hand while standing out there in the dark, cold evening. He hadn't raised his voice when he'd greeted me. There was a kind of quietness in his voice that was soothing. I shook his hand once and tried to let go and get inside, but he just stood there smiling, being glad to see me, and we shook and shook and shook until finally he let me in.

Arthur was sitting at his usual spot at the kitchen table, with a can of Pabst's in front of him. There was another can in front of an empty chair at the table, and Carl walked over and sat there. Mona was at the kitchen sink. Watching her turn to me and smile hello, her stomach big, back reared, face pregnancy-puffed, I realized that practically every Negro woman in Trumbull Park was having a baby, including mine. I said to myself, even as I said hello to Arthur and Mona, Is this what hard times turns us to—having babies? But there wasn't time to answer that question then, and I don't know if I ever did. Arthur smiled. That cat seemed absolutely too calm and unconcerned. He said:

"Hey, man, how you doing?"

"*I'm* doing all right. How're *you* doing?"

"*I'm* straight, Daddy."

I looked at Carl. He was wearing as big a grin as I had wanted to wear when Helen told me about what Arthur had done. Mona was going on about washing the dishes like nothing had happened. I looked around for their children. Mona said:

"They're upstairs in bed."

"*Upstairs?*"

I guess I sounded *too* concerned. Arthur laughed:

"Ain't nobody going to be breaking any windows around here tonight."

He sounded as if he hadn't the slightest bit of doubt about it. I tried to crack a joke:

"Well, I guess there aren't any more windows here to break, are there?"

"Mona, are there any more windows around here to break?" Arthur sounded like he had just won something—I don't know what. Well, I do know too.

Mona sounded a little self-conscious, but she went along with Arthur's program:

"I think there're one or two around here some place."

Carl was the one who couldn't hold it any longer:

"Arthur, did they run?"

I think he asked that just for my benefit. Arthur laughed halfway inside himself.

"Boy, coat tails were flying and flapping in the wind and wasn't a one of their feet touching the ground. I swear I haven't seen——"

Mona shushed him:

"You know these cops listen at the doors and windows, Arthur. For all we know they might have the house wired for sound."

Arthur lowered his voice a little, but he was laughing so

hard by now that the tears were rolling down his cheeks.

"Boy, I have never seen a bunch of hunkies scatter so fast in all my life! One long lanky cat had his head thrown way back. You remember how Stepin Fetchit used to run? Well, this cat had those big feet of his lifted three feet off the ground. I swear he left a trail of dust behind him when he cut around that corner—a livin' trail of dust! You hear me?"

Mona stopped washing dishes and turned around to snicker, putting a red-bordered dishtowel to her mouth. Tall, round-shouldered, olive-colored Mona—that black Indian-looking hair cut short and curling around the side of her face and pressing close to her cheeks. She reared back and laughed so hard that her stomach just bounced up and down like a thing apart from the rest of her, jumping all by its natural self.

Boom! Boom!

And then:

BAR-ROOOMM!!!

Carl got up from his seat so fast that he scared me almost as much as the bombs did. Arthur stopped laughing. He clamped his hands across the top of his head the way I had seen him do so many times before; then he laid his head on top of the table. Carl walked to the back door and reached for the shade, then he caught himself and turned and tried to laugh:

"Well, this looks like one of those nights. I hope you-all will excuse me. I got to get back to Ernestine. She's expecting any day now. I oughtn't to have left her alone."

He turned to Arthur:

"I took care of everything. Don't you worry about nobody finding nothing over at my house."

Arthur got up and shook Carl's hand:

186

"Man, if you hadn't been home today, I'd a been up a creek."

"Whenever you want it just let me know. They can't put you in jail if they can't find the evidence."

Arthur laughed:

"You remind me of a joke they used to tell about the cops down on 'The Stroll' when you said 'evidence' . . ."

He waited. We waited. Then:

"There was this old cop that was supposed to be on the narcotics detail, and one day he was arrested for being an addict himself, and the 'Black Dispatch' had big headlines the next day: COP RAIDS THE PEOPLE'S RESIDENCE—— AND SMOKES UP ALL THE EVIDENCE."

We all screamed and just fell out. I laughed so hard I hardly heard the next bomb go off. Carl said:

"Man, the next time I need a good joke to tell, I'm going to tell that one!"

Arthur was only *half* kidding when he said:

"Shee-it, that ain't the joke to tell. The sight of those paddies tearing-ass after trying to gang up on me is the best joke *I* know."

Mona filled in:

"He was minding his own business, Buggy. Just going to the store. Five of them tried to gang up on him. Not a cop anywhere."

Arthur broke in:

"Now all you can see is cops."

Mona kept talking right over Arthur:

"Two of them started walking beside him, and three stopped right in front of him."

Arthur had told her the story well. He picked it up as if they were both thinking the same thing at the same time:

"One of them said, 'We're getting awfully brave,

187

aren't we? Don't even need a police escort nowadays, do
we?' "

Carl just stood there looking serious. Arthur went on,
using different voices for each of the people he talked
about—a high nasal voice for the white people and a deep
bass voice for himself. I didn't know how much of what he
said was true, and how much was one of those everyday
lies we all tell each other when we say what we said to
somebody else who has done us wrong. But I knew one
thing for sure—somebody had shot at somebody else that
day, and Arthur and Mona and Carl and I were pretty
glad about it.

Arthur told his tale with gestures and voices—the whole
works:

"'Yeah, I'm brave,' I said. I had ol' smoky right under my arm with a newspaper folded over it. So these fools
start to push me, see? And this long, lanky one grabs my
arm—not the gun arm but the other one. Meanwhile, the
other three in front of me pick up some bricks. Oh, they
were going to have a *good* time! One brick just misses my
face, and that's when I jerks out ol' smoky."

Arthur swung his right hand under his left armpit, then
jerked it out, whirling around and jabbing his forefinger
hard into my stomach.

"All right, you somitch! You're going to get yours—
now!"

He laughed:

"That beanstalk bastard broke out faster than
Buddy Young! 'Look out!' he says. 'He's got a gun! Jeezus
Christ!' And I——"

There was a hardness in his eyes, and he closed them to
a slit and clamped his teeth together and pulled his lips
down showing his teeth, and bent his finger four times as
he described what he did next:

188

"——and I shot at those hunkies as long as I could see 'em. Four times! *Bam! Bam! Bam! Bam!* Bullets went every-which-way!"

And in his deepest, bassest voice:

" 'Come on back, you somitches! Thought you wanted to kick my black ass!' "

And again:

"*Bam! Bam! Bam! Bam!*"

14

THE FIRST MEETING of the "Vigilantes" was a comical thing in itself. It was comical and yet pitiful. We all met at my house two nights after Arthur was arrested—Arthur and Mona Davis, Terry and Nadine Watson, Carl and Ernestine Burton, Buggy and Helen Martin. It was nighttime, and the bombs had been blasting away for three hours straight. I'd tried to count them, but I gave up after I got to one hundred and five. I was nervous and mad at myself for not going out there and beating the hell out of a couple of those people. I was mad at Arthur for shooting at them, when I'd run away from them. I was mad at Helen because she'd seen me run, and I was mad at her for trying to have a baby here in Trumbull Park. I was especially mad at Carl Burton for what he'd done to me that morning.

Carl had seen me stand up to a cop who'd left the window down in the paddy wagon while one of those nasty November snows blew in on us as we rode in together to work. Carl said that I had snarled like a natural bulldog, but it wasn't a snarl—not really. It was a cry that sounded like a snarl. It was a cry of bewilderment, of hurt inside and out, of desperation. It just sounded like a snarl.

"You are the best guy to run this group," Carl had said. "Arthur is a hot-head. He'll get us into a lot of trouble.

You know Arthur by now. I don't mean to talk about Arthur. I just think you would be the right guy to head up this bunch, and I'm going to nominate you to be the leader. Excuse me for putting it like that, but will you do it? Huh?"

And I had said:

"Well, okay I guess—if you think I'm the guy."

But now that Carl was saying it to everybody, I didn't think so at all.

"Well, gentlemen," Carl—the big-shouldered, square-headed Carl—began, "gentlemen, I think we have here with us a very intelligent young man who . . ." I watched his fingers rub in and out of themselves and looked at him opening and closing his mouth and twisting that heavy moustache this way and that, talking ever so softly of how it was: ". . . the day I moved in here, when there was *really* trouble, gentlemen . . . I mean we have suffered, gentlemen . . . but I think we have fresh blood out here—someone with new ideas—and he ought to be our leader . . . Buggy Martin! What do you say, gentlemen?"

And who could have anything to say after *that?*

"I second it," Terry surprised me. "I'm no crusader, but I believe that in unity there is infinitesimal strength! And consequently I feel that I must support any individual who is willing to undertake the serious responsibility of providing leadership to our"—he laughed here—"organization."

And Kevin, the doer, sat half salty in the corner. And Helen stood in the door of the kitchen looking at me and smiling like a momma hen. Arthur sat surprised. Betrayed again! This time by his buddies, the guys whose "turn" it was. No one had asked him if he thought I should head the group. In fact, it was the other way around. Carl had figured that Arthur would want to head up the group himself and had led him to believe that there wouldn't be any planning ahead of the election, that everybody would have an even chance to run for president, that nobody would plug for anybody else.

Arthur was hurt. Wasn't it Carl's house that Arthur ran to whenever the mob threatened to break in the front door while the police begged for order? Wasn't it Carl's house where Mona left the children when she had to go out? Wasn't it Carl that Arthur talked about, the way one talks about a big brother? "Wait 'til you meet this Carl," he had said. "He's a big cat, and he don't take nothing off of nobody. He was in the Pacific during World War II and he killed fourteen men. He was a sniper. He's one Negro who is as straight as the days are long, and he'd just as soon die out here in Trumbull Park as in the Pacific. He said so!"

And I had felt bad because I had no such war tale. My military service had consisted of smashing my knee-cap at Fort Leonard Wood back in 1946 after all the commotion was over, and then spending ten months in the hospital hating myself for having volunteered for the Army in the first place. But Carl had a real war tale, and yet he wanted me to be the leader. There was something churchy about that guy. There was something that folks have when they come from good families, not society families but really good families. Carl was a good man—yet he'd killed in the army. Boy, we were all an odd bunch!

Me. The leader. Louis "Buggy" Martin. Leader of the tenants of Trumbull Park! If I had only the hell known.

The first thing I had to do as the leader was to end the riot as soon as possible:

"Fellas," I said, scared to death, "I called you together tonight because I have an idea. I think we ought to try to get in touch with some of the people that's behind this thing. You know—I mean like that big, fat gray-headed guy that's always in every crowd that gathers out there."

End the riot in one big punch, with one big idea, by one big something—that was my plan. And now as I talked, I was deciding at the same time that even white people would listen to reason. That was my feeling, my hope, at that time, at that minute, on the night I was talking about it. The idea, fuzzy and slow in coming at first, put itself together in my mouth—and Helen looked at me like she wanted to spank me. I caught that look, and cut my eyes at her; and she looked down at her stomach and I went on, listening to my own voice as I went on, wishing that Carl hadn't said a damn thing to me about being a leader.

"If we could get to some of the guys that's leading the others on and tell them that we're not going to mess up their neighborhood—I mean, tell them that we will take care of our places and that our children won't be always running in other people's yards and . . ."

I was sweating; and it seemed that what I was saying was sweat too, and it was coming out; and, to tell the truth, it looked and sounded like sweat, and nothing else. Kevin coughed and yawned, making a lot more noise than he had to. Arthur started laughing. He pinched his cheeks and got up from the couch and walked to the window, and looked out. I knew that this time it wasn't because he was scared. Nobody in that room was scared right then but me.

And I went on, looking at Ernestine and Mona, and Nadine, and then Beverly as I talked; but they wouldn't look at me . . . and finally I stopped. I was so mad I could have beaten everybody's brains out in that room.

I had to be mad. There was no other way to feel.

"Damn it, this isn't my problem all by myself! What do *you*-all want to do? I don't care! Hell, this isn't my problem all by myself!"

Still not a word from anybody.

Arthur turned away from the window. I tightened up. I wasn't ready for none of his smart crap. But he fooled me. He knew that I was down, and he smiled and clamped his hands on the top of his head and mashed down his hair, and breathed in and out real loud, and said:

"Buggy, you and me ain't got no business out here. We are too good for these people! I talked to one of them hunkies for two hours one time right in my back yard. He was just as nice as could be while we were talking, but the next day who was the first face I saw leading a mob up to my door?" He didn't wait for an answer to his question. "You're damn right! That somitch.

"Look," Arthur looked real-*real* serious. He scared me, and everybody else looked scared too. "Look, I didn't want to have to shoot at those people! I had to. There wasn't a damn thing else to do."

He walked to the middle of the floor. He looked like he was on a stage. He looked around at all of us and spread his arms out and took another breath; and then like all of the air had been let out of him, he dropped his arms and said:

"Shee-it!"

And sat down.

Ernestine Burton put her hand over her mouth and snickered. Nobody else said a word. Yet the air was cleared. Arthur had cleared it for me, and I tried to look at him to say thanks. But there was no way to say it, and so I asked Arthur:

"Well, maybe we ought to put together to help you take care of your lawyer."

"I don't need no help, man! The NAACP sent a lawyer out here as soon as they heard about the shooting. All I need is for another one of them bast——" He waited until everybody knew what he was going to say, and then he stopped and put his hand over his mouth and said: " 'Scuse me. One of them people to mess with me. Then I'll need a lawyer. 'Cause I'm going to do the same damn thing all over again: shoot ass."

Carl said:

"That NAACP is all right, Arthur, but, man, get yourself a white lawyer. Don't nobody listen to 'Ol' Home.' "

Arthur slapped his forehead:

"You and your Uncle Tom crap, Carl! You holler about what white folks do to you and now you're bullcorning about 'get a white lawyer'! Make up your mind!"

Terry started his signifying:

"Then, again, Arthur, I don't know. Color chasms are figments of the American imagination, young men. Many people who Americans imagine are white are not, and many who Americans imagine are Negro are that in name only."

Smiling through his permanent frown, Terry turned to Arthur and said:

"Now, for example, take——"

"Yeah," Arthur snapped, "finish what you're getting ready to say and get the shit kicked out of you!"

"Fellas, fellas, there's no need for all this!" I had to break that up—quick. "We got to figure out what to do about Arthur's case."

"I don't want you to figure out what to do about *my* goddamned case! I've figured out my case already. I shot at a somitch. That's my case. Figure out your own damn case."

Such a silence you never heard before.

Kevin stood up. He took out a comb with some broken teeth and started combing his thick, funny-cut hair. He tilted his head to the side, just like I'd seen some white

guys do. I wanted to laugh, but what he said killed everything funny that I had inside me.

"Ain't there nobody but Arthur here got nerve
enough to be a man?"

There was no doubt about what he meant. Helen looked
at me at about the same time I looked at her. I saw the
funniest kind of scared look in her eyes.

Carl stood up. He hitched his pants up and then he sat
back down, saying nothing.

I knew that all it took was for one guy to agree with
Kevin and that we'd be into something that would change
things in Trumbull Park like they'd never been changed
before. But would we survive the change? Arthur was the
first one to answer Kevin's challenge:

"Well, I'll tell you. The only way to straighten these
people out is to give them their own medicine—double."

Arthur seemed to be throwing a curve at the rest of the
men. It was shrewd, because now he had sealed the deal
before anybody could back out.

I remembered all of a sudden that I was supposed to be
the leader. Terry must have remembered it before me, because he too was looking at me when I turned to look
at him.

Boom!

I sure didn't need *that!* But there it was, blue-white and
loud, and just one more than I could have counted—if I'd
tried again. I spoke up:

"White people don't understand nothing but an eye
for an eye."

And Arthur, the slick dog, said:

"And a bomb for a bomb."

The fever was setting in. I could feel it in the pit of my
stomach, in the wet palms of my hands. I could see it in
Helen's face, looking now the way it had looked when she'd

told me about the snake. I could feel that fever in Louella and Diane, who sat close to Helen now, looking around at each of us as though even they knew that something was going to happen. I remembered those faces staring at me, not believing that their daddy could be scared, could cry, the day the mob chased me across the courtyard and into the house. I remembered the mobs yelling at the patrol wagon as I sat in the filthy black rolling cell, coming home from work; the brick through my window; the hundreds of bricks through Arthur's windows; the sight of Mona, fat and awkward with her big stomach and her two children clinging to her.

Yes, the fever was setting in!

Boom! Boom! Boom! Boom!

Kevin stuck a hand into one of his back pockets and pointed his shiny wing-tipped shoes in front of him and looked at each of us and laughed:

"Anybody here ready to go back to war?"

I stood.

"I think we should take a walk—a long walk."

Carl stood.

"Gentlemen, if you'll let me stop by my house I think I'd like to go along with you."

Terry remained sitting. He'd gone stiff, and his jaw quivered.

"I'm not going."

I tried to squash him:

"So the 'brain' has got no guts! Boy!"

Terry stood up.

"What do you guys think this is? What do you think you're doing? Don't you know you have families? None of our children are school age this year, but what about next year? Are they going to school out here without fathers to take care of them? Or will your wives have to move out because they can't take this alone? Then what'll all this prove? Arthur"—he seemed to blame Arthur for the whole thing— "you're a brave guy, Arthur, but why do *we* have to be? How do you get on, telling us that we have to be like you? You die your way and I'll die mine! I don't see what it will accomplish, and—and—I'm not going!"

The little Bugs Bunny face was almost crying now. Something had gotten through to Terry, and he didn't like it. He was thinking beyond what we were getting ready to do, and he knew that it couldn't work. And he was right, as far as he went; yet he was wrong for thinking that much. I knew that—how, I don't know—but I knew it. I didn't want to think too much. Here was the chance to do something— to hit back hard. And I couldn't let myself think about tomorrow, and Kevin couldn't either, and neither could Carl: their faces said they couldn't, and they said it by heading for the door; and I walked fast to get ahead of them—after all, I was the leader.

Terry sat down but then stood up again; and the women watched us like we weren't any kin to them at all. First they started talking among themselves and then Nadine, Terry's wife, spoke up:

"I don't know what you men think you're going to accomplish! You're just going to make matters worse!"

Carl's wife, Ernestine, started to say something; but she looked at Carl, and he looked at her and something went on between them; and she smiled and looked at me and smiled; and *that* pretty, dark woman kept her mouth shut.

And Helen called me:

"Buggy? You're not going to get that gun, are you?"

I didn't answer her.

Mona looked at Arthur and smiled, and looked away. We all knew that his going was out of the question. No one even brought his name up. It wasn't that he wouldn't go; he just absolutely couldn't.

And Beverly, Kevin's wife, said nothing. It wasn't hard to see who ran that family—for better or for worse.

I looked at Helen and she looked away. I knew what she was thinking. I knew that she knew that if she really put up a fuss I might change my mind; and yet I knew that she knew I'd hate her for making me change my mind. I knew, because I *would* have hated her for making me change my mind.

The fever had struck, and we were all drunk or hypnotized by the sudden chance to go for broke. We wanted to, yet we didn't want to, and now we had to.

"I think we ought to walk up to 106th and Torrence and back." I was surprised to hear myself sound so calm and sure. "Don't bother anybody if they don't bother us. But you know they're going to bother us, and when they do——"

And Carl put his hand on the doorknob, but I put my hand over his and pulled the door open and stepped out first. I had to. I was the leader.

Terry started walking toward the door.

"You guys are crazy!"

Kevin stepped out behind me and Carl followed him; and Terry, looking like someone was taking him somewhere to get a whipping, followed Carl.

"Sign out, boys."

For the first time, I didn't mind signing the book. We all signed real quick and walked forward, two in front and two in back.

15

I T WAS NEARLY dark now, and the wind was laying down a thin spray of snow. It was two weeks before Christmas and we were going for broke.

We got into step with each other, and I could hear Terry's teeth chattering. It was cold, but not *that* cold.

We stopped by Carl's, and the three of us—Kevin and Terry and I—stood outside feeling the dark and the wind and the snow, shuffling our feet and saying nothing while we waited for Carl to come out again. It was dark inside his house, and it stayed dark inside. I thought about Helen and said, more or less to myself:

"Helen was worried about me going to get my gun; but, man, I want one of those bastards so bad that I can feel his nose on my knuckles right now! I don't want to shoot him. I want to hit him." I felt trembly! "I want to hit him with these." My fists looked bigger to me then than they ever had before.

"I've got my gun, gentlemen." Carl, coming up behind us, said it so soft and quiet that at first I thought I was imagining him saying it.

Kevin said:

"I've got a knife. I don't need nothin' else."

Terry said something that was the most honest thing I'd ever heard come out of his mouth:

"My gun's at home. But I'm telling you, if I go home after it, I'm not coming back."

Kevin laughed.

"In that case we'd better get on with it. What the hell! Let's go."

And we turned left, out of the project, into the face of one of the coldest December winds I'd ever felt, toward the sanctified streets of the rioters. I looked around for the policemen who were supposed to be on guard in front of our houses, but there wasn't a one in sight. Only the wind, and the lonesome sound of our heels on the sidewalk going along the outside of the project, disturbed the dark, scary quiet of Trumbull Park. The smell of steel burning in the mills made my mouth pucker, and my face was hot, and I thought I felt a stream of heat in the cold winds. My mind was racing like a subway train zooming past a tunnel full of toothpaste ads.

A nervous kind of excitement took over me. I was scared, but I was eager. I was eager, but I was grateful for the long stretch of empty dark sidewalk in front of me. Yet I could hardly wait to see the faces of the first bunch of white folks we ran into, to see their faces when they saw us on their street. I imagined them running to fight us and all of a sudden catching sight of Carl's gun and Kevin's knife, and me and Terry empty-handed but with our fists doubled up ready for some heavy scuffling; and I imagined them screeching to a stop on the backs of their heels and ducking and dodging the fire from Carl's gun, and Kevin waving his knife at them, and me and Terry sitting back laughing so loud that you couldn't even hear a bomb if one happened to go off. I laughed under my breath and, right at the same time, Carl laughed, and Kevin laughed. Terry took a deep breath, but no laugh came out.

We walked on, two by two, and it felt good—safe. I don't

think I ever felt more like three guys were my friends than I did right then. Up Bensley we walked—or rather marched, because that's really what we were doing—marching just like the army—only here we had no doubt about why we were going to fight.

All around us the tall trees whispered. It grew even darker, and the wind blew even harder. Peering ahead and squinting my eyes against the spitting snow, I suddenly became aware of a shadowy mass at the far end of a corner four blocks away, and just as suddenly I knew it was a crowd of people. Kevin saw it too, and broke the clickety-clack of our heels upon the sidewalk:

"It looks like our action's up the road a piece."

He looked across the street at the dingy houses, with their half-naked shrubbery and ghostly gangways, probably remembering, as I did, the white trail of the bombs streaking upward from behind those very houses.

Carl sounded the way he must have sounded in the South Pacific:

"There's the bastards!"

Terry finally managed to get a word out:

"Let's stick together, fellas! Let's not panic and leave each other stranded out here when the going gets rough!"

I thought about how smart and thoughtful he had seemed when I first met him, and how scared he was now. And even though I was, most likely, just as scared as he was, I got disgusted and really aimed one at him:

"Just make sure *you* don't panic."

"*Niggers!*"

The word sounded so close that I looked around to see if the man who yelled it wasn't marching right behind us. He wasn't. He had come out of a store up ahead across the street—a short, sawed-off little squirt; and five big, red-faced, hatless guys in leather jackets and plaid jackets came out behind him.

We headed for the corner just like we hadn't heard or seen a thing. We hadn't talked about it, but it was understood that we wanted them to make the first bogish move. And then? My hand could feel flesh already. Kevin slid his hand into his right pocket.

"*Niggers!*"

Again this one little guy hollered—so loud that the crowd at the corner four blocks away began to bunch together; and I could tell by the way it moved that it had become a mob. It headed toward us from the faraway corner and the plaid and leather jackets took a couple of steps from their side of the street to head us off. We couldn't kid around any more. We moved across the street toward them. The stuff was in the fan.

The biggest white guy took a couple of steps toward us, his thick black hair fluttering across his forehead as the wind blasted down the street. Carl rushed a little and headed for him, and the big guy stopped and looked around for his buddies. They hadn't moved. I caught up with Carl. Kevin hung back a little, but the look in his face said that it wasn't because he was scared.

I looked around for Terry, but he was right at my side, and now he wasn't looking scared—just wild—crazy, big-eyed, bundle-of-nerves wild. He was almost leading the rest of us, and his little Bugs Bunny fists were clinched into the tiniest little balls I'd ever seen.

Four-to-six tally-up time was here, but the enemy wasn't coming. Carl stood in the middle of the street and bellowed:

"You ornery sapsuckers, come on! I said, come! Let's get this show on! Come on! We gon' have it now!"

The little loud-mouthed one backed away, and he had

started to lead a run, when a lot of footsteps resounded from out of the gangways around the project.

"*Get back over here, Burton! You hear me, Burton? I said——*"

Boom!

Along with the flash, half a hundred little brass mirrors burst out at us from the gangway, and seven or eight cops and one gray-haired plainclothesman ran up to us before we knew what was happening. Where had they been? When had they seen us? Why had they waited till we had those six guys backing up and getting big about the eyes? The plainclothesman was the first to reach us. He pulled his club out.

"I said get back in there! Get!"

Carl stopped, I stopped, Kevin stopped, and Terry stopped. Stock-still.

Things had gotten hazy for me. There were no longer voices and bodies that looked like bodies across the street— only the cold-flushed pink of the enemy faces; and I was being drawn to that pink as if someone had a string tied to me and was pulling it with all his might. I had trouble making out the policemen and what they were saying. But I knew that something had happened, had come between me and the pink faces pulling the string across the street. So I stopped and the other policemen surrounded me, and someone pushed me lightly back to where I'd come from. I felt like I had been asleep and was still half asleep. I un- clinched my fists and turned around, and I saw that my buddies had turned around too. The mob reached the cor- ner nearest us just as we walked into the narrow gangway that led to the heart of the red-bricked fortress-looking project. Voice added to voice and grew louder as we walked inside ahead of the policemen.

"Black niggers! We dare you to come over here!"
"Come back, you black cowards!"
"Nigger, nigger, nigger!"
Boom! the bombs went off like firecrackers now.
Boomboomboomboomboombbbooommmm!
I looked at Carl; his bottom lip was trembling. Kevin walked taller, straighter than ever, his face aimed directly in front of him, his eyes at once blank and full with a kind of fierce unconcern. Terry still had that wild, wound-clock look about him, and now his teeth chattered more than ever. It was the first time that I realized that his teeth hadn't been chattering because he was scared, but because all that tightness had to come out of him some way.

The gray-haired detective snarled:

"What were you boys trying to do out there? Start trouble? Incite a riot? Whaaat? Come, you heard me! Where were you boys going? What were you doing on that street?"

None of us answered.

Night had come on all the way, and the lights in the apartment were on now; and as we passed under a weak, yellow street lamp, I saw Kevin slip his hand into his pocket. I suddenly remembered his knife and Carl's gun. Aw, hell . . . Now what? I glanced at Carl as we passed before a light that slanted out of one of the houses along the walk, and he glanced at Kevin.

I turned to see the gray-haired detective staring at me, then retracing the look I had passed down the line. He was just about to frown an angry, I mean real ferocious frown, when we stepped into the shadows and his face disappeared from sight. But while I didn't see that look, I just about heard it, because the next thing I knew, this gray-haired squatty little sawed-off I-don't-know-what hollered:

"Hold it! Hold it right here!"

With that he ran up to Kevin and grabbed Kevin's hand while it was still in his pocket; then with the other hand he pulled out something from under the left side of his coat, and I didn't need light to tell me what it was. He kind of spoke under his breath, but it felt like he was screaming:

"What you got there, boy? A knife? You got a knife there? Huh? That's what it is, ain't it? A knife!"

He pushed Kevin away from him, snatching that tall, still unconcerned cat's hand from his pocket. The knife came out with Kevin's hand and fell upon the cold dark walk with the loudest, echoingest clang you ever heard.

The other policemen shoved Terry and Carl and me into the light of another window. Now all of them had their flashlights out, and shined them into our faces. Six or seven little suns seemed to be floating around in front of my eyes, and I closed my lids and opened them again, and tried to put my arm across my face to block that hurting light. A hand grabbed my wrist and snatched it down.

"Don't move, you son-of-a-bitch!"

Then:

"See if *he's* got a knife. He may have a gun even!"

"Hey, this one's got a gun!"

For some reason, it all began to get funny—like these policemen had been playing a real exciting game of cops and robbers, and all of a sudden someone had run across a real gun. *A real gun!* What the hell did they expect?

Hands slapped my ribs, hips, and legs and poked around my waist; but, as the guys in the movies put it, I was clean. But Carl wasn't, and Kevin wasn't, and the gray-haired man ran from one of them to the other, talking about their mothers something awful. He barked, actually barked:

"Take 'em to the station!"

So we marched again: Terry, with his teeth playing a regular Art Blakey drum solo, and me beside him; and, in front of us, with only their straight backs showing, Kevin and Carl. Now there was no rhythm to our steps; and the white folks had our gun and our knife, and they had their guns drawn on us.

"Come on, come on!" the gray captain grumbled; and off we went to the station, broke, busted, and disgusted.

16

THE MAHOGANY BENCH where the judge sat needed shining. Out of the window, I could see the streetcar tracks, the 12th Street overpass, the El tracks, church steeples, the filthy roofs of the warehouses along State Street, television antennas sprouting upwards—the whole smoky, junky, smudgy, crisscross, lopsided mass of long, short, and middle-sized domino-looking homes, huts, apartment buildings, and factories.

The dingy courthouse windows were smeared with finger-writing that spelled words we used to scrawl on the walls of the washroom in the Owl Theater out on 47th Street. The judge had big red bags under his eyes, and he kept looking around the courthouse like Somebody Important was missing. The bailiff had made us stand, had brought out the two prisoners, Carl Burton and Kevin Robinson. Terry, letting well enough alone, had sat down a good distance from the bench; but in the heavy quiet that grew while the judge waited for the Important Person, I could hear a faint clackety sound. I'd be willing to swear that Terry's teeth were still chattering. Escape from jail had been too close for him, and for me. They'd let us go "with a warning."

But Kevin Robinson and Carl Burton were "criminals," "menaces to society," "trouble makers," "agitators"—so the rioters' little "community newspaper" had said. And so Ernestine and Beverly waited, and Nadine, Terry's wife, Mona and Helen side by side. Arthur wasn't there. I didn't know where he was. Other Negroes waited too. Some were down there on business of their own; but the way they smiled at Kevin and Carl from the long benches behind the mahogany gate that separated the defendants from the audience made me know that they were with us, and it made me feel good. I felt ashamed too, for they seemed to feel sorry for us.

A gray-haired Negro man with brown skin came in, wearing a tan porter's jacket and carrying a cup that spread the scent of coffee all over the place. He smiled when he reached the judge, and the judge smiled and grabbed the coffee, and smelled it and smiled again and turned the coffee cup up and sipped it. The gray-haired brown man opened a tall mahogany door and stepped out of sight. The Important Person had come and gone. The judge cleared his throat and swallowed the last taste of the coffee and looked at Carl and Kevin, at the old detective who had frisked us two nights before, and at the two young policemen who had been with him. The smile lines bent down around the corners of the judge's lips, and he sounded like he'd caught all of us peeping through his window:

"What *is* this?"

One of the young cops shuffled his feet and put his hand over his mouth and coughed, and a fat man wearing a light-tan jacket like the porter's whispered:

"Trumbull Park, Your Honor."

The expression on the judge's baggy red face said, *Oh no!* But the judge himself, turning toward a long lanky guy in a brown sports jacket, said:

"State's Attorney, how were these men apprehended?"

"Your Honor, Captain Silo here can testify to those facts, if you please."

"I don't care who testifies. Just give me the facts of the case."

The gray-haired detective stepped forward and smiled:

"We apprehended these men in the process of creating a disturbance, Your Honor. We arrested them and searched them and found a gun and a knife."

The NAACP had sent us a lawyer, a short, dark, Indian-haired little man, who had spent his time telling us why we shouldn't be Communists. Now he jumped to his feet and shouted in a beautiful bass voice:

"I object, Your Honor!"

"You're the attorney for the defense?"

"Yes, Your Honor; and I object to the captain's charge that he apprehended these men in the process of creating a disturbance!"

The gray-haired detective whirled around:

"Well, they *were* creating a disturbance!"

"That's a lie and you know it!"

"Who're you calling a liar?"

"Order in this court!"

Everybody got quiet as soon as the judge hollered. For a second he glared at us with his gavel poised in the air. Then he decided to bang it down anyway.

Bam!

"Now let's get this thing straight. Captain, what were these men doing when you arrested them?"

"Your Honor, they were preparing to cross the street."

"And what else?"

"What else? Why, that's all. There were some people on the other side of the street, and if these boys had crossed that street, there'd have been trouble. Why," he turned to Carl, "you know that!"

"And then what happened, Captain?"

"Well, Your Honor, we got there just in time, and we stopped them and took them back to the station. You see, Your Honor, there is an emergency station in the Trumbull Park project, and that's where we were taking them."

The NAACP lawyer took a deep breath and let it out, loudly.

"When did you find the concealed weapons on the men, Captain?"

"Your Honor, we found the concealed weapons when we searched them. You see, there was four of them, but two of them were clean—I mean, they were not carrying arms, and we let them go; but the other two had concealed weapons, Your Honor. Why one of them had a knife *this* long!"

The captain held his hands about fourteen inches apart.

A fat Negro woman in a cloche hat down the row from Helen and Mona mumbled over the testimony:

"*That* long? Ain't this a killer?"

The bailiff looked around to see who'd said that, but now the woman was looking at the judge, and there was a holy look about her fat mischievous face.

"Order in the court! Now, Captain, I gather you then filed charges against the men after you found the weapons. Is that right?"

"Yes, sir, Your Honor."

The NAACP lawyer called:

"Your Honor!"

"Yes?"

"I'd like to crossexamine the witness."

"All right."

The NAACP lawyer's dark skin was beginning to sweat, and a vein at his temples kept bulging and shrinking with a regular rhythm. He moved closer to the judge's bench, and the sun caught the faint silky stripes of his single-breasted suit. He slipped one hand into his coat pocket and moved the other hand, palm up, toward the captain.

"Now, this man, Your Honor, has said that he arrested these men just as they were about to cross the street. Then he says he found the so-called concealed weapons on their persons when he searched them and consequently arrested them. Right?" He didn't wait for an answer. "Right. Now, on the basis of that testimony alone, I move to suppress the evidence on the basis of the fact that the seizure was illegal, and therefore the search was illegal, and meaning, of course, that the evidence, to wit, the so-called concealed weapons, are inadmissible in this court."

The State's Attorney sprang up:

"Your Honor! These men are trouble makers! They could have caused a race riot out there! That Trumbull Park is a serious situation, Your Honor, and——"

"And what?" the NAACP lawyer snapped. Then he answered his own question. "Is it a crime for two Negroes to cross the street in the city of Chicago?"

"It was four!"

"I don't care if it was fifty! I ask you, Your Honor, is that a crime? These men live in that neighborhood. By the captain's own testimony they were crossing the street when they were arrested. Then they were searched. What overt act did they engage in that prompted the captain to decide that they were breaking the law? I'll tell you: they are guilty of just one thing—being black!"

Somebody at the back of the courtroom grumbled:

"That ain't no lie!"

"Order! Order in the court!" Another rap of the gavel. "State's Attorney, what do you think?"

The State's Attorney fingered the lapels of his brown

sports coat. Then he looked around at us—me, Helen, Mona, Terry—all of us. Then he looked at Kevin. Kevin looked at him and shrugged, and a laugh came through his nostrils: "Your Honor, these boys have learned their lesson." Carl looked at me at the very moment the State's Attorney said that. We both knew what was next. They were free! I was glad, and I smiled at Carl.

But Carl sucked his bottom lips into his mouth and shook his head, and just that quick his eyes got full of water; and I realized right then and there, that Carl Burton, deep down inside, was broken, whipped, beaten, done up, goofed, did in, messed with—through.

The rest of the State's Attorney's words just sort of droned outside my ears without actually coming in. And after some more words, I heard the judge say, "Dismissed," and I saw somebody shake Carl's hand and Kevin's. And while Mona Davis and Nadine and Terry laughed and started telling each other about how the NAACP lawyer had got them told, I felt—all of a sudden—the guiltiest, most sickening feeling I'd ever felt.

The boys on the streets say of a man whom a woman has begun to rule, whose boss can and does cuss him eight hours a day, whose neighbors bump into him without saying "I'm sorry," whose children talk back to him, and whose dog won't come to him when he calls—the boys say that a guy like that has been de-nutted.

Carl had been de-nutted; and when I saw Kevin turn away from my eyes, I knew that he had too. I wanted to cry, but I felt too guilty to cry. We, the four of us, had started out to fight together side by side. The white folks had stopped us, but I was clean, and Terry was clean, and so they couldn't touch us. But our buddies weren't clean. They were dirty. Dirty with pride. So now the enemy had cleaned them. And I wanted to cry.

17

DECEMBER MOVED ALONG in a rough way. The weather changed from a chill that scooted over the collar of my coat and slipped down my back and tingled my skin, to a hard freeze that hurt when the wind banged the snow against my face and squeezed the cold up my sleeves and made my wrists hurt and my ears ache around the edges and my nose feel like it was running all the time.

Instead of the bombs slackening down since it was so doggoned cold out there, more and more went off every day and night. The patrol wagon that took me to and from work was icy inside, and there were lumps of coal strewn all over the floor. The police on guard around the houses had chipped in and sent the patrol wagon drivers to buy coal, which they burned in cans they set up right near our houses.

Here and there you'd see shacks popping up, leaning against the buildings, and built by the cops from scraps of wood, tin, pasteboard, and anything else they could get their hands on. There was one laid up against my house, and one stood under the tree in front of Arthur's. Sometimes there'd be more than eight or ten cops inside and just outside one of these shacks, laughing and joking; and every now and then talking a little too loud and letting out the same kind of words the rioters used: "black son-of-a-bitch" . . . "nigger" . . .

The police worked on three shifts. Every morning at seven o'clock you could hear the first shift coming on and the old shift going off, and they'd shout jokes to each other as they met and then parted. The new shift would often come early, and the two groups of cops would talk and laugh loudly, and tell jokes. The second shift came on at three-thirty and worked until twelve o'clock at night. This was the shift that had to handle most of the trouble. People came home from work while this shift was on duty; people gathered in mobs and set off bombs and set fire to stores and garages in the neighborhood and broke windows. These cops didn't joke much. They were pushy and mean-tempered when I came home from work, and they handed me the book to sign with a look on their faces that said they would have given up two weeks pay just to have me down at the precinct station under the lights behind closed doors. The only time these guys would perk up was when it got close to twelve o'clock; and then me and Helen and the kids would wake up scared into a sweat by a loud guffaw or a shouting back and forth that started up when the twelve-o'clock shift came on.

The twelve-o'clock shift was the jelly shift—law students, taxi-cab drivers, and small store-owners, who also worked for the police department. These men were tired when they got there. There'd be no laughing and loud talking out of them. No, sir. These fellas would come quietly to work and start up the fires in the shacks, or sit in their cars with the motors running. Helen and the kids and I would often hear one growling like some big purring cat early in the morning before the sun came up. As soon as these "sideline" cops got settled in the cars or shacks, off to sleep they'd go until daylight; the seven o'clock shift would wake them up, and then there'd be the hollering and laughing and the jokes about "the nigger I arrested down on 63rd Street, who . . ."

Round and round the clock, night after night and week after week, this merry-go-round would twirl: first shift—bombs; second shift—bombs, mobs, bricks, and curses; third shift—sometimes quiet broken only by the coming and going of the cops, but sometimes bombs, garages burning mysteriously down to black smoldering stubs. The shifts went round and round. Hundreds and hundreds of policemen, Negro and white, mad-looking all the time, confused most of the time, making up their own rules and regulations when something blew up in their faces over and over again, rules which always wound up in somebody's feelings being hurt—usually ours.

Christmas slipped up on Helen and me so fast that we hardly had time to get the kids downtown to have their pictures taken with Santa Claus (white) and bring home their toys (in the patrol wagon), and find a Christmas tree (and bring it home in the patrol wagon). We had become so wrapped up in our own growing anger that we hadn't had time to get the feeling of closeness with the world around us that had been one of the best things about living in the Gardener Building. Living almost in each other's laps, the way the people in the Gardener Building had, made Christmas everybody's Christmas. The smell of everybody's turkey blended in with that of everybody else's, and those places which had no turkey smell were soon known to those places that did. Christmas Eve would catch Mrs. Palmer and Bertha and Mrs. Jackson and Helen's mother easing in and out of the apartments with big platters piled high with pieces of turkey, and bowls of dressing, and saucers of cranberry sauce, along with a shot or two of some of that man-sized egg nog.

But now we were free from the Gardener Building—free from the stench that returned when the Christmas smell of sage and celery had died and the scent of Christmas trees, used for stove wood after, had soaked into the walls and disappeared. Free from the dampness, the rats, and the broken bannisters; but we were also free from the home folks who spied on us to make sure that we had "ours" and slipped a little down to us when we didn't. Now the only people who wanted to make sure we got "ours" were the white men who slipped along the sides of the buildings at night (even Christmas Eve) and lit up gasoline-soaked rags and dumped them into the gratings underneath our windows—men who went off into the Christmas Eve night, most likely home, where little children and turkeys and Christmas trees waited for them.

So we hurried through our celebration Christmas morning and had our Christmas dinner and hurried off to visit Helen's folks Christmas afternoon. Church music from Reverend Boddie's church beat from the radio with a warm, comfortable, solid swing. The Gardener Building was the same, and people were glad to see us. Mrs. Palmer was worried about us:

"Why don't you kids come out of there? You're no better off than you were here. At least you didn't have to worry with a lot of fools breaking your windows and setting off bombs and all that stuff, when you were here."

And I don't know why I said it, but I did:

"I don't want my kids to fall off of a bannister, Mrs. Palmer."

"Shucks, that was the first time that had happened in a long time! Bertha's a lot better now, and old Mr. Gar-

217

dener finally got around to fixing those bannisters. Yes, he had all of them fixed and painted up, real nice."

"What about the windows, Mrs. Palmer? Did he put glass in the windows yet?"

"Well, some of the people put glass in them themselves."

"With their money, Mrs. Palmer? Out of their own money?"

Why was I so snappy to Mrs. Palmer? Was it because I didn't like her trying to tell me that I hadn't decided right, by moving out to Trumbull Park and catching hell rather than staying here in the Gardener Building?

Then, Helen's mother and father. Not old, but not young. Mr. Reed still holding that cigarette tilted upward from his lips; hair brushed back and rippling in pretty black narrow waves; still squinting those narrow eyes of his, and squeezing those lips tight upon that cigarette; sitting in the big chair near the window overlooking State Street, narrow house-shoed feet propped upon the window sill; relaxed in a soft white open-collared shirt and blue creased pants, staring across the street at the green-shaded windows of the opposite third floor; staring across the street at some narrow-eyed man over there, who sat with his feet propped up at the window behind a lace curtain staring back at him.

Mrs. Reed—short, chubby, dark-skinned, with black shiny curls all around her full, dark face; glancing at Helen every now and then, and then at me—smiling quickly and sweetly when I caught her at it. She wore a brown wool dress with white buttons running down the front and a large white collar that was lightly smeared from the rich clay-colored powder on her neck. Not asking many questions about what was going on in Trumbull Park. Afraid to. Passing by me and squeezing my shoulder, like I was a son in blood and not in law.

218

There were things they both wanted to say, Mr. and Mrs. Reed; but they knew both Helen and me better than to step in where only Mrs. Palmer was not afraid to tread. Finally Mr. Reed said, as if to himself:

"If one of them hunkies bothered me, I'd have to load up my 'brother.'"

He'd called his gun his "brother" ever since I'd known him. He'd said it so many times that I really believed he felt that his gun wasn't a steel thing with a trigger and a handle that could punch holes in "just about anything." No, indeed! This slim, light-skinned man, who moved in and out of the building, to and from work, like something apart from life itself, felt that his big, blue-steel, oily automatic was his honest-to-goodness brother! And the thought of it made him pass his lips ever so coolly down upon his cigarette and tilt it upwards toward the sun, and prop his feet in the window sill and stare out at the lace curtains of the apartment across the street from his apartment, with all the confidence in the world. He seemed to feel that if things got too bad for us out there his brother would take care of everything—and that would be that.

"Honey," Mrs. Reed said to me—after giving Louella and Diane two big Christmas stockings full of everything, and me a flat box that had a sharp button-down-collar sports shirt in it, and Helen a pink slip with a waist line that I truly doubted would ever go around Helen's waist again—"Honey, I want you and Helen to stay in close touch with me. I'm not going to say I'm not worried. I am. I'm worried to death. I can't sleep at nights even."

Something in me got scared when she said she couldn't sleep. The Gardener Building was no place to be if you couldn't sleep at night.

"Aww, now," I objected, "don't you go worrying about us and not sleeping at night. That's not——"

"Just a minute, Buggy. I'll be all right. I know how to take care of myself. Don't you worry about that! I just mean that I've been thinking a lot about you kids." She looked over at Johnny Reed staring straight ahead, but with his head kind of cocked to one side so he could hear good—"and your father has been thinking a lot too. We know that you can take care of yourselves. Anybody who can take care of himself here in this crazy house can make a way any place. We know that. We know that you did the right thing by leaving here . . . I only wish . . ."

She threw another glance at Johnny Reed, and a thick puff of smoke bloomed from his cigarette, and she didn't finish that line. Instead she hugged me, and she hugged Helen, and grabbed underneath Diane's arms and lifted her up and kissed her face, and bent down and kissed the top of Louella's head.

"You're out there now. You're away from here. You've got a chance. Stay out there. Fight if you have to; but for goodness sakes don't start anything. Do you hear me, Buggy?"

She seemed so much like Momma!

"I hear."

"Well, it's not every day you get a chance to fight back against—against——"

Johnny Reed said:

"Oppression."

Helen's mother didn't even look at him:

"You kids are doing something different—important. Just be careful. Just keep your mother wits about you."

And she put her arms around Diane and Louella, who were standing at her side looking at Helen and me as though we had come to visit *them,* as though they lived here with Helen's mother and father.

"And," Anna Reed said, "if you let anything happen to these kids, we're going to have it."

Helen said smiling firmly:

"Don't worry about a thing."

Helen looked at me and smiled and then looked at her mother. Helen was tall; her mother was short. Helen was slim; her mother was heavy. Yet both of them had the same soft, determined eyes that could stare you down five times out of six, the same rich-brown skin and coarse glossy hair, the same soft face that made you want to hug that face close to yours, and look at it and study the new things that came and went across it darkly. I don't know—those two women seemed like what real women ought to be!

So Christmas had come and gone—almost, and me and Helen and the kids kissed her folks goodbye and took the State Street car to 95th Street. When we got there, Helen and the kids waited outside, blinking and squinting through the feathery wet snow that floated into the light of the street lamps, while I went inside the tavern on the corner of 95th and State and pushed my way through a happy crowd who were finger-snapping to a rock-and-roll "Jingle Bells" so hot and groovy it could have melted all the snow at the North Pole. To the telephone booth and *Essex 5-5910*.

"Headquarters Nine. O'Grady speaking!"

"This is Martin. Can you send the wagon to 95th and State?"

"Yeah, Martin. 95th and State. That right?"

"That's right!"

And you know what? The patrol wagon came staggering around the corner of 95th Street an hour and a half later.

"Hey, didn't you tell Headquarters Nine that you were at 95th and Cottage Grove?"

221

And the sound of that hot "Jingle Bells" followed us out to Trumbull Park, trailing away out of our ears and taking up again inside our minds. What a gassing deal! Hot "Jingle Bells" and people dressed up and laughing and having a ball, and us riding home—Louella, Diane, Helen and me—in a cold, filthy patrol wagon that came an hour and a half late.

And then, with the kids home and asleep, we sat on the couch and tried to get warm from being so cold outside, and stared at the Christmas tree, and waited for the bombs. Five went off twenty minutes after we had gotten into bed and kissed and said good night.

That night I dreamed I kicked the hell out of old man Gardener.

18

I DON'T KNOW whose church radio program it was that was swinging so nice that January Sunday morning. I mean, organs and choirs and people clapping—not that off-the-wall holyroller kind of clapping, but that happy-in-time easy-going everything-together kind of clapping. Whosever church it was, it was going. I felt happy in my bones, like I had just been sent a message from home. From home? I don't know from where. Maybe from the South; maybe from the past; maybe from those people I used to see in Helen's father's Negro history book, with that thick bushy hair fixed up there some kind of way, and those thick curly moustaches, and that proud look that's just beginning to get back in style.

Sunday morning! Bacon frying. The *Tribune* spread all out over the floor; comic strips everywhere—on my bed upstairs, on the kitchen table—just everywhere. The kids looking like they were trying to find something else to mess up. I was going to have to talk to Helen about those kids. But not now—not while that organ was spreading the word the way it was.

I walked to the kitchen. Helen was just a-going—taking the bacon off the stove, breaking the eggs, looking in the oven after the biscuits. I snapped my fingers in time with the music:

"Good morning, Miss Pretty!"

She turned away from the stove and walked up to me, that big stomach getting all in the way. Then she hugged me and put her face in the curve between my neck and shoulders.

"Hi! What are you so happy about this morning?"

" 'Feel the spirit, Doll! That's all—just the spirit."

I kept snapping my fingers even while she hugged me. She laughed:

"Well, you've given it to the kids. Look."

That Louella! She was holding her hands straight up in the air the way those real holyrollers do. Her head was pointed straight up at the ceiling, and she was walking around in circles in time with the music. I felt a little bit embarrassed. Where had she seen that? I hadn't really liked to see those old women in that church down on State Street, in those stores in the Gardener Building, do that. But there was Louella; and she was really doing it, too! What the heck, I thought. She's mine; and it was my old holyroller people that she got it from. So what the heck! Would I be happier if she were doing the Twelfth Street Rag?

I snapped my fingers along with the music.

"Go—go—go!"

And, man, that chick really went!

And that organ was going!

Old Diane was playing it cool. She was standing in the kitchen doorway leaning on one foot, watching as if she really objected to the whole disgusting affair. But her left foot, the one she wasn't leaning on, was wiggling right in time with the rest of the music!

Well, look-a-here, I thought. Are we actually happy here in Trumbull Park? I guess so.

Ba-rooom!

What the heck was that? Oh, I knew that it was a bomb. But what did it mean—now? In the middle of our church music? In the middle of one of the few little good times we were able to have nowadays? Bombs don't have any respect for happy times, so why should happy times have any respect for bombs? So:

"Yez—yez—yez!"

But Louella had stopped dancing; Diane had stopped patting her little foot; and now the organ music stopped, and a commercial came on. The man was selling the best lard that money can buy.

I went to the living room window. The house got quiet, except for the sound of the oven, where Helen had just taken the biscuits out. I shouted back to her there in the kitchen:

"We haven't seen Arthur in a while. I wonder why?"

"I saw Mona yesterday."

"How is she doing? I mean how are they doing?"

What was getting wrong with me? Women were beginning to be on my mind more and more.

"They're doing all right, I guess. Mona didn't look too hot though. I think she's going through a lot, Buggy—a lot more than just this riot."

And what business was that of mine? But, do you know I got just as mad as I could be? The idea of Mona—that tall olive smooth-skinned quiet woman, whose face seemed so innocent you wanted to take your hat off whenever she came around even if you didn't have one on—suffering more than the riot could cause, made me mad. At Arthur? Maybe.

"I think I'll go over there after lunch and see Arthur."

"And Mona?"

I practiced nights just to be ready for questions like that. I shot right back:

"Sure, Mona. She's our friend too, isn't she?"

"She *sure* is!"

Ouch! The way she said that!

Arthur was sitting at the kitchen listening to a table radio when Mona let me in. The little boy, Bobby, was sitting in one kitchen chair marking up a whole page of funnies with black crayon. The little girl, Sharon, was standing behind her mother, wearing a little apron, jam all over her bright-creamy face.

"Well," Mona smiled, "come in."

"I just thought I'd drop by to see how my friends were doing."

Arthur had his head cocked a little toward the radio, but he straightened up when I walked through the little storage room between the back door and the door leading to the kitchen.

"Grab a chair, man."

That music seemed to have him in a fog. I tried to hear what it was, but Mona turned the water on in the sink and I couldn't hear. By the time she turned the water off the music was over. Arthur leaned up from the radio smiling like he had just come back from somewhere.

"Man, that Count Basie! He's going to really be great one of these days."

I said:

"I think he's great already."

"Oh, sure. But I mean when people really start to digging what he's doing. What he needs is one of those real swinging vocalists like, say—have you ever been to Club DeLisa?"

"Who hasn't been down there?"

"Well, you know that real dark cat that sings with Red Saunders' band? Joe—Joe—"

"Joe Williams?"

He brightened up. Did this kind of talk mean that much to him?

"Yeah, yeah, that's him. Now you put a cat that can whale like that with a cat that swings like Basie and—shee-it, man!—talk about some swinging sounds!"

Mona cut in:

"I think Lonnie Satin would sound better with Count than Joe Williams."

Arthur whined:

"Aww, Mona, you don't know what you're talking about! Now why you want to say that?"

Mona looked at me and smiled. She seemed *so* much like Arthur's mother right then.

"All right, Mr. Einstein, you know it all!"

Boom! Boom!——Boom!

Arthur sat there. It seemed to take everything he had, but he sat there, and there wasn't the tiniest wrinkle on his face as those bombs went off. But Sharon whined and pushed her head in between Mona's legs and tried to close them shut, to hide herself inside her mother.

Bobby breathed real hard and loud. He tried to copy his father. Bobby was about four; his hair was straight and shiny black and parted on one side. He tried to seem as cool as his father had seemed, and he said, real disgusted:

"Ho—hum."

But there was that same Arthur Davis tremor in his voice; and when I looked closer at him, there were tears blocked up at the rims of his eyes. I wondered if he did this every time a bomb went off.

It was exactly two-thirty—the man on the radio said so.

Arthur got up, feeling in his pocket as though he had forgotten something; then he went into the living room. I was surprised to see that the board was lying against the wall on the other side of the room, and that there were window panes in all the windows. They had the shades down, and that's why the room was so dark. I got up and followed Arthur into the living room. It was so bare! There was still nothing in there but that one broken-down chair and the two orange crates against the wall between the front and the side windows. They had never lived in the living room, I thought. That kitchen was the whole house as far as they were concerned. I wondered what upstairs looked like.

Arthur peeped along the side of the shade and looked north toward 107th Street. There was nothing down there, I suppose. Then he looked south and stepped back from the window looking absolutely white in the face—I mean, that ashy kind of white!

He didn't say anything, but his expression changed, and he went upstairs, still without saying anything. I went over to the window and peeped out. I stepped back feeling like I had just stepped off of the "Bobs" at Riverview Amusement Park.

Arthur came running down the stairs and started into the kitchen, but then he stopped. It seemed as if he hated to have to be the one to tell Mona and his kids that 106th and Bensley was full—and I mean full—of white people. Three squad cars were lost like corks on the Washington Park Lagoon in that twisting, turning, shoulder-bumping, fast-walking mob. Way down the street toward 105th, I could see a patrol wagon driving toward the crowd real, real slow.

I looked at Arthur. It wasn't fear that had put that ash on his skin and turned his lips dry and dusty white. At least, it didn't look like fear. It was more just plain sadness. Does that make sense? Sadness? Finally he was able to get it out. He'd lost the tremor in his voice now; you might have thought that he was telling Mona that the biscuits were burning or something:

"Well, Mona, let's get the kids together. Here comes the South Deering Improvement Association."

Mona sat down the dish that she was washing with a bang, but there was no fear in her face either. I wondered how I looked to them; then I got ashamed for wondering at a time like this. I said:

"What are you going to do?"

He sounded like he had already worked it all out:

"Mona'll take the kids over to Carl's house, and I'm going to stay here and wait for them."

Did I call this guy scared? Did I think that?

Mona didn't waste any time, but she didn't act like she was out of her head either. Arthur went back to the window. The crowd was moving right pass the squad cars, and already rocks were hitting the front yard of Arthur's house. They were coming close.

The house seemed so defenseless I felt like I was not really there. Well, there, but just as an observer—invisible, maybe.

Mona's voice was soft and calm, and she was even smiling a little, like she wanted to apologize for having to leave so soon:

"Well, we'll be going . . ." Then she stared at Arthur with that sweet mother's look. "Arthur, you be careful, hear? Don't do anything foolish—hear?"

He walked away from the window, over to her, hugged her. I was surprised at how much Mona looked like Helen right then, with her big stomach sticking out and keeping Arthur's body from really touching hers, except at that point. Arthur kissed her forehead, and she pulled away from him, still smiling, and grabbed her two babies by the hand and opened the back door just as a bomb went off.

Boom!

Three more followed that one.

Boom! Boom! Boom!

Then two more *big* ones:

BA-ROOM! BA-ROOOM!!!!

Arthur stood at the kitchen door watching her walk across the back yard, down the cement walk that ran between the fences around each of the back yards. Two cops stood on the walk looking a little worried. I stood beside Arthur watching Mona go. Could it be, I wondered, that these cops are worried about Mona and her kids too?

I laughed out loud, and Arthur turned away from the window and laughed back at me:

"Hell, Buggy, you're getting to be as 'buggy' as I am!"

Crash went a front window!

"Aww, damn!"

Crash! Window pane number two. Glass flew everywhich-way, and a loud thump hit the living room wall, and the brick (I knew that it was a brick) rumbled over a couple of times and lay still.

Arthur went to the kitchen cabinet and took out a halfpint bottle. He seemed a little ashamed to drink in front of me. I set things straight with him:

"Listen, Arthur, you're my friend whatever you——"

Crash! Window number three. This time a side window. Another brick slid across the floor. Arthur smiled, unscrewing the cap.

"*We want Davis! We want Davis! We want the nigger! Nigger, nigger, nigger!*"

Arthur waited until they stopped for breath:

"What did you say? I didn't get you."

There was a new kind of smile on this cat's face. What was happening? I said:

"Take your drink, man. Like that song goes, 'Ain't nobody's business if you do.'"

But he had taken his drink by the time I said that. Already he was putting the top back on the bottle and putting it back into the cupboard. His Indian-colored skin was red already, and there was a terrible look in his eyes. His eyes seemed to say what his voice had said just a few minutes ago: "Awwww, damn!"

Crash—crash—crash! Wow! Windows three, four, and five.

There was something different about all this. Everything was too calm in this house for all that was going on outside! Arthur walked into the living room. The shade was ripped with explosion-looking holes. Part of the shade hung down as though someone had ripped it with a knife; and the Sunday sun was just as bright as ever outside, and I bet that that church organ on the radio was still whaling! I noticed that Arthur didn't even try to cover himself when he went into that room. He didn't seem afraid, didn't seem to care about being hurt. Has this cat flipped? I wondered. But why does it have to be that anyone who does something that somebody else doesn't dig, has to be nuts? Why is that—huh?

He stood at the side of the window—watching, just watching. The sunlight hit his cheeks and chin, I could only see the side of his face, standing in the kitchen door the way I was; but there was a murderous hardness in his face, and the muscles in his cheeks bulged and shrunk and bulged again. And don't think that it wasn't noisy outside! Over and over and over again, those people screamed:

"*We want Davis! We want Davis! We want Davis!*"

"Come here, Buggy. Look at these fools."

I went over to the window. There was a fight going on right across the street from Arthur's house. There were hundreds and hundreds of people there. The paper said the next day that there were over five hundred people out there, but I saw a thousand or more if I saw one. Why the streets were jammed with people going north and south all the way out of sight; and they all seemed to be yelling the same thing at the same time:

"*We want Davis! We want Davis!*"

Arthur snickered:

"Look, Buggy. Look at those fools fighting. Look!"

Again, I looked at the men fighting. One was a medium-sized, stocky guy with a dark coat and a white shirt and tie; and four or five jacket-wearing, hatless guys were punching this dressed-up guy everywhere they could hit him— on the head, on the neck, in the face, in the chest—everywhere. He tried to swing back at them, but he was having a hard time doing it, because he could use only one hand. In the other, in behind his back, he held onto a little writing tablet, and it seemed that every time they'd hit this guy he'd grip that tablet even harder. Arthur asked:

"You know who he is?"

"A newspaper reporter?"

"That's right."

Crash—crash—crash! Six—seven—eight. Those were the upstairs windows. Why was this guy so calm! Why? Why? I couldn't get scared for watching Arthur. Bricks just banged against the walls outside!

Crash! One flew through the window right above Arthur's head. I screamed. I couldn't help it.

"Let's get out of here!"

Crash! Number ten.

Arthur said nothing. A screechy man's voice outside shouted some orders:

"*Taaaake cover, men!*"

Another voice near the front door mumbled:

"*Shee-it!*"

232

From all I could see, there was a line of policemen standing in the muddy January snow, piled up in the street along the curb nearest Arthur's house. Some of them were squatting; others were swinging wildly at little groups of four and five that attacked them. Others were ducking the bricks that kept flying across the street from the mob.

"*Aaaaaaeeee! Son-of-a-bitch!*"

A real nasal voice cried out. I found the man who had cried it just as he slapped his hands against the bloody splotch that a brick had opened on his forehead.

Way off somewhere there was a fire engine going; and above the house across from Arthur's house, two black twists of smoke with orange at the bottom were belching up from somewhere behind. The paper said next day that the garage of a "sympathizer" had been set afire for the fifth time. I thought, when I read that, that he must be a hell of a brave cat to let it be known that he sympathized with us out there in Trumbull Park.

Windows breaking and people shouting and screaming, and the cops just standing there taking it. Not breaking up the crowd, not throwing the rioters in those big paddy wagons that sat parked, surrounded by screaming crazy people, on the corner of 106th and Bensley.

I was watching a movie. I was sitting in some dark show somewhere watching a movie, and I didn't like what I saw worth a damn. It got dark before I knew it. Five more windows had been broken. Total—fifteen. All at once I noticed that it was night and that the crowd had thinned out, and I suddenly realized that Arthur hadn't said a word to me for hours. I tried to see his face, but it was already too dark, and the kitchen light had never been turned on, so all I could see was the dark shadow of him standing there in the smashed-up living room. The whole house was the broken-bottled, brick-strewn shambles of a Federal Street tavern after a real serious argument. I heard him step out

233

into the mess, heading for the kitchen; and I followed him. His feet sounded as if they were walking in a back alley.

His face looked dirty when he turned the light on, and tear-streaks striped his cheeks with two-toned crooked lines that all met at the bottom of his need-a-shave chin.

I knew what was wrong with Arthur, but I asked him anyhow. And he knew what was wrong with him, but he looked surprised and said:

"Explain yourself."

"I—I can't. I—I—oh, skip it, Jim!"

He stood directly under the kitchen light, and his nose made a long shadow across his lips. He took a deep breath and raised up on his toes, and clamped his hands across the top of his head. Then, all at the same time, he let out the air he'd filled his chest with, eased down on his heels and slid his clenched fingers from the front of his head to the back and down his neck.

I watched him. I wondered if he knew that he was shaking off, right there in front of me, all the water in his eyes, all the hurt on his face, and a hell of a lot of the droop from his tall, not-so-big body. He spoke, louder than the moment called for:

"Let's go over to Mr. O'Leary's house. I want to *will* you something."

"Will me what?"

"Knowledge, Daddio, knowledge. Mr. O'Leary's got it. You remember the white stud I told you about next door?"

"Yeah, but what's he—I mean how does he figure in this?"

Arthur flicked off the kitchen light and stepped out the back door of his wrecked house just as somebody outside his front door yelled:

"*Nigger! Nigger-lovers, nigger! Niggerrrr-lov-errrrrs!*"

19

M

R. O'LEARY'S HOUSE was dark. A dim light
shone from the front room to the kitchen where we had
come through the back door. Struck by the flickering light
from a kerosene lamp, was an old woman sitting in a wheel
chair; a shawl covered her shoulders, and her head drooped
and raised and drooped again. Against the front room
window was a large wooden board. I hated to see that
board. Once again I had to sift my hatred of white people,
whom I was beginning to hate as a race. Here was another
I just couldn't hate. Here was a man who was white, who
had to put wooden boards against his window just as Arthur had.

He was wrinkled, and white haired, yet he walked
quickly, with a silly kind of swagger, and his voice sounded
like a silly kid's:

"Hi, boys. Come on into the front lounge."

He walked ahead of us. There was a gloomy torn couch
in the corner.

"Sit down, boys." Then: "Oh, yes. This is my wife,
Baby."

Baby. Babydoll! I wanted to run out of there. What kind
of foolishness was this? The old lady's face started quivering as though a smile was trying to break out from behind

those sagging cheeks and that juicy slobbering mouth. Arthur touched her white hair, and Mr. O'Leary laughed.

"Arthur here, is her beau."

I said:

"Glad to meet you, Mrs. O'Leary."

Arthur said:

"This is Buggy Martin. He's taking over out here."

I glared at Arthur. He looked back at me and smiled. I sat down.

"Mr. O'Leary," Arthur jumped right into the subject, "you know you were telling me about all the goings on out here? I knew Buggy would think I was nuts if I tried to explain all that stuff to him, so I brought him over here for you to put him hip to just what's behind all this."

Mr. O'Leary stared at me, then at Arthur. He sat down beside me, silent for a minute, then:

"Buggy—it is Buggy, right?—Buggy, I'm an old man, old enough to be your grandfather."

He turned to Arthur and laid his hand on Arthur's head. I wanted to get out of there. They seemed like they honestly liked each other.

"I've been around this neighborhood a long time— since back when horse and buggies trotted up Bensley. A long time ago, before Mascari, before the project here. Yep, I used to be a South Deering Resident. Owned my own home out there."

He glanced at his wife, and then at the wooden board at the window.

"But a lot of things happen in a lifetime"—he hit Arthur lightly on the knee—"a lot of things. It's the combine-boys. I mean it. It's the land-boys, the speculators. Listen . . ." He looked around as if he thought that anyone who heard him would just automatically clap him into jail. "Listen . . . I know what I'm talking about." He walked to

236

a chest and opened it. I heard a paper rustle. "Listen, I've got something here that'll bear me out. I say that we're fighting an organized conspiracy . . . Look!"

He spread a wrinkled *Daily News* on the floor in front of the couch. Then he got the kerosene lamp and set it on the floor beside the paper. His old lady seemed to disappear into the darkness of the room. The paper was folded back to the part he wanted me to read:

HOW TWO GROUPS STIR UNREST AT TRUMBULL PARK

I stared across at him, kneeling there on the floor, the paper spread out between us like we were playing an eerie crap game there in the half-light, half-darkness:

"Where'd you get this?"

"Read it! Read it, boy!"

So I bent over and read real fast until my eyes were caught by some words that slowed me down:

"The disturbances at the Trumbull Park Housing Project are not spontaneous but are being fostered by two small organizations. The campaign of police harrassment, window smashing, rock tossing and barn burning that began last August can be traced, at least in part, to them. . . . The campaign appears to be organized—A group advocating race superiority theories and other extreme racial measures, although having only a tiny membership, lends its support to the campaign—The two organizations in the background of the disturbances are: 1. The South Deering Improvement Association. 2. The National Citizens Protective Association, a small group founded in St. Louis, Missouri."

So this was it. What had been guessing and rumor was at least printed rumor, and most likely fact.

"They have plans, Buggy—big plans. And the Negroes in Trumbull Park figure in those plans. You ever hear of the *Southend News?*"

I had seen one at Arthur's house.

"Well," he went on to say, "there are plans to do away with the Chicago Authority altogether, and a couple of guys down in Springfield have already drafted a bill to abolish the CHA. In fact, this *Southend News* said that these guys were among a group of senators who have already made a law which prevents public housing from being built in any area where the majority of the voters don't vote in favor of the project being built there."

"What has all that got to do with Trumbull Park?"

Mr. O'Leary answered my question with another question.

"Why are you having so much trouble having the law enforced out here?"

"Oh—I think I see what you mean."

"Look"—he looked around himself again like a man expecting to be arrested any minute—"look, boys, wake up! There are no accidents in society. Whatever happens—mobs, riots, stuff like that—happens because of something somebody did, or didn't do. And in all cases you know what's underneath it all?"

I answered without thinking:

"What?"

"Bread, baby—bread."

I whispered to Arthur:

"Who has this old cat been hanging around with?"

Arthur's lamp-lit face winked an eye:

"Me."

"Now get this . . ."

I almost laughed at Mr. O'Leary.

"Now get this"—he grabbed my arm and leaned real close—"it's a two-pronged attack—understand?"

He got up, walked away, and returned with a large piece of brown wrapping paper. He took out a pencil and drew a square.

"Now this is us."

"Us?" I turned to Arthur. "What the hell?"

Arthur frowned:

"Wait a minute."

Mr. O'Leary put his hand to his mouth and laughed into it.

"I haven't lost my mind, Buggy. I just mean this to be a diagram of the project—see?" He drew a circle up at the top of the square. Then he drew one all around the little circle and the square. "Now," he said, "take this square. As a public housing project this square stands in the way of this circle." He pointed to the little circle with the pencil.

I whispered to Arthur:

"What is he talking about?"

Mr. O'Leary kept his pencil on the little circle. He leaned to me:

"You ever hear of the Cal-Sag Seaway?"

"The who?"

"Never mind. Now you watch this carefully. I'm going to play a little game." He took his pencil and drew a line from the little circle straight up the paper for about a foot. "Do you know where that line ends?"

"Uh—no."

"In the Atlantic Ocean! Listen. I've got this so-called riot figured out, boys. Listen. Nobody starts a riot for nothing, you understand. I've got friends—well, I used to have friends—in the South Deering Improvement Association. We used to drink together; we used to talk together. I thought they were drunk when they bragged, 'We're gonna buy that project right out from under you, you ol' coot!' I'd kid back. 'A public housing project can't be sold,' I'd say. And then they'd look at each other and at me and suddenly burst out laughing. I thought they were drunk—then."

Mr. O'Leary was trembling now, and there was no cheerfulness in his face. He looked very, very old, and sad. He was teaching me something, or at least trying to—but what? He pointed to the middle of the line he had drawn:

"Here in between Canada and the United States is a bunch of lakes. You know 'em—we had to learn 'em in school, remember? The Great Lakes? Lake Michigan, Lake Superior, Lake Erie, Lake Ontario, Lake Huron? Well, at the other end of this line . . ."

He ran his pencil down the line until it reached the circle that sat just above the little square that was supposed to be me—or, at least, Trumbull Park.

"At the other end of this line is a little lake called Lake Calumet—you boys know—where those people fish—that lake along Doty Road leading out of Stoney Island."

"Yeah?"

"Well, that is Lake Calumet. The government, *your* government, is now getting ready to spend a lot of money widening the river that runs into the Calumet Lake, the Calumet River. You know why?"

"Go on."

"Because at the other end of the line"—he ran his pencil up again to the outer edge of the paper—"is a pot of gold for Chicago, for the United States. You see, Buggy, what I found out, just by doing a little talking here and there and reading a few old newspapers, is that when this line is made wide enough, ships from all over the world will come from the Atlantic Ocean"—he started bringing his pencil down again—"through the St. Lawrence Seaway . . . through Lake Ontario . . . through Lake Erie . . . heading for Chicago . . . through Lake Huron"—slowly that pencil crawled, slowly, slowly—"through the Straits of Mackinac at the top of Lake Michigan . . . across Lake Michigan . . . into the Calumet River"—pencil crawling

slowly, slowly getting closer to the square where I was—
"and through the Calumet River into"—he slapped the paper on the floor with the palms of his big hands—"Lake
Calumet! Boys, Lake Calumet is right at your back door!"

I still didn't get the picture.

"So what's the big deal?"

Mr. O'Leary whispered:

"Look . . ."

He then ran his pencil around the big circle that surrounded both Trumbull Park and Lake Calumet.

"Then, my two little pawns, then the land in this
area will be worth millions and millions and millions! Do
you know New York?"

Arthur spoke up:

"Do *I* know New York!"

Mr. O'Leary didn't pay that any attention at all. He was
excited now, and his face was about to catch fire it was
so red:

"Boys, New York will be a nothing town after the
Cal-Sag Seaway. Shipping, shipping, Buggy! . . . Tulips
from Holland, perfume from France—if you go in for that
kind of thing—bells from Belgium . . . Look, Buggy, Arthur,
what I'm getting at is that the products of the world will
no longer stop at New York, but will come inland through
the Cal-Sag Seaway and park right at our back door. This
means jobs—lots of them." He leaned back. "Jobs for Negroes. Who else does the labor for this country? What other
race has enough people, poor enough to do the stevedoring,
the warehousing, the boxcaring. Where are those people
going to live, Buggy? I'll tell you where. In Trumbull Park!
But"—he started whispering again—"suppose Trumbull
Park wasn't a *public* Housing Project but, say, a *private*
housing project? . . ."

Then real quick:

"How much do you pay a month, Buggy?"

And before I could stop myself:

"Around fifty. . . ."

Then he started some fast figuring.

"Let's see. Four hundred and sixty-two units in Trumbull Park at, say, a hundred dollars a month or more. Let's see—$42,620 a month for, say—forever. You get it Buggy? We're pawns—all of us. If public housing can be made to seem troublesome enough—disruptive enough—to enough communities, then these guys down in Springfield can work a law like their referendum deal so that the people in each neighborhood will be able, not only to decide whether or not projects are to be built there, but also to decide whether or not a project can *stay* in a neighborhood. Then, my good friend, Trumbull Park will be sold, because of the trouble caused by Negroes living here, to private enterprise, which will be happy to take it off of the government's hands. As you might know, Congress has already passed a law permitting sale of government projects, so it would be a simple matter for some good-hearted riot-backer to step in and say, "Well, I'll just take that l'il ol' project off your l'l ol' hands; and the South Deering people would gladly vote Trumbull Park into private pocketbooks. Then"—he tapped at the circle that went around Trumbull Park and Lake Calumet—"then, my friend, Negroes would be perfectly welcome to live out here—for one hundred dollars and up a month!"

Wow! My head was spinning!

"Mr. O'Leary, you mean that there are folks behind this that got *that* kind of money to spend?"

He spoke back at me, in my own tone of voice:

"Did you say that bombs go off here every night?"

I mumbled:

"Hundreds."

"Well, Buggy, tell me this: who in the hell pays for them?"

"The Association?"

"And where does their money come from?"

"The neighborhood people—I guess."

"Yeah, Buggy; but the *Daily News* said the South Deering Improvement Association has a tiny membership."

Old Mrs. O'Leary shuffled, and Mr. O'Leary picked up the lamp and went to her. I said:

"You got me all confused." I turned to Arthur. "It's time to go back. Let's go."

The old man stood there and looked at me, one hand holding the kerosene lamp, the other resting on the shoulder of the old lady slobbering in the wheel chair.

"I don't think you're confused, Buggy. I just think that you don't want to face up to the fact that there's a real heavyweight at the other side of the ring. And he knows how to box, Buggy. He's got our mayor in his hip-pocket, and he's whipped the police so far, hasn't he, Buggy?"

I started out of the room, toward the back door, and Arthur followed me. Mr. O'Leary, still holding that lamp, passed him by, caught up with me, walked along beside me. Grabbing my arm, he whispered to me in that let's-start-a-jailbreak voice of his:

"I love this country, Buggy. I've watched it grow. There's a lot of my sweat in those paved streets out there. I've carried my share of mortar and cement in my day. So have your people, Buggy. This"—he pointed his open hand toward the front where Bensley was—"this isn't what I looked forward to when Isabelle and I were young. These greedy, selfish people are making a joke of our dreams, boy, the rights we've all suffered for, the good name we once had throughout the world"—the old man was almost growling—"down the drain now! 'America the Beautiful'—what a

243

lovely song—so much like my America! But"—he turned to include Arthur in his words and almost whined like a girl—"where is my America, boys? I'm seventy-three years old. And I'm an outcast, for trying to be American!"

I pulled away from him for the door, and he let me go; but as Arthur and I went off into the night, I heard him screech after us:

"Don't let 'em get away with it, boys! Fight 'em! Y'hear me? Fight 'em!"

And when I looked back at him, I saw him standing there in the doorway, peering out after us into the dark, that lamp lifted high in his old hand—a perfect target for anybody who wanted to throw anything his way.

20

CALLED THE GROUP together right after that absolutely out-of-sight talk with Mr. O'Leary. It seemed true, yet it was fantastic. I decided not to talk to the group about it until I had it clear in my own mind.

I had wondered whether or not it would be wise for the women to come to the meetings. After all, most women will tell you themselves that when men want to get together, leave them alone—all women do is gossip and gab anyway. But the women had done something that we men didn't have to do. They had put in twenty-four hours a day in good ol' T. P.—no husbands, no nothing—and had faced up to the mob *and* the policemen, all day, every day. My walking with Carl, Kevin, and Terry was almost as bad as the women's grind; but we'd been stopped, and it had only been that one time. We had not even fought them, and so, although that loud-mouth, supposed-to-be-bad white cat had broken out and run when we started to cross Bensley to get him, we still had not given or taken what the women had. That fact stayed with me.

The women had fought the mob in their own way and had won out. So I was glad to see Helen come out of the kitchen and sit beside me, and to see Mona sit beside Arthur, and Nadine beside Terry, and Ernestine beside Carl

Burton, and Beverly beside Kevin Robinson, plus now Christine and William Thomas.

Christine and William just showed up one night like they had always been there. One night it got dark; and when it got light again, there were Christine and William Thomas. Christine was the biggest—I knew that the first minute I saw them. She had opened the door and let me in, and William had come out of the kitchen wearing an apron and a handful of soapsuds. His eyeglasses and his young smile were just trimming to his natural-born, all-over kind of littleness. He was a very nice guy. And when he passed my house early in the morning on the way to work, he wore a leather jacket with a zipper on it.

Christine was big, dark, and as loud as the days are long. She was boss, and even her laugh said so. I could see 35th Street written all over her face, and I was glad that now there was a real gone gal in Trumbull Park.

Arthur was in his usual Georgia Pine condition. It looked to me like he'd had a couple. We hadn't even settled down before he brought up Carl and Terry's arrest. Theirs seemed to have nothing to do with his; his arrest seemed to him a different thing altogether.

"Yes, yes, yes . . . here we are, gentlemen! It's the same old story . . . the two baddest hombres . . . west o' th' Pecos! One-Gun Pete . . . and One-Knife Cassidy . . . they tell me!"

I didn't go for that noise no kind of way, and I glanced at Kevin; he had never been known to take "that much" off of Arthur. But now he sat stiffly, one arm around his little girl, staring as hard as he could at the zipper on the leather jacket of William Thomas, who sat across the room from him. And Carl just looked Arthur straight in the face and smiled without showing his teeth—one of those I-ain't-nothin'-no-way kind of smiles.

I felt the heavy weight of being president, as I sat there

listening to the women gossip and gab and watched the men glance at me and talk awhile and glance at me again . . . waiting. I felt like somebody had asked me to speak some algebra or explain how babies are born. These Negroes hadn't walked past dark gangways and taken a chance on being mobbed just to hear some vague ideas from their leader. The more I thought about being president, the more I wondered whether or not the guys weren't playing a real dirty joke on me that day when they agreed so readily that I should be the leader. Leader of what? For what? How? But there I was, and there they were; and there Trumbull Park sure in the devil was. So I started the meeting, unsure of what I was going to say even at the second I opened my mouth to talk:

"Well, I guess we'd better get along with the meeting . . ."

So far, so good. A few coughs and some restless shuffling of feet; then, silence. Nothing going but those boxcars banging up against each other in the train yard behind the house. I went on:

"As you probably know, we formed this little group to try to see what we could do as a group to end all this—this——"

Arthur cut in:

"Bullshit!"

Mona hunched him hard. Some of the women giggled. Some of them looked at Arthur with ice-cold eyes. I was glad I hadn't said that. I went on:

"Anyhow, you know we—that is, some of us—had a little trouble . . ."

Christine Thomas snickered. I didn't look at Carl and Kevin, and they didn't look at me. I did look at Terry, and he rushed a real serious frown into his face and uncrossed his leg and crossed it again on the other side.

"Well, as you know, we had a pretty close escape

that time; and, well, I think we oughn't to give up. I mean—
well, I mean—like——Take those books they make us sign
everytime we come in or go out of our houses—I don't think
we should sign them anymore!"

Now how on earth did I think of that? I felt pretty good.
I started to work on this idea; but big, husky, soft-talking
Carl interrupted:

"I don't mean to cut you off, Mr. President, but last
month on a Sunday my mother came out here to see me,
about the—uh—trouble and even she had to sign in. I think
it's a shame when your own mother has to sign in to see
her own son."

Arthur's voice had that slow-hard-to-get-it-out way
about it; but what he said, put this signing up business in
a new light.

"Who are they . . . protecting? Us . . . from the rioters? Or the rioters . . . from us? Like . . . they won't protect
us; but . . . they put us in jail . . . for protecting ourselves?"

I open my mouth to say that he had made a good point,
but he wasn't through. He had just taken an *extra* long
pause.

"Person'ly, I think that . . . this whole thing . . . is
a . . . plot to drive us back . . . into the shorts."

Terry raised one eyebrow real high:

"Drive us back where?"

Arthur's head nodded, and his eyes closed on him.
Then he jerked his head up and his eyes open, and drawled
at Terry with a sickly smile:

"To the shorts, square . . . back to where you came
from! You know . . . 43rd and plum-nelly."

Terry put on that famous frown of his:

"I know, plum out of the city and nelly out of the
state!"

I jumped in to head off an argument:

"So what should we do about this book-signing mess, you-all?"

Carl almost whispered:

"Excuse me, Mr. President. I think you have a good idea. I don't mean to put words in your mouth, but don't you mean that we oughtn't to sign the books? Yes, that's a good idea; but how are you going to do it? You know we're up against some mighty big people out here. There are some strange things going on behind this riot."

I hadn't thought of *how*. I had just gotten the idea. I felt that Carl had asked that question to goof me. Maybe he was salty, because he got put in jail and I hadn't. Maybe I was just feeling guilty. All I know is that I got mad:

"Well, don't ask me! I'm just supposed to keep order. I'm not supposed to do all the thinking!"

Helen didn't like that one bit, and I heard a dig at me in her voice:

"Well, Mr. President, I think that if we *all* put our heads together, we could figure out a way. One thing—going out to shoot them sure doesn't work—not here in this place anyhow."

I said:

"Well, I didn't mean it the way it sounded, I just——"

But Arthur with his drunk self had figured out the answer, and he tossed it into the meeting like you'd do a lighted match into an unlit oven:

"Just don't . . . sign . . . th' g'ddamn books! Thash all! . . . N'body can grab you by th' hand . . . an' make you sign y'r name. They can't keep you out y'r own house. It's 'gainst . . . th' consh-tution!"

Terry knifed Arthur real hard:

"And to what particular section of the Constitution are you referring?"

Arthur clubbed back:

"Ask y'r mother . . . man!"

Terry got that dark frown and glanced at his wife Nadine, but Nadine was looking at her little girl who was sitting on the floor leaning against her mother's leg.

Kevin, who hadn't taken a seat, was standing near the kitchen door, both hands in his suit-coat pocket. Now he reared back on that one leg and, looking down on all of us as if he was a visitor from outer space, said in his smooth, heavy, room-filling voice:

"Now that's a right idea!"

Those whose backs were turned to him, turned around to see where this approval was coming from.

"This was the same thing I was telling you guys last time. Don't spend all your time sitting up talking about this stuff. Talking doesn't do any good. Act—that's all—act! If you don't want to sign, don't sign, that's all."

Kevin's wife sat in a kitchen chair right beside where Kevin stood. She was tall like Kevin was, but while Kevin's hair came to that unbelievable sharp point right at the tip of his forehead, her hair had something of a receding hairline that gave her a high, tan forehead she tried to cover up with thin bangs. She looked up at her husband with pride spread all across her thin face when he got through talking.

Carl's wife, a dark-skinned, keen-featured women with two braids crossing the top of her head right over a part that ran down the middle, raised her hand. I thought, What a polite family, the Burtons! I said:

"Yes?"

"Mr. President, I don't want to sound like I'm putting cold water on the suggestion that Kevin just made"— she smiled at Kevin, a smile so sweet and innocent that she looked like a little girl—"but I would like to know—what are we to do if the police arrest us for not signing the books?"

250

Kevin jumped to defend Arthur's idea like it had been his own:

"Awww, they can't arrest you for something like that!"

Terry's hard bass sliced in:

"Friend, you've broken the law in the first place just by being a Negro! Don't you know that anything else you did—*anything*—would but compound your offense?"

Kevin snarled at him:

"Aww, that's what's wrong with you guys now! Scared! Scared to go to jail! Scared to get hurt! Scared! If you are that scared, why did you come out here in the first place?"

Arthur joined Kevin's attack:

"Prob'ly scared . . . t' stay where they were."

I could see Will Thomas' expression growing more and more disgusted and disappointed in our meeting and everything we said. Yet I couldn't stop Kevin and Carl and Arthur and Terry and their families from bringing these problems down front. And, I thought, that's where they needed to be —down front. We needed to know where everybody stood, what everybody thought, how everybody would act when the deal went down. Any day we might be standing side by side, shooting or brick-throwing or fist-fighting whoever it might be, the mobs or the police. I had to see what kind of guys I was in with in this thing.

"Well, one thing"—Terry was frowning, but his voice was steady, and very deep—"trouble is easy to get into but it's hell getting out of—if I may proffer a colloquialism."

Helen's soft voice almost went unheard:

"But isn't that what we're trying to do now? Get out of trouble? Aren't we already in trouble?"

Nobody answered. I could see Mona smiling—you would have thought she said it. Kevin's wife Beverly smiled too. So did Christine Thomas. It seemed to be a special victory for the women—a silent joining up that made me uncomfortable. I suggested in a loud voice:

"Well, why don't those who agree that we should not sign—just not sign. And those who think that we should sign—sign. That way, if the ones who don't sign get away with it, then the others can follow suit. If they don't get away with it——"

You would have thought that Terry would have had enough of his smart remarks, but he finished my sentence:

"They go to jail."

Kevin pulled his hands out of his brown single-breasted and straightened his tie. I could tell that he was getting ready to go:

"Well, I for one don't intend to sign any more."

Boom!

A bomb slammed its hollow blast against the walls of the room. A couple of the children whimpered and crawled closer to their mothers. The second the bomb went off, I realized that I had closed my eyes. Helen sat with her hands pressed between her knees, and her lips mashed hard together, looking like something was hurting her. William Thomas' eyes were wide, and they looked like agate marbles behind his thick glasses. His mouth had dropped open and there was an uncertain smile that kept starting across his lips and disappearing while he looked from face to face to see whether, I guess, we took the explosion serious or had come to take it as a joke.

Kevin unbuttoned his coat and hitched up his pants, and his wife reached for his hands as soon as he dropped them to his side. Carl bent over and covered his forehead with one big rough-looking hand; he looked like he was praying. Everybody in the room did something, and whatever they did told the same story: those bombs bit down into your guts and pulled until the pain made you feel that you had to do something to hide the pain and the fear that poured into your face from the pit of your stomach.

Will Thomas placed both hands on his knees and turned his toes in, and said as if he had just figured out why the bomb had gone off:

"That bomb was for *us!* That was our welcome from certain people!"

From that minute on, until Mr. and Mrs. Thomas moved out of the project a year later—broken, nervous, talking about divorce, not speaking to each other, not speaking to any of us—William Thomas was never—not even in the closest room, not even in a moving car driving away from Trumbull Park—able to say that the white people were breaking the windows, or setting off the bombs, or gathering in the mobs that once surrounded his wife and threw a bomb straight at her. Always, always were they "certain people." It reminded me of the part of that old blues that went: "I'm in love with a woman, but I'm afraid to call her name . . ." William wasn't in love with the rioters, but he was strictly afraid to call their names.

Boom!

The blue-white flash turned the back of Nadine Watson's neck a chalky gray. I expected her to wince, so loud was that *bar-room!* She hunched her shoulders up and bent her head down, but she didn't make a sound. Arthur Davis began to get his walking heebie-jeebies again. He got up from the couch slowly, trying to act unconcerned; but his eyes were watery, and the lines that had pulled his face so tight that night at his house while he told me about his experiences, had begun to sink underneath the curves around his mouth and nose. His lips were pressed tight together and when he tried to smile, he looked like he was getting ready to tune up and cry instead.

"Excuse me," he said.

He stepped out of the close circle of men, women, and children to the front window to look around the shade, and then to the front door, and across the room to the side window, and then to the front door again. He opened the door and peeped around the sides of it, and stepped outside, leaving the door open, and came back in and started all over again, looking out of the front window and the side window, walking slowly, like he wasn't doing anything in particular, like he was just doing what any normal person anywhere in the world had done millions of times. Nothing to it: nothing to the water in his eyes, to the tremble in his knees that made it hard for him to walk; nothing to the way he pushed his hands into his pockets and then snatched them out and ran them across the top of his head, crushing his straight dark hair like grass underneath a steamroller. No, nothing. Nothing at all to it.

But the gloom had started to settle—the hopelessness, the loneliness, the fear that the happy people on the corner of 95th and State would not be around when the deal went down—fear that the names the *Chicago Defender* might print as the "dead and wounded in the Trumbull Park racial disturbance" would be the only thing that would get through the cool sounds of Ahmad Jamal at the Pershing Lounge down on 63rd Street, through the bluesy tastes that Johnny Griffin laid down at the Basin Street on Cottage Grove. And then it would be too late. Then it would be too goddamned late.

21

So Arthur Davis walked, and the rest of us
watched, and another bomb went off—*Boom!* And another—*Boom!* And it seemed to be raining bombs out there
in the cold night, so that while everybody wanted to go
home, nobody wanted to go before it stopped raining. So
there was silence again, except for the sound of Arthur's
feet clomping from window to window, and the choking
sound of his breath trying to push past the strain-lines running up and down his throat.

It took Nadine Watson's little girl to break it up, in a
harsh, hard, demanding voice:

"The meeting is over, Mother. Let's go home—hear?"

Hadn't she heard those bombs outside? Didn't she care?
Hadn't she learned to understand that they were meant for
her? I think she did understand, but she wanted to go
home—bombs or no bombs. The grown-ups laughed.

I was embarrassed. I should have thought of that. Maybe
I shouldn't have said it, especially since they were at my
house, but I *should* have thought what that child had
thought and said. She had said, "Let's go home." But she
had thought—I'm sure she had—bombs or no bombs.

Kevin led the way out:

"Hey, there you! C'mere and sign this book!"

255

The policeman was a late-shift man. He was angry at not having been able to get his sleep. Kevin didn't answer. He kept walking—his wife walking close beside him, his little boy holding his hand, and his little girl walking—just waking up from a long sleep and holding Beverly's hand. Another voice rang out:

"Hey there, fella! You hear the officer callin' you! C'mon back here and sign that book!"

I went to the front window. It was the captain. Two silver bars on his shoulders picked up the light from the street lamp nearby, and his white hair hung in mid-air over the dark uniform and apart from the darkness that surrounded it. There were other people there, a lot of them, mostly policemen, but others in overcoats and hats and scarfs, holding flashlights and mingling in with the policemen. Detectives, I thought.

Two or three other voices shouted at Kevin:

"*Come back here! You sign that book! Hey you, come back!*"

Terry came to the window beside me. He looked out:

"It seems we had an audience, huh?"

"It looks like it."

Arthur and Mona were next to step out. The policeman stepped in front of Arthur:

"All right! Sign this book!"

Arthur turned around to Mona and grabbed the hand of his little girl, Sharon:

"Come on, Mona."

"I'm coming."

The captain ran up to Arthur, his voice snapping a whip over our heads:

"Now look, Davis! You've been nothing but a trouble maker since you've been out here. Nothing but a trouble maker. I don't want any trouble out of you. You heard

256

what the officer said. It's not my rules. It's orders from downtown. We got to make everybody that comes in or goes outa these houses sign the book. Now sign up! I don't want any trouble outa you!"

"Come on, Mona."

"I'm coming."

The policeman grabbed Arthur's arm and spun him around, tearing his coat. Arthur screamed:

"Get your goddamned hands off of me! I mean it, goddamnit! Get your hands off of me! Why don't you spend your time keeping those hunkies from breaking people's windows and setting houses on fire instead of spying on us and pushing me around?"

The captain forgot all about Kevin and his family and poured all of his resentment upon Arthur:

"Pushing you around?" he shrieked. "Pushing you around?" He shrieked even louder. "Nobody's pushing you around!"

Arthur pulled and twisted trying to get free, but the cop wouldn't let him go, and Arthur screamed again—at us:

"Now you see what I've been going through—huh? Look at them! Look at them now with them smiles on their faces! Standing out here eavesdropping, grabbing me, tearing my clothes!" He screamed at them: "Get your goddamned hands off of me!"

Carl stepped out of the house and walked over to the cop holding Arthur:

"Officer, why don't you let the man go?" So quiet and cool his voice was. So big he looked with that thick neck sitting on top of his wide husky shoulders. The officer looked at the captain. The captain gave a quick signal with a nod of his head, and the officer let Arthur go; but he covered himself right away by shouting at Carl:

"You want trouble, gun boy? Huh? You want

257

trouble? Next time you go down, you're staying down. Get it? We let you off easy last time. You didn't just *get* off!"

I saw Red standing by the truck looking to me for help, for just one quick second, the first day we moved in. I saw myself running away from the mob halfway up the stairs in my own house the time I'd been chased home. I couldn't stand the idea of seeing myself standing there inside the house like any other bystander while these friends of mine were outside fighting to carry out the decision I had been so much in favor of just a few minutes ago. I took a deep cold breath and pushed past Helen and Christine and William Thomas.

"What are all these men doing around my house anyway? Were you spying on us?"

One of the plainclothesmen in the shadows snarled back:

"Whadda yuh having in there—a convention?"

Helen's soft voice raised above mine:

"That's right—we're having a convention, and we're going to keep on having them too!"

And Carl's wife, Ernestine, standing on the sidewalk beside her husband, backed up what Helen had said:

"That's right."

And a loud, grating woman's voice screeched out from inside the house:

"And there's not a damn thing you can do about it!"

Was that Christine Thomas? It had to be. Nobody else out here had a voice like that!

The policemen started moving in on us, hitching up the gun belts that held their shoulder holsters, and spreading their legs wide ready for Freddy; but Arthur walked past them, and Mona, Sharon, and Bobby followed a step or two behind:

"Come on, Mona!"

"I'm coming."

And not a policeman touched them.

Terry and Nadine stepped out behind Arthur and Mona. Nadine held her two-year-old red-faced baby girl high up in her arms as if she was trying to hold it up out of all this; but that baby—all of us—were in it for keeps now!

Carl Burton and Ernestine were the next to go. Carl went back into the house to get his little boy, asleep on the couch. Ernestine waited outside, and the light from the house caught the straight, even lines the snow made in the air as it began to fall out of the cold blackness beyond the ring of policemen that were watching us. Things were moving slow, but they were happening fast!

The captain did not go after Arthur and Kevin as they walked past him; he stayed right there in front of the door like he was getting ready to grab the next person that tried to get past his ring of cops without signing. But some people had already gone by, and it wouldn't have looked good to grab some for not signing after letting others go. Then too, all the people who had walked past him had been carrying or leading little children—and what would happen if one of the children got hurt while he was scuffling with one of the men? He stared at Ernestine, and then at me, and then at Helen standing in the door behind me, and then he turned to his men standing side by side—big and dangerous-looking in their uniforms and plainclothes, bulging with guns and with black jacks fixed so that they could get to them as soon as they needed them. But they couldn't help the captain get out of his fix; and there was Carl Burton rushing out of my house with his son, a four-year-old little giant, running and rubbing his nose with the palm of his hands and sniffling behind him.

Ernestine led the way through the ring of uniforms and plainclothes, and Carl waved at Christine and William Thomas:

"You-all planning to spend the night?"

Christine hollered back so loud it made everybody jump:

"Don't worry 'bout the mule goin' blind, Honey!"

She grabbed William with one hand, almost knocking his glasses off she jerked him so hard. William fumbled at his thick horn-rims, and just managed to lay hold of his five-year-old daughter's arm before Christine plunged out— looking for all the world like she was playing fullback for DuSable High. She almost knocked me down as she rushed by—taking long, loud, clomping steps that cut through the thin layer of snow on the walk and banged against the cement like a pair of horseshoes. I heard her laughing as she walked out of sight past the policemen into the almost pitch-black courtyard of the project, dragging her husband and daughter behind her:

"Let the good times roll, Honey!"

What a long way I had come in a short time! Things were becoming clear to me that I had never given a second thought to. Ideas about Negroes—born into me, breathed into me from my earliest days at the Gardener Building—were beginning to turn, ever so slightly, so that I could see the other side of them. What I had told Helen about Negroes not sticking together was beginning to soften at the edges and melt away before the hot, happy goofy kind of way things were happening.

Now who on earth would have thought that we really could have gotten away with standing up to the cops— *white* cops. Us! Colored folks—brought up to fear white people, whether we lived in the North or the South. The stories of our people being dragged through "back home" streets behind cars full of white people; the stomach-turning picture Mrs. Palmer brought up to Chicago from Oxford, Mississippi, of two young Negro boys dangling with heads down and mouths wide open and eyeballs pushed

over the edges of their sockets—these tales had burned—
and you know it—a horrible dread into our minds that not
even stories about white people who were shot down in
fields by "unknown niggers" could ever cover completely
up—kill our dread of the kind of human being who could
burn another, and drag his smoking remains down the
streets behind a car, not caring who saw.

No need to deny it—the dread was there. But so was the
hatred, and with it a never-ending push against the body-
burners and their kin and their images, though sometimes
the push was so light that you hardly knew it was there
at all. Now I knew that the push was always there—sometimes as soft as the drip of water from a broken faucet,
sometimes as foamy and giggly as little waves breaking up
against the rocks at Jackson Park beach. Sometimes the
push was half an hour of gunfire up and down the back
porches of the Gardener Building that started us praying
out loud or inside ourselves, to God or to the lodestones
that Mrs. Lowe's Fortune House sold for one dollar apiece,
that the black man would get at least one of the white uni-
formed cops or plainclothesmen who had come into our
neighborhood to shoot one of ours!

Oh, yes, this was really something—this walking past the
white policemen without signing the book. It wasn't new,
but it was us doing it—not somebody else, but us—the Negroes who wouldn't stick together! I went to bed for days
after that meeting singing "Let the good times roll!" I felt
that foamy laughing kind of pushing going on inside me.
But it was a push. Lord have mercy, it was a push!

22

I T WASN'T FUNNY—what happened to Terry, and it sure wasn't funny to Beverly Robinson, Kevin's wife; but it happened, and Terry came over to my house early one morning at about one A.M., sweating in the hard January winds like it was the Fourth of July. I let him in and he walked past me without even saying hello and flopped down on the couch and squeezed his cheeks between the palms of both of his hands. What little I could see of his dark homely face was twisted up into the deepest frown that Terry Watson ever had, and he'd put on some deep frowns since I'd known him.

You know about his deep, bass-drum voice. Well, he started talking in a bass that sounded like somebody was scraping sandpaper across one of those big kettle drums:

"Young man"—as little as he was, he loved to call people "young man"—"I'm here because I don't want to send my wife into hysterics. But I must, I simply must tell someone. I'm about out of my mind. I swear to God, I'm going insane."

All of a sudden he pointed at me and roared:

"Did you know that Beverly Robinson, Mrs. Kevin Robinson, was *enceinte?*"

Naturally I didn't know what *enceinte* meant, but the way he put it, and as deep as that frown sank across his brow, I automatically figured that it had had something to do with her being pregnant, so I, acting on the idea that that was what Terry meant, said:

"Well, I guess so. I mean she's been sticking out a little lately. Actually, I haven't paid her much attention. Why?"

"Believe me, young man. I've paid Mrs. Robinson considerably less attention than have you. I'm sure of it. Yes, I've been a friend of the family. I've kept an eye on the house inasmuch as Kevin has been working on the night shift. But pay Mrs. Robinson attention? As God is my witness, I've paid her as much attention as I have the configuration of the planet Jupiter! Yet do you know what has just happened to me?"

I shook my head, really confused by now. Terry then answered his own question:

"I have just given birth to a child!"

"You what?"

I looked at the bottom of the stairway, afraid that all the loud talk had awakened Helen. Terry stuck his right hand out and with his palm upward waved me towards him:

"Come here, come here. Sit down."

The first thing that came into my mind was that this Negro had flipped, blown his natural top. I sat on the couch, but way down on the other end, and he began to tell me how he'd "given birth to a child":

"I was in bed reading Killens' *Youngblood,* and Nadine was asleep, when there came this loud knocking at the door. Thinking that something had happened to one of you, I rushed to the door, to see Beverly leaning against the door—her little girl beside her—wracked with pain and holding her stomach. I guessed immediately that this was a matter for Nadine, so I helped Beverly inside and got Nadine up. Beverly herewith complains to Nadine that she suspects that she has miscalculated the date of her impregnation and that instead of having two weeks to go before delivery, she has ample reason to believe that she has about fifteen minutes.

"So Nadine, ever the tactician, anticipating that Beverly is going to ask her help to get to the hospital—which, by the way, happened to be Cook County—offers to keep Beverly's child Irma, and offers my services as escort-attendant."

By this time Terry was beginning to sweat around his ears and neck. He was talking just above a whisper, but the heavy growl of his voice buzzed against the wall like an idling motor.

"What was there for me to do but accept—indeed, to accept enthusiastically, instantly? There was no time to waste asking questions such as what I should do in the event the unexpected—no, the expected—happened, as it most assuredly did. So accept I did, and off we went—first to the police headquarters, then to the paddy wagon—that abominable dungeon on wheels—and straight up Bensley to 103rd Street, and from there to Jeffery, and from Jeffery to the Outer Drive—Beverly sitting on the hard ledge along the wall of the wagon that they call a seat, moaning and crying and twisting in agony, and me sitting there beside her holding her hand—yes, holding her hand—and trying as best I can to console her. As you know, I'm not one for height—that is, one might say I am a rather diminutive man, particularly in comparison to Beverly, who, as you know, is almost as tall as her husband.

"Well, there I was holding hands with this woman who, *sitting*, towered over me, and who at last asked me if she might lay her head in my lap. I won't say that I wasn't embarrassed, but I truly felt pity for Beverly, and I would have been glad to do anything I could to alleviate her suf-

264

fering. The wagon's red light was on, and I could feel us taking those sharp curves and turns along the Outer Drive on two wheels. I could see only the globes of the street lights as we shot down the Drive, but they whizzed by so fast that I'm sure we must have been going at least sixty miles an hour. And all the while poor Beverly lay with her head in my lap and twisted and turned and cried so pitifully that it made me feel altogether helpless and out of place sitting there in the flittering light of the street lamps we passed looking down on her face.

"We finally took that very sharp turn at 12th Street on the Drive, and I knew that we had only a few minutes to go before we'd be at County Hospital. But wouldn't you know it?"

He was sweating under his eyes now, and the collar of his shirt was dark from the water that had run down from his face.

"Wouldn't you know it?" he shouted, and then put his hand to his mouth startled by the sound of his own voice:

"She gripped my hand, and squeezed it till it hurt, and cried out: 'I can't hold it! I can't hold it!' 'Well, hold it! Hold it!' I pleaded with her. 'I can't! I can't!' She was screaming now, and I had to hold her by her waist—well, actually it was her stomach—to keep her from rolling off that narrow ledge and falling into that filth on the floor. And now she was twisting and writhing so I felt that I'd be unable to keep her from falling. The street lights flashing by the wagon window had changed to the yellowish kind you see along Harrison, and I knew that if only she could hold out for ten minutes more, we'd be at the hospital. But she couldn't——"

He stopped and put his hands in front of his face and mopped the sweat with the palms of his hands. I said:

"What?"

"She couldn't. She couldn't hold it any longer, and she didn't!"

"She didn't? Uh—what did *you* do?"

"What did I *do*? What would *you* have done?"

"I would have died."

"Would that I could have! Then and there. But there wasn't time—I—I——"

"You what?"

"Well, I—like I said there wasn't time for the formalities and the niceties that usually prevail under normal circumstances. I shouted for the cops to help me, but they didn't hear me. So finally I—I had to——"

"You had to what?"

"I tore her panties off!"

"You *what?*"

"I tore her panties off."

"You—wait—let me get this straight! You snatched Beverly Robinson's panties off? *Kevin Robinson's wife?*"

"The baby was—the panties would have been in the way—the *baby's* way. As it was, I had to catch it in my hands to keep it from falling on the floor. Oohhhhh, if I ever——"

He pressed the palms of his hands hard against his cheeks pushing his mouth into a tiny red doughnut, covering his eyes with his fingers, squeezing his nose with the edges of his hands.

"The doctor and nurse ran out and cut the child's umbilical cord—"

"Birth string?"

"—and finished the job right there in the back of that open wagon. They wrapped the baby in blankets and rushed it inside, and shortly afterwards took Beverly in. Somebody asked me if my hand had been clean before I

266

touched the baby, and I told them that the only thing I'd held in my hands since going to bed was Killens' *Youngblood*. That's all anybody said to me. Well. The patrol wagon got a good washing, and I rode back here hearing Beverly's screams in my ear every inch of the way, feeling every beat of that young baby's wet body in my hands, shaking like a leaf, and sweating to and through my absolute socks . . . Do you have a cigarette?"

"I don't smoke."

"Oh, hell!"

He got up to go, and as he opened the door, he growled over his skinny little shoulders:

"We've got to get rid of those patrol wagons. A woman could catch peritonitis having a baby in one of those things!"

"I never did like those paddy wagons. Why don't we call a meeting about it?"

"We'll talk about it later, Buggy. I'm going to bed, and I'm not getting out until spring!"

He closed the door. I stood there for a moment, numb from what he had just told me. Then I ran to the door, opened it and called out after him:

"Hey, Terry!"

"What?"

"Was it a boy or a girl?"

"Go to hell!"

23

WAITED a couple of days to let Terry get himself together after that wild "giving birth to child" he'd got hooked up in. But what had happened to Beverly stayed on my mind. Suppose something like that should happen to Helen? She'd flip! I'd flip! And I knew Terry'd flip if he happened to get caught in the same shuffle again. I called the meeting as soon as I could get the word to Arthur to tell the folks near his house to come. I told William and Christine Thomas about it, and Helen told the rest of the people during the day.

The bombs were going off more than usual the night we met. Arthur and Mona and their kids came in first. Arthur seemed in a nervous mood:

"Man! Those people are out there in all that snow and cold, screaming and fighting policemen up a storm!"

"What are the cops doing—cracking heads?"

"The last thing I heard when I left was the Sergeant hollering——"

I knew what Arthur was going to say, and we both said it together:

" 'Take cover men!' "

We all laughed. It wasn't funny worth a damn, but we laughed.

The others came in right after Arthur and his family, and we got into the meeting. Terry started things off:

"Mr. Chairman, might I interject here to say that in view of certain recent developments——"

The story had gotten out, and Terry's wife giggled.

"In view of certain recent developments, there is an acute danger implicit in the continued use of the patrol wagon for transportation purposes. I feel that the squad cars would be much more satisfactory for transportation, though God knows it's a shame that we must have need for either. In essence, Mr. Chairman"—his deep voice rolling softly—"I think that we should visit the captain at headquarters relative to the substitution of squad cars for patrol wagons."

Christine Thomas piped up in a rough high-pitched voice:

"Besides, what kind of dignity can you get out of riding to the hospital to have a baby in a paddy wagon?"

Nadine Watson took it a step further:

"What kind of dignity can you get out of riding in a squad car?" But then she bent the point into something else: "At least you have protection in those paddy wagons. It's not as easy to throw a rock through that grating in the paddy wagon as it is to throw one through a squad car window. Besides, I've heard of them smashing squad windows more than once. No, I frankly prefer the protection of the paddy wagon to the dignity of the squad car."

Ernestine Burton raised her hand:

"Mr. Chairman?"

I nodded for her to speak.

"I don't mean to interrupt, but I'm not feeling too well, and I wonder if we couldn't just take a vote and decide what we want to do?"

Kevin, standing at his usual spot near the kitchen door,

pulled his hand out of his side pocket and ran a finger along the inside of his collar, saying at the same time:

"You ain't just lying. I haven't got time for all this lollygagging! Let's take a vote and decide. I'm going to do what I want to do anyway; and I'll tell you right now I didn't go for it a bit—my wife having a baby in a dirty, nasty paddy wagon."

Christine Thomas said:

"Hell! First thing, I wouldn't have gone all the way to County. Didn't you have insurance on her?"

"Yes, I had insurance on her; but I still went to County. I wouldn't risk my wife's life in one of these white hospitals arguing with them folks: 'Does she have a doctor in residence? . . . No? . . . Oh, well, there's nothing we can do except in case of emergency!'—crap like that. I had a cousin in Altgeld Gardens out on 130th suffocate trying to get emergency treatment from that white hospital out in Roseland. I *know* I can get in at County, and that's where they took her, and I'm glad of that. But did they have to take her in a paddy wagon?"

Carl Burton asked:

"Why didn't she go to Provident Hospital?"

Kevin snapped back:

"Because she went to County!"

I broke in:

"Well, all in favor of going to see the captain about using squad cars instead of the paddy wagons say 'aye.'"

The ayes and the noes were about even, so I called for them to raise their hands. They did, and you know what? Terry raised his hand for, and his wife Nadine raised hers against. Christine Thomas raised her hand for, and her husband William raised his hand against. Arthur Davis and Kevin voted for, but then Ernestine and Carl Burton both voted against! So it was four for, and four against.

I didn't dig all this—I mean, how the wife voted one way and the husband voted the other. Were these wives voting different from the way their husbands were voting just to be contrary? Was there something coming between them, that made one do the opposite from the other just for spite? I looked at Mona and Helen; they were the only two who hadn't voted. Hell, if they did like some of the other women, they just might vote against too. I looked at Helen, and she looked away. What the hell was this? I looked at Mona, and she smiled, sort of polite-like. Everybody was staring at something in front of him. Nobody was looking at anybody else. I said:

"Well, it looks like we got a tie here, but——"

Kevin cut in:

"Mona and Helen haven't voted."

I remembered the bruise I noticed on Mona's cheek the first night I saw her. Would she pick now to get back at Arthur? Did Arthur put the bruise there? I was afraid to try to find out. But I had to. I said:

"Well, that's just what I was going to say, man."

Why was I afraid? Was I afraid of Helen too? Didn't I trust her? Maybe I'm going crazy, I thought.

"Okay," I said, "Mona you and Helen have to break the tie. Are you in favor of trying to get rid of the paddy wagon or not?"

Helen answered first:

"I'm for."

Mona looked at her and smiled. Then:

"I'm for."

William Thomas cleared his throat. Christine looked at him and rolled her eyes. I smiled.

"I guess we may as well go on over and talk to the captain tonight—huh?"

Kevin didn't answer. He just went into the closet and

took his coat out. Arthur got his. Carl just sat where he was.

Arthur had hard feelings in his voice when he asked Carl:

"You getting chicken, Jack?"

Carl didn't look afraid, but he didn't answer. Terry got up, and Christine did too. Mona said:

"Maybe Helen and I ought to stay here with the kids." Nadine complained:

"Isn't anyone speaking to me, any more? Just because I didn't vote in favor?"

Terry opened his mouth to explain, but Nadine raised her hand, and that cat clapped shut tighter than Dick's hat band. That worried frown passed across his face and settled down between his eyes.

My door sounded extra heavy and loud when I shut it behind me. There were two policemen standing alongside the window, their faces almost smack-dab against the window pane. They had been trying so hard to hear what we had been talking about that they jumped when Terry, Arthur, Kevin, Christine and I stepped out and slammed the door.

Arthur spoke in the direction of the two policemen:

"Don't freeze your ears, men!"

"Whadda yah mean, Davis?"

None of us answered. We headed toward the police headquarters. I sure felt good walking in a bunch. It got awfully lonely sneaking through that project all by yourself.

The captain was the same cat who had given us the business over signing the books.

"Come upstairs!"

He walked ahead of us, up the stairs toward what would have been our bedroom in my house. The walls had pencil marks all over them—phone numbers, ladies with mous-

272

taches, and all kinds of chicken-scratchings. I thought, I'd whip one of my kids for putting all this junk on the wall!

The captain walked over to a chair against the wall and pointed to a bench on the other side of the room.

"Sit there."

We sat down. I felt like we were in jail, getting ready for the third degree. He didn't say a word, leaving it to us to start it off:

"Uh, Captain—I—uh—we came to find out——"

"Just a minute! Just hold it a minute!"

I shut up, while this cat just sits there staring at us with those ice-cold eyes. Finally, a chubby, school-teacherish-looking stud, wearing a solid-color blue sports shirt under a tan gaberdine double-breasted suit, came in carrying a pencil and a little notebook with spirals at the end. He sat down beside the captain, and the captain whispered something to him. He nodded, and the captain turned to us:

"All right. I want each one of you to say what you have to say, *one at a time.*"

Terry said:

"Well, Captain, Mr. Martin here is our spokesman. I think he can satisfactorily state our case for the rest of us."

The captain frowned up. He looked a little like Terry when he did that.

"This is a free country. If these other men want to talk, they may. I don't believe in dictatorships!"

The captain's cap was off, and his white hair was thin on the top and real heavy at the sides. He was on the chubby side, but he wasn't sloppy. He had on his uniform, and every button was shining like new money. His hands were folded across his knees and his legs were crossed. I had to fight back the feeling that I was in the principal's office back at Colman Grade School.

"Uh—Captain . . ." I waited for him to snap me up.

He didn't. "We want the paddy wagons taken off. They're——"

"You want *what?*"

"The paddy wagons taken off. We want to use the squad cars instead. Beverly Robinson—uh, Mrs. Robinson—had a baby in one of them, and the wagon was—well, other women out here might have to go to the hospital any day now, and we just don't think that——"

"Are you trying to tell me how to run the police department? Now look, Martin! I've had my eye on you, and you're getting to be as big a trouble maker as Davis here, and I don't mind telling you——"

Arthur jumped:

"What do you call a trouble maker? Any Negro who ain't scared of you?"

Kevin whispered:

"Sit down, man! Damn!"

The captain kept on talking just like Arthur hadn't said anything:

"I don't make these rules out here! I'm assigned here just like any other policeman. If you have any complaints about the service you're getting out here, see the supervising captain. But I'm telling you now"—he uncrossed his legs and leaned towards us, both hands on his knees, his neck stretched out, his head aimed right at us—"I'm telling you now," he shouted, "those paddy wagons are not going to be removed! Is that clear? They are not going to be removed! And"—he sat back now, looking worn out—"I think you people would do yourselves a lot more good trying to get along out here instead of antagonizing."

Arthur got up and started out:

"It's the same old story . . ."

We followed Arthur. Kevin's voice surprised me, it was so soft, when he said over his shoulder:

"Can't nobody arrest us for walking . . . Can they, Captain?"

The captain jumped up. He looked absolutely scared:

"Walk? Walk? Why, why you can't do that! I'm responsible for your safety! This isn't the time to walk. Do you want to get yourselves killed? Walk? Why, you can't do that!"

But none of us answered him.

24

ALMOST TWO WEEKS passed without anything frantic happening. Oh, yeah, bombs went off—lots of them; and Arthur's bathroom windows were broken out—the last windows in his house. But, as Arthur said, it was just the same old story. I mean nothing unusual happened—like a snake being put in somebody's mail slot, or a fire being set in somebody's grating outside his window.

Then one evening a mysterious white man knocked on my door. Terry and Nadine and their kids were over, and we had been trying to figure out a way to set off a few bombs of our own. We had almost decided that the only way to get those bombs stopped was to get them blamed on *us,* when there was this white guy—tall, around fifty, wearing horn-rimmed glasses something like Arthur's wife Mona wore. He had on a blue Homburg with a dark-green double-breasted overcoat. That combination—a blue Homburg with a green coat! That was the first thing that made me suspicious of this cat; and the next thing was that great big smile on his big red face. He reached out to shake my hand and spoke in a voice so soft and cultured that it didn't match the way he looked at all.

"Mr. Martin? Mr. Louis Martin?"

Terry cleared his throat real loud. I knew he was laughing. I stiffened my own voice up and tried to sound real high class when I answered:

"That's right."

We were still standing in the doorway, and that January wind wasn't kidding. I said:

"Uh—come in. It's cold out there."

He was taller inside than he had looked outside. His shoulders were thick, and so was his neck, and when he took his hat off I saw that his hair, parted on one side, was that limp silky blonde hair you usually see on white actresses and models and all. He bowed slowly to Helen and to Terry's wife, Nadine, and said, still smiling:

"How do you do? I'm Hiram Melange—heh, heh—some monicker, eh?"

What a character! He then turned that grin off and stared at me, taking his coat off at the same time. I took his coat and hung it up in the closet, and Terry slid over on the couch to make room for him to sit down. He sat down between Terry and Helen—this Melange, or what ever his name was—and scooted his long lanky legs up and put his hands right on top of each knee, and started right in asking questions:

"Well, folks, how are things out here?"

Nobody answered. How do you tell a stranger how things are in Trumbull Park? So he asked another question—of me this time:

"Mr. Martin, you're the leader of these people out here—that is, the Nig-groes, right?"

He pronounced *Negroes* just like my foreman at work, half *nigger*, half *Negroes*. I was standing by the kitchen door. Terry looked at me when the guy said that, and gave me one of his famous sour looks. I answered carefully:

"Well, I wouldn't say that I'm any *leader* . . ."

I *started* to explain to him that our little group wasn't

actually any organization, or anything like that—it was just a bunch of us that decided to get together to figure out how to keep from getting killed or running crazy. But then, I asked myself all of a sudden, how did he know who I was? Who told him that I was the leader? And who told him that the Negroes had gotten together in the first place? I shut up right quick. Maybe, I decided, I ought to ask him a few questions.

"Uh, Mr. Mel——"

"Melange, Melange—as in *hodgepodge*. Heh, heh, heh! May-lahn-juh!"

Helen tried to cross her legs and then remembered that she couldn't because of her stomach and just flopped back on the couch instead, taking a loud breath. I said:

"Yeah . . . Well. Uh—what is it you want? I mean, who are you? Like where did you come from?"

He sat straight up and started fumbling in his inside coat pocket. He took out a thick leather wallet that was stuffed full of papers instead of money, and handed me a dirty, folded-up bunch of letters:

"Read those!" He leaned back on the couch—and relaxed.

One letter looked like it was from the Attorney General of the United States, and I don't remember all that letter did say, but I do remember that it was addressed to Mr. Melange and went something like this:

"*In response to your inquiry as to your political affiliations, this office is pleased to inform you that you are not a Communist.*"

The letter went on to tell Mr. Melange that his organization wasn't Communist either. I read through the rest of the letters, and most of them seemed to be saying the same thing. I thought, Here is a cat that's so twisted he don't know what he is—has to ask somebody else what he is, and then carry papers around with him so he can prove to other folks what he is—or isn't. Good Gordon's gin!

"Well, folks, I think that explains who I am—huh?"

No one else had read the letters, so Terry and Helen and Nadine looked at me. I said:

"Yes, I guess so."

"Well!" He started smiling again. "I've come to offer my services. There are certain forces in this town that would love to exploit your—ah—problem . . ." Then he got an idea: "Well, I suppose it's actually the white man's problem, isn't it? After all, Nig-roes certainly didn't *ask* to be brought here . . ."

No answer.

"Did they?"

There wasn't anything we could say. This cat looked to me like he had really flipped. Still no one answered. That was the longest pause I'd heard in a long time. Things got so quiet that there actually seemed to be noise in that quietness—like the quietness itself was deafening. Finally Terry lit into this guy:

"Well, Mr. Melange, the trouble out here may be the white man's problem, but I don't recall hearing about any snakes having been put through any white man's mail slot, or about any rocks breaking his windows, for that matter. Aren't you being a bit academic? When have you had to ride a patrol wagon to work?"

Mr. Melange was ready for that one. He grinned.

"I've ridden in plenty of patrol wagons in my day, young man."

But he wasn't ready for the next one.

"And when has your wife ridden a patrol wagon?"

I wondered if my face would get red all over if I were

279

white and somebody had said to me what Terry had just said to Mr. Melange? That man's face absolutely turned on!

But he was a game stud, and I was beginning to feel bad about the way we were doing him. After all, we hadn't even given him a chance to be friends with us. He came right back with a sad, worried look, saying in a whispery, heavy voice:

"Do you people have to ride in *patrol wagons?*"

Nadine mimicked his voice when she answered:

"Yes, we *do.*"

Helen just kept quiet. Melange said:

"Well, I think we can do something about that. You see, I know Captain Silo, and I think I might be able to swing a little weight with him."

Helen smiled at this. She asked:

"Do you really think you could?"

Melange opened his mouth into that wide smile again:

"Well, let's see . . . Today is Tuesday. Give me until Thursday, and I think I might have some good news for you."

He got up, and I got his coat. He shook my hand and Terry's and bowed again at Helen and Nadine.

"Good evening, all," he said. "I'll see you Thursday; and, remember, don't let these forces ruin the beauty of the magnificent courage you're showing out here!"

Terry said:

"What forces?"

He looked at Terry with all kinds of surprise on his face.

"Why the Commies, of course!" He felt for his bunch of letters, and when he saw that they were still there, he smiled and pulled on his heavy overcoat. "You can trust me, though. I'm all right. You know that." He turned to me:

"Don't you, Mr. Martin?"

I guessed he was talking about that bunch of letters he had shown me, so I played along with him:

"Yeah, yeah. Sure. Mr. Mel——"

"Melange, Melange as in hodge podge. Heh, heh!"

"Yeah. Sure. You're all right."

He left smiling, and we just sat there for a while looking at each other trying to figure out what in the hell it was all about.

25

THURSDAY took its own good time getting there, and when it came I was a little disappointed to see the patrol wagon still sitting outside just as big as you please, waiting to take me to work. That evening Helen and the kids and I took a little trip. Terry and Nadine had been over to see us a lot of times, but we had never been over to see them; and Terry and some of the other people were beginning to get a little salty about it. We decided that Thursday was as good as any other day. So we waited until it was dark and bundled up real good in that January cold and walked real fast, Helen holding Diane and me holding Louella, to Terry's house. Nadine let us in. I was surprised to see such a sharp house!

These people had taste! Everything was modern. They had those kind of lamps that went way off on an angle, and it looked to me like the cocktail tables did the same thing. The couch was a light-gray sectional job, and there was a great big comfortable-looking chair against the wall—away from the window—to match. Practically everything was away from the window. I sure didn't blame them, thinking about Arthur's bare jail-looking place. This was a pure-D mansion by comparison.

Terry was sitting in the big chair with his shoes off and

his stocking feet plopped as cool as you please on the pale blue carpet. He got up when he saw us.

"Well, well, well, so the mountain has come to Mohammed! Come in. Come in. I'm glad to see you."

I laughed:

"Don't call my wife no mountain!"

Terry frowned and explained:

"Wait a minute! I was talking about you, Buggy—not Helen."

"Oh, don't take everything so seriously, Terry!"

Squeezed-faced, the little dark man smiled at Nadine, not saying anything, and went back to his seat. He sat down like he was tired. I hadn't noticed it when we first came in. He looked at Nadine, and Nadine looked at him, like each of them was asking the other to *please* say *something*. Helen and I felt as if we'd broken in on a serious family talk. Finally, Terry spoke. There was a wobble in his deep voice, and there was fear there, too—I was beginning to know fear whenever I saw it and in whatever way it came.

"Buggy," Terry tried to smile, "I guess our white friend does have influence—eh?"

"What do you mean?"

"Didn't you know? The patrol wagons are off. Now we ride in nothing but squad cars. Carl called and told me just a few minutes ago. He gets in after the rest of us, you know. Works way out—you know?"

The first thing I wanted to do was smile. But the second thing I wanted to do was to run. Fear flickered inside me like the static on old Mrs. Palmer's radio back at the Gardener Building. All I could think of now was what Nadine had said about it being easier to throw bricks through the windows of a squad car than through the iron walls of a patrol wagon.

I looked at Helen, she looked as if she felt the same way

I did. I looked at Nadine, and she just had that disgusted look, as if she knew what we were all thinking and was saying I told you so. Terry looked sicker by the minute. I tried to perk things up:

"Well, isn't that what we all wanted? I'm glad."

Nadine's voice was hard and mean when she answered me:

"It isn't what *all* of us wanted—just our leaders, I think."

I looked to Terry to answer this. I'd gotten into the habit of counting on Terry to take up for me whenever somebody tried to criticize whatever we were doing. But I had forgotten one thing: Nadine was his wife. I had forgotten something else too, and Terry's face was reminding me of it every minute that I looked at him. Terry was scared to death!

Why should he be scared, I thought. After all, if he hadn't come over to my house that night telling me about Beverly having that baby in the patrol wagon, all this might never have happened. That's right, I thought, it's only what he had suggested in the first place. In fact, wasn't he the one who brought it up at the meeting? Didn't he go to see the captain with the rest of us? Sure he did. Then why the hell is he so upset now?

Terry must have known what I was thinking. Maybe I was looking at him real funny or something, because he started to explain:

"You know," he started off real casual, "I'm a great one for painting myself into corners . . ."

There he went again with that kind of talk that sounds like those real weird paintings look down at the Art Institute: you know they're saying something—but what? I waited for him to explain himself. I had also gotten into that habit with Terry.

284

"Buggy"—he smiled at Helen—"and you too, Helen . . . I think I've had it."

Nadine said:

"I've long since had it."

Terry cut his eyes at Nadine and went on, that deep, deep frown beginning to find its way into his face again:

"I mean it, Buggy. You may not have noticed it." He smiled. "But then again you may have. My nervousness, I mean. I'm as fidgety as a—I don't know what. And what's more——"

I broke in:

"But Terry——"

He raised his great big growly voice and sort of cut the air with the side of his right hand, and I shut up. He went on:

"I'm not the heroic type, Buggy—that's all there is to it."

Hadn't Nadine told Helen that very same thing? Helen had said that she had.

"But Terry," I said. "Didn't you——"

He cut me off again:

"Yes, I suggested it. Oh, man, don't you get it? I'm the idea man—the brains! I'm—I'm—I'm no good for anything else!"

All the time Nadine sat quiet, looking straight at Terry, not smiling, not frowning, just looking, just looking.

"Buggy," this little dark man said, "I don't think I can explain myself to you. I don't even know whether or not I should try to. I know what you're trying to do out here. I know what we're all trying to do; but I'm scared; Buggy—pure and simple, there it is. I'm scared. Maybe it's because I'm a little man—I don't know. Maybe it's a lot of things. But everytime I hear a bomb go off do you know what happens to me? . . . I have to go to the toilet."

He turned to Helen.

"I'm sorry, Helen, really I am, to have to put it that way, but there is no other way that it can be put. I have to go to the toilet every single time I hear a bomb."

Nadine began to look like she was going to cry. I didn't know whether it was because she was ashamed of her husband or because she felt that way herself. I started to say something again. I started to tell Terry how I felt when the bombs went off; I started to tell him how I felt when I was chased home and ran halfway up the steps into my pregnant wife's arms. But as I got the words together and took that one long breath you need for telling such things, Nadine started talking:

"Buggy, we're not going to be in on all the things that you and the rest of them are doing out here. It's futile. And worse than that, it's about to drive Terry and me out of our minds. I——"

I had to break in then:

" 'Things'? 'Things'? What 'things'? You know what we're doing out here! Trying to stay alive—that's all. Anyhow, don't lay it all on me! We all started this stuff. You came to meetings just like everybody else. I didn't start this. I was just elected president. And another thing—I'm as nervous and upset as anybody else! What started all this anyway? Me? Did I do something? Huh? Tell me if I did? I'm not perfect."

"Oh, no, Buggy," Terry broke in, "it's not that at all. I don't think you get it. I don't think you even know what we're getting at. You haven't suffered enough yet. You're still fresh, and full of fire."

He paused, and no one could fill in the blank space he'd left.

"Of course, you couldn't see what we're talking about, Buggy! And I hope to God that you never feel the way I do. Because if you do—then it will be because you are as—as—as goofed as I am! Forget it, Buggy. Nadine and I are just talking crazy. Forget it."

He smiled, but that frown between his eyes didn't budge. I looked at Helen. She had water in her eyes. She knew how Terry and Nadine felt. I knew too, but I think Helen *really* knew. She got up, and said to me something she never does:

"Let's go home, Buggy."

Nadine went to the door right away and opened it. Terry didn't even look at us. I said:

"Well, I guess we'll be going."

I was so confused that I had absolutely forgotten our kids were with us. They had been so quiet—or maybe they hadn't been—anyway, things had happened so fast that I felt now as though I'd been asleep and was just waking up to find my kids standing by me patiently waiting for me to get myself together. I grabbed Louella's hand, and Diane grabbed Helen's.

That night not a single bomb went off. And I lay awake all night listening to the trains banging against each other in the train yard, and waited for a bomb *to* go off—just one—so that I could go to sleep.

26

LIKE THAT song goes, "It was early one morning, and I was on my way to school." Except I was on my way to work. The first days of nervousness from riding in the squad car past those people along Bensley had settled down into a sort of permanent nervousness that ran all night and all day just like a Frigidaire—a low humming everlasting nervousness that I'd gotten used to, that didn't scare me much any more even though it made me sit straight up in bed at night, cold as I could be and sweating to beat the band.

Now I sat in the corner of the squad car leaning way back in the seat, telling myself that I sat that way because I liked to sit that way, and not because I was scared that one of those red faces steaming in that late January ice-wind would follow up the spit it spat at me with a brick. The squad car cruised slowly, often driving close to the curb where the South Deering people stood, the men huddled up in faded plaid mackinaws and leather jackets, and the women in stubby-collared cloth coats that looked worn at the elbows and cuffs even from where I sat.

"Nigger, nigger! Nigger's got a new taxicab!"

And the harsh icy laugh would follow, and someone else would take up the cry:

"We'd better not catch you walking, black boy!"

And freezing-steamy voices would raise up out of that shivering, foot-stomping, hand-rubbing crowd:

"*Black boy, black boy! Nigger, nigger, nigger!*"

And the cops in the car would smile and glance at me through the rear-view mirror, and I would look as mad as I could at them and then at the crowd and then at the cops again, and notice only after the car had pulled into the driveway at 107th and Bensley how tightly I'd been gripping the seats.

Yes, riding that squad car was something! Terry and Nadine knew what they were talking about when they said that the glass windows of the squad cars offered you a hell of a lot less protection than the iron walls of a patrol car.

And do you know something else? Since we were in the squad cars now, instead of the patrol wagons, I didn't appreciate it worth a damn. Now it seemed to me that getting rid of the squad cars was what I had really wanted in the first place and that actually nothing had changed—that I was still the same crook that well-dressed Negro lady had warned her little boy about when she saw me slipping out of the patrol wagon one day down on Cottage Grove.

It was getting dark when I sat down to dinner. Helen was toddling around in that kitchen like every step she took strained every muscle she had. Louella was sitting at the table not eating—her first two fingers stuck in her mouth, sucking away.

"Why don't you eat, Louella?"

She said I don't-know-what with words; but that kind of *umm-ou-ummm* noise came out of her mouth—you know what I mean?

Diane was going to town on her dinner. I tell you, that Diane wouldn't care if the wind blew the room off over her head. I could still remember her, whenever I thought about it, telling Helen:

"Momma, Ba'doll fall. Go boom!"

Helen wasn't herself. But then who was? I sat down at the table, and when she passed by me, I grabbed her hand:

"What's the matter, Mommy?"

Helen pulled her kitchen-wet hand away and headed toward the sink:

"Oh, nothing . . . There's been a lot of activity today."

"Like what?"

She wiped her hands on the dish towel and looked at Louella and shook her head and pressed her lips together and smiled a sort of grim smile:

"Well, let's see . . . Beverly and her baby are home, and . . ."

"What is it—boy or girl?"

"Girl."

"Whew! I've been worried for days, wondering what that little thing was!"

She laughed, but it wasn't *her* laugh.

"And a lot of bombs have been going off today . . ."

"I didn't hear any when I came in."

Talk about a fierce look! The one she gave me! Man!

"Buggy, do you think that I'm lying about the bombs?"

"Lying? No, I don't think you're lying. I just said that I didn't hear any when I came in, and I usually do."

"Well, that's just saying the same thing. I can't help it if you didn't hear any. After all, you've been at work all day, and I've been here all day, doing nothing but listening to them . . . Just look at these kids!"

Louella's sucking got louder. I didn't want to look at her. It did something to me to see my baby suffer. I tried to get out of looking by saying something else that would make Helen forget she had told me to look:

"Well, what are you getting all on your you-know-what about?"

She said it slow and even and very, very distinct this time:

"Look—at—those—kids!"

It actually hurt my neck to turn my head toward those children and look at them the way Helen had told me to. But I did. Diane was eating with her hand and her spoon, but there was something frantic about the way she was eating. I mean, her head was pushed down in that plate like food was going out of style. I didn't want to ask Helen what I asked her next, but it was all I could think of:

"Well—did you feed her today?"

She smiled so bitterly that she didn't even look like my Helen:

"Yes—I—did."

"You mean she's eating like that because she's nervous?"

"Buggy, when she's not eating she's pulling at her braids—taking them down . . ."

Helen got up and walked around to the back of Diane's chair. Diane didn't pay us any more attention than she would have if we hadn't been there at all. Helen lifted a stubby raggedy-looking little braid at the back of Diane's head and turned to me. Did I see water in her eyes? No, I told myself, I don't see water in her eyes.

"Look at this braid, Buggy. Has it ever looked like that to you before?"

I shook my head. Then she went over to Louella. My brown-skinned little stubby-nosed baby looked up underneath her eyelids, still sucking those two front fingers. She hadn't even *started* to eat that food.

Something in me started yelling at that child:

"Eat your food! *Eat* it!"

I stepped back—scared of my own voice. How did that get out? Helen didn't even look at me. Neither did Diane. Louella kept sucking her fingers, looking at me with that real baleful look. Helen went back to her seat. She sat down:

"Another family moved in today."

I wasn't hungry now. I sat down in front of my food, but not at an eating angle.

"Yeah? Have you seen them?"

"No, but Carl's wife Ernestine has. She's the one who told me. She also said that there's something in today's *Defender* about Arthur."

"What did it say?"

"Something about some kind of committee recommending that Arthur and his family be put out of the project because they're some kind of symbol—oh, it was foolishness-like! I don't remember what all it did say."

"Boy, that *Defender* don't know whether it's coming or going!"

"Wait, I didn't say the *Defender* said that Arthur should be put out. In fact, they had an editorial saying that Arthur *shouldn't* be put out, not *should*."

"Ohhh, I see. Well, now, that's more like it. I didn't think the *Defender* would say a thing like put the man out."

"Buggy." Uh-oh! There it was. There was that big decision kind of sound in her voice. "Buggy! What are we going to do about the kids? I mean us—well, we're supposed to be able to take it—and I can take my medicine as well as any woman. But the kids, Buggy. Honey, I—I—I'm worried. I can see how Terry and Nadine felt."

"I'm going over to Kevin's to see the baby. Do you want to go?"

"I guess that's as good an answer as any."

292

"I don't know, Honey. I just don't know what to say. What should I say? Should I say, Move? Move where?"

She smiled at me. I was *so* glad.

"Why don't you eat?"

Louella, remembering I had gotten after her for not eating, stopped sucking her fingers long enough to see what I would do now. I hadn't intended to look right into her eyes when I looked at her, but I did; and she held me there with her eyes—her sad, sad eyes. I felt guilty. What was I doing to this baby?

"Okay, Louella," I sure sounded cheap! *"I'll* eat if *you* will. What do you say—huh?"

She smiled as if she felt sorry for me. I looked away from her and imagined I had heard her say okay, because the next thing I said was:

"That's fine."

And I scooted up to my food and started eating it. It was cold now, and the grease from the lamb chops had gotten gooey, and the green peas and mashed potatoes had gotten hard—old-looking already. Or was that just the way I felt? But I ate. I ate and ate and ate, and I didn't look up from my plate. I didn't want to see anything but that harmless, unmoving, lifeless plate in front of me. I looked up just once: at Diane—two-year-old—well, two-and-a-half now—Diane. She was looking down at her plate eating and eating and eating. I put my fork down and got up from the table. That diesel was after me, the diesel train from the Gardener Building, but now in Trumbull Park. I had to run. Damn everything! I had to run!

"I'm going to Kevin's house."

Helen didn't answer me. She got up and walked over to Diane and took the spoon from that baby's tiny hand. Diane looked up at her. Surprised—hurt. Helen picked

Diane up and lifted her up over the other baby that lay—still safe—in her stomach. She held Diane high in her arms, the way Ernestine had held her baby high the night she and the rest of the Negroes of Trumbull Park walked past the cops without signing the book.

Helen went into the living room, but I went outside. I had to. I couldn't stand it.

27

HOW YOU DOING?"

That Kevin was so cool it was a shame. Here it was the first time that I had been over to his house, and he says just like I live there:

"How you doing?"

"Hey, man. Let's see that little trouble maker."

He took my coat and hung it in the closet. His house was really different from Terry's and mine—and Arthur's, for that matter. There was a radio-television combination in the living room and a linoleum that looked like varnished wood on the black-tiled floor. Helen and I hadn't even gotten a rug yet. His couch was one of the let-out kind. It had flowered slip covers that were repeated on a rather uncomfortable-looking chair in the corner. I noticed that the nice space near the window was vacant.

Kevin's hair was carefully combed and brushed as usual, and he wore a heavy wool maroon bathrobe, with maroon house shoes to match.

"Wait here a minute. I'll go upstairs and see if Beverly's decent."

There wasn't the least bit of excitement about this cat, no kind of way. He came down right away:

"Okay. Come on up."

Beverly was in the bed. The furniture up here was heavy—not modern, but polished and pretty. There was a thick inexpensive-looking rug on the floor, and all kinds of do-dads—perfume bottles, face-cream jars, mirrors, and all —sat on the wide dressing table in the corner across from the bed, away from the window.

Boom!

That bomb seemed profane. *Boom! Boom!* Lightning flashes flicked the white wicker basinet beside Beverly's bed like whip-tips. The baby, red as it could be and with a whole head full of hair, whined softly and then cooed. I tiptoed over to get a better look.

Beverly said:

"Isn't she cute?"

I whispered—I don't know why I always whisper when I'm around little-*bitty* babies:

"Yeah, she sure is."

The baby poked its fingers into its poochy wet mouth and started sucking. I got scared to death. Wasn't there any place to run to? She was doing exactly the same thing that Louella had done—the same thing that chased me out of my own house over here. I looked away from the baby to Beverly.

"I hope that ride wasn't *too* bad, Beverly."

"You mean when I went to the hospital?"

"Yes. I've been worrying about Helen ever since I first heard about what happened to you. I mean, suppose she couldn't wait until she got there? She'd—she'd——"

Beverly, long and lanky just like her husband, smiled and finished my sentence for me:

"She'd have it."

Her hair was thick and yet fine. It had that fluffy-light look about it as it crowded around her face there on the pillow. A pale light from the wall socket softened the flat yellow of her skin and brought out the freckles and the Boston tanness of her eyes. For the first time I saw that Beverly was really pretty. I couldn't imagine her lying on that ledge in the patrol wagon. I couldn't imagine Terry pulling her panties off. She did nothing to make me feel the way I was beginning to feel, but all of a sudden I wanted to go home to my wife, to hold her tight against me. I didn't know what we'd do with the baby, meanwhile! Kevin had been watching me closely; but when I looked at him, he had no expression at all that would have let me know that he didn't go for the way I looked at his wife. Instead there was the warmest, friendliest look I had ever seen on that guy's face. He looked as if he knew how I felt and was feeling sorry for me.

Beverly said:

"Well, Ernestine Burton is next, Buggy. When is Helen expecting?"

Why did I get embarrassed when she asked me that? I knew that Helen had three long months to go. She always looked big before time. That's what made it so hard. She looked like she would have the baby any day, but she went for months looking like that. I didn't know what to say to Beverly. I stuttered:

"Well, I think she's got about a couple of months."

A couple of months didn't sound as long as three months. Beverly looked at Kevin standing beside me and smiled. Then she said:

"You tell her she'd better hurry up! Even Ernestine is going to beat her. I think Ernestine is going any day now."

That just goes to show you how much attention people paid to each other. I hadn't noticed Beverly, and she went. And now Ernestine was going to have a baby any day, and I hadn't had the slightest idea before now.

Kevin and I went downstairs, and another bomb went off just as we hit the bottom step. His little girl had come down from her bedroom and was sitting at the far end of the couch, pouting.

"Man," Kevin sounded worried, "that one there." He nodded at his little girl.

"She thinks the world is coming to an end every time one of those things goes off."

What was this? Was everybody cracking? How could we expect to hold out if we—or our children—were all going to go nuts?

Kevin explained:

"Me—I don't care. They don't bother me. I think that those people are ignorant for setting them off in the first place. Don't they know that white people can hear the same as we can? Hell, I can stand a loud noise as well as any man."

Then he nodded his head at his angry little light-skinned girl sitting at the other end of the couch.

"But, man," he said, "that one there!"

28

SOMETHING WAS GOING ON! We were all dying
without knowing it. On again, off again. Sudden plans: the
sign-in books, visiting the captain. Sudden mess-ups: the
bombs, the squad cars, the mobs outside the door. Mys-
teries: Mr. Melange, the non-Communist, Mr. O'Leary's
idea about the Cal-Sag Seaway—those two scared me to
death. Big Boys, Big Plans, Big Mobs, Big Deals—whew!
Just for not wanting to live in the Gardener Building.

What to do, what to do? Shooting them sure didn't help.
Look at Arthur. Trying to shoot them sure didn't help
either. Look at Carl. He looked the same, acted the same,
talked the same, but he was not the same Carl who had
started across the street after that loud-mouth white cat
on 106th and Bensley—not after that trial, not after they
made him feel, made all of us feel, like our big move, our
willingness to fight and die on the street that day, was nothing. A nothing not worth taking up the time of the court
with, not worth a damn. And so they'd let us go: me and
Terry at the very beginning, and Carl and Kevin after
they'd got them into court. A slap on the booty and a don't-
do-that-no-more-children and—and—nothing. Kevin never
looked me in the eye after that day, and I never looked

Carl in the eye, and Terry—well, Terry had never looked anybody in the eye no way. Yet Terry knew one thing: Terry knew himself, and he didn't lie about himself, to himself. Awwww, man! Damned if you do take the crap, and damned if you don't! I sat at my machine thinking, watching the metal casting open up little holes beneath the spinning silver tongues that sank into them, and I thought and thought and thought.

We were dying, dying on the vine, and only Mr. O'Leary seemed to offer a way out. His pointing out the gray-flannel boys behind, in, with, on top of, and underneath all this three-six-nine, gave me my only something to work on. And the machines went and the going-home whistle went, and I went, but I was working on Mr. O'Leary's Boys. I had to—there wasn't any other way. January left, and February started its lonely way, and Carl stayed out of everybody's sight, and the bombs did their natural numbers, and I thought and thought, but nothing came out—not a damn thing. So I decided to call a meeting.

We all got together at Carl's the next night. Helen and I brought Diane and Louella. Beverly Robinson was out of the house for the first time since having her baby; and Kevin—long, tall, proud cat—held the baby, wrapped in a pink blanket with a white stripe along the edges, just like it was the first one his wife had ever had, instead of the third. Norman and Armela Douglas, the new family, were there. Norman wasn't too tall—about my height, but real wide and strong-looking. His voice was kind of high, but it was rough-sounding. He smiled and laughed a lot, but I wasn't surprised when Arthur told me that Norman had just gotten out of the Veterans hospital from fighting in the Korean War, and that this cat had a top drawer full of medals and certificates and things from all the hell he raised overseas.

Norman's wife, Armela, was very young. She looked to be no more than seventeen or so. I found out later that neither Norman nor his wife had been in Chicago any longer than a couple of years, that they had come from Little Rock, Arkansas, after the Army sent Norman from overseas to Hines Veteran's Hospital to get that shrapnel out of his chest—they never did get it all out. Armela, like I said, was very young: she wore bobby socks and a sloppy-Joe sweater, and she had great big dreamy eyes, and full, natural red lips—and she was pregnant.

Looking at her and thinking about my own wife, and remembering Beverly and Mona made me feel sort of guilty. I mean, you hear people talking about Negroes having a lot of babies, and not having control, and all that, and here we were—almost all of us fathers and mothers, or at least fathers and mothers to be. Poor wives. Poor colored wives. After the white folks got through calling us out of our names, and pushing us up in Gardener Buildings and all; after we get through watching our folks fall, or at least stagger, from seeing each and every day bring nothing but the same old jolly rag—bad jobs for most of us, "bad luck, and troubles," like this blues singer, Joe Williams, says; after, we, man and wife, both feel sometimes like packing our bags and running away, only to find that there's no place to run—then we husbands got to add just one more straw to our women's back. Babies. You ever do any thinking like that? I mean about why? Love? I guess so, but that love gets awful thin at about two o'clock in the morning when the baby starts to crying, and you lay in bed waiting for "the baby's mother" to get up and "see about it," and she's laying up there waiting for you to do the same thing. And finally *she* gets up. Love gets awfully thin, awfully thin at times like those. But anyway, there we were with our babies: Arthur and Mona, and Terry and Nadine, and Christine and William Thomas, Norman and Armela Douglas, me and Helen.

We were there on a Saturday night. Everything down on 63rd was just about getting ready to start jumping. Everything out here was getting ready to start jumping too. But we were there in Carl Burton's house to see what we could do to back Arthur up in his troubles. The children were squealing and giggling and running all over the house. The women right away bunched themselves together in a corner of the room, and started talking about stitches, breast feeding, contraception, miscarriages, camphorated oil "to dry you up," and goodness knows what else. But they all seemed so glad to see each other, to see somebody else out in Trumbull Park in the same fix as they were—bombs, babies and all—that they couldn't stop talking. And so they talked and giggled and laughed hard and rough sometimes, and their laughing mixed up with the kids' noise. And we men gathered together on the other side of the room, talking low and dignified: women were present.

After Carl let the first bunch of us in, he disappeared. I didn't know that he had been out of sight for so long until I heard one of the women mention Ernestine's name, and the women grew quieter and quieter as Mona said something to them in a low voice. They grew even quieter when Mona began to tell them something in that low voice, and one by one the women got the funniest, far-off, sad-scared, tormented look on their faces, and one of them—Beverly Robinson—started crying, and another one of them put her finger to her lips and said, "shhh!" and Beverly stopped and bit her lips and smiled a hard-to-make polite smile when Arthur looked up from the little circle we were in and hollered across the room:

"Hey, what're you young girls whispering about over there?"

302

Mona joked back:

"Oh, you men just mind your own business! We're talking woman-talk."

Kevin, who was sitting on a kitchen chair, right across from me, stood up. He looked like a flagpole:

"Hey, where's Carl? . . . Hey, Carl!"

Arthur, sitting right next to where Kevin had sat, got up too:

"Maybe he's upstairs in the bedroom . . . Hey, Carl!"

Arthur started walking toward the stairway that led to the upstairs bedrooms. Carl met him at the foot of the stairs. He didn't have his usual smile. He looked like something was hurting him, like he was getting ready to cry. When he came into the room, he still didn't smile. He just spoke to all of us and sat down on the arm of the couch where the women were. I looked at him, curious, remembering how the women were talking about Ernestine, and how they looked as Mona told them *something*. I then looked at Arthur, and I could tell from his face that he knew whatever it was that was bothering Carl.

Terry and William Thomas sat with their backs to the wall near the side window. They were still talking in low and whispered voices. Both looked worried, both looked like they had a secret. Doggone it, I thought, things change so often and so fast out here, that you don't know from one minute to the next what is on anybody's mind. Just a minute ago, everybody was laughing and giggling and at least acting like they were in good humor, and now everybody is sullen and whispering, and Carl is sitting around looking like they had just lynched every Negro in the South, just like my father used to say my mother used to look.

Well, I thought, if I'm the leader, there's no better time to start. Take the mule by the tail. So I did:

"What's the matter, Carl? Something wrong?"

Mona got the funniest look when I asked Carl that. I

looked at Arthur, and he looked away. **Carl** didn't open his mouth. Even the kids got quiet, and one by one each kid found its way to its mother or father. Carl looked like an old man, with his round head, his hair cut close, his heavy moustache, his thick neck, and his fat chin, dark with a new beard. Even his eyes looked old, sad, and hurt. His great big hands grabbed each other and made fists, and then he made a fist with one hand while the other hand gripped that fist, before opening up to be hit by that fist—hard. Then he opened out and spread all his fingers and clamped them in amongst each other like a man getting ready to pray. He stretched his legs out stiffly in front of him as we all watched him. It was plain he was getting ready for something, and we all watched and waited for him to get ready. It came to me just as he opened his mouth to tell us what had happened, and I blurted out:

"Where's Ernestine?"

Carl's nose was wide at the nostrils, and those nostrils flared wider, and his mouth opened almost as if he couldn't help himself, and he took a long breath through his open mouth. I thought I heard a tremor in that breath. When he let the air out he said, not to me, but to all of us:

"Well, you-all—I guess this is it. I'm moving out. I mean to say me and Ernestine and the kids—we're moving out of Trumbull Park."

As big and strong—inside, I mean—as Carl was, I had never thought of his sitting there in front of all of us and saying *he* was moving out. I didn't feel anything when he said it, because I didn't believe I was hearing Carl Burton say it—not the guy who had risked going to jail to step in and help his friend hide a gun that he had used to protect himself with. I didn't believe Carl, but I listened. He went on:

"I don't know how many of you here believe in God. But I do."

There was such deep-set fire in those waterless crying eyes, that I felt a tug of something inside I had never felt in church—at least not for a long time. He even began to sound like a preacher as he talked:

"Last night I had to pray to God, to keep from killing a bunch of people out here—policemen and all. I mean it, you-all." That "you-all" was thick and warm and real Southern. "Ernestine had the baby last night." He looked like a bashful little boy when he turned to the ladies, with a sad quick smile, and apologized: "I hope I'm not embarrassing you ladies."

Christine Thomas' raw voice piped up:

"Oh, no—we all been through the same thing you know."

"Well," Carl went on, "like I was saying, a man can only take so much, and after last night I know that if I stay out here much longer, I'm going to kill somebody, and that'll mean going to jail and leaving my wife and these children here to look out for themselves. It happened right after I got home. I thought Ernestine looked kind of funny when I first walked in, and sure enough, it wasn't half an hour before she told me that her stomach was hurting her. I remember I asked her: 'Are you sure?' But believe me, she was sure, all right."

He stopped talking and stared at the front door, and I felt that he was going back in his mind to whatever it was that had happened last night, because his eyes got real watery, and he pressed his lips together and looked so mad that I thought he might get up and start hitting the door with his bare fists or something. For the first time since I'd known Carl, he cursed. I noticed, because I had never heard those words spoken in his voice the way he said them then:

"Those ornery son-of-a-bitches!"

He said it slow, and quiet, and with so much feeling that

the words meant something foul, dirty, and rotten to me that they had never meant before. He went on with his story:

"Well, after Ernestine kept complaining that way, I called Headquarters Nine for a squad car to take her to Provident. Well, this policeman, I don't know who on earth he was, said in a real nasty voice: 'We can't send a squad car all the way to Provident Hospital. You have to call the Ninth District.' So I called the Ninth District: 'Whatta yuh call here for? We don't handle that Trumbull Park detail. Call Headquarters Nine—they're the only ones can help you.' By this time Ernestine was really in labor. I mean she was in agony. Poor thing couldn't sit down and she couldn't stand up. Crying, the kids crying, and getting in the way, and right about that time I hear people outside the door, right out there where that grating is, and I know it's these people out here up to some more foolishness, but I'm so excited about Ernestine and I'm so mad about those cops giving me the run-around I can't pay them too much attention.

"So I don't know what to do. I run and hold Ernestine awhile when the pains start to hitting her hard and then I run to the telephone and try to get a squad car. I call Headquarters Nine again: 'Listen, fella, there's nothin' we can do. We're out here to protect you people. We can't send cars all over town for yuh! There's nothing we can do.' I told that guy: 'Listen you! If you don't send somebody over here after my wife I'm coming over there shooting! I'm not going to sit here and watch my wife suffer like this! This woman is in pain, Mister, don't you have any pity or nothing in your heart?'——'There's nothin' I can do. Why don't you call a taxi?'——'What damn taxi is going to come out here to take a Negro any place! There's a crowd of people out here right now—right in front of my door!' And right then . . ."

Carl turned to us:

"Those people started that same kind of hollering they do in front of Arthur's house. I figured somebody must have told them that this was the first place Arthur ran to after he shot at those peckerwoods. I don't know what it was, but I swear I started praying to the Lord to keep me out of trouble. I prayed that He'd keep me from getting my gun and shooting those silly peckerwoods. I called back and forth and back and forth, Headquarters Nine, Ninth District, Headquarters Nine, Ninth District; and all the time Ernestine was twisting and turning and crying, and those hunkies were outside my window hollering, and acting the fool, and . . . and . . ."

He lost his voice and just sat there swallowing hard and beating the palm of his hand with his fist. Finally he got himself together:

"This went on from seven to nine o'clock. My wife suffered right on that couch there, rolling and turning. Her water broke, and I had to run around looking for a towel for her, and the kids were crying, and the floor was wet, and the cops still saying: 'Call Headquarters Nine . . . Call Ninth District . . . Call Headquarters Nine . . . Call Ninth District!'

"Every time I called Headquarters Nine they'd tell me: 'Look, Burton, I told you there's nothing we can do.'——'Well, let me talk to the captain then. I want *him* to tell me that there's nothing you can do!'——'The captain's not in.'——'All right, let me talk to the lieutenant then. Let me talk to him!'——'Lieutenant's not here either. Look, did you call Ninth District?'——'Hell, yes, I called Ninth District! And every time I do, they tell me to call you, and you say call them. Do you-all want my wife to die?'——'Look, Burton, I tol' you a thousand times. There's nothing I can do! And the captain and the lieutenant ain't here. Call Ninth District.'

" 'Hello, Ninth District, this is Carl Burton. I don't know what to do! My wife is going to have this baby right here on the floor! There's a mob outside my door! Headquarters Nine won't help me! They won't send a squad car, and they got squad cars all over the place! They keep telling me to call Ninth District. What am I supposed to do? I can't get a cab! I don't have anybody to come out here and take my wife to Provident Hospital! I'm going to get my gun and go out there and start shooting those people in a minute if something don't happen quick! I——'
'All right! All right! Just hold it a minute. We'll send somebody out. Just don't get excited. You don't want to get in trouble, do yuh?' "

Carl's voice preached the gospel of misery like I had never heard it preached before. I wanted to cry, but I had cried so much lately I guess there just weren't any tears left. Still, I felt that swelling rise in my throat; it had come so often that it seemed like some old friend, something so familiar and painful that I wouldn't know how bad it hurt until it finally went away. But I was mad at Carl too—praying to the Lord to keep from shooting those white people outside his door, screaming and raising sand while his wife was in agony inside. It seemed to me a godlessness like nothing else in the world could ever be.

Nadine and Beverly were crying openly, with all kinds of sniffling noises. Their kids were snuggled up against them, looking worried at their mothers and looking mad at Carl for saying they didn't know what—whatever it was that was making their mothers cry. Mona and Helen and Christine and the new girl, Armela, just sat staring in front of themselves—bottom lips jammed hard against top lips, tiny hands clamped tight together or nervously picking at long-ago pulled hangnails.

The men looked even more stunned and stepped-on than the women; and it made me mad to see such despair. Yes,

I guess that's what I saw—despair, sitting like a big fat man on top of all these people. I pulled myself away from them in my mind. I pulled and pulled until I was far enough away from them to be angry at them for feeling only sadness and not boiling, scalding anger. But maybe they did. I only knew that after I swallowed the tears that gripped my throat, I felt anger, anger, anger—anger, anger, anger!

Carl preached on; and we, his disciples, listened with bowed or too stiffly-straight heads:

"Finally, after an hour, the police came. It was snowing out there. And as you all know, the lights in the project were out. And these five police came stomping in the house, talking loud and rubbing their hands: 'Okay, Mr. Burton, you ready to go?' Those people outside started yelling then, for real. *'Get out, nigger! Get out, nigger! We want the nigger!'* And I said: 'Well, what are you going to do about those people out there outside my door? I'm telling you if they hurt my wife——' 'Awww, don't worry 'bout that! We're just here to take your wife to the hospital.'—— *'Nigger! Get out! Nigger! Get out!'*——'Why don't you men go out and chase those people away? Can't you all see what condition my wife is in?' And poor Ernestine was moaning and calling me all the time.

"Finally, one of the cops went outside and started *pleading* with those ornery peckerwoods—*pleading*, you hear me? *Pleading* with them! I put a coat on Ernestine, and the kids were running around hollering, and I had to tell my biggest boy—he's six, you know—to watch the other four. Poor thing . . ."

The boy, a little model of his daddy, with a blue-denim unironed shirt and creased short pants, moved bashfully toward his father, and Carl reached out and pulled the boy to him and rubbed his head without looking at him:

"He was a real little man last night."

But then that fire swelled up in his face all over again, as if the thought of his son's courage was painful to him, as if the very idea that his son needed to have courage so early in life hurt him; and the hurt twisted his wide hard chin and quivered his hard-pressed bottom lip.

"They carried her out on a stretcher. The white people stood in front of the patrol wagon and wouldn't let them put her in. I prayed to the Lord to keep me from killing them. The policemen pleaded with the people to let them put Ernestine in the wagon. She was hurting; she had been crying in the house, but she wouldn't cry out there. Not in front of those white people. But she was in agony—Lord knows she was. I prayed, 'Lord, keep me from killing one of these people!' And the cops said: 'All right, people. Come on, the lady's having a baby. Now, come on, let us through! Don't be that way! You wouldn't want anybody to do this to you, would you?' The snow was falling on her face, and the kids were out there with no coats on, and these people were calling us names—calling her names while she lay there flat on her back. And the policemen *pleaded* with the mob to let her get in the patrol wagon. Well . . ."

He looked as if he was happy to be almost through telling us about it:

"She had the baby at Provident all right, and it's a boy, and it's all right, and she's all right. So thank the Lord for that."

And after that not a one of us said a thing for a long, long time.

29

ARTHUR, as you might know, was the first to speak. He spoke quietly, still in the mood that Carl had set with his low, solemn voice:

"Why," he asked, "why didn't you shoot the hell out of them? Cops and all?"

Kevin was *really* bitter when he answered Arthur:

"Shee-it! You heard him say he was praying!"

But Terry was working on an angle of his own, and he made his move:

"I don't think it was like that." His deep voice just automatically attracted attention. "I think we all understand what the situation is out here."

Terry shifted his little frame in the kitchen chair, and that deep, deep frown creased his skin like crayon marks, and he dropped his head and stared at the sharp edges of his cuffs as he talked—working, working, working on something:

"I think this proves as conclusively as possible the dilemma in which we find ourselves. Arthur shot at some people. If he had been white in a Negro neighborhood, and shot at five Negroes who had surrounded him, he would not have been arrested, but more than likely awarded a medal for heroism. Buggy and Carl and Kevin and I go out to stand up for ourselves and they warn us not to do it again. Out here we are faced with this kind of problem: if we shoot or defend ourselves in the only way that even tends toward a successful defense—that is, with weapons—we will most assuredly end up in jail——"

Arthur cut him off:

"Go to jail then, damn it!"

But Terry's little face was as cool and stony as a frowning Abraham Lincoln statue in a downtown park. He overruled Arthur, and there was a knife in his growling rolling voice:

"Yes, that's easy to say . . ."

Arthur snapped:

"*I* did it. *I* shot at them somitches, and *I* went to jail, and if I go to jail to stay when my trial comes up, I'll still be glad I did it!" He mumbled something about "cowards."

Terry was in the saddle, though, and he wasn't about to get off. He was working, working, working:

"Why should we make our families suffer any more than they have? Who's going to feed them while we're in jail? Who's going to buy their clothes and pay for a roof over their heads? The NAACP? I doubt it. The Negroes we think we're fighting for?"

He looked straight at me when he said that and went on:

"Oh, yes, I know it hasn't been said; but some of us think we're in a great crusade! Some of us think that this is a great game which we are sure to win because right always wins, but"—and he looked at Carl—"does right always win?"

Carl looked hard at the door out of which they had taken his wife last night, while Terry went on:

"Heroism is vanity. Most of us came here not to

fight the great fight for racial equality, but because we needed a decent place to live. Well, I think we now realize that this isn't a decent place to live. In fact"—and he looked at Carl again—"Trumbull Park is one of the most *indecent* places that a Negro could possibly find to live!"

Kevin was getting mad. He snapped:

"All right! All right! What are you getting at?"

Terry raised his hand to shut Kevin up; and Kevin shut up. What did Terry have on big bad Kevin that could shut him up the way he always did?

"As I was saying, we are in a dilemma. If we fight, we go to jail. If we don't fight, we suffer, our windows are broken, our women cursed, our evenings blasted by those endless bombs. Then where are we? What should we do? Sit here and slowly go mad? Or go mad quickly and hurt somebody out here, and go to jail or maybe even be killed by some law-enforcing policeman?"

Now it was out in the open. Almost. Terry had talked about moving the last time I was at his house, but I didn't fully get it then. Now he was seeing a real chance to get out. He was, for all his deep voice and serious frown, a pretty scary cat. He would never risk having one of us say that he turned chicken, simply by telling everybody that he was going and then cutting out. No, he wasn't that kind of guy. He was this kind of guy, the kind he was being right now. He would go, but in a crowd—make all of us decide to go. There weren't too many to convince—only six families, only twelve grown-ups. Then he could go. But where? Back to where he came from? Where would Helen and I go? Back to where Babydoll fell four flights down through a hole in the bannister on *my* porch, where *my* Diane, Babydoll's very same age, could just as easily have fallen as Babydoll? Oh, I saw where this cat was leading, but I

313

wasn't going! The more he talked the madder I got. But I held my peace until he really brought his program down front:

"Well," Terry was making his big point now, "all I say is that a wise man knows when he has been beaten. He retreats and gets a new bearing on his situation and then proceeds to advance again—refreshed, stronger. I say that we have been beaten——"

Arthur blurted:

"I'll be damned!"

"Wait! Wait, Arthur. I don't mean that we've been beaten by the mob. I mean by the combined force of the mob, antagonism, and police apathy—indeed, complicity. To make a long story short, I say that the greatest single thing we could do to bring this whole problem to the attention of the citizens of Chicago, and in fact of the whole United States, and at the same time save ourselves more grief and"—once again he looked at Carl—"grief and pain would be for *all* of us to move at the same time."

So there it was. He'd said it. I waited to see what the others would say. I was surprised to see Christine Thomas' husband William stand up to talk. I don't think I'd heard him say five words since they moved out to Trumbull Park over a month ago. Christine had done all the talking for that family up to now.

"*Welllll.*" His voice was like a child's, airy and whiney. "I think Mr. Watson is right. I *meeeeaan,* look. What have we got? No protection from the police. Can't even take a walk around the *block*—if you want to come back *alive.* After *all,* there are some pretty big *people* behind this thing! Else why would the police department let this thing go *on* for this long? Six months. We are just little people. We got nobody *behind* us. Like Terry said, I didn't

314

come out here to *crusade*. I just wanted some place to *live*."

Carl said:

"Well, I didn't mean to start no argument, and I don't want nobody to follow my lead. I just said that *I'm* leaving. I'm not scared of any man with two feet. I've killed many a man in the war. But this isn't a war. This isn't Saipan. This is the United States of America, and what I did in the war, I could go to the electric chair for doing now. I mean, like shooting people. No, I got too much to lose by getting in any trouble. So that's why I'm getting out of here before I get in a whole lot of trouble. I——"

He looked at the floor:

"I'm sorry."

He looked at me for one quick second, but I guess I was looking like one of those big grizzly bears down at the zoo, because he looked away real fast. I could have spit on that man. I had forgotten all about how scared I was at the time those people chased me home. I forgot all about being too scared to help Red out, the day I first moved in. I forgot about how the sound of the bombs made everything tighten up inside me, and cut off my breath so much sometimes that I thought that I was going to choke to death. Now I was scared in another way—scared that the little spark of manhood in me that was beginning to light up like a match on an airy day would be blown away by these men sitting about me. I could see myself with my tail tucked between my legs just a-skidooing it back to the wine bottles, broken bannisters, bogey-man diesel noises, and clangety-clack-clack of the streetcars grooving it down State Street by the Gardener Building. I could see Mrs. Palmer's old grinning mug kissing hello on my cheeks, and hear Mr. Gardener— old gray-haired, shriveled-up, bony-handed Mr. Gardener

315

come shuffling down the hall, going from door to door, hand out, knocking like he owned not only the apartments we lived in, but us too—knocking, knocking, knocking for his rent.

"Hell, no!" I said out loud, and everybody looked at me. "Yes, I said it. Hell, no!"

I got up from my seat. I didn't care what they thought, how I looked, who I hurt. Trumbull Park could mean death—that I knew; but already it meant life, and I wasn't dying!

"Hell, no!"

I waved my hand at the men who sat looking up at me, waiting. Nobody was surprised at anything anybody did any more. So they just looked.

"Hey, you!" I pointed at William Thomas.

I knew I sounded like a fight, and I didn't care. William got up on his rear end too after I called him like that. He answered roughly:

"What do you want?"

I didn't answer him. I pointed at Kevin and Carl:

"And you; and you too, Norman Douglas—all of you men, come on into the kitchen. I've got something I want to say. And I don't think it's for ladies to hear."

I got up and went into Carl's kitchen. Dishes were all over the kitchen sink, unwashed. They followed me. The lights had been turned on again in the project, and the lamplight right near Carl's back window slipped in alongside the curtain like a butter-colored knife. I knew where the light switch was in my kitchen, so I knew where Carl's was. I turned it on and walked over to the sink and leaned back on it, facing the middle of the kitchen and waited for all of them to come in.

I studied their faces as they shuffled in, one by one: Kevin—tall, high-pointed crew-cut looking as perfect as

316

ever, thin hollow cheeks looking more sagged than I'd ever seen them before; Carl—still with that sad, worn-out defeated look on his face; Terry—short dark hairline going back-back-back, his deep frown now a part of him, buck teeth showing underneath his lips even though his mouth was closed; William Thomas—light-skinned, thick glasses, thick curly hair looking like he hadn't combed it at all that night; Norman Douglas, a teen-age-looking guy, wearing a leather jacket unzipped, showing an open-collar, heavy green-and-gray-striped sports shirt underneath, a part on the side of his head, with his hair brushed flat and waved ever so slightly in the front, over his big square face—something like Carl's face, only much more younger looking; finally, Arthur—still wearing that double-breasted gray suit with a yellow sports shirt underneath, pointed-toe shoes, straight black hair hanging over his forehead, setting off his olive-brown skin. There they were—the soldiers of Trumbull Park—six of them. Seven, with me. Hundreds and hundreds of words were being written in papers and magazines because this bunch in front of me were out here in Trumbull Park. What a tired bunch, what an unprepared bunch for the battle with the Big Boys that old man O'Leary talked so frighteningly about, that William Thomas just somehow felt to be behind the riot, that I was feeling more and more each and every day to be behind the every-night bombing and the do-nothing policemen that had to take cover whenever the mob kicked up its heels! What an uneven match we seemed right then! But there we were—escapees, refugees from Gardener Buildings all along "The Stroll," as the boys put it. I wasn't going back. That's all there was to it!

"All right! So some of you guys want to go."

Nobody said anything.

"All right! Get out!"

Still nobody said anything.

"Get out, so that we can get some men out here! We've got too many cowards as it is. Get out!"

Still nobody said anything.

"Look, do you think that I'm not catching hell too? How do you think I felt being chased home? Being called nigger? Having my windows broken? Do you think I like it? What am I—iron? Hell, no!"

I felt blood banging so hard inside my arms and neck and cheeks that I thought I would just start bleeding from my pores.

"Carl! You especially should get out. Do you think that I would give a damn about what might happen later on, while a bunch of hunkies were calling my wife names and keeping her from getting in a squad car to go to the hospital to have a baby? My baby? Get out. Get out! I hate cowards!"

I hadn't wanted to say that, but I had said it, and it was too late to do anything about it now.

"Look, guys, we are all veterans—of World War II or of the Korean War. We had to fight, huh? Didn't they tell us to kill or be killed? Do you think our own officers wouldn't have shot us down like dogs if we hadn't gotten out there and fought and risked our lives?"

I answered myself.

"You're goddamned right they would have! When are we simple-ass Negroes going to wake up and do a little fighting for ourselves? Huh? Crispus Attucks died for American Independence—at least that's what they tell you in the books. Negroes been dying for this cause and that ever since any of us can remember. When in the hell are we going to fight for a cause of our own? Look, I know you guys wouldn't have come out here if you hadn't needed a

318

place real bad. Because, just like me, I know you knew what was happening out here before you moved in.

"There's only one family that didn't know what was happening before they moved out here and that's Arthur Davis's. But, look, the rest of you must have decided that Trumbull Park was better than wherever it was that you came from. I mean, didn't you?"

Nobody answered. I looked at Carl:

"Didn't you, Carl?"

He mumbled:

"Yeah."

"Well, do you think it's going to be any better when you go back? Hell, no! It's not going to be any better; it's going to be worse! Because you will have tried and quit. That's right—quit. And you, Terry——"

"Don't get on my back, Buggy. I'm not for it!"

"Damn what you're not for! I'm in this too. I wouldn't give a damn what you do except that what you do will affect me, and I'm not letting you pull what you've been trying to pull without bringing everything right down front. Now you talk about making an impression on the city of Chicago by moving. What kind of impression? I'll tell you what kind of impression! Everytime a bunch of hunkies decided they don't want you somewhere they'll just do what these people out here are doing, and after a while you'll hightail it out of there too—just to make an impression. Hell, yes! You'll make an impression all right—right in the middle of your behind! I don't think you're worried about making any impression. I think you, and you, Thomas, and—yes, you, Carl—you're chicken! Well, get out. We don't need you. I, for one, am not moving. I don't care if I'm the last one out here! I'll fight it by my-self!"

Terry muttered:

"Well that's all right—if you want to crusade."

"You're goddamned right I want to crusade! Shee-it! People crusade against *me* don't they? Well, I'm not crusading *against,* I'm crusading *for*—for a decent place to live—some place away from that alley that I lived in down on 57th. I'm not going back there, and I don't want to see any of you go back to wherever you came from. Yes, I'm a crusader! And this is no place for anybody who ain't one. So get out!"

Carl walked toward me. I doubled my fists.

"And I say just this one thing. If there are any other cowards, let them get out now. Because if you don't go now, if you stay around and get chicken later and mess up what little fight might be left in the rest of us—I—I——"

Was I going to say it?

"—I'll beat the living hell out of you!"

Carl was just about on me now. I looked right at him:

"I'm not a big man, but I'll tell you this—I'll beat the living pure-D shit out of you if *you* don't leave with the rest of the cowards!"

Was I crying? Where in the hell did that water come from running down my cheeks?

"I—I—I—I—I——"

I couldn't talk! What was happening to me?

I kept my fists doubled up, and I tightened them even more as Carl got within reaching distance.

"Buggy!" he snapped.

I snapped—maybe, sobbed—right back:

"I don't want to hear a damn thing you got to say to me. You goofed on me! Anybody—anybody woulda killed any one of those peckerwoods that tried to stop them from taking their wife to the hospital to have their baby. Then on top of it you come up with this mess about want-

320

ing to move. I don't want to hear a thing you got to say!"

"I ain't moving, Buggy."

Terry screamed:

"Don't listen to him, Carl! He can't tell us how to run our lives. He doesn't pay our rent!"

Arthur screamed back at Terry:

"Well, move then—damn it!"

But Terry couldn't move by himself, and he shut up and sat down hard on the edge of the kitchen table.

Carl put his arms around my shoulders:

"Look, son, I killed a lot of Japs overseas. Maybe I should have saved some of those bullets."

"You ain't moving, Carl?"

Kevin snarled:

"Where in the hell could he go? These Housing Authority folks aren't going to give this Negro a transfer."

"You're not moving, Carl?" Now I couldn't believe he wasn't moving.

"I guess I *am* a crusader, after all. But, listen, you little fart buster . . ." He put his big fist against my nose. It felt like a rock. "Listen . . . You're the one always talking about fighting. You're our leader. You got guts—I know that now. We better win this fight, man. I mean, you better lead . . . and lead your ass off . . . from now on!"

Kevin was always ready with the answers for other people:

"Hell, he can't lead without somebody to follow."

Arthur got up and went back into the other room, saying over his shoulder as he walked out:

"Leader or not, I'm always going to take up for myself."

Norman Douglas and William Thomas were quiet. They were new families and they knew it. They seemed to agree to stay, but I noticed that from that time on neither of them

321

seemed to want to say much to me or to visit me, and they weren't too happy the few times I visited them.

But the storm had come, and we had survived it. Nobody was moving out—at least, not right then. Carl said:

"Buggy, we ought to sit down and get ourselves a little program. I mean sit down and figure out just what the hell we're up against, and what to do about it, don't you think?"

Carl had changed. I knew he had. He was cursing more—yes; but there was something else. There was something strong in him that was pushing its way to the front. I felt like a man coming up out of deep water. I was soaking wet from sweat. I was crying. I was laughing. I was a man. A real man. One who had offered to get his butt kicked—for a point.

Terry was quiet. He hadn't given up the idea of moving; but now he was alone. He was hurt because he had been beaten at his own game—talking. But he wasn't through, no kind of way.

"Well," Carl announced to the women as we went back to the living room, "we're going to give it another fling."

"Yippee!" shouted Christine Thomas.

"Hump!" grumbled Nadine.

"Well all right!" said Mona, smiling.

"That's nice," mumbled Armela, Norman Douglas' teen-age wife.

"I wasn't going nowhere no way," Beverly Robinson announced.

Helen said nothing. She just kept looking at me and smiling that old lady's smile at me.

I felt ashamed, remembering what I had said in that kitchen, sounding like the big hero, the brave man, the rough-and-ready guy. But I had had to say it. I said to

322

myself, Lose or win, it was the only thing I saw to do. I looked around at the guys—Carl, Arthur, Kevin. They looked back at me and smiled those kind of it's-all-right smiles. I wanted to say thank you. I guess my eyes did say it.

It was a Saturday. We knew the bombs were going to start going off any minute; in fact, it was funny that they hadn't gone off before now. But do you know what we did that night?

We partied!

Terry and Norman thawed out, and those two went with Arthur and Kevin—in the squad car of course—and got a few cans of Bud and a few Pepsi-Colas, and I went home after some records, and we put the kids in Carl's bedroom on his kids' beds, and had a real, live Saturday night party!

30

Mona's going to do what?"

Kevin sat—long-leg thing—straddling his kitchen chair.
He told me again:

"Mona's making a speech at the Greater Urban
Church down on 42nd and South Parkway."

"About what?"

I don't know why I was so concerned about Mona making a speech, but I was.

Kevin didn't answer me right away. He got up and
turned the chair backwards, criss-crossing his arms and
resting them on the high back of the chair.

"Some kind of businessmen's society, or something
like that, is having some kind of march on City Hall, and
they are trying to get a lot of people interested, so they
asked Mona to speak. So she is, I think."

He'd started this conversation, but now he sounded like
I was prying into his business by asking questions.

"When is the meeting?"

"This coming Sunday."

"You going?"

"Naw."

This Kevin was really a character! I asked him:

"Why not?"

"Man, meetings and all that stuff—it's nothing but a lot of talk! When I get ready to do something, I don't need no meeting. I mean, like if one of these people push me too hard, I'm just going to turn his head upside down, or shoot the hell out of him and forget about it. Meetings? Me? Shee-it!"

"Why do you go along with the meetings we have out here, if you feel like that?"

"Why not?"

Well, that was an answer! And this guy had 'em!

Friday's *Defender* gave notice of the meeting. It was to be held at two o'clock. I went to Arthur's house Saturday night to see if we could go together, but he wasn't there. The house was empty. Kevin had said what he was going to do, and Ernestine had just come home from the hospital with a fat, brown cute little boy, so I knew that Carl couldn't leave her there alone to take care of five kids now. I didn't feel like visiting Terry since we had had it at the meeting at Carl's house, and Norman Douglas—well, I didn't know him too well, so I decided to go by Christine and William Thomas' house to see if they could go. Even though William was sort of down on me, he wasn't the kind of guy who would or could show it face-to-face.

We all left Trumbull Park at one o'clock, giving ourselves plenty of time to get there. That squad car was jammed-packed with our two families, the Thomases and the Martins. Kids were stacked two-high on our laps, and some even had to stand up holding on to the back of the front seats. There was a holiday-ish kind of feeling inside that car, even though dressed-up people from the neighborhood, returning from church, yelled the usual "*nigger! nigger! nigger!*" as we rode north on Bensley. By the time we got to 95th and State and waited for a streetcar going north, and got off at 43rd and waited for one going east again to

325

South Parkway, we were late anyway. It was two-fifteen when we walked in the Greater Urban Church.

A big, muscle-necked man, in a neat brown single-breasted and a glowing white shirt set off with a red-and-black tie, was talking. He had one of those pipe-organ voices that kept making me want to clear my throat. He was just finishing up when we finally found seats.

The big-balconied church had a high ceiling with dark-brown rafters that contrasted with the cream-stucco ceiling. Behind the pulpit was a row of real high organ pipes, gold and rich looking, rising up in glowing stripes behind the white-robed men and women sitting in the choir box. One or two of them was asleep or at least that's the way they looked from the third row on the side where we were sitting.

The sunlight from outside lit up the deep, dignified stained-glass pictures of Christ in the meadow, Christ crossing the sea of Galilee, Christ on the Cross. The light caught the blood from Christ's wound and laid it gently across the bald shining head of a dark-skinned man in a navy blue suit. It looked like the man was bleeding.

The big man speaking was almost through. I tried to stop thinking about how quiet and peaceful everybody in the church looked, and how loud and ornery the people were where I lived, and put my attention on what the big man on the stage was saying:

"And I say to you . . ."

Great big voice!

". . . that if the mayor and other elected officials of this city of Chicago . . ."

He paused after every sentence as though he were drawing his last breath and was plumbing his lungs to see if there was just one more left.

". . . don't wake up! . . ."

"YEAH!" some of the people cried.

"AMEN!" moaned some of the others.

". . . this city is going to see one of the most cataclysmic . . ."

Cata—who?

". . . upheavals since 1921!"

Many people gasped at this, as if they had heard it for the first time.

"There are evil forces about!"

"AMEN!"

"*Evil* forces!"

"YES, LORD!"

"Forces that feed on strife! . . ."

"YES, LORD!"

". . . and discord among the working men and women of our great nation! . . ."

Everybody waited for the next sentence.

". . . There are forces that are moved by greed . . . Almighty love of the almighty dollar!"

"AMEN!"

". . . and they would turn brother against brother . . ."

The preacher in the storefront church downstairs in the Gardener Building used to say that.

". . . and Negro against white . . ."

Pete, the white guy at the airplane factory had said that.

". . . for the love of the almighty dollar! Trumbull Park . . ."

One lady screamed at the name. Others moaned. I felt that it was some place other than the place I lived that they were so upset about.

". . . is a disgrace!"

"AMEN! . . . YES, LORD! . . . LORD JESUS!"

I remembered how Babydoll's mother had cried "Lord

327

Jesus" when she looked down from the top floor at Babydoll's body lying on the concrete below.

"Men and women . . ."

He turned and pointed to Mona, who had been hidden
from view right behind him.

". . . this young lady! . . . can't go to the store for a
bottle of milk for her baby . . . without hearing that *awful*
name . . . that has signaled our degradation . . . for three
hundred years . . . three hundred years too long!"

He was sweating now. He pulled out a handkerchief
and stopped talking and started wiping his face. People
mumbled to each other, and the sun moved the stain of
Christ's blood from the dark bald head of the man in the
navy blue suit to a little baby sound asleep in the arms of
a young girl in a pink hat with a veil.

I looked at Mona. She was beautiful. She wore a black
maternity suit with a wide white collar sweeping to the
front and coming to a point just above her full breasts. Her
soft hair curled around to the outer tips of her eyebrows,
and her skin was as rich looking as a piece of olive-colored
silk that had a soft light shining behind it. I found myself
straining to see her every time the big man stepped in
front of her. I turned to see Helen looking directly at me.
My neck burned and my ears rang, but she just smiled and
slipped her hand over mine and squeezed it real tight.

The man was almost through speaking now. What I
heard him say stuck with me for a long time afterward. His
voice stayed big, but he let flow like a river now:

"Don't you think for one minute that our white sisters and brothers don't suffer when they allow themselves
to be fooled into breaking ranks with us, their fellow suf-
ferers! When they permit themselves to be persuaded to
join the shadowy, hooded, schemers who would turn the
clock back to the days before the Civil War and shortly

328

thereafter! Don't you ever think that our young white youths who heed the exciting lure of tormenting their dark sisters and brothers won't one day discover who their real enemies are—who it is that is really responsible for white slums, white unemployment, white hopelessness, white despair! It will come to pass my friends. It will come to pass."

There weren't many *amens* after these last words. The day this big man talked about seemed too far off for any of us to see, too far off to me to make going back to Trumbull Park any easier. I couldn't see any of the twisted faces in the mobs out in Trumbull Park waking up and discovering any real enemy but me and my folks. I squirmed uncomfortably, squeezed Helen's hand, and waited for Mona to speak.

She was a tiny thing in all that crowd on the platform. And when she spoke, her voice, though loud enough to hear, was so soft and warm that even the thought of the other speaker's voice jarred me and made me squeeze Helen's hand before I could help myself.

"I'm not a public speaker," she said, "but I do appreciate having the opportunity to speak to you." She paused as if to be thinking of what she would say next. "I—I don't know how to start telling you about Trumbull Park. I suppose the best way would be to explain how we happened to move out there. You see, Arthur, my husband, and I have two children, and we were living in a two-room apartment on the South side, paying much more rent than we're paying now. It—it wasn't a very nice place, and so we thought we'd put in for a public housing project, and since I had friends who lived on the other side of Trumbull Park near the steel mills, we thought it would be nice to move out that way, away from—well, to give our children a chance to grow up in a nice neighborhood . . . Well, I

329

went to the office out there, and they took my application and in a short while we were told that we could move in. After we were there for about a day or so, the clerk called Arthur in, and Arthur could tell by the way that she was talking that they hadn't known that we were—well, colored." Mona paused and laughed to herself. "I don't know what they thought we were."

One or two other people laughed. Then Mona said, not laughing at all this time:

"But I don't know what difference our color should have made anyway. After all, I thought that Negroes had as much right to the facilities of the government—I mean like a government housing project—as anybody else."

And the people started applauding, and saying *Amen* and *Yes, Lord!* And one or two ladies in the choir behind the speakers' stand started dabbing their eyes with frilly little handkerchiefs.

"Well," Mona went on to say, "nothing happened for the first few days after we moved in. Then—well, then things happened. People broke out all of our windows, and every time the Housing Authority would put them in, the mob would break them out again. So now we can't even *have* windows in our house. We have a big board across the place where the windows are."

A low mumbling set in; people were turning to each other and asking each if the other had heard what Mona had said, just like they didn't trust what they thought they themselves had heard. Two more ladies in the choir started dabbing at their eyes.

"We can't even eat dinner in peace. I remember once when we were eating—my husband, my children, Bobby and Sharon, and I—the mob gathered outside our door and started calling Arthur, and chanting and throwing rocks against the door, and setting off bombs and

330

aiming them at the windows. We stood it as long as we could, but when things started exploding upstairs in the bedroom—I mean, it seemed that the world was coming to an end out there that night—well, we just decided that we were going to finish our dinner no matter what happened. Other colored families had moved in by then, so we just took our plates and went out the back door and went over to the apartment of one of the other Negro families and finished eating. . . ."

I was sure I heard a man behind me—in church!—say: "I'll be damned!"

"LORD HAVE MERCY! LORD JESUS!"

I hated to hear people say "Lord have mercy!" It kept bringing back Babydoll's mother, fat and crying, running down those steps screaming:

"*Babydoll, Babydoll, Babydoll! Lord have mercy! Kind Jesus, have mercy!*"

Mona went on—calmly, steadily, as if it were someone else she was talking about:

"Now I don't mind—well, I do mind too, but it isn't so hard to take as an adult, when someone chases you away from your dinner table, and you have to carry your food outside in the cold wintertime to a friend's house to eat—but when you think of what this does to the children, that's when it's hard to take, believe me. The police department has been derelict in its duty out there. I've actually seen sergeants tell their men to take cover when the mob has stood in front of our house throwing rocks, lead pipes, ball bearings, and everything else that they could get their hands on. I've actually seen sergeants send Negro policemen back to the headquarters, after the Negro policemen stood up and said they weren't going to take cover but were going to try to stop the mob from throwing bricks at us. I don't know how I can explain this thing to you—

explain how it is to walk down the street like a criminal, surrounded by policemen and people standing all along the street calling you names. Every night they set off loud, bright bombs, hundreds and hundreds of them, one after another, trying to wear our nerves down, trying to get us out of there."

Now practically all the ladies in the choir were crying, and a lady sitting right behind me had started. 'Way in the back I heard a woman sobbing out loud. Mona went on:

"Just last week one of the ladies, Mrs. Burton, had to go to the hospital to have a baby. The mob wouldn't even let the policemen take her to the patrol wagon, so that they could take her to the hospital. In fact, Mr. Burton had to call from one police station to the other for over an hour before one of the policemen finally agreed to send a patrol wagon after her. Take a taxi, the policeman said. The mob wouldn't even let the policemen put the lady in the patrol wagon until one of the policemen begged them—please believe me—*pleaded* with them to let them take this pregnant woman, in pain as she was, to the hospital."

Now some of the men, the men who had sat with no expressions, staring hard at Mona as if she herself were the white people she was talking about—now the men started blinking and coughing, and one man pulled out a handkerchief and started blowing his nose and dabbed at his eyes real quick just as he took the handkerchief away from his nose to put it back in his pocket. Most of the women were crying out loud now—not hollering and screaming, not making a show of it, but just sort of quietly, sort of deep inside themselves.

Mona herself was crying now. She stopped and took a long breath and reared back. She was getting tired. The weight of the baby was beginning to pull at her muscles, and she seemed unable to bring her talk to any kind of close:

"I have some questions which I would like to ask: first, would this riot be allowed to go on this long in a Negro neighborhood?"

"NO! NO!"

That same guy behind me muttered:

"Hell, no!"

Mona waited awhile and then:

"Then why haven't the police done something to enforce the law in Trumbull Park? Isn't six months long enough to torture a group of people for moving into a white neighborhood?"

"LORD YES! LORD HAVE MERCY!"

I trembled!

Mona's voice was quiet now. Calm. She sounded as if she had just finished running, or crying:

"All we Negroes in Trumbull Park want is to live like other human beings. We're not bothering anybody. We're not hurting anything. Yet we can't even get the same kind of police protection other people in Chicago get. Well . . ."

Now Helen was crying. Christine was too. William Thomas was wiping his nose with his handkerchief, looking around, waiting until he thought that there was no one looking at him so he could wipe away the tears that brimmed in his eyes. I looked away from him. I didn't feel a thing. I couldn't cry any more. Something had been burned out of me. I couldn't feel any pity any more—not for anyone—not even for myself. Mona said:

"Well . . . I'll say just this one thing, and then I'm through. . . ." She almost whispered. "It'll take more than this to get us out of Trumbull Park."

A coarse, loud, rough voice from the rear of the church shouted:

"Say it louder! Say it! Say it louder!"

"I said it will take more than bombs and mobs to get us out of Trumbull Park!"

Helen screamed, and then fell over onto my shoulder and cried loud and hard. Other ladies who had been crying just let out louder wails. The men were grumbling. Someone said something about getting "a bunch together and going out there and shooting a bunch of them hunkies." The church was in an uproar.

All this time, I hadn't said anything to Helen, but I put my arm around her, as Mona sat down and the choir started singing. Helen wasn't crying now. I looked across her to Christine Thomas. She wasn't crying either. I looked at William Thomas. He was stern-faced as he put his handkerchief in his pocket. Diane and Louella were smiling. I felt very good inside.

I was very proud to be living in Trumbull Park.

31

THAT PETE! His eyes got bigger than half-dollars when I told him that the Negro Businessmen's Society was going to have a march on City Hall.

"March on City Hall!" He grinned like a young boy. "That'll do it—mass action. Mass action!"

Through all this, through all the hate I'd begun to feel for all white people, this goofy Pete and I had stayed friends. Whenever I told him about what the mob had done, he'd frown all up and stand real close to me and absolutely plead:

"Let's kick their asses tonight, Buggy! C'mon, let's you and me go out there late tonight and grab a couple of 'em and kick their asses!"

The big presses and drills were grinding out the engine parts by the thousands, row after row of castings—big ones, little ones, rolling down the long leather belts that were strung from one end of the plant to the other. Everybody worked fast. Everybody walked fast. *Clang bomp!* went the presses.

Pete walked by me again later that day:

"Mass action and ass-kicking, Buggy! That'll stop 'em like nothing else will!"

Mass action. March on City Hall. It seemed to me

that the City Hall was just the place to march to. After all, I thought, who tells the police what to do? The mayor. And where is the mayor? At City Hall.

Helen had to stay home with the kids. Naturally Mona, as far along with her baby as she was, couldn't go. The Douglasses were still a little new to this thing, so they didn't go. Arthur didn't want to leave his home unprotected, so he stayed with Mona. So Terry and I went, along with a guy from a new family, named Harry Harvey, who asked to go with us.

It was still February, but a sunny morning that made you feel that spring might be thinking of setting in. Harry, a short stocky guy with a dark-brown baby face and a heavy moustache that shagged over his top lip, wore his red-and-black high school sweater from DuSable. He talked in a flat low voice, but whenever you could hear what he said you heard each word being pronounced sharply, like his tongue was a knife slicing each word off of a loaf—neat, even, clear.

Terry, the idea man, still wanted to move. I knew that. But he liked crowds. I think he would have gone to the picket line even if it hadn't been about Trumbull Park— just because it was something big and acceptable that he could belong to. Terry liked to belong. He hated not belonging. That's why he hadn't moved yet. He belonged to the group of Negroes who lived in Trumbull Park, and he couldn't stand not belonging to a group.

Terry wore a neat well-fitting raglan-sleeve topcoat, one of those skinny-brim hats, which were just beginning to get a play around "The Stroll" on the South side, a white button-down shirt, and a bow tie which I thought was spread just a little too wide. I mean, in spite of all the dressing-up he did, that cat still looked exactly like Bugs Bunny.

336

Cops were lined up all along the sidewalks and against the wall of City Hall. I noticed that there were a lot of Negro policemen. So did Terry.

"Well, look—so this is where they've put all the Negro policemen! No wonder you don't see many in Trumbull Park."

Harry, the new guy, said:

"Well, I've only been out there a little while, but I've seen quite a few Negro policemen near where I live."

I had been over to Harry's, but Terry hadn't. Terry asked:

"And where do you live?"

"Over by the power house. You know, don't you—where the back of the project is?"

Terry laughed and rubbed his narrow, pointed little chin with the palm of his hand:

"Yes, I suppose there would be quite a few Negro policemen near where you live. My friend, you live in Limbo. You know where that is?"

I said:

"That sounds like a nice way of saying way on the outskirts of town."

"Precisely," Terry answered.

"Oh," Harry seemed a little confused by all this, "I see."

We walked over to a spot where a man was handing out picket signs. More and more people were coming up. Many of them seemed to know each other, and all of them seemed friendly and sort of excited. I heard one stocky, light-skinned Negro woman say to a leather-jacketed man beside her:

"Looks like the old days, huh?"

I wondered how many picket lines she had been in. I wondered what the old days were like that would have brought out people in the numbers that these people were coming out in. I felt safe—secure—being in this crowd. It seemed to give me a feeling of protection—the same feeling that I felt whenever all the Negro tenants got together in the Gardener Building in somebody's rooms to "see what we can do."

Soon the streets were full of people; and a minister, a young man wearing hornrimmed glasses, got up by one of the columns and raised his arms and shouted:

"Now, ladies and gentlemen, I'd like to advise you that this picket line is being sponsored by the Negro Businessmen's Society!" He didn't need a microphone. His voice was loud, and he spoke with pretty, clear words. "We are not here to provoke incidents or to cause any unlawful disturbance. As you know, our right to assemble here is guaranteed us by the Constitution of the United States. We are here to see if we can't get some more of the rights guaranteed us by that same Constitution!"

I went for that, and I clapped loudly. Others clapped, and some cheered, but there was a feeling of self-control over the whole group that surprised me and made me feel as I imagined Terry felt. I looked over at Terry, but he was busy tying a picket sign around his shoulders. He looked like an old vet, and I wondered where he had ever been in a picket line before. I never did get around to asking him. I did say, though, when I got close to him:

"Hey, man, I thought you weren't a crusader."

He yelled back in his biggest voice:

"I wasn't when I said I wasn't!"

"Well, how about tomorrow?"

"It depends on the circumstances!"

"Oh."

Somebody gave Harry one of the signs that you carry on a stick. They gave me one too.

338

Pretty soon the preacher and some other men—dignified-looking chaps wearing printed badges that read "Picket Captain"—started lining everybody up. Nobody got mad when one of the captains pushed him, and the captains seemed like they had rehearsed all this somewhere before coming downtown. The young preacher with the horn-rimmed glasses got out in the front of the line. Terry and Harry and I weren't too far behind him. I looked behind me. We were on LaSalle. The line, two-abreast, ran all the way to the end of the block south to Washington Street, and turned the corner going west toward Wells.

There were people in line who were dressed up; there were people wearing jackets from unions; there were old ladies with cloth coats and babushkas; there were young ladies in those sharp-looking poplin car-coats; there were dark men with bald heads and mean faces; there were light men with sandy hair and baby faces. Negro men, Negro women; white men, white women; Mexicans; all sorts of people. Where had they come from? Why were they there? They didn't even know me. Why were they so concerned? These questions swirled and turned in my mind as the young preacher started walking and singing:

"We shall not be, we shall not be moved. . . ."

Slowly and unevenly the people behind the preacher—Harry, Terry, me, all of us—started moving, and one by one we joined him in his singing:

"We shall not be, we shall not be moved. . . ."

I remembered that I had thought that that was just about one of the squarest songs this side of the Pershing Ballroom, when I used to hear the scrawny cluster of people downstairs in the storefront church in the Gardener Building singing:

"Just like a tree that's planted by the waaaaaaa-terrrrrs. . . ."

339

But now that song seemed like a new song. No Gardener Building bunch now: no two or three out-of-tune old ladies singing that song now. The sound of the singing rose over the steady noise of rubber tires underneath the Yellow cabs and Cadillacs slapping the smooth LaSalle Street pavement, over the sound of the El on Wells Street clacketing by, and over the thousands and thousands of leather and rubber heels clicking against the sidewalk as the Loop started to wake up. The people, who had been rushing into and out of and right on by those tall serious-looking gray buildings that looked so much like big cement trees with all the branches cut off standing over the stream of people and cars down below, stopped to watch and listen. So I sang the song, and liked it, and walked in the crowd feeling like a little boy who was returning to the place where the gang had beat him up—only this time with his mother, his father, his sisters, and lots and lots of brothers. Somebody made up some words to the middle of the song:

We shall not be, we shall not be moved!
We shall not be, we shall not be moved!
ENFORCE—THE LAW—IN TRUM—BULLL!
We shall not be moved!

So we sang and walked and sang and walked and I felt a silly buzzing in my ears, and a goofy thumping in my chest, and a foolish urge to cry—from happiness this time. I turned to Terry, right behind me:

"We're not altogether alone, are we?"

He seemed caught up in all this himself. He had to think a minute to get himself together. Then:

"Nothing beats mass action, Buggy—absolutely nothing!"

Where were these guys getting all this stuff?

It was dark and cold when we finally sat on the State Street car heading south to Trumbull Park. Harry went to sleep right away, laying his head against the window in the seat in front of Terry and me. Terry didn't say anything for a long time. Finally, when we hit about 47th and State, he started talking:

"Buggy, I guess you've seen that I'm a sort of Dr. Jekyll and Mr. Hyde."

"Why do you say that, Terry?"

"Well, you know that I want to get out of that place. It's driving me crazy. I can't stand prolonged tension. I'm a one-shot man. I will fight as hard and as desperately as the next man within a reasonable length of time; but this— this, Buggy, is a war of attrition."

"At—what?"

"There is an evil, shrewd mentality behind all this, Buggy, that has had experience in psychological warfare. I don't mean figuratively. I mean literally, actually."

"Well, there's a guy named Pete at work who said——"

"And furthermore, Buggy, the technique that mentality is using is foolproof."

"Well, this guy named Pete thinks that there is big money——"

"For example, Buggy, you ever hear of a thing called selective perception?"

"No. This guy Peter, he has got it all figured out where these guys are trying to create disturbances out here that will lay the groundwork for turning Trumbull Park over to private——"

"Selective perception, Buggy, is that tendency on the part of an individual to pay attention to one particular thing even though there may be many other things competing for his attention."

"Pete, and another old guy Arthur introduced me to, have both been saying something about land around

341

here being worth a lot of money soon, when the government gets through building some kind of seaway; but the main point was——"

"We are being trained by those bombs to attach a significance then—to select the noise of the explosion as a noise especially directed at us. It's almost as if the rest of the neighborhood—the whites in the neighborhood—are being taught that the bombs are *friendly* noises, and we are being taught that they are *enemy* noises. Don't you get it, Buggy?"

"Terry, the main point was that——"

"Buggy, this means that we are being attacked by sound, and because of what that sound means, and the constancy of the explosions. Our own ears carry that attack to us; and our knowledge that enemies, not friends, are responsible for that sound makes it a painful, wearing, ever-present strain on us, Buggy. Now why would a bunch of rowdies go to such lengths? Who among those idiots is that smart? Who's buying all those bombs? . . . Buggy, you know what?"

"Terry, I'm trying to explain something to you! You won't give me a chance to talk at all!——"

"Yeah, yea, yeah. Listen, Buggy, maybe getting us out of here is not what these guys have in mind at all! Oh, certainly they hope that some of us move! Maybe getting us out *was* the way this thing first started. But now, Buggy, now! Listen, maybe they want to feint us into killing someone, into starting a riot, so that then they can finish it! Yes, Buggy, maybe that's it! Drive us crazy enough to try to retaliate in kind, Buggy—but why?"

"I'm trying to tell you why!"

"Huh?"

"I've been trying to tell you why for half an hour! Now . . ."

342

I was disgusted at this guy. He was smart all right. Figuring out all that psychological warfare stuff was pretty
good. But listen? Not Terry.

We were at 95th and State. So I shook Harry and he
crawled, still half-asleep, out of his seat, and we got off of
the car, and Terry went into the tavern to call the cops to
come after us.

32

THE PICKET LINE made the rioters as evil as six
mad bears, and they blew up twice as many bombs after
that and broke out twice as many windows, and the cops
were twice as slow in breaking up their whooping and
hollering. March shot by like a late C.T.A. bus, dragging
with it a nightly blasting of bombs and crowds in front of
Arthur's front door. Even from where I lived I could hear
them screaming and chanting:

"WE WANT DAVIS! WE WANT DAVIS! WE WANT
DAVIS!"

The meetings we were having kept our spirits up—
mainly because when we were together, the other guy
always looked so much worse off than we did to ourselves.

The next time the meeting was held at my house, I
bought a couple of cartons of beer and some potato chips.
It was Saturday night, and I decided to make a little party
of it.

"Buggy"—Helen was fat all over now, but still full
of her foolishness—"you act like you're getting ready for
a real ball."

344

"Well, I . . ."

"I haven't seen you work around the house so hard since we were married."

"Do you want me to stop?"

Now was that called for? I mean, snapping her up like that?

"No, go ahead"—and as she walked to the door to see who was knocking, she threw in one of her choice signifying lines—"with your feet sticking out!"

She opened the door. It was Arthur and Mona—an hour early!

"Hey!" I put the dust rag in my back pocket, and then thought how funny that looked and put it on top of the radio, and then snatched it off of there and stuck it back into my pocket. "How you people doing?"

Arthur didn't even answer. He sat on the couch and crossed his legs and waited. For what? Don't ask me. Mona looked at me looking at Arthur, and she laughed and tried to smooth things over.

"Don't mind him."

And that's all the explaining *she* did.

Pretty soon the others started drifting in: Terry and Nadine and Kevin. Then Carl came. Beverly and Ernestine never did show up. All this time Arthur sat in that chair. A bomb went off. He still didn't move. He didn't even start walking and looking out of the window.

I started talking:

"Well, good evening, you-all. Well, that picket line didn't exactly settle things out here, but I still think it was a——"

"Buggy . . ." Arthur spoke so soft, yet the sound in his voice stopped me just like that.

"Yes?"

345

Arthur said it as if it was yesterday's weather report:

"I don't think I—we—me and Mona, that is—are going to be with you very much longer."

ARTHUR DAVIS MOVING?

"You what?"

"We got a notice to move in thirty days."

Mona laid her hand on Helen's arm as if to say she was sorry that she hadn't told Helen when they first walked in, but that it was Arthur's place to do that.

Helen just sat there on the couch beside Mona with her eyes closed tight, frowning, not moving, sitting so still, breathing harder and harder.

Kevin straightened his blue tie and ran his finger around the inside of his white shirt and pulled the collar down underneath his Adam's apple.

"You what?"

"We got a notice to move."

And I felt like I was in the Gardener Building again. Floating fast as hell on nothing—all the way back to nowhere!

"Well," Terry sighed, "if this doesn't take the cake!"

"It's the same old story," Arthur added it up.

"What are you going to do, Arthur?" Helen sounded like she saw Arthur as a nice guy for the first time.

"What *can* I do, Hattie?"

"Helen."

"I mean, Helen. The big wheels are rolling. They couldn't get me out with bricks and bombs so now they're doing the next best thing. It's the same old story."

"What are they putting you out for?" I wanted to know why the Housing Authority had done the rioters such a hell of a favor.

"They say I got out here by fraud."

346

"*Fraud?*" This was the first time Kevin had raised his voice since I'd known him.

"They say Mona was working when she said she wasn't."

I asked Arthur like *he* was the one who had accused Mona:

"How could she have been working when she was supposed to be . . . ?"

Arthur helped me:

"Pregnant? That's right. But you see there was a guy down there that made like Sam Spade, the detective. Put in a lot of time, even after working hours finding out everything he could about our business. Went to places where Mona used to work. Visited our friends and our family and finally got what he figured was enough dope to prove that Mona wasn't *technically* off of her job when she applied, even though she wasn't *actually* working. Well, she couldn't have worked, she's been sick with that kid ever since she's been pregnant. Anyhow, they fixed it all up . . . and now they say I got in here by 'fraudulent and illegal means.'"

Terry cut in:

"The only thing fraudulent about your coming out here is that you are Negro."

Arthur answered:

"Don't I know it? But the thing that gasses me was the slick way this cat down at the Housing Authority came down with that 'I'm your friend' crap, and me and Mona trusted him. You know?"

Carl complained:

"You *trusted* him? Was he white?"

"Yeah. But you can't go around not trusting *all* white people. Some of the Negroes I know would goof you

347

ten times faster than some whites—and there'd be much less in it for them at that. Carl, *you* know that."

But Carl wouldn't let it go.

"Yes sir, but there's a difference. A Negro, you can see why you'd have a little trust in him. After all, he's been kicked in the ass as much as you, and he knows how it feels. So you most likely can recognize a Negro who could forget about his own ass-kicking and start to kicking on another Negro—that kind of Negro's got a certain stink about him, a certain whorish look. . . . 'Scuse me, Helen. . . . All this bad language. I'm sorry."

Then to Arthur again:

"But Arthur, you *need* your ass kicked—trusting a *white* man. Arthur, those folks will goof you and not even know it. This country has ruined them people. Suppose *you* had been told that you were God, each and every day for three hundred years?"

"I don't think I could live that long," Arthur poked fun at Carl; but Carl went doggedly on:

"Gentlemen, you see what I mean. I mean, suppose someone had been feeding you a lot of stuff for as long as you could remember, about how much better you were than—say, the Chinese. Do you think you could get that stuff out of your mind just by being friendly with one of them? Do you think you still wouldn't believe that Chinese are just natural-born laundry men, even though you ate, slept, and maybe even got a little piece from some Chinese doll? God yes, you would! You couldn't help yourselves, gentlemen. And it's the same way with these white folks. Even when they *mean* well, that old poison pops up in their minds. And when it does, there you are—sitting high and dry with a thirty-day notice in your hands! Goodness, gentlemen, don't you know that?"

Nadine sat in a kitchen chair close beside Terry. She

348

hadn't said anything all night. When she spoke, her voice was loud enough to hear, and the words she spoke said it for all of us, even more than Carl had.

"What are we going to do now?"

What was so funny was that she wasn't even looking at Arthur or Mona when she said it. She sat near the kitchen door and the light from the kitchen lit one side of her face and she seemed to be staring at the light like that was what she was talking to. The light.

33

HELEN started keeping a little record of things that happened. She kept it for about a month, but then things started happening so fast that she couldn't keep track:

March 5: Mob around Arthur's house. Arthur's windows broken. Man throws iron pipe through Arthur's window.
March 6: Forty-five bombs. Last bomb: 2:10 AM.
March 7: Mob threatened Arthur.
March 8: Bombs (too many to count).
March 9: Mob outside Carl Burton's house.
March 10, 11, 12, 13, 14: Bombs, bombs, bombs!
(Damn it!)
March 15: Two of Kevin's friends working at Wisconsin Steel at 106th and Torrence beaten up. (Nobody arrested.)
March 16: Housing Authority replaced Arthur's windows. Wonder how long they'll stay in this time. Paper said two cars driven by Negroes stoned at 106th and Torrence.
March 17, 18, 19: Mobs in front of Arthur's house. Arthur's windows broken again. (Bombs getting louder.) Mona looks terrible.
March 20: Chicago Defender said six Negroes beaten

up at 103rd and Torrence. (No one from the project, thank God!)

All through that over-and-over-again March, we got together every Saturday night. We didn't talk about Arthur Davis, but we didn't talk about anything else either.

Christine Thomas took over as the cheer-er-up-er of the bunch. Her dark dimples weren't sexy-and-at-the-same-time-sweet-and-little-girl-looking like Helen's; but when she smiled, she made me smile; and the night we had our meeting at her house, a "Little Walter" record was playing some Down Home guitar that wouldn't have sounded right in anybody's house but Christine and William's.

Helen and I sat close to each other, and we reminded me of Terry and Nadine, the way they huddled together when they were at my house. But I liked to feel Helen close to me, and she was, and Diane and Louella were upstairs lying across Christine's bed.

Arthur was busy talking to Carl and Kevin in the kitchen, and they were busy digging into their pockets, and Arthur collected the money and slipped out the back door.

I'd saw it, and didn't believe it; but it had to be true. Somebody out there in the middle of all that bombing and mobbing and everything else was selling Arthur Davis fifths of Old Taylor!

When he came back, nobody asked him any questions, and the cap of the Old Taylor was busted, and Arthur informed everybody that he was Arthur Davis and that "My trial for shooting at those hunkies was continued all the way from October!"

It was now April.

Helen's baby was due in a few weeks. And by counting the fifths of Old Taylor, Arthur was downing, I could tell that his thirty-day eviction notice was just about up.

351

But we didn't talk about it. We just waited. And Arthur waited. And so did Mona. But we didn't talk about it.

Before long it was meeting time at my house again. I didn't fix up so much for this one. Kevin was the first one to come, and when the others got there he acted like he was mad at all of us.

But we didn't talk about Arthur Davis moving.

"The thing to do," Kevin said, "would be for us to get ourselves a bunch of forty-fives, get out of those squad cars, and start walking in. That way we'd show these people that if they want to whip ass they'll have to bring ass, and by the time we shot up one or two of them, even if we did have to die for it, this stuff would be broken up for once and for all."

Big fat Christine Thomas agreed:

"Yeeeessss, Honey! That's what I say. Get something to protect yourself with and walk those streets; and if somebody jumps wrong, that's all she wrote . . ."

But Mona had an announcement to make.

And the second before she made it I knew it: her quietness, her extra sweet smile for everybody; the way she looked at me when I looked at her . . . for the very first time; the grip of her hand on her other hand; the dark in her dark eyes . . . I mean, you don't know her! Arthur was standing in the door and she looked at him. Her hair was curled fluffy with a soft black—or was it brown?—kind of shine to it. No, not that look either. And looking up at Arthur that way made a curve along her neck that . . .

But I knew she was going to say something, that she had an announcement to make. I knew as she made it. I wanted to tell somebody that I knew what she was going to say . . . before she said it. But I kept quiet, and everybody else kept quiet, as Mona made her announcement:

"I hate to break in here with this kind of news . . .

But I just . . . well, wanted to tell you that Arthur and I are moving out . . . Monday."

I looked at Arthur. He looked away. I looked at Mona again. She looked at me. I looked away.

Terry said:

"So it's come." He tried to smile, but that made him look so bad that he must have felt it, and so he went back to his regular frown. "Maybe if we all moved——"

Kevin cut him off—for the first time:

"Damn, man! These people have been *through* some stuff. *Suffered!* You know? And *fought!* You ain't done nothin' but suffer—and not much of that."

You ever hear a man with a bass voice whine? Well, that's what Terry did:

"Ooohh, I didn't meeaaan——"

But Kevin had his number today:

"Yeah, we all know what you mean!" Then to Arthur: "Man, you get the hell out of here if you want to go. Let some of *these* rusty-leg Negroes begin to carry the load a little. Good luck, man."

Arthur had those hands clamped together across the top of his forehead looking down at the floor, shaking his head from side to side. He shook a little all over. I think he was crying.

One by one each one of us spoke up.

Helen said:

"Well, I hope you two will move into a friendlier neighborhood than this—thing. But I know one thing— South Deering will never forget the name Davis."

"Don't you worry, Art," young Norman Douglas walked up to Arthur and patted his shoulder like a soldier, "you don't have a thing to be ashamed of. You 'held the perimeter,' like they used to say in Korea, and now your replacements are here. I fought in Korea. I haven't forgot

353

how, yet." Then Norman looked at me. "I just have to have a little time to understand what's going on out here." He smiled. I smiled back.

Harry Harvey—short, still wearing that DuSable high-school sweater said:

"Good luck, man! We're sure going to miss you."

Arthur looked up and laughed sort of quick-like and pulled at his ear; and one by one the brave ones, the not-so-brave ones, the hip ones, the square ones, the men and women—one by one, we all said thanks in our own off-the-wall ways:

Thanks, Arthur Davis. For showing us how to fight. How to lose, but fight. How to win, but fight. How to suffer, but fight. How to drink, but fight. How to cry, but fight. How to fight—fight—fight—fight.

Arthur looked at each of us, eyes watery. He seemed to be counting us: Terry-Nadine, Carl-Ernestine, Me-Helen, Norman-Armela, Harry-Margaret, Kevin-Beverly, Christine-William: seven families. Seven against South Deering. It had been eight. Arthur and Mona Davis were the eighth.

Boom!

Soon Arthur wouldn't be hearing those bombs.

Boom . . . Boom . . . Boom . . .

Soon his kids wouldn't be squinching their eyes and hunching their shoulders the way they were doing right now.

BAR-ROOOOM!

Christine Thomas sang out, loud and bluesy:

"Big stars fallin'. It won't be long before day . . ."

Arthur got up and started his walk to the front door:

We all followed him with our eyes as he walked. Kevin didn't sound too far off-base when he said to Mona:

"He won't have to do that much more will he?"

Mona shook her head:

354

"No. No, I guess not."

BAR-ROOOOOOOOOOOOOOOMMMMMMMM!!

Everything and everybody in the house shook with that one!

Carl stood up after a while and, rubbing his hands together, said:

"Hell, no need to sit here cryin'. Let's have a party!"

Freckle-faced Beverly—almost slim again, full lips shining, dark hair curled and cut into one of those Italian haircuts—snapped her fingers and said just as cheerfully as you please:

"You *know* yes! Let's have a party!"

Christine looked at me and said:

"Mr. Chairman, you got anything to say?"

I laughed:

"Well, I think I've already told most of you about what's really happening out here." Someone had turned the phonograph on. It was playing real softly. I went on though: "I guess this is as good a time to have a party as any. But some of us are thinking more about walking than dancing. We're thinking about walking in. But we'll talk about it at our next meeting."

And so we had that party.

Beverly was free again, loose from that big baby, getting slim again. She had a right to celebrate, and she did. She danced with Terry and Carl, and Norman, and Harry. She even danced with her husband Kevin. She even danced with me.

Christine sang along with Ella Fitzgerald's bebop piece "How High The Moon," and that Christine *whaled!*

Harry and his wife snuggled up close and whispered—I can't imagine what—in each other's ears, giggling like a couple of teen-agers.

Nadine and Terry sat side by side on the couch—Na-

355

dine's light-brown skin looking a little faded in the dim light of the lamp next to the couch, her eyes sad, her hair shiny and new looking. Nadine was unhappy about something. She *always* seemed to be unhappy about something.

Ernestine and Carl, changed now from their Down Home politeness and bashfulness, but not altogether, stood near the phonograph, leaning close to each other, looking at each other every now and then, and—I do believe— blushing whenever they caught each other's eye.

William Thomas put on one of Christine's aprons and started washing glasses in the kitchen, grinning to himself and taking a taste out of a glass filled with some kind of brownish-looking stuff.

A little later on, Arthur and Carl and Kevin went into one of their famous private talks. Money started changing hands, and after a while Carl and Kevin eased out of the house, to come back about a half an hour later with a bag full of what they called "groceries."

Boom! Went those bombs outside!

Go! Went a bunch of us watching Christine Thomas dance inside.

Boom! Boom! Boom! Boom! White-blue lights licked and jabbed at us through the windows.

But Sonny Rollins and Thelonious Monk were playing "Get Happy"; and I, of all people, was trying to tap dance! And Helen was laughing so hard that she was crying. And Mona and Arthur were laughing so hard that they were crying.

Barroooom!! Went one of the Trumbull Park specials.

But Norman Douglas was doing an imitation of Joe Carroll doing an imitation of Louis Armstrong and we were all screaming—I mean, screaming!

Harry Harvey had a recording machine and went home

356

and brought it back, and we all sang "Auld Lang Syne" to
Arthur and Mona, and they both joined in and sang it to
themselves, and—

    Boom . . . Boom . . . Boom . . . Boom . . . Boom . . .
All night long.

    I asked Mona:

    "Do you think those folks out there are celebrating
too? Maybe they know you're moving."

    Mona threw her arms around Helen and me and said:

    "I don't know *why* they're celebrating." She pointed
at me and at Helen and then moved her arm all the way
around the room. *"You're* still out here."

    Boom . . . Boom . . . Boom . . . Boom . . . Boom!
went the bombs!

    "Go . . . go . . . go . . . go . . . go!" went Kevin and
the rest.

    And Beverly danced and danced and danced.

34

I WAS GLAD to go to work Monday so that I wouldn't have to say the last goodbye to Arthur and Mona, but when I came home Helen said:

"They weren't out here themselves. The moving men just came and took their stuff away. A few people hollered and called the moving men names, but they seemed disappointed that Arthur and Mona weren't there. They wanted to boo Arthur and Mona, not the moving men."

I asked:

"And that was that?"

"That was that."

That was that. What an empty solemn sound! That was that. What would we do now? Now that the careless man was gone? Now that the guy who took chances was gone? Now that the fabulous Arthur and Mona Davis were gone?

"Helen, it's going to be hard, now."

She sat down on the couch:

"Mona and I were close, real close. Buggy, do you know why they moved?"

"I don't hardly know why they *stayed*. Why *did* they move?"

"They were dead, Buggy, dead. Those people died for us, just as surely as they say Christ did."

"I hope we get better results."

"Buggy!"

"I mean it, Helen. I hope that if they died we have more to show by their death than we have for Christ's!"

"Buggy, we can't wait for Christ or Arthur or anybody else to win our battles for us."

"These aren't our battles alone! Hell, other folks profit from our struggle—not just us! I just said I hope we get better results from Arthur and Mona's death than we got from Christ's. Look what we got now—Trumbull Park."

"Buggy, I don't mean that they died like—well, like your mother. I mean, they have suffered so much, their children have suffered so much, that they'll never be the same. On top of it all, Buggy, that trial was hanging over their heads, along with the bombs and window-breakings and mobs. The whole thing, Buggy. It was too much. A human can only stand so much. Poor Mona. You should have seen her while she was telling me about all this stuff. She could hardly talk. Buggy, she asked me not to tell anyone—not even you—but, well, I never could hide anything from you. The trial, Buggy—somebody, Mona wouldn't say who, told Arthur that he could have his choice of going to jail for at least a year for firing a gun in the city limits, or if he moved—of getting off with a disorderly conduct charge."

"You're kidding!"

"Didn't you say we were playing with Big Boys?"

"I guess I did."

The newspaper said that Arthur said:

"We decided to move, since our family was the main target. I hope that our family, by moving out, can help bring peace to Trumbull Park."

I read that statement till it got blurry before my eyes. I knew what it said. But I knew that what Arthur Davis really meant was:

"It's *really* you guys' turn now!"

35

WALK, WALK IN. It scared me to death to think
about it. But the more I thought, the more it seemed like
the only thing to do. We were living in a jail, and we went
out of Trumbull Park in a cage and came back to Trumbull
Park in a cage. The South Deering people got their natural
kicks leaping at that cage, trying to get at us, throwing
rocks at that cage and daring us to come out, pretty doggoned sure that we weren't thinking about coming out,
no kind of way.

We held our next meeting at Harry Harvey's house.
Everybody was there. No, not everybody. How could we
be everybody, with Arthur and Mona gone? Harry's house
was on the modern side, though not as fancy as Terry's.
A pretty lamp sat on a table near the couch, and underneath was a metal ashtray that had the words "Illinois—
The State of Lincoln" stamped on it in green paint. This
was the first time I had seen Harry without his DuSable
sweater. He looked absolutely burly in a white short-
sleeved sports shirt and slacks—great big arms and a thick
neck almost as big as Carl's.

The people dragged into the meeting late, unsmiling—
mouths stuck out, half-speaking to each other, half-speak-

ing to me. There wasn't much talk before the meeting started, and I got to the point right away:

"We've been just sitting here taking it so far. We haven't had a plan. No program, no nothing. Now——" Now was the time to talk about walking in. "Now is the time to start showing these people that we aren't scared of them. They actually think we're scared of them. Some of us have been talking about walking in and out of the project instead of going in squad cars. I mean, to and from work and the stores and church—wherever we go—you know what I mean?"

Nobody said a mumbling word!

"Well, what I mean is this: as long as the people behind this thing can keep these people encouraged, keep them thinking that they have any kind of chance of winning, they can keep them out there in those streets raising sand until kingdom come. But suppose the people out there started to feel that there wasn't any use in standing on those corners night and day, or marching up and down the streets each and every night? Suppose they were shown that, no matter what they did, we weren't going to move, that they were going to fail—then do you think they'd be out there for long? I don't."

Still not a peep!

"I mean—like look at this—if we walked, the cops would *have* to protect us, because the eyes of the city would be on them."

Terry coughed real loud right here. I went on:

"Well, let's don't count on what the public might think, then. The *Daily News* has a article about Trumbull Park where it says that we can sue the police if we get hurt out here."

Terry coughed loud again. I went on:

"I know nobody wants to get hurt just to be able

to sue the cops; but, look, are we going to sit here and take this stuff until we all go crazy and have to be carried out? We're going to have to start standing up for our rights some day. The guys behind this thing are counting on our being too cowardly to take up for ourselves. As long as we don't make *some* effort to fight back, we're just the same as helping these people kick our rear ends."

Kevin finally spoke up:

"Well, I for one will walk any time anybody else will. I just say we should take our guns to make sure that we won't go down on the humble if someone should try to start some stuff."

Terry was ready now. He had his arguments all lined up:

"And you may rest assured—they will try to attack you."

Kevin shot back:

"Attack *me?* Why not you? Where are *you* going to be?"

"In a squad car like I've got some sense! Listen. He who fights and runs away lives to fight another day!"

Kevin snapped:

"How about he who talks and runs away, never does anything but talk?"

Terry growled:

"I'm *not* walking!"

Christine Thomas said:

"Suppose we get caught with the guns on us? Then we'd go to jail and still wouldn't accomplish anything."

I don't know whether I really felt this way or not, but something made me answer:

"We can't carry guns."

I scared myself!

It had been quiet anyway, but now it *really* got quiet.

Kevin looked at me real hard. He kind of laughed when he said:

362

"Say, Daddy! We didn't say nothing about people not carrying some *protection*."

I answered, trying to sound as unconcerned as I could:

"Well, you heard what Christine said, and she's right. If we carry guns, we're going to be arrested before we get started—like the last time, you dig? Then that would discourage everybody else from even *trying* to walk."

"Getting kicked in the booty would be mighty discouraging too."

"We're not going to get kicked in the booty."

Christine's husband William sighed:

"Oh, no?"

Kevin said:

"Man, I tell you, I don't mind going along. But I'm not going out there among those fools with nothing to take care of myself with. So I go to jail again. So what?"

Then everybody—Carl, Terry, Norman, everybody—started mumbling and talking among themselves.

Up to now I hadn't even dreamed of walking out there with nothing on me. Now I began to see it clear. Walking in would have to be a game of bluff. We had to count on the white folks wanting *us* to start trouble so that *they* could finish it—the shooting way I mean. Walk with nothing on you—that's what I was arguing, knowing I was right, even though I didn't know exactly why. That's what I had said.

Now Norman was ready to say something:

"No, Buggy, I can't go along with that myself. I mean, I was wrong about wanting to move out, I admit that. But walk in unarmed? Man, do you realize what you're asking us to do? Hell, even in Korea, we had something to shoot with!"

Terry snarled:

"He's asking us to prepare to die. And for what?"

I answered him before he could get through talking:

"Die for that dark face of yours, man! What are you worth anyhow? We're all going to die some day, but——"

"Yeah," Christine bellowed, "but why rush it?"

"*You're* rushing it by sitting here letting these people wear on your nerves this way. You're dying by sitting up in those squad cars like a bunch of wet, scared rats hiding from the Great White Father! Is death any worse?"

William Thomas threw in his two cents again:

"Yeah. Yeah, it is. This is a hell of a world, but I don't want to leave it."

Now it was my baby. Walking in—not using the squad car, not carrying a gun or a knife or even a good baseball bat.

"All right! All right, all of you! Forget it! I don't care! You wanted a leader. A leader's got to have plans. I told you mine. You didn't want them, so get yourself another leader! I'm through!"

But Terry was too slick to let a good bet go by, so he said:

"No, no, no, Buggy! We don't want you to feel that way!" He turned to the group. "Do we?"

They mumbled back:

"No . . . No . . . of course not."

Then Terry swung his Sunday punch:

"Why don't *you* try walking in—unarmed, I mean. Then maybe if you—uh—make it, then——"

I wasn't ready for this. A man needs time to think about going out alone by himself among a bunch of screaming, rock-throwing, bomb-shooting people unarmed, maybe to die. But Terry hadn't given me that time. Had I given it to him?

They waited.

I could hear that diesel whining in the distance. It always knew when to whine—just like a dog near a deathbed, or a place where death is to come.

Terry said:

"Well?"

Helen said:

"Now, just a minute, this isn't Buggy's——"

"*Hold it, Helen!*"

"But Buggy, after all, *you've* got a family too! If these people don't want to——"

"*HELEN!*"

"Don't holler at me, Buggy!"

But she sat back in her chair, silent, head bent, breathing hard, loud, holding Diane's hand, standing beside her. Louella started sucking her fingers.

"All right! All right! I didn't say I wanted you—any of you—to do anything that I won't do. Sure it's a chance, but I think it'll work. I don't think that the Big Boys will kill any of us—not unless we give them a real good excuse, like trying to shoot one of those people. Arthur was lucky. If there had been a cop around, what would have kept him from shooting Arthur and telling everybody that Arthur had gone berserk and that he had to shoot Arthur to save innocent people? To save himself?"

Nobody answered. They wanted to hear just one thing: Was I going to walk or not?

"I don't think these people intend to kill us. I think they want to scare us, yes. Put pressure on us, yes. Man, listen to what I'm telling you! It's a big money scheme, and murdering us in cold blood would bring headlines and investigations so fast it would make your head swim! These guys have to play it cozy—go so far and no farther. I say that by walking we can force their hands—make them put up or shut up . . ."

Carl said:

"Don't you mean shut up or kill us?"

"That's just what I mean."

Beverly gasped, and then started giggling, holding her hand over her mouth and bending over in her lap.

Terry said:

"Are *you* going to walk?"

I asked the group:

"If *I* walk, will the rest of you?"

Kevin asked:

"Without guns?"

"Without guns."

Kevin hunched his shoulders and breathed loudly:

"I want to see *you* do that—first."

"*Then* will you?"

"Hell, if *you* do, I *got* to!"

"All right. I'll walk."

I sure missed Arthur then. What would he have said? Would he say he'd go with me? Would he have said that he wouldn't walk without carrying a gun? That bothered me.

It was Saturday night, but we didn't have a party. Helen didn't speak to me all the way home—not even when, just before we reached our house, a voice shouted from the darkened area near 106th Street:

"*Get out of here, you black niggers!*"

Helen didn't say a word to me, not even when a bomb shook the soft ground under our feet and turned the bare tree branches above us from black to blue-white against the nighttime gloom.

36

I DIDN'T DIG HELEN no kind of way. I mean, one day she's telling me to fight, and then the next day she comes up with this "you've got a family too" stuff. Oh, I knew all about not looking for trouble and all that. But, well, I wasn't looking for trouble—I was looking for peace, *my* peace; and right now it seemed that crawling out of those rolling jails they called squad cars, and walking the streets like a man, by myself, was the only way I was going to get any peace. But still I didn't know. Many a time the next day I thought I was all wrong.

It was thoughts like these that were just a-going in my mind the next day—at work, and in the squad car riding down Bensley. And there they were—just as faithful as you please—the mob, out of winter jackets now and wearing spring jackets; gloves and scarfs gone; no vapor coming from their mouths now. Just words:

"*Nigger, nigger, nigger!*"
"*Why don't you come on out here like a man!*"
"*We'd better not catch you on the street!*"
"*Go back to Africa!*"
"*Blackieeeee!*"

It was at times like that that the thought of walking down that long street—four blocks to the project, five blocks to my house—seemed like a junkie's nightmare.

The squad car dragged by the people. Buggy Martin was on parade. Black nigger Buggy Martin on parade in a black cage with a red light on top, and outside screaming on the street were the men and women who came out every day at the same time to watch the animal go by.

Walk in that? Not me!

Tell me not to walk the streets—the free, American streets of South Deering? Not me, I'll walk anywhere I please!

Trust these mean-looking cops to keep the mob from grabbing me on those streets and killing me? Not me!

Let these grinning, yelling white folks tell me where to walk and where not to? Not me!

Back and forth. Back and forth.

Walk. Don't walk. Walk. Don't walk. Walk. Don't walk!

Be smart. Play it cool . . . Be a man. Fight for your rights . . . Don't be a square. Live this thing through safely . . . It's your guys' turn now!

This way and that way, and this way and that way!

"Okay, Martin, this is it!"

We were in the project already. I got out of the squad car and started for my house, sick at the stomach. What had I done; telling those people that I would walk in? When was I supposed to start? Today? Tomorrow? Next week? When? When? And what for?

But I knew what for. I had told all of the others what for.

"You're *still* the ugliest man in the world!"

That voice! I felt ten years roll off of my back like rain water! I felt the wildest leap in my chest where my heart is! I turned to see where that voice was coming from.

"Over here, Buggy!"

Standing in the doorway of Headquarters Nine.

"Ricky!"

My little brother Ricky, taller than me, was standing

there in the doorway of the project police headquarters. I knew he'd become a policeman since he ran away from us at the Gardener Building. But out here? He sure *was.* I ran over toward him, and he broke over to me.

"Ricky! I'll be damned!"

He grabbed my hand, and we stood there like two fools, just shaking hands up and down and up and down. The first thing I noticed were the wrinkles underneath his eyes, and then the cigarette yellow of his teeth. But the rich red was still there in his skin, and his eyes, even with the wrinkles, were clear—a little hard, maybe, but right now bright and maybe a little watery. And what a heavy rough voice he had!

"Your *little* brother?!"

He raised up on his toes and put his fists on his waist and looked down at me. I pushed him and he staggered back a bit. I laughed:

"You'll always be my little brother! What the hell are you doing out here?"

He clamped his arm around my shoulder, and laughed.

"Well, you see I *am* in jail—only not on the side of the bars where Daddy said I'd be."

"Come on, boy! I know Helen's goin' to flip when she sees you."

"You mean she hasn't put you down *yet?*"

"She'd better not."

"Buggy, I'm sure glad to see you. It's been a long time, man."

"You're not kidding!"

And we almost skipped as we walked through the project to my house.

Helen had only a few more weeks, and she looked it. Talk about big! Ooooou-whee! She had on a pink maternity blouse that looked like a fat man's shirt, and she had bought a pair of those Toreador pants for pregnant women. I had teased her when she first put that outfit on, but now it looked kind of sharp; and on top of that she had her hair fixed—even that wild part that hung down over her ear was in its rightful place. She looked pretty good, if I do say so myself, when she swung the front door open and ran as best she could down the short walk from our door to the sidewalk where we were and almost knocked Ricky down, she hugged him so hard.

"Ricky! Ricky!"

"Helen! You're still the world's prettiest!"

"Come in, come in, both of you."

She grabbed Ricky's hand with one hand and grabbed mine with the other.

Inside Louella and Diane looked with big eyes and mouths wide open at this strange man in a policeman's uniform. I picked Louella up:

"Honey, this is your Uncle Richard."

Ricky took her from my arms, and she took to that guy right away. He always did know how to handle women. He kissed her and tickled her chin, and she giggled and hugged him.

"Louella," he told her in his deep voice, "you can just call your Uncle Richard 'Ricky.' Everybody else does."

Louella giggled and said:

"Ricky?"

"That's right, you pretty thing! Hey, who's that little butterball standing over there by the couch?"

Diane, seeing the treatment Louella got from this tall, laughing man in a policeman's uniform, ran over to him and hugged his leggings, giggling, and squealing like it was something big just to hug those shiny, black, leather-covered legs. Ricky picked her up with his free hand, still holding Louella in his other arm. I stared hard at him, at his broad shoulders and big arms, at his great big chest, at his cap tilted slightly back from his head. I tried to compare the squeaky baby voice I remembered with the rough, tough-guy's voice that now came from this good-natured giant.

"Hey, Ricky, how'd you get to be so big?"

He put the kids down and took his hat off and walked over to a chair near the table on which the record player sat. He hitched up his pants over his long legs and slapped them lightly on the sides with his wide thick palms.

"Well, you remember how everybody was always saying that *you* looked to be the spitting image of Daddy?"

Helen sat on the couch across from Ricky and I sat beside her. The kids hung around the chair where Ricky sat. Helen said:

"I remember that."

Ricky went on:

"Well, I just decided that you could *look* like Daddy if you wanted to but I was going to be as *big* as he was, and"—he changed his voice and twisted his mouth to one side—"and, by cracky, I am too!"

Time was when that would have made me mad, but now I was so glad to see that guy I didn't know what to do. I said:

"The last time I saw Daddy, he was drinking 'blood' like water. I think it was down on 58th Street under the El. I haven't seen him for quite a while though. When's the last time you saw him?"

Ricky's face lost its laughing look, just that quick.

"I saw him last night, Buggy."

"Last night? Oh yeah? Where?"

He lifted his policeman's cap from his knees and started

371

fumbling with the badge on it. He kept his eyes right on that cap, and a trace of the little brother's thinness came back into his voice:

"Daddy's in the hospital, Buggy."

Helen dug what was happening right away. She pulled herself up and called Diane and Louella:

"Come on, girls, let's wash up for dinner."

Ricky got up and sat down on the couch beside me:

"Buggy, you wouldn't believe it was Daddy. He— he's nothing but a skeleton, Buggy. The doctor says it's a wonder he's alive today—or at least alive last night. He might be dead now, for all I know. I went by Helen's folks' house and they told me you were out here. But Daddy, Buggy—he's in bad shape."

I told myself I didn't care, that it wasn't Daddy who was in bad shape, that it wasn't nothing but a goddamned lushhead stranger who was lying in a hospital, and I didn't care. But even as I told myself I didn't care, I got cold all over and knew that I did.

"What's wrong with him, Ricky?"

"He asked me to tell you to come and see him. He wants to see the kids too."

"What's wrong with him?"

"Cancer."

"Cancer? Daddy? Our Daddy? Cancer?"

"Cancer. Cancer of the throat."

A bell went *ting!* Right inside my head it went. *Ting!*

"Awwwww, Ricky! Are you kidding? You're teasing me, aren't you?"

"I wouldn't tease about a thing like that, Buggy. I saw him myself. He looks pretty bad."

"How they treating him? What do the doctors say? Is it going to kill him? Can't they stop that stuff from spreading sometimes? What did the doctor say?"

"I just saw him for the first time last night myself. A lady from the Social Services Committee called me at home. I don't know how they found me. The doctor wasn't there when I went there. I'm off duty now—I work the seven to three-thirty shift—and I'm going down to see him again this evening. You want to go with me, Buggy? Daddy said he wanted to see you."

"I wonder if we ought to let Helen and the kids go?"

Helen said from behind the wall that ran alongside the steps leading to the upstairs bedrooms:

"Yes, I *would* like to go."

Then she came down and walked, tired-looking and sad, over to the couch. Ricky and I made a place for her. She explained:

"I thought you two would like to be alone for a while. I was just coming down when I heard—what Ricky said about your father. I'm sorry, both of you, I'm so sorry."

I hugged her, and she laid her head on my shoulder:

"Honey, do you think you ought to go? I mean being the way you are and all? Do you think that——"

"He's your father, Buggy. He's my father-in-law."

She got up and started back upstairs:

"I'll have the kids dressed in no time. We'll fix sandwiches from the meat loaf we were going to have for dinner."

She yelled from the top of the stairs:

"I'll only be a minute."

Ricky said:

"I'll pull my car around the back."

When he was gone, while Helen dressed the kids upstairs, I went into the kitchen and washed my hands in the sink. I took the meat loaf out of the oven. I opened the bread box on top of the refrigerator and took out the bread. I got the mayonnaise and relish out of the refrigerator and a knife out of the utility cabinet, and laid the bread in a row on the table. I remembered how Momma had laid the bread and meat and mayonnaise and all out on the table once back at the Gardener Building. We were going to the "Bud Biliken parade" over on South Parkway; and after that we were going to the "Bud Biliken picnic" in Washington Park. Joe Louis was going to be there. And we saw him, too—and his wife Marva Louis, too. They were still in love then, Joe and Marva; and Momma was alive then, and Daddy hadn't even met this 61st Street girl.

I listened for the sound of the diesel train, that sound I had heard so many times before when death was about back at the Gardener Building where the tracks the diesel rode ran along Lafayette over the viaduct at 57th Street, right near the Gardener Building, where Momma lay in bed at night, alone—dying. I listened for the diesel to start buzzing by, the way it did while Momma cried in the dark— the way it buzzed now here in Trumbull Park while the bombs spit blue-white on everything around me—trees, grass, buildings, us, and even around the very people who set the bombs. But there wasn't a single sound—no diesel, no bombs, not even the clanking of the trains in the train yard.

I said the words out loud to myself:

"Daddy's got cancer of the throat."

Ricky came in the front door, and Helen came downstairs. The kids were dressed. I slapped the sandwiches together real quick, and we turned out the lights and locked the doors and went around the back in the darkening evening—too light yet for the street lights to come on; too dark to see good—a heavy, thick, foggy, gray evening. The grayness hung about the branches of the trees in dark spiderwide splotches. The grayness darkened the corners of the

374

building and sank into the ground. In the apartments where the lights were not yet turned on the grayness turned the glass panes black. Black tree branches, still bare from wintertime, stood out against the lighter gray of the sky, and as the branches moved in the lazy, damp, wet wind, their black reflections waved in the window panes like bony witches' fingers from haunted houses.

37

RICKY'S CAR was a brand-new, shiny, jet-black Lincoln Capri. I was scared to get in it, it looked so good.

"Hey, man! The Gardener Building was never like this!"

"Get in."

The kids climbed into the back, and Helen and I sat in the front with Ricky. Helen turned to the kids:

"Don't you kids put your feet on those seat covers."

Ricky laughed:

"Don't worry about it. Those are dirt-proof seat covers."

Helen laughed:

"Show-off!"

Ricky asked us in an excited little boy's voice:

"No kiddin'. How do you like it?"

"Jim," I said, "it's a gas!"

Ricky laughed and hunched Helen:

"Will you listen to the hippy-dippy?"

Helen joked back:

"Oh, he's a real hippy-dippy, all right."

But the way she said it let me know that she was still thinking about my intentions of walking in—an unarmed hippy-dippy. I know that what she really meant was: Oh, he's a real fool, all right!

Ricky started the motor, and leaned way back in the seat, and the big shiny black Lincoln hushed away from Trumbull Park like anybody's magic carpet. We glided up Oglesby behind the project up to where it ended at 105th Street. I hadn't ever been back there before, and now I could see how the great prairie ran right up to the project and stopped. In the middle of the prairie the silhouettes of boxcars in a train yard, stood still as sleeping cattle in one of those old Gary Cooper movies—black shadows against the sky, each separated from the other by the same-sized patch of gray; each coupled to the other at the bottom by the same little thin black line. Behind the boxcars was a bunch of buildings: low, square-topped mountains. Beyond the buildings was a water tower, caged by thin girders and high rising frames, all black against the gray sky.

The Lincoln rolled alongside the park that ran on our right from 105th to 103rd. There were trees and bushes everywhere, and a couple of teen-agers chased each other on the wide, wide lawn beyond the trees. An empty swimming pool surrounded by a fence sat high on a cement base, and a fieldhouse with yellow lights at its windows stood just to the north. North of the fieldhouse was a ball park; and as the car pulled to the corner of 103rd Street, two men coming across the ball park yelled:

"*Hey, nigger!*"

I looked at Ricky to see how he would take being called a nigger. He and I had said when we were very, very young that we'd kill the first white man that called us a nigger. Ricky just laughed:

"Those silly sons-of-bi—— Oh, I'm sorry, Helen! I forgot you and the kids were in here. I'm sorry."

"That's all right, Ricky, I know how you feel."

We crossed the high bridge at 103rd Street going sixty-five miles an hour. I said:

"Man, you're going to get a ticket!"

Ricky laughed:

"There's only one cop who'll give his fellow policeman a ticket—under normal circumstances, of course. You know who that is?"

We all said it at the same time:

"Muller!"

Ricky said:

"Right! And right now Muller is way on the other side of town."

When we hit the top of the bridge I looked back at Trumbull Park. I felt as if we were escaping from prison, and that any minute someone would be chasing us and catching up with us and making us go back to our cells.

The train yard was right underneath the bridge now. It seemed so dark and dead down there that I couldn't believe that those tracks were the same tracks the diesel rode. Somehow riding away from Trumbull Park in a private car was altogether different from riding in the squad car. You could see things around you. In the squad car all you could think about was that you were riding with a couple of policemen . . . But we were riding with a policeman, weren't we?

Down Stony Island to 95th, west on 95th to State, north on State to 63rd, across the cobblestones at the streetcar junction at 63rd, on past the Gardener Building at 57th Street. Helen asked:

"What hospital is he in?"

"County."

We hadn't talked about Daddy all the way from Trumbull Park; now, passing the Gardener and all, it seemed I just had to say something, but all I could say was:

"Poor Daddy."

Ricky's voice was soft when he asked, staring straight ahead:

"Do you feel sorry for him, Buggy?"

"I guess so. I mean, no matter what he did he was our father."

"He was surprised to see me in a policeman's uniform."

Helen said:

"I guess he was. You know, police-work doesn't exactly seem to be your line."

"What do you mean, Helen?"

I answered for her:

"Remember the time those policemen shot——"

"Just a minute! I didn't make the police department. I just work for them. That's all any policeman does—work for the——"

I cut him off:

"Work for the who? The real estate boys out in Trumbull Park? The rioters? The people who bomb us? The people who——"

Ricky laughed:

"Wait, wait a minute! Like I said, I didn't make the police department, I just work for it."

"But," I snapped, "who does *it* work for? Not me. Not Helen. Not Mona or Arthur or any of the other Negroes out where I live. Do you think that a bunch of Negroes could bomb and bother a bunch of white people in this city for almost a solid year without more being done about it than these policemen are doing out in Trumbull Park?"

Ricky was still good-natured:

"Look, the mayor is the one responsible for law and order in Chicago. He appoints the police commissioner, and he gives the commissioner his orders. The commis-

379

sioner gives me and all the rest of the poor working guys on the police force our orders."

"Well," Helen said, "what *are* your orders? The only orders I've ever heard them give you policemen in Trumbull Park is——"

And Helen and I both said at the same time:

"Take cover, men!"

Ricky stopped smiling now:

"So what do you want me to do? *Not* take cover, and get fired? Listen, I'm not any different from you. I know what's happening."

I said:

"But you *are* different. When you're on duty, you're very different!"

"Every policeman is. It's his job. A policeman has no friends. He's there to enforce the law, that's all!"

Helen said:

"He's not there to enforce the law. He's there to take orders."

And I filled in:

"And in the case of Trumbull Park your orders are not to enforce the law. Your orders are to——"

And Helen and I again:

"Take cover, men!"

Ricky said:

"Awww, now look! You two aren't being fair. You know what I'd do if I had the chance. You know what any Negro cop out there would do if he had the chance. That's the whole problem. The guys in the district, when they come back from Trumbull Park, say that most of the colored cops are stuck way back in one of those cubby holes. Now isn't that right?"

Helen answered:

"Sure, but——"

"Well, then. Why do you suppose they've got us

back there? I'll tell you why: because they know we wouldn't turn our backs when one of those people started some trouble."

Helen said:

"Yes, but I've heard a lot of the colored cops talking just as bad about us as some of the white policemen. I didn't tell Buggy about this, but I had to set a couple of them straight for starting the same kind of talk about Buggy that they used to keep up about Arthur."

"*Arthur Davis?*"

"Yes, Arthur Davis. What's wrong with Arthur Davis? Why are all of you policemen so hard on him? All he's done was to defend himself. You'd do the same thing if you were in his place."

"Arthur Davis is a trouble maker! Do you know what he thinks about colored policemen? Listen, Buggy, don't you ever get the colored policemen down on you the way they are on that Davis!"

Helen asked again:

"So what did *he* do?"

"He turned two colored policemen's names in to the commissioner."

I cut in:

"Well, what did they——"

Ricky cut me off:

"And that's not all. Do you know that that guy peeps out of his window every five minutes just to see if we're out there? And if he doesn't see us—wham!—right on the phone to the commissioner's office! He's a smart-aleck, talks bad—smart. He struts like he owns the world, and he hasn't got a pot to—cook in. Arthur Davis? I know all about him! And I'll tell you this—none of the other Negroes out there like him. His own people—even they think he thinks he's cute."

Helen spoke in that dangerous low voice of hers:

"When did you come out to Trumbull?"

Ricky laughed:

"Oh, I know what you're going to ask next! How do I know all these things? Right?" He didn't wait for Helen to answer. "Well, every cop in the project can tell you the same thing—even the sergeant knows."

Helen's low voice flicked out:

"Who told you?"

"Lemme see. Oh, I know"—his voice sort of died away—"the sergeant."

"And who told the sergeant all these things?"

"Helen, I don't know. I'm just taking the sergeant's word."

"The *white* sergeant's word about a *colored* man in *Trumbull Park?*"

"What reason would he have to lie?"

She rode him like a sparrow on a hawk:

"What reason would he have to tell you men to take cover? What reason would he have to send the Negroes back to the boiler room?"

"What are you getting at, Helen?"

"I'm not getting at anything . . ."

"You must be."

Helen stopped talking for a minute or so. We were at 46th and State, passing the Owl Theater. I remembered the old Friday night serials in that place. I also remembered the time a policeman hit a colored boy in the stomach—where he'd been cut in a gang fight, because the boy wouldn't tell who the other boys in the gang were. I remembered how the blood squirted out underneath the boy's sports shirt and ran down the front of his pants.

Helen finally answered Ricky:

"Let me ask you something, Ricky. Did you know that Arthur and Buggy were something like leaders out there?"

"I heard that today."

"Did you ever stop to think that the police department might have a whispering campaign going on against Arthur, and maybe even Buggy, so that they can isolate them from the rest of the Negroes, isolate them even from the Negro policemen?"

"Oh, I don't hear anything about Buggy!"

"But you do hear things about Arthur, Ricky. I just want to ask you these few questions: first, why would the cops be hostile against a *Negro* in Trumbull Park, when he's not the one throwing bricks, or setting off bombs, or anything else? And next——"

"Look, Helen, I know what you're getting at! Yes, there's prejudice in the police department. I know it as well as you, but how can you change men's minds about you?"

Helen was looking straight ahead, and as we passed 39th Street the light from the Church of God in Christ flicked across her face, and I saw her stiff, tightly-pressed lips, and the hard set of her chin.

"Ricky," she said still softly, "the prejudice I'm talking about is not in the mind. It's in the *acts* of those policemen. And it's permitted by everyone, from the sergeant to the lieutenant to the captain—all the way up to the mayor's office. Prejudice. Let the Negroes move out if they don't like the way they're being treated! Let them start a race riot and get killed if they're tired of being kicked around! Let them suffer if they insist on living in white neighborhoods! That, Ricky, is what your police department is saying when it lets the mob get away with tormenting us! But more than that, Ricky: they've added one more thing—hate. Create hate among the Negroes between themselves. Lie on them. Turn the colored cops against them. Create stories. Tell young cops new on the force: they'll pass it along; they want to get in the know; they want to be one of the boys. And look at you, Rick. Look at you! Why you took that sergeant's word like it was the gospel. You haven't even been in Trumbull Park a whole day, and you are already down on Arthur Davis. Why? Because you were told to be! Oh, no, nobody came up to you and said, 'Now I want you to be down on Arthur Davis.' But it amounted to the same thing. One of your own gang—a policeman—told you. A *sergeant* told you, and you tell somebody else, and they tell somebody else, and Arthur gets to be the big bad wolf of Trumbull Park. Well, you can stop now. Arthur's gone, Ricky. There's another big bad wolf of Trumbull Park now. It's Buggy now, Rick—your own brother. Are you going to believe what the sergeant says about *him*? Are uniforms thicker than blood?"

We were crossing 22nd Street now. The silhouette of the El platform on the right strung across the street like a clumsy bridge. On both sides of the street in front of us were taverns, the bottles piled high in the windows—nice full clean bottles of drinks for men of distinction—and the men who drank the drinks were lying outside the doors of both taverns as if someone had driven by and shot them dead. A few left standing leaned heavily against the windows of the taverns, "just about ready to die." On the floors over the taverns were the homes—yellow lights behind windows without shades; cracked walls sat behind the windows; and little dark-skinned children sat in the windows watching all the cars go by. Once Ricky and I had sat at the windows in the Gardener Building watching all the cars go by.

The reflection of Ricky's long black Lincoln whizzed by in the storefront windows of State Street like a long black ghost. I wondered, ghost of what? Me? Ricky? Our family? Momma? Daddy? What was that floating black Lincoln the ghost of? Ricky sat staring straight ahead. The lights from other cars lit up his face, and there were wrinkles there—confusion. Guilt? Maybe. Finally he said:

"A man has to make it some way or other in this

384

world. What should I do? Hold somebody up? Drink whiskey so that I won't know that I'm hungry, that I need a place to sleep? That I need someone to—to love me?" Helen was sitting in the middle next to him. He leaned over her and said to me: "I didn't tell you, Buggy. I'm married. I got a couple of kids myself."

I said:

"Hey, man, that's nice."

He said:

"Helen, I don't have the answer. Like you say, as a cop I just follow orders—good orders, bad orders, no orders. I follow them if I want to eat. Okay, so the police department *is* prejudiced, but they are just as hard on whites as they are on colored. I've seen some of those guys down at the station beat those white guys something awful. It's not just colored they discriminate against. It's—it's——"

Helen said:

"It's what?"

I said:

"The nobodies. The no-bread squares. The cats on a humble. The lushes like those guys back there on 22nd."

Helen said:

"But *we're* not lushes, Buggy."

I put my arm around her and hugged her tight:

"No, we're not, Baby. But we don't stick together to take care of ourselves. None of us—white or colored."

Helen mumbled against my shoulder:

"How can we, when we're trying our best to kill each other?"

We were at 12th Street now, and Ricky waved at a white policeman on a three-wheel cycle. The white policeman waved back, grinning. Ricky turned to us:

"That guy and I were in police school together. He's going into the detective bureau next week."

Helen said:

"When are you going?"

"Me? Oh, well, he's got a better clout, I guess. I mean, I put my application in a long time ago—even took the exam; but I haven't heard from them. Maybe he's just a better man than I am. I don't know. I know one thing, though: my name wasn't on the list that came out in the paper last week."

Helen laughed:

"How many Negro police captains are there on the force?"

"One."

"And how many policemen?"

"Oh, I don't know—four or five thousand."

"Uh-huh!"

Ricky laughed:

"What are you two looking for? The revolution?"

Helen answered:

"I'd like to see even the *evolution*, in *this* town."

Ricky turned left at Harrison three blocks north of 12th Street. He stopped at the stop light at Harrison and State. I said:

"I'm going to stop riding the squad car next week, Ricky. I'm going to walk the streets—like a man."

He said:

"Well, from what I've heard of those people, you might start out walking like a man, but you've got a damn good chance of ending up lying like a corpse."

"Well, that's all right too."

"For crusaders, yes; but not for me."

Helen said:

"Well, I've got to admit I don't think Buggy should walk in myself—at least not right now. They're still mad because Arthur shot at them, and they're just itching to get at one of us for that."

We were at Canal Street west now. The raggedy shadows of the Congress Street Expressway being built stood between the tall buildings that sat on the western edge of the Loop and Harrison Street where we were. Ricky said:

"Buggy—I didn't want to tell you this, but I *did* hear something about you. Some of the guys think that you're trying to be another Arthur Davis. And they say that you'll be very sorry if you make the wrong move. I mean, the word is out on you, Buggy. They say that Buggy Martin is next."

We were at Halsted and Harrison, waiting for the light to turn green. I said:

"Well, I haven't really decided definitely to walk in yet; but I'm thinking pretty hard about it."

Ricky laughed:

"Now, don't change your mind on my account."

Helen had ice in her voice:

"No, he's changing it on his account. Buggy, I've told you these same things before. Why are you thinking of changing your mind now? Did it sound truer coming from Ricky?"

"I didn't say that I was walking in for sure, or that I wasn't. I just said that I was thinking hard about it. But after all, Helen, a policeman does have the inside track on what's really happening out here—at least, as far as what the mob is going to do, and I don't want to walk into trouble when I *know* there's going to be trouble."

Helen said:

"Buggy—you have less and less room every day to change from one thing to another—less and less room—each and every day."

"And," Ricky added, "less and less time. I'm not like you. I've taken my choice. There's no doubt about it in my mind. *I'm* going to make it—the whole works—car, home of my own, fine clothes—the whole works. And I'm not going to jail getting it either. Let those dumb spooks out there in Trumbull Park take care of themselves, Buggy. If they want civil rights, they know how to get them. Fight for them themselves. But you can't teach those people new tricks. The white man has kicked us in the ass so much that a lot of us think that that's the way it's supposed to be! Well, I'm not giving my life to a bunch of goofs like them. If our people ever decide to stand up and fight, then you can count on me. Till then—stuff! But you, Buggy—you're the worst kind. You're too honest to be a good scuffler, and you're too scary to be a good hero. You're too proud to take this crap lying down, but you're too confused to know what you want to do about it. Man, I don't envy you no kind of way! In a way you're as bad off as—as—Daddy."

We were at the hospital, a great big tall place made of yellow bricks, with lights at all the windows, running three blocks west and three blocks south—people going in and coming out, squad cars with red lights flashing, screeching around the corner of Wood Street heading for the emergency room.

Ricky parked the car, and we all got out. The kids had fallen asleep a long time ago. Their sandwiches, still wrapped in wax paper, lay in the back seat beside them. I looked at my own sandwich. I looked at Helen and Ricky. I wasn't the least bit hungry.

"Poor Daddy," I said.

"Yeah," Ricky answered, "poor old Daddy."

Helen said:

"Maybe I'd better stay here in the car with the kids, since they're asleep—huh?"

38

THE ELEVATOR on the Harrison Street side of the hospital was new—new plastic, new buttons with nice shiny numbers for the floors that you wanted to go to. But the old, old blended smell of sick people and dead people and dying people, and of people who were just getting well and babies who were just being born—all that mixed-up smell was still there, and not even the new smell of the plastic and the hot smell of the soft white light inside the bright-green elevator could do away with that hospital funk. The odor of Lysol grew strong when our elevator reached the second floor.

Ricky got out first. He looked real official in his black shiny leggings, his dark-blue riding-looking pants with the light stripe down the side. His wide shoulders strained the shoulder-pads of that heavy, short jacket, and hanging from underneath the jacket, through a little slit along the side, were two guns—one on each side—pearl-handled and polished till they sparkled.

"Little brother," I called as he walked in front of me.

"What?"

A pretty nurse passed and smiled at him. He smiled back and turned his head as she went by. I answered his question:

"Oh, nothing. Where's Daddy's ward?"

"It's 221." He stopped at a door right near the elevator. "Here it is."

A long dim-lit hallway with a lot of doors on each side led way down into a large room where the sick people were. I could see an old white man on crutches way down there—white-haired and skinny, head bent down, crutches hunching his shoulders up even with his ears, one leg bent, walking slowly toward the hallway. Another man came up from behind me and Ricky in a wheel chair—a young man with big arms and real big hands:

"'Scuse me."

Ricky stepped to one side, and I to the other. The brown-haired young guy rolled by.

"Hey!" Ricky called to him. The young man stiffened, the back of his neck got red, and he started turning around. "You know Charlie Martin?"

I spoke to Ricky under my breath:

"What you asking him for? I thought you saw Daddy last night."

"I did."

Then I remembered. Ricky was a policeman, and a policeman has to let the world know he's around. Testing, testing, always testing—they all do it, the cops. Testing—got to make sure that people respect them, fear them. Ask a question, call somebody back, take an apple off the fruit stand. Free beer, free cigars, free Christmas presents from the merchants on the beat. I had seen all these things, but I hadn't thought much about them, until I saw Ricky the cop. The old Ricky I knew. Now I was getting to know the new Ricky—Ricky the cop.

The man in the wheel chair whirled around and hunched over with quick strokes to where we were. He studied Ricky as he came, and the cop-fear in his eyes went away.

"You mean the Champ?"

I looked at Ricky. The Champ? Ricky looked at me, then at the young man:

"Yeah, the Champ."

"Oh sure, I know 'im. Everybody does." That cat spun that chair around so fast it would make your head swim. "C'mon, follow me. I'll take you to 'im."

We had to really put on some speed to keep up with this guy. He slowed down just before he reached the ward:

"You guys kin to 'im?"

I didn't know what to say. Sure, he was my father all right; but behind not seeing him for years on top of years, I remembered that 61st Street girl, and how Momma cried herself to death worrying about him, and I had more or less disowned him as far as any feeling goes. But now, this: "You guys kin to 'im?" It made me remember that there was someone in this world who was older than me and kin to me. Winehead or not, deserter or not, two-timer or not, in that room was where I came from—my father. I looked at Ricky and I thought, His father too. My brother—Ricky. My father—Charlie Martin. Louis Martin, known as Buggy— brother and son. I *was* something, *did* come from some place. Trumbull Park and the Gardener Building were not just nightmares waiting till morning so that they could go away. They were real, and so was my father.

I put my hand on the wheel-chair guy's shoulder, and finally got the words straight enough in my mind to answer him:

"Yeah, we're kin to him. We're his sons."

Ricky really sounded like a little me-too brother when he said:

"That's right."

The man looked up at Ricky, smiling. Then he dropped his head and shook it from side to side:

"Ain't that somethin'! The Champ's got a cop for a son!" Then he looked up at Ricky real fast:

"No offense, officer. I mean, it jus' seem like the Champ wouldn't be having no kid that was——C'mon." He wheeled his chair through the door of the ward: "I'm glad you guys could come out to see 'im. He's one hell of a swell guy."

He pointed at a bed that was right near the front door on our left.

"There he is."

I walked in front of Ricky. Daddy's eyes were closed when we got to his bed. When I was near enough to him for a good look, I just stood there and looked. My father, Charles Martin. Big, good-looking Charles Martin, the only one in the family with good hair, we used to say. Now look at him. Just look.

Ricky stood with his hat in his hand, and he kept moving it around and around in his hand—not saying anything, just looking.

Great big Daddy. Could lift his end of a piano all by himself, while it took two men to carry the other end. Good-looking Daddy. Women stared at him like he was something good to eat. Laughed all the time, except when Momma asked him where he was going. Six-foot-five anyway you looked at him. And big—that was the main thing I had remembered about him. Big!

Now look at him. Just look.

His hair was white as snow, and his head was twisted over to one side, like it was broken. A black lump bulged out from his neck that looked like someone had jammed a great big grapefruit or something underneath his skin. His mouth was twisted down at one end, and it was open, and a milky-colored stuff ran out of his thin almost-black lips, turning the shaggy tips of his thick white moustache yellow and

392

faded. The bottom of his narrow teeth—those teeth that had smiled so prettily when he was feeling good—were brown now, and the brown lay in between each tooth.

Daddy was a little man now.

He looked to be no more than a hundred pounds. The cover sunk in where his chest was supposed to be, and it fluttered with every quick-short breath he took. One hand was out from under the cover, and it reminded me of the way those black branches looked, reflected in the windows back at Trumbull Park—skinny, knobby fingers, lumps at the joints, gripping the sheets tightly the way Momma had done once in the Gardener Building just before she died.

Those eyes looked so tired.

Everything had sunken deep into his skull. Once full, round, strong cheeks. Now—bones covered with sagging, rough-lined, wrinkled skin. It looked like chicken skin without the feathers.

Only his nose refused to change. Straight, bent down a bit in a little hook, wrinkled slightly as though it was concerned with something that had nothing to do with hospitals or cancer or death. You could have seen a nose like that right now on a man at a bar, taking Pabst from the barmaid instead of Hamms; on a man in a taxi, watching a pretty lady tell him she was sorry for stepping on his foot. Oh, you could have seen a nose like that 'most any place where a man was happy and healthy, and not dying. But the nose would go too, I thought; and thinking of this made me say to Ricky:

"Why did it happen, Ricky?"

"The wages of sin are——"

"Well, I'll be! Look who's here!"

Daddy's eyes were open and he was smiling. His voice scared me. I had already begun to think of him as dead, and now he was talking and smiling and trying to wipe the yellow from his mouth. He raised up, ever so slowly on one elbow, and pulled a towel from under his pillow, and wiped his mouth, and plucked the crust from his moustache and smiled.

"Buggy, I haven't seen you since I don't know when." He spoke in a sandpaper whisper.

I didn't know what to do. I just stood there trying to stretch a grin across my face:

"Hi, Daddy. How you feel?"

"Much better now, boy. I was sick there for a while." He looked at Ricky, and turned to me and laughed: "You ever think we'd have a bluecoat in the family?"

Ricky laughed—a flat, hollow, unhappy laugh:

"Watch out there! I'll lock you up."

Daddy twisted around on his back slowly. Everything he did was slow. He pointed to the end of the bed:

"There's a handle down there some place. Jack this bed up a little, will you, Ricky?"

Ricky jacked the bed up—not much. Daddy said:

"Sit down. Sit down. Take a load off of your feet."

Ricky sat in the chair near the bed. I got one from the empty bed beside Daddy's.

"Yeah," Daddy laughed, "take that one. He won't be needing it any more. He checked out last night."

The bed was so smooth and empty it was the emptiest bed I ever saw. The cover was made up, and the sheets were so white, and the pillow was so soft-looking. It was just waiting for someone else to get in it. Daddy explained:

"I used to be way down at the other end."

Rickey asked:

"How long you been here, Daddy?"

"About a month now. Anyway I used to be way down at the other end, and as soon as they roll me up here this son-of-a-gun hauls off and dies. He's the second one in a week to die up this way. I don't know why they don't take those guys out or something when they know they're going to die. It's—it's bad for the rest of the patients." He looked at the young man in the wheel chair who had met us at the door, sitting now near his bed two beds down from Daddy. "That kid cried all last night after this joker died. Now you see what I mean—it's not good for the rest of us to be that close to that sort of thing."

Then he stopped and jerked and closed his eyes, and water ran from his eyes, and his bottom lip pulled downward showing his teeth. His hands choked the sheets and his toes wiggled underneath the cover, and finally he took a deep breath and opened his eyes and smiled again. I said:

"What's wrong, Daddy?"

"Well, it was just a little pain that hit me. The nurse will be by here after a while and I'll get some pain pills. The doctor said that there's some new stuff that has helped a lot of people that would probably help me if I took it. Of course, it's special, so you can't get it here. You have to get a prescription." And he looked at me, pleading with his eyes. "If one of you boys has an extra buck or two—I can have the doctor make out the prescription, and you can get it at the drugstore across the street. It doesn't cost much, and the doctor said that it's a new medicine that not only kills that pain, but actually helps rebuild those tissues and things."

Ricky said:

"I'll get it, Daddy. Where's the nurse?"

Daddy frowned:

"Don't bother her now. These nurses have more work than they can handle. She'll be by here in a few minutes."

I said:

"Daddy, what happened? I mean, how did all this start?"

Daddy laughed, his watery eyes squinting and sparkling almost the way they had—before.

"Well, it's the darndest thing." He opened his mouth slightly, and tilted his head back.

"There was a tooth in there that I wouldn't have pulled. See that hole up there at the top?"

I bent over and pretended to see. The sour smell of sickness made me dizzy, and the sight of Daddy straining to move his head back just a little bit set my heart beating hard. I wanted to go, but I bent down and looked into his mouth and squinted and stood up and said:

"Yeah, I see it."

Ricky just sat there twisting that hat around and staring at Daddy's bony face. Daddy went on:

"Anyway, that doggoned tooth kept biting down on the top of my tongue. I guess I should have done something about it; but, well, you know how you put things off. Anyway, that little bugger did it, kept biting my tongue and biting it till finally infection set in, and one thing led to the other. And, well. . . . But the doctor's been using the X-ray on me, and I've been taking those medicines he's been giving me. Getting a lot of rest—that's the main thing—rest. And, hell, the doctor hasn't said it right out yet; but I can tell by the way he talks—I'll be well enough to get out of here before you know it! And boys"—he looked at me and Ricky—"I'm settling down, this time. No more of that running around with those wine-heads out there on 58th Street. Do nothing but ruin your health running around with those people. No more of that for me!"

Once again that pain struck him, and he closed his eyes, and the muscles in his face tightened like wires. He bit his lip so hard the blood came. I said:

"I'm going to call a nurse, or somebody. It's no need to let Daddy suffer like this."

"No!" he grunted, shaking his head and twisting his head as far as that black lump in his throat would let him.

Ricky got up and went into the hallway. He turned into one of the doors, and he stayed there a long time.

The pain let Daddy go, and he smiled again, eyes wet, forehead shining from the sweat:

"What was I saying? Oh, yes. I guess I've been feeling sorry for myself long enough. You know what, Buggy? I started working when I was eleven years old. Your granddaddy died when I was eleven, and I started working the week after he died—I mean working hard! Things were rough in those days, and I had your grandmother and your Aunt Bobby to take care of, and your Uncle Eddie. I was the oldest—the sharpest thing on the block! Always had money in my pockets, when my daddy was living, got anything I wanted. When he died, I took his place. Mother was sick, couldn't work. I was the oldest, had to work. I sent my sister and my brother to high school; and they were looking good every day they went, too! Started working on an ice truck. Then in a garage—learned how to fix cars—you know how good I can fix cars, Buggy. I'm going back into that business when I get out of here—good money in fixing cars. But, Buggy, I got weak after I got married. Your mother was a good woman—too good—made me want to give her big things: new clothes, fine furniture, and all—you know what I mean. That was before you were born, Buggy."

The pain hit him again, and I turned my head, and everybody in the ward was looking at me—and looking at him. Some of them were shaking their heads; others smiled when I looked at them.

"Buggy—everything I touched turned to you-know-what. I mean, everything. Then, well—I guess I just sort of gave up . . . My mother needed things, getting older—Bobby —Eddie. Then your mother—and you kids. Too much,

Buggy! I tried, but everything . . . So what the heck! Live! I said."

Ricky came back with a tiny paper in his hand. Daddy waited until he came near, and then:

"But, boys, I've had some good times!" He turned his head and laughed, or tried to. "People have tried to beat me. Thought ol' Charlie nothin' but a fool. But I fooled *them*. This girl up 61st Street . . ."

The 61st Street girl! How long, how long had I waited to hear the story of this girl. She was the one that had broken up my family, killed my mother, destroyed my father. I held my breath hoping that Daddy wouldn't change his mind about talking about her.

He didn't:

"Tried her best—that girl—to make me leave your mother. Young. Smart. Pretty. Not prettier than your mother, though! Worked in a laundry. Always gave me what I needed. 'Leave her! Leave her!'—that's all I could hear. I left all right. I left *her!* Early one morning. Took a long time to make up my mind, but I did. I left that 61st Street girl. But it was too late then. Your mother thought every time I went out that it was with this chick. It wasn't. Lots of times, just gambling. Or drinking. Should have told her. *Did* tell her once. Wouldn't believe me. Nobody believed me. Mother needing things. Kids hungry all the time . . . My friends: 'C'mon Charlie, who's the boss in your family?'—— 'Me!'——'Well, all right then! Let's go get a taste.' . . . Never had real friends. Had to work too early, too young, too much responsibility . . . But I quit that 61st Street girl!"

He turned to Ricky:

"What was I looking for, boys?"

Ricky said:

"I don't know, Daddy."

"What, Buggy? What was I looking for?"

398

"I don't know, Daddy."

"Was it the big things? The *new* car?" He laughed. "You know, I've had ten cars—not a one of them new. Don't worry about those cars, boys. They'll be here when you're gone . . . Got families, haven't you?"

He turned to me:

"You marry that little gal downstairs?"

"Helen?"

"Yeah."

I nodded, and Daddy smiled and shook his head slightly:

"Good girl. Ricky, you get married?"

Ricky took a wallet out of his back pocket and pulled some snapshots out. Daddy squinted his eyes as Ricky held them close to his face. I know he didn't see the two babies and the light-skinned long-haired woman who held them smiling out from that shiny, grey paper, but he pushed out a grunt that was supposed to be a laugh.

"Hot damn! You boys are doing all right! The girls— Doris, Johnetta—hear from them? Tell them I said they'd better come out here to see me. But I'm getting out of here soon. Tell them anyway. Okay?"

Both Ricky and I nodded. Ricky said:

"Daddy, I'll go get the medicine."

I don't know why I said:

"I'll go with you."

Daddy said:

"You boys see this lump on my neck? This is the bugger that's got to be whipped. Me and it—we fight all night long sometimes. And all day. Me and it. It's a tough one, all right! Don't play the least bit fair." He laughed at this supposed-to-be joke. "Waits till I get sleeping good, then— wham! And that's when we tussle. But feel this lump, Buggy. You, too, Ricky. Feel it. I just want you to see how hard it is. Feel it."

399

He reached for my hand and I put my hand in his. It was hard, rough. He pulled my hand upwards and placed it very lightly on his neck. My fingers touched his flesh—no, skin— skin as thin as it looked, soft and rough with shaving bumps, but thin and lying across the hard rock on his neck like tissue paper. I touched that lump and felt it with the tips of my fingers while he gripped my wrist tightly. Then he did the same thing to Ricky, while Ricky held on to his policeman's cap with his other hand as if it was his only protection against the wave of sorrow and fear and love that rose in me and seemed to rise in him.

Daddy let go of Ricky's hand and laughed:

"Feel that? But I'll whip him! You *bet* a man I'll whip him! Never seen a fight yet I didn't win! I'll whip him, 'cause I'm getting out of here."

Ricky said:

"We'll be right back. The doctor told me where to go. We won't be long."

"Bring me a pack of cigarettes back—Camels."

When we were out of the hospital, Ricky said:

"I asked the nurse about him and she said get him anything he wants, if it'll make him happy."

"What did the doctor say?"

"He wasn't there. The nurse said he'll be back before visiting hours are over, though."

And when we got back from the drug store, we stopped by the doctor's office. He was there—a short fat smooth man with a wide face and a wider smile. Ricky said:

"We're Charlie Martin's sons."

The smile vanished.

"Yes, yes. Well, have a seat."

We sat.

He sat at the desk and without wasting a minute said:

"I'm sorry to have to give you news like this but——"

400

I wanted to stop time right then. Grab the guts of all the clocks in the world and hold them so that they wouldn't go. I wanted to put my hand over the doctor's mouth. Get up and run out. Anything to stop him from saying what the *but* meant. After that *but* nothing would ever be the same. I could imagine that Daddy would get up from there like he said he would—if only it wasn't for that *but* . . .

"But your father is not going to be with us for very long . . ."

The doctor pulled some eyeglasses from the pocket of his white jacket. He put them on and then took them off again.

"It's been the talk of the hospital that he has lived this long . . ."

We shook the doctor's hand and went back into the ward. Daddy's eyes were closed, and I leaned close to him to hear his breathing. He breathed in short, jabbing breaths, as if he was trying to sneak his breath past that big black bulge in his throat. His head was turned to the side, and one hand lay outside the cover with the fingers bent like a claw, ready to grip the sheet when the pain came back strong.

Ricky bent over and kissed Daddy's cheek. I bent over and kissed his cheek too. Ricky laid the medicine and cigarettes on the table by the bed and we went out.

39

Ricky didn't say anything to me as we walked down the hall and waited for the elevator and got on and rode to the first floor; and I said nothing to him. There wasn't enough time to talk; there wasn't enough time to think; there was only time to feel. But there wasn't even enough time then to know that anything was being felt, so we just stood there in the elevator and listened to the cables scrape against each other and to the hiss of the door sliding open. Only, just as we stepped off of the elevator, I turned to Ricky, still holding his hat in his hand:

"Ricky, I'm going to walk in and out of that project."

Ricky said:

"Poor Daddy. Poor, poor Daddy."

Helen rubbed her eyes and blinked and patted her cheeks as Ricky and I got into the car on either side of her and slammed the heavy cushioned doors.

"How is he? How is he, Buggy?"

Why couldn't I open my mouth? Why couldn't I say anything to her? She turned to Ricky:

"Ricky, what's wrong? Is he—is he all right?"

Ricky flicked the switch and pressed the gas pedal, and the black ghost eased away from the curb at Harrison and Wood streets, whipped in the middle of the street, and headed back where we came from—Trumbull Park. Helen sat back in her seat. She stared straight ahead for a while and then she looked first at Ricky and then at me. Then she asked in a pitiful, low voice:

"Isn't anyone going to tell me how my father-in-law is?"

I saw about ten answers swirling around in a white, yellow, and green whirlpool of Lysol and black cancer lumps. I was busy—real, real busy. I wanted to stop what I was feeling, seeing, tasting, smelling, hearing; to put some words together; to answer my wife. But I couldn't seem to grab any answers out of the rainbow whirlpool that had the rhythm of the wheels of the car and the sound of its low hum; out of the burning heat that seemed to raise up from the dashboard and the thick leather seats, burning my ears and the back of my neck. Say something to her, something said. *Daddydaddydaddydaddydaddydaddydaddy*, something else said. I knew that Helen was going to cry in a minute if I didn't say something to her, but I didn't know what muscle to use to make my mind pull a thought out of the noise-picture-feeling that had me locked up. Then she did cry, and I guess it was the sound of her crying that set the right muscles to working in me. I put my arm around her and laid my head on her shoulder. She rubbed her cheek against my forehead, and a sweet smell of talcum arose from her dress.

"He's real sick, Honey—real, real sick."

Now *she* didn't say anything. She just kept rubbing her cheek against my forehead, as Ricky—at 57th and State Street now—turned his head toward the gloomy, yellow-light spotted mountain that was the Gardener Building; turned his head toward the place where Babydoll had died, and Momma, and—well, a lot of people. There was water in Ricky's eyes when he cursed in a little brother's thin whine:

"You dirty rotten son-of-a-bitch."

But that Helen—that Helen!

"Don't blame the building, Ricky. Blame the owner, Mr. Gardener. Blame the people who let him operate a thing like that. Blame all the Mr. Gardeners. They're the son-of-a-bitches."

Ricky said:

"It's the system, the whole rotten system."

Helen said:

"It's not the system, Ricky. It's us—you, me, Buggy, all of us. Who makes up the system, anyway?"

I said:

"The people."

Ricky said:

"Like hell! Look what's happening to you two for trying to act like you make up the system, trying to live in one of the system's projects."

Helen sat up straight. She turned back to look at the Gardener Building as we waited for the light at 59th and State Street:

"Look what happened to those who didn't try to act like they make up the system."

Ricky got quiet again. I did too. Helen did too. When we hit 95th Street, Ricky said:

"Poor, poor Daddy."

Louella stirred in the back seat. Then she screamed:

"G'way, bombs! G'way, g'way! Momma, Momma, Momma!"

Helen tried to turn around to reach her, but she was trapped between me and Ricky. She struggled frantically for a minute like it wasn't just Ricky and I that she was trying to get aloose from; then she sat back and breathed hard and said in a worn-out old lady's tone of voice:

"Don't cry, Baby; Momma's here."

I turned around to pat Louella, but she was asleep, and she didn't wake up all the rest of the way home.

When we got home Ricky said:

"I wonder how he is now?"

I said:

"Maybe we ought to call and find out."

Helen came downstairs from putting kids to bed—stomach as big as it would ever be. I thought, It won't be long now. I wondered about Mona. She should just about have had hers by now.

Helen picked up on the conversation and walked over to the telephone. Reared back and swaying from side to side, she walked, flat-footed, dragging her feet across the floor, over to the big lounge chair beside the table with the lamp and the telephone on it. Dialing a number she turned to Ricky:

"What ward is he in?"

"221."

A pause. Then:

"Can you tell me how Charles Martin in Ward 221 is doing?"

Another pause. Then:

"Can you tell me how Charles Martin is doing?"

Another pause.

"Yes, I'm a relative."

Still another pause. Then Helen looked at me. Her eyes watered, and she handed me the telephone.

"Hello, hello?" a woman's voice complained.

I said:

"Hello?"

"Oh . . . I was talking to a young lady."

"I'm her husband, Mr. Martin's son. What's happened? Is he all right?"

"Oh, I'm sorry, Mr. Martin. I was just trying to tell

the lady that Mr. Martin died at nine forty-five . . . I'm
very sorry. I've been trying to reach you for the last fifteen minutes, but I didn't get any answer."

I said:

"He's dead?"

Helen cried out:

"Oh, no! Lord, no!"

Ricky started walking around in circles, still holding his
hat in his hand:

"Poor Daddy. Poor Daddy. Poor, poor, poor Daddy."

The lady on the phone said:

"I know I'm not supposed to say this, but no one in
the ward expected your father to live this long. Are you
the one who was down here tonight?"

"Me and my brother."

"Well, I believe that all he was holding out for
was just a chance to see you."

"Daddy's dead."

"I know I shouldn't be talking to you like this—it's
against the hospital rules—but no one else may tell you, so
I feel like I just have to. Mister, your father fought death
like nothing I've ever seen before. He wrestled with it! Tonight it waited until he was half-asleep, lying back in that
bed so exhausted and out of breath that he couldn't even
keep his eyes open. Then that attack came. But, Honey,
that man wouldn't go down. He just wouldn't go down!
This way and that way he turned—and he suffered, Lord
knows he did! All of a sudden I saw him sit straight up in
that bed and open his mouth wide. And you know he
could hardly move when you were here—that's just how
hard those pains hit him. But do you think he cried out?
Not a word. Not a word, do you hear me? Mister, your
father was a man. I know I've got no right to be talking
like this, but your father was a man! He fought to the very

end. I mean, the very end. And when it did finally catch up with him, he died with his fist clinched, and his eyes wide open, and not one time did he cry out. And that's the way he died, as God is my witness! I know I shouldn't be talking to you like this, but I knew no one else would tell you how he died. I knew you'd want to know. I know I shouldn't be talking to you like this but——"

"Thanks, lady. Thanks a lot."

I handed the phone to Ricky. He put the receiver to his ear, but the nurse had already hung up. He hung up the phone and started walking.

"Poor Daddy. Poor, poor Daddy."

Helen sat stiffly in the chair by the telephone. The lamp was on, and there was a bunch of yellow flowers painted on the shade. I sat on the arm of the chair beside her and traced the outline of the flowers with the tip of my little finger:

"Helen . . . Daddy's dead."

She put her arm around my waist and rested her head against my chest. Those yellow flowers felt real to my fingers. I had never noticed how pretty those flowers were before. Pretty, pretty flowers. Nothing else in the whole wide world was pretty then, except those flowers.

Ricky walked round and round and round, still holding his policeman's cap. Little brother Ricky. Poor Ricky. Poor Daddy. Poor Momma. Poor Babydoll.

Ricky stopped walking in circles and walked over to me. He was crying. He knelt on the floor beside me, got down on his knees, and put his hands on my knees, and looked up at me crying. He looked so much like Momma right then.

"Buggy," he said, "I—I don't know who to blame. I don't know who to hate for this. I don't know who to get even with, who to kill. Whose fault is this, Buggy?

Mine? Yours? Daddy's? Mr. Gardener's? God's? Whose, Buggy? Who's to blame?"

I said:

"Helen said it's the fault of all of us—them for doing it—us for letting them."

Ricky said:

"Poor, poor, poor Daddy."

Then he got up and walked out. He didn't say another word to either of us. He just walked out. I looked at the door after he shut it. I looked at the spot where he had knelt. I had answered his question, in a way. But I hadn't really, and I knew that. But answering his question wasn't really important then. Staying alive inside was. I started fighting to keep from letting Daddy's death do to me what his Daddy's death had done to him. I could see the gray skeleton the artists tell is how death looks, staring through the whirling crazy business going on inside my head; and I knew that just one word, just one word not said but thought, and I'd be next on the list. I sat very still and breathed very slowly and tried hard to keep from thinking that word. Didn't even know what the word was, and that made it even harder to keep from thinking of it; but I couldn't let myself think of it. I'd be lost if I did. I sat very still, staring ahead inside my mind watching the artist's picture of death's hollow-eyed skull stare back at me—grinning, waiting, waiting.

I knew I had won when I noticed I was staring at the place where Ricky had knelt, and I saw that his cap was lying there on the floor. He had forgotten his policeman's cap.

40

ALMOST A WEEK had gone by since Daddy died, but I had no more gotten in the house—still riding the squad car back from work—when Helen, after taking just one look at me, sat down on the couch and turned around and laid her head in her arms across the back of the couch and cried and cried and cried. I tried to hug her, but she still cried. I kissed her, but she still cried. Nothing I did would make her stop crying.

"Daddy," Diane was getting just as big as she could be, "wha's s'matter wi' Mommy?"

"I don't know, Baby—just tired, I guess."

Louella sat beside Helen on the other side of the couch from me and hugged her with one arm and sucked the fingers on her other hand. I got up, and Diane followed me into the kitchen and stood beside me, holding my leg as I washed my hands. She followed me around the kitchen as I went from refrigerator to cabinet to table, fixing us something to eat—spaghetti and franks.

Nobody ate them, and we all went to bed as soon as it got dark.

Boom!

The mob was still on the ball. The bomb's blue-white

409

flash slapped the foot of the bed; and the perfume bottles, jammed beside each other on the dresser, clinked from the force of the blast.

Boom!

Helen sat up just as this one went off. The light hit her stomach and her neck and the bottom of her chin.

"Buggy." I couldn't tell how her voice sounded. She didn't sound mad. She sure didn't sound glad—and not especially sad. I sat up beside her:

"Huh?"

"What are we coming to?"

"What do you mean?"

"Where are we going? Where have we been? What are we going to make out of life?"

Now what kind of questions were those at this time of night? I didn't have any answers. Why should I have? Working everyday. Taking care of my family the best I could. Didn't drink much. Didn't even have a girl friend. Never been in jail. Never got fired from a job. Kept myself clean. Paid my bills, when I had the money. Make something out of life? I said:

"Make what out of life? I don't get you. What do you mean?"

She laid her head on my shoulder:

"I know you're doing all you can to provide for us. And God knows I'd die without you, and it's because you're so sweet that I worry about you. I don't want you to have to struggle day in and day out, going to work, getting paid, paying bills, going back to work, and on and on and on like that. Buggy, you've got something—maybe even I don't know altogether what it is—I mean, the way these people out here look up to you. They see it; I see it. But, Buggy, you must *use* talent. Use it, and make it strong, make it do for you. I don't want you to wake up one day and see nothing but bills and babies and say 'Aw what the hell!' and throw up both hands——"

"Aw, naw, Helen! I'd never do that."

But she shook her head from side to side, there on my shoulder.

"It can happen, Honey . . ."

And she waited, and I knew that we were both thinking of Daddy, and how he had thrown up hands, wife, kids—even his life—when he looked up one day and saw nothing but bills and babies.

Helen said:

"It *did* happen Buggy."

I said:

"I know."

"Where are we Buggy? What are we going to do?"

"Helen, what are you getting at?"

I knew what she was saying, but I couldn't bring myself to admit it. Here I was almost thirty and still a boy, still waiting for my ship to come in—in Trumbull Park because it was the only place to run to, like a crab that had crawled out of the drying mud to the wet mud in the shade, but still in the mud. I never had anything, never did anything but just enough to get by on. A has been already? A has been? A never was? A never would be? Oh, yes, I knew what she was talking about! But the thought had never been more than an uncomfortable fear that brushed through me like any passing cold wind.

Helen, seeing that I wasn't going to answer, said:

"You know, sitting in this house, all day, every day, doing nothing but listening to the radio for recreation, gives me a lot of time to think about what's going on in the world. Everything is moving, Buggy, backward, forward, up and down. We're moving too, but not of our own accord—not because we sat down and said we're going to

411

move. We're being pushed—pushed out of the Gardener Building—pushed out here—pushed out of the paddy wagon into the squad car . . ."

And—I said to myself—pushed into the street.

"When are we going to take hold of the reins, do some pushing of our own? Go someplace, right or wrong, good or bad, because *we* want to go, not because we are pushed? . . . You ever hear of Bandung?"

I hadn't.

"That's where the man on the radio says that a whole bunch of colored folks from all over the world—Africa, India, China, America, all over—are getting together to figure out how to keep from being pushed by all the things that are happening in the world. They are getting together to figure out how to do some pushing themselves, how to make the wagon go the way they want it to go. Down South, Buggy, the radio talks about how down South Negroes are pushing, trying to get the Supreme Court to outlaw segregation in schools. Everywhere everybody is doing *something*—everybody but us, Buggy. Buggy, what are *we* going to do? I don't want a Lincoln, or even a fur piece like some people have. I just don't want to sit by and watch life pass me by without doing *something* about it."

"What should we do?"

"You tell me."

"Trumbull Park *is* important, you know."

"I know. Buggy, Honey, Trumbull Park is what I'm talking about!"

"You mean I could walk in?"

"And help the others walk in, Buggy."

"It won't make us any money, like Ricky's got."

"It's better than money, Buggy."

"I may go to jail . . ."

"I'll take care of things till you get back."

"Tomorrow, Helen?"

"Tomorrow, Buggy?"

"Yeah. Tomorrow."

My heart was beating so hard that I absolutely heard it! A joy swept into me that made me dizzy, and water ran down my cheek, happy water.

"Helen."

I turned to her. She slid down in the bed. I slid down in the bed. Her big stomach pressed close to me. I felt that little so-and-so in there just kicking to beat the band. I hugged her as tight as I could without hurting. She hugged me and kissed me, and I felt tears on her cheeks, and I smelled the sweet talcum rise from her body. Oh, I hugged her so *tight!*

"What have I been scared of, Helen?"

"Yourself."

I kissed her hard—and just that quick she was in that soft green dress, and we were in the hallway back at the Gardener Building, and she was kissing me with her eyes closed, and I was feeling the *funniest* buzzing sensation under my skin . . . And here after all these years . . .

"Helen . . . Does 'I love you' sound silly?"

"It sounds awful."

What mob was big and bad enough to move me back from where this dark woman had taken me? What fear of death was greater than the crazy screaming and beating, and laughing and singing, and jumping up and down that was going on inside me right then? I felt drunk. I was anxious for morning to come. I was going to get in line with all those people that Helen had heard about on the radio, the ones from Down Home, the ones from Bandung.

I heard it. Yes, I heard it, that diesel, that bastard. But do you know who wasn't scared of any more diesels? Me!

41

AND THIS WAS THE DAY. I'll never forget it. I mean, never. Walk in. No more squad car for Buggy. No more listening to guys start whistling "Old Black Joe" and "The Darktown Strutter's Ball" and all that. No more people gawking at me at 95th and Cottage Grove. No more. No more.

I got up feeling evil—I mean, evil. I went to the bathroom mirror and looked at myself in that mirror. My goodness! Hair sticking straight up. Bags under my eyes. Hard lines around my mouth I had never seen before. I didn't even smile at myself. Didn't *try* to look good—"Ready for Freddy," like they say down on 58th. But my heart was driving the blood through me in hard and fast jabs. I could feel that blood gushing in my ears and in the ice-cold tips of my toes.

There's no need to lie. I was scared. But what a delicious kind of fear! *Winning* fear. You ever feel a winning fear? Like a boxer facing a real big bad cat, but knowing all the time that he *will* whip that cat, whip him to his knees, whip him till the blood runs like water? That's the kind of scared I was—*winning* scared.

Helen called me after a while:

"Hey, you better hurry up! It's getting late."

I didn't answer.

She didn't call me again.

At breakfast she said:

"This morning?"

I said:

"May as well get this show on the road."

She smiled and looked down at her plate.

When I was through eating I started upstairs to kiss Louella and Diane, but they were both on their way downstairs. I picked Louella up and hugged her tight. What was *her* heart beating so hard for? I kissed Diane, and she kissed me and got my cheek all wet. Then I kissed Helen, and hugged her tight, but I let her go real quick and slipped my jacket on. At the door I said:

"It may take me a little longer getting home today, so don't get worried if I'm not home at exactly five."

She snatched a piece out of Joe William's song "Every Day":

"Ain't nobody worried!"

And I said:

"And it ain't nobody cryin'!"

And I cut on out singing under my breath:

"Every day . . . Every day I have the blues . . . Ev-ev'ry daaaaa-ay . . . Ev'ry *day* I have the bluuuu-ues . . ."

Scared? Whistling in the dark? Shee-it!

I had to make up my mind as soon as I stepped out of the house. No time to walk and think about it. To my left was 106th Street, the bus stop, and the mob. To my right was the squad car and "Darktown Strutter's Ball."

I turned left.

"Nooooooooo-ooo-ooo-body loves me! Nobody seems to care! No-obody loves me! No-obody seems to care! Speaking of bad luck and trouble—well, you knooooo-ow, I've had my share! Seems to me that every day, every day,

415

every day, every day . . . I have the blues . . . every day!"

I could just see that big, dark, smiling, sweating, strong-looking crinkly-haired Joe Williams at DeLisa's singing that song. Holding the mike in one hand, and walking with that head way, way up in the air, carrying the mike with him as he walked, chest way out, shoulders way back, singing "Every Day"!

And everybody would be screaming and throwing money up there on the stage and he wouldn't even look at the money. Step over it, singing and swinging, preaching a natural gospel of power—that finger-popping, hip-swinging, bust-you-in-the-mouth-if-you-mess-with-me kind of power!

And I walked and sang, "Well, it ain't nobody worried . . . and it ain't nobody cryin'!"

It felt like I was walking through the mob already—and it wasn't bad at all.

When I took the last step out of the project, I looked around for the cops. There weren't any to be seen. Who'd be silly enough to riot that early in the morning?

I turned to my right and crossed the street to a vacant lot where a path angled through to Bensley, the street where the mob hung out. So far I hadn't seen anybody—not a soul. I walked with my fist clenched, and I felt the sweat on the underside of my fingers, and the beating—heavy, hard, thumping kind of beating—in my chest. I kept on until I reached the end of the vacant lot, and then I turned left and started walking north up Bensley, toward the park where the mob stood each and every day and jeered when I passed in the squad car. I heard them in my mind:

"We dare you to walk, nigger! Nigger!"

I felt a little like a kid walking a freshly waxed floor, walking on the white folk's holy ground. It didn't feel any different from any other ground; but, I thought, that's what makes it so good to walk on. It's ground that don't feel any different than any other ground, yet they want to make so much fuss over it—something over nothing.

"Noooooo-body wants me. Nobody seems to care!"

Then I saw a white man.

Young—about twenty-five or six. Blue-denim jacket over a blue-denim shirt. Light-brown hair, and stubble on his chin. Holding a cigarette in one hand and a heavy metal lunch pail in the other. Walking straight at me down the narorw sidewalk, two blocks from home, not a policeman in sight, and houses of the rioters running down both sides of the street as far as 103rd.

He stiffened when he saw me, and I thought I saw him get a tighter grip on that lunch pail. I felt in the breast pocket of my jacket. Maybe there'd be an old pocket knife that I'd forgotten to take out—maybe, at least, a sharp pencil. But there was nothing, nothing in my side pockets, and nothing in my back pockets, except one very soft dollar bill.

We were almost within arm's length. I looked into his face. This was it. I rehearsed in my mind real quick what I would do to him. Kick him first in the stomach, and then hit him across the back of the neck when he bent over in pain. But suppose he didn't bend over in pain?

"Good morning!"

And just as if I was used to saying good morning to young white men in Trumbull Park who walked straight at me with heavy lunch pails in their hands, not smiling or anything, I answered him:

"Good morning!"

And the cat went right on by and never looked back.

What the hell was this? Where did he come from? How many more were there out there like him? I forgot all about "Every Day." This goofed my double-barreled hatred of

white folks—especially those in Trumbull Park—in a hurry.
I wasn't ready for this kind of stuff. Now how would I
know who to hate and who not to? Now was I going to
have to wait to see if they said good morning every time
before I kicked them in the stomach and hit them a hard
blow on the back of the neck when they bent over in pain—
if they did?

I didn't pass anybody else all the way to 103rd. The
street was so quiet that I had to think hard to remember
that this was the same street that Arthur Davis had seen
jam-packed with thousands, with old ladies trying to ride
the bumpers of Kevin's car to keep him from getting into
the project. I could hardly believe that this was the same
street that I had seen full of people screaming at the squad
car and throwing bricks and bottles and everything else
as we rode by.

I crossed 103rd Street and waited at the bus stop for
the westbound bus. A squad car came cruising up Bensley,
and I could see somebody sitting in the back. It was Harry
Harvey, the new guy who had gone with me and Terry to
the march on City Hall. He rolled the window down just
as the squad car stopped at the stop sign at 103rd:

"Hey, Buggy!"

"How you doing, Harry?"

"Hey, Buggy, I don't appreciate what you did!"

"What did I do?"

"You didn't ask me to go along!"

He opened the door. The cop sitting by the driver
shouted:

"Hey, fella! What're you tryin' to do? C'mit suicide?
Why'nt you take a squad? Whadda ya think we're out here
for?"

I said:

"I don't know what you're out here for! Besides, it's too nice a day to ride."

It *was* a nice day. The sun was turning everything in sight a warm whitish yellow. Harry crossed the street. The cop shouted:

"You guys trying to start trouble or somethin'? C'mon, both of you! This squad car is for your own good."

The cop opened the front door and started to get out. His face was about ready to catch on fire it was so red. But right at the same time, a bus which we hadn't seen pulling around the corner from 103rd and Torrence moved between me and Harry and the cop across the street, and we got on.

There were about three Negroes on the bus. I figured they were from the Wisconsin Steel Mill around the corner. Everybody else on the bus was white. One or two of them looked real hard at us. One dark-haired narrow-nosed woman hunched a short gray-haired one, and they both giggled when we passed them; but no one else said anything, and we sat in the middle of the bus, figuring that the Negroes behind us would warn us if anybody tried to start anything. After we sat down Harry said:

"Man, I didn't believe you would do it! I saw you from about two blocks back, and I got cold chills when I saw this white cat coming your way, but he didn't open his mouth, did he?"

I nodded, and Harry went on:

"You going to walk in this evening?"

"Yep. I'm walking from now on."

Harry laughed:

"Well, *all*-right!"

The bus hit the top of the high bridge heading for Stony Island Avenue, and Harry and I both looked back at Trumbull Park. It looked like a tall gray prison rising out of the fog, out of the rows of trees that ran all the way from the park to the other end of the project. The bus coasted down the bridge and along the level street toward the stoplight at Stony Island, and Harry said:

"Do you mind company? When you walk in this evening, I mean?"

I was so glad that that man said that I didn't know what to do; but I was real cool about it:

"Well, sure, sure! If you *want* to."

"I want to. Where'll we meet?"

"I get to 79th and Cottage about four-thirty or quarter to five, depends on whether or not the first bus out of the plant is too crowded to get on."

Harry laughed:

"Say, that's right up my alley! I get to 63rd at about four, and it takes about half an hour to wait for the southbound car and get to 95th, so I should be at 79th at about four-twenty. I could wait for you at Walgreen's on the corner of 79th."

I felt good. Company! I never thought this Harry guy had it in him. I mean, so quiet and all. Harry Harvey— short; still wearing that DuSable high-school sweater; moustache trimmed just as neat as you please; no hat to cover that thin spot at the top of his head; caramel brown, with a short wide nose that just matched his full, dry lips. Harry Harvey—just moved out here, and walking already. Here I had to decide and undecide and decide, and this guy ups and, just like that, says he'll walk in. Boy, I felt good! Company! Maybe, I thought, there'd be more company, if me and Harry made it alive.

We got off of the bus at 103rd and Cottage Grove and waited near the tavern on the west side of the street for a northbound car. One came fast, and we hopped on it and sat near a window and watched the Jays Potato Chip place roll by, and the Armstrong Linoleum place, and the yellowed, water-stained bricks striped with crooked, brown water-marks, on top of which the IC trains ran carrying the people who lived in the suburbs to the Loop to work.

Harry Harvey said:

"Man, these people are running just as far out of town as they can, just to keep from living by us."

I said:

"They may as well come on back, 'cause that black belt just can't hold us any more."

Harry giggled:

"Now ain't it the truth?"

The bus hit 79th Street, and I got off:

"Four-thirty—huh, Harry?"

"Just like downtown."

And in a while I was standing in front of that multiple drill, drilling away.

All morning I practiced in my mind what I would do. Meet Harry. Ride to 103rd and Cottage. Get off and transfer to an eastbound bus and ride to Bensley . . . I couldn't imagine it any further than that. I couldn't imagine what would happen after that. One thing I did know: the streets wouldn't be empty *then*.

Buzzzzzzzzzz!

Lunchtime! Pete came over.

"Hey, Buggy, c'mon let's eat! What're you doing, day-dreaming?"

I laughed:

"Cool it, Daddy!"

Pete said:

"I'm always cool, Pops!"

That doggoned Pete. Who had he been hanging around with?

At the lunch table, I gave Pete the news:

"I walked out today, Pete."

He almost choked on his ham sandwich. He set his coffee down slowly and said:

"You *what?*"

"You heard me! And I passed a guy and he didn't open his mouth."

Pete's face darkened into a frown, and he clamped his jaws together and talked through his teeth:

"That's because he was by himself. He'd have kicked your teeth out if he had been with his crowd!"

"Well, like my mother said, you can whitewash a paddy all over but he'll still be a paddy——"

Oops! I put my hand to my mouth. I *knew* that one of these days I would forget that Pete was white and say the wrong thing. When Momma used to say that about white people, she meant *all* white people—white friends, white enemies, white wives, husbands, children—the whole works. I hadn't thought of it as an idea so much as just a way of talking—a way to fill in when you couldn't figure out a way to separate the feelings of one white person from another. I didn't want to hurt Pete. He had been a real friend, but now I had said it, had thrown all the friendliness we had had between us into the same pot as the way I felt about the rioters. Shee-it! How can I let somebody bust me in the mouth before I say he's a wrong cat? But there were other cats—maybe they ought to wear signs saying, I ain't a wrong cat. It's these Petes that mess a cat up. I looked at him. Apologize? Not apologize? But he kept on chomping that ham sandwich like he hadn't heard what I said. Then:

"Hell, Buggy, don't you know you'll get your ass whipped if you try to walk in there! Listen, if you'd just *listen* to me one time." He gritted his teeth and leaned close to me and frowned and pleaded through his closed teeth: "Let's go out there—tonight. Let's go out there and catch one of those guys alone and kick his ass. Why don't we Buggy? Kick—his—ass!"

I put my hands over my eyes and shook my head. Thoughts were about to burst my skull. I shook my head from side to side to side. I didn't answer Pete.

As we went back to our drills, he shook his fist at me in a stomach-uppercut and frowned.

"Don't be a fool, Buggy! Those bastards will kill you!"

And so I drilled and drilled, and thought and thought, and worried; and finally the four o'clock whistle rang. It was time to go home.

I felt a surge of that old-time fear just gush into my body. I wanted to go to the toilet, but I knew that it wouldn't do any good. This was a feeling that would go away only when I wasn't scared any more, and I was going to be scared as long as I still had it in my mind to walk into that project; so I was going to walk into that project if I never did another thing in my life again.

Punch! went the stamp on my time-card. Oh, what a feeling—what an awful feeling!

I dragged my feet while walking to the bus; but it waited for me. I looked out of the window at the stores going by. They had gone by so slowly that day when I was trying to get home to Helen, the day after we moved in and they put the snake in our mail slot. Now I couldn't even see the street good, the bus was going so fast.

Time was running, running, running, and I was right on top of it—a cork from an old bottle floating down the edge of a sewer into a black hole where I didn't know what was!

"Cottage Grove!"

Already? Yes, already. My hands were slick, and the skin

on the back of my hands trembled. That pounding in my chest was making me too weak to walk, and my throat got just as dry as it could be. Maybe, I thought, maybe Harry won't be there. So what? I thought, then you'll walk by your own damn self. But Harry was there, looking *worried*.

"Hey, man!" Harry's voice cracked on "man." And he giggled.

I said:

"Well, are you ready for the picnic?"

He tried to steady his voice, but he couldn't. That wobble made it hard for me to understand him. I wondered how I sounded to him.

"Man, I'll tell you the truth. I'm scared shitless."

"Me too."

But neither of us even joked about not walking in. I knew, and Harry seemed to know, that this was it. We were going to walk today even if the sun went out.

The streetcar that I had had to wait so long for, the day I was trying to get home to Helen, came just a-speeding up the street, lickety-split! Damn streetcar—didn't never come when you wanted it!

There were still a few Negroes on the streetcar; the 95th Street bunch hadn't gotten off yet. 95th was usually the last stop for the Negroes on the Cottage Grove car, and then it would be all white the rest of the way. But now there was another outpost—Trumbull Park. And we—Harry Harvey and I—were heading there as fast as that rocking, humming, clank-clanking green devil could go.

4:35 the clock in the cleaners at 93rd Street said.

Two white people got on and two Negroes got off.

4:40. The car stopped at 95th Street, and eight Negroes got off. Three white people got on.

4:45. The car, having whipped around the bend at 95th and Cottage Grove and zoomed past Jays Potato Chip place and the linoleum factory, sped between the factories on the left and the yellow brick IC tracks on the right like something was chasing it. Suddenly I noticed the two white women in front of me. They were the same two who had ridden the bus with me and Harry in the morning. The dark-haired one, the one who had laughed when we got on, started talking a little louder to the gray-haired one with the crisscrossing wrinkles in the back of her neck. I thought I heard her say something about "nigger."

I had that feeling, and I had it bad! Stomach itching on the inside where I couldn't scratch it. Nerves in my arms trembling like tight telephone wires quivering on a cold windy day. The sun was still bright and warm, and this made me feel worse, for there would probably be a lot of people in the park playing baseball on such a warm day.

4:55. The car stopped at 103rd. I felt myself getting more and more tight inside, more and more nervous, more and more feeling that thumping in my chest, and that tremor under my skin. What a feeling!

"Harry, this is it."

We got off of the streetcar. The two women got off in front of us. Harry said:

"This sure is it! Hey, did you hear those two chicks saying something that sounded like 'nigger'?"

That awful feeling deep down in my stomach! I looked around for some place to go to the washroom, but the bus was coming from the west, going east, our way—going to Trumbull Park. I answered Harry's question:

"I thought I heard the same thing. I hope we don't have to kick any *women's* bootys!"

Harry said:

"Me too."

The two women got on the bus in front of us. There were nothing but white people on this bus, and it was full! That

425

feeling! Ooooh that God-awful feeling! I looked at Harry's watch.

5:00. The two women sat behind us now, talking quietly now, saying things that sounded for all the world to me like "nigger." Now getting home seemed to be the most important thing in my life, getting home to my Helen, Diane, Louella. Harry laughed:

"Got you insurance paid up?"

I said:

"You?"

"I've got the payment in my pocket. I forgot to mail it."

"Well, you can mail it when you get home."

Harry looked at me. He wasn't smiling now. He said:

"I hope so."

The bus driver yelled:

"Next stop, Bensley!"

I sat up, trying to see whether or not there was anybody near the bus stop, but I couldn't see a thing, and I sat back in my seat again. The two women got up and walked to the door. Harry got up and I followed him.

Sick! Sick-at-the-stomach feeling!

"Bensley!" the bus driver said.

I looked at the watch on Harry's arm as he held on to the pole near the door.

5:10. The two women got off first. Now they didn't whisper! They both screamed at the top of their lungs:

"*Niggers, niggers, niggers! Here come the niggers!*"

I couldn't see before, because of the crowd and the funny angle of the bus; but now I could see everything. The mob was there in full force. The park was nothing but a bunch of heads—bald heads, black-haired heads, long-blonde-haired heads, crew-cut heads. Nothing but heads, and shoulders, and chests, and big hairy arms and hands. And in those hands, baseball bats, broken bottles, tire chains, bricks.

Nobody was saying anything but those two women. Nobody seemed to believe what they were seeing. Harry and I didn't believe what *we* were seeing: hundreds and hundreds and hundreds of people standing all over the street and on the sidewalk and in the park—looking, waiting, for us. And even they didn't seem to believe that two Negroes were getting off of the 103rd Street bus, in broad daylight, at 103rd and Bensley.

The rear doors of a patrol wagon banged open, and about a dozen policemen climbed out slowly, looking at me and Harry as if we were the ones breaking the law. That bus sure made a lonely sight as it pulled off and disappeared around the corner of Torrence Avenue. Harry looked at me and started giggling:

"Hey, let's go back and try this some other day—say, a month from next Tuesday!"

I whispered:

"You fool."

A police officer with silver bars shining in that April sun snapped:

"Okay, men, here they are!" He walked up to us, looking angry, holding a shiny club with a red tassel across his chest. "You boys want a ride into the project?"

A hoarse voice back in the crowd started it off:

"Get out of here, you black son-of-a-bitch!"

Someone else joined in with him:

"You'll never walk these streets, niggers! Never!"

I told the captain, a tall, stocky, gray-haired man, with smooth red skin:

"We're walking."

427

He looked at Harry. Harry started walking toward the sidewalk that led toward the project. The captain yelled:

"All right, men! Surround them!' '

The policemen formed a square around us—four on the left, four on the right, one in front, and one in back. The captain walked on the side nearest the curb, and a sergeant walked inside the square just in front of Harry and me. The streets, jammed as they were, got even more crowded as we started walking.

"Hey, niggers! Get out of here! You're not going to get our homes, you black Africans!"

I could see the face of the guy who said that—a fat, muscle-bound-looking guy with a gray-haired crew-cut.

People came running from the other streets, running and screaming. Men, women, children, running from everywhere, out of backyards, down front steps, out of cars, off bicycles. The screaming got louder and louder as they pushed closer and closer to Harry and me. Noise louder than I'd ever heard at any football game, at any playground, in any movie. Voices of every tone and pitch—high, squeaky voices, growling bass voices, young children's cracking voices, screaming and cursing.

"Black jungle bunny!"

"Get out of here, son-of-a-bitch!"

"Go back to Africa, you black bastard!"

I saw an old lady with her hair drawn up in a ball at the top of her head. Her eye caught mine, and she spat at me. She missed. I glanced at Harry, but he was watching a big bald-headed guy with no shirt on, who kept tromping toward us, talking and shouting to the others. Harry said:

"Buggy, watch this bastard on my left. He's going to try something."

There was no point in asking Harry what should I do if he did start something. I had no time to wonder what I should do, how I felt. I was too busy watching each face as we passed, too busy keeping my stomach tight, my feet moving on and on.

We were about at 104th Street. The two women were right on our heels. The policemen elbowed their way through the mob, elbowing through but arresting no one, and the names kept coming:

"*Get out of here, you black jungle bunny! Get out! Get out!*"

And me and Harry kept walking.

The bald-headed man saw the chance to make his move. He broke past the policemen in front of us and walked up to Harry, his reddish face shiny with sweat, his breath smelling like an old brew of cigarettes and stale whiskey. He bumped into me, and I staggered back a few steps. The people in the mob screamed and laughed.

I stopped, and things got quiet. One by one the screaming voices stopped, the cops stopped, and Harry stopped. I shouted at this guy:

"Okay, you son-of-a-bitch! Now what?"

The guy looked around at the mob. Some of the guys he looked at looked down at the ground.

I screamed it!

"Okay, you son-of-a-bitch! You bumped into me. Now what?"

The sergeant walked over to where we stood facing each other, his big lean face twisted in anger:

"Come on, Martin, come on! What are you out here for—trouble?"

He grabbed my arm. But this was it; and everything went: I didn't want anybody grabbing me then—not anybody. I knocked his arm off of me, and he stood there a minute not saying anything. Then somebody in the crowd yelled:

"Kill the black bastard! Kill him! Kill him!"

The sergeant stood right in front of me, not saying a word to the guy who had started it. He stared at me as if he was trying to work up enough steam to blow me out of sight. Then he turned to Harry, and then back to me. We both stared back at him, and he didn't open his mouth. He turned to other policemen and said in a loud voice:

"Move on!"

And we moved on—the cops, the mob, and Harry and me.

Trumbull Park was in sight. Just a few more steps. If we could make it, we would have won. It was supposed to have been our first move. We were supposed to strike that first blow, draw the first gun, pull out the first knife. This wasn't in their plans. No fight. No first move. Just walking . . . walking . . .

We got to an alley near the vacant lot right across the street from the project, and another mob crowded the streets in front of us, blocking the way between us and home. The cops slowed down, and as Harry and I stepped into this alley:

"Look out!" one of the policemen screamed.

A wave of bricks flew at us from the vacant lot. Harry and I never stopped walking. We were too close to Trumbull Park to stop now. If the bricks killed us, then that would be the way it would be. But duck? Now? It was too late. There was no place to duck behind, no place to run to. No diesel, no mob, no bricks—nothing could stop us now! It seemed like it wasn't really me and Harry walking, but somebody else in a scene on a movie screen—somebody else who walked while we *felt*.

And even as I stared the faces down that would have liked to make us start the one little act that would have turned this mob on us and the policemen as well, I felt no hatred for them—nor pity. Just anger—the kind that one

430

feels when you see somebody blocking the way between you and home. Anger—but no hate. These faces that moved by me and Harry were tired faces. Grime and filings from the steel mills lay on their faces like black veils—the old folks and young ones, screaming still. Once a rock hit me, and I almost fell it hurt so bad, but I didn't. I couldn't. Harry couldn't. To fall would have been to die; and we didn't want to die—we wanted to live. And we were going to, no matter what.

And we walked and walked and walked—walking through the great Trumbull Park, Buggy walking to Helen, Harry walking to his wife Margaret, walking to all of our friends there. Walking. Mobs screaming, throwing things, pushing us, pushing the policemen who had orders to take cover or else. Walking past 104th, past 105th, past the alley near 106th, almost there, almost home. Walking.

The Big Boys couldn't afford cold-blooded murder, and the Little Boys were afraid to commit cold-blooded murder—by themselves—and that's what it would have taken to stop us. That's what it would have taken to get Mona and Arthur Davis out before we came, and cold-blooded murder was what it would take to stop the others now—Kevin-Beverly, Terry-Nadine, Carl-Ernestine, William-Christine, Norman-Armela—all of them. They'd walk now. I knew they would. So would the other "new" guys like Harry. So would guys not yet in Trumbull Park, and their wives, and their children. They'd walk. They'd follow the path that Arthur and Mona and Harry and Helen and I had made—widen that path and wear it smooth. They'd let these people, the Big Boys and the Little Boys, let them know that death is not enough any more to keep Negroes from walking—and running and crawling and flying and singing and crying and even dying—for what we know is ours.

431

Oh, yes, the mob was still screaming; but now I heard singing—Big Joe William whaling:

"Every day, every day . . . Well, it ain't nobody worried, and it ain't nobody cryin'!"

And we walked with our chests stuck out, and our heads way up in the air—just like that big, dark, blues-shouting stud.

And we took the long hip strides that Joe took as the women at the DeLisa screamed. There were women screaming at us—men too. So I started singing out loud, in the middle of cops, mobs, and everything else. Ol' Harry joined in, and I noticed a little water in his eyes. I felt a little choked up myself as we both sang loud and clear:

"Every day, every day . . . Well, it ain't nobody worried, and it ain't nobody cryin'!"